Fletcher and the Samurai

Also by John Drake

Fletcher

and the Samurai

JOHN DRAKE

LUME BOOKS

LUME BOOKS

This edition published in 2021 by Lume Books
30 Great Guildford Street,
Borough, SE1 0HS

Copyright © John Drake 2019

ISBN 978-1-83901-373-7

Typeset using Atomik ePublisher from Easypress Technologies

www.lumebooks.co.uk

In fond memory of
David Burkhill Howarth

----------- DBH -----------

1946 – 2009

PATRIFAMILIAS AMATISSIMO
MAGISTRO DOCTISSIMO
INGENIOSISSIMO TECHNITAE
OPTIMO AMICO

INTRODUCTION

This fifth book of the Fletcher series presents Admiral Sir Jacob's memoirs from the period May 1797 to December 1799, as bellowed into the face of his reluctant clerk Samuel (later the Rev. Dr) Pettit, during the early 1870s. Pettit then transcribed Fletcher's memories into twenty-five volumes, at first in elegant hand-writing but later using a Sholes & Glidden typewriter: the very latest in Victorian technology.

Pettit himself has therefore attracted the attention of many readers, who have asked what sort of man he was. So I quote from a letter of 1871 written by the Right Reverend the Bishop of London, Sir Alfred Atherson-Jones to his wife, after Pettit had applied to Sir Alfred to become a candidate for ordination.

'Pettit is in his early twenties and is long, thin and lank, with damp hands, and he stoops to lower himself down among the rest of us dwarves. He is tremendously efficient as Admiral Fletcher's clerk, being tremendously speedy at Pitman shorthand, tremendously adept at fingering the type-writing machine, and he is tremendously well paid for it by the admiral. Also Petit is tremendously diligent, tremendously polite, and tremendously enthusiastic in his churchgoing. He claims to be Anglican but he is very high, and exudes an odour of genuflection and the confessional.'

Whatever Pettit's religious inclinations, he was gravely embarrassed by much of the content of the memoirs and, after Fletcher's death at the age of one hundred years (and vigorous to the last) Petit found courage to add chastising notes into the volumes. These notes I have included:

[in this different font, inside square brackets, signed by his initials: S.P.]

i

In Chapter 18, Pettit reports the only occasion in all his employment by Fletcher when he refused to transcribe a phrase. He describes Fletcher's fury at this refusal and the means whereby he was able to stand fast: a considerable, if solitary, victory for Pettit and I have therefore left this phrase of vulgarity exactly as Petit finally did, with the words struck out by crosses. But I would be grateful for any suggestions from readers as to what the actual words might have been.

Moving on, I am frequently asked why Fletcher addressed readers as 'my jolly boys', and called himself 'uncle Jacob'. Chapter 18 offers one answer to this question, but note the following from an 1875 letter written by Benjamin Disraeli, Earl of Beaconsfield and twice Prime Minister under Queen Victoria. The letter was addressed to Disraeli's brother Ralph.

> 'Regarding that rascal Sir Jacob, whom all the ladies admire: I asked –
> on sight of his memoirs – for whom are they intended? Whereupon he
> declared that they were for the young of England generally, in the hope
> to breed boldness into them, and to all such as them – he said – then
> I'm their uncle!'

I now turn to Fletcher's profoundly strange account, in Chapter 28, of 'The Bald Man in the Cable Tier'. This story – famous in its day – has received many explanations including the following, and readers may take their choice of them:

'a crossing between this life and the next'
Editorial, 'New England Spiritualism', September 1913.

'visitation by aliens'
D.I.K. Hed's 'UFOs Among Us' McLowre Press, 1955.

'communal psychotic delusion'
A. Nutte's 'The Mass Mind' Oxford Academic E-Print, 2019.

Finally, as in previous books, and drawing on my ever-growing archive of Fletcher papers I have extemporised some third-person chapters to give a rounded view of events. These chapters are merely my own best guesses but they are as accurate as I can make them. I have also included extracts of documents in 18th century Japanese, kindly translated by experts at Sidings College, Cambridge who also converted traditional Japanese measures and dates into modern eqivalents..

John Drake, Cheshire, England, May 2019.

– 1787 –

CHAPTER 1

'I go to distant and mysterious lands where I shall be guided not only by the honour of a samurai but more powerfully still, by the words that you – my Lord and father – have spoken and which shall sustain me in my task, even if, by fate, we never meet again.'

(From a letter of June 12ᵗʰ 1787, from Masahito Hitamoto, aboard the Dutch East Indiaman *Oosterhout* in Nagasaki Harbour, to his father Lord Hayato Hitamoto.)

Okonoma castle on the south-westerly extremity of Hito Island, was huge and invincible. The stones of its pyramid base rose out of rock on three sides, over the ocean two hundred feet below. On the landward side, the castle was defended by four lines of entrenchments: V-bottom ditches fifty feet deep, fortified with redoubts to sweep attackers with flanking fire. The single road through these earthworks, zig-zagged via gates and draw-bridges, past still more redoubts, forming a death trap to any force which sought to enter the castle without permission of its master, Lord Hayoto Hitamoto.

This same Lord Hayoto, the *Daimyo* – absolute ruler – of Hito Island, now stood with his five sons and a dozen of his leading samurai, at the apex of the castle's keep on the seventh floor of its pagoda-like levels. Each level was slightly smaller than the one below, so the keep sloped inward as each level rose through the middle of the one below, fringed by blue-tiled, up-curving roofs. The keep was timber-built, white plastered, richly painted, and beautified with gilded sculptures of the exotic monsters of Japanese mythology.

Thus the keep of Okonoma castle differed in every imaginable way from the keeps of European castles. But it served exactly the same purpose as barracks, store-rooms, and living quarters. Likewise it was defended

3

by every architectural trick that its builders could contrive, including dropping-ports for grenades, and loopholes for *Tanegishma* – match-lock arquebuses – which were stored on racks behind the loopholes, with powder, shot and match-cord. They waited in their hundreds, as patient as the castle's samurai who were expertly trained in their use.

So Lord Hayato should have been secure within his castle. But he was not: not in these dangerous times when every daimyo was looking for defence with entrenchments and gunpowder. But Lord Hayato's plans went far beyond that. His plans went beyond Japan itself.

'So,' he said, and gave a brief bow, profoundly returned by his sons and samurai. The chamber rustled with the silk of each man's formal gown: wide shoulders tapering to a waist bearing two swords within a sash. The gowns were plain black embroidered with the Hitamoto clan badge – its *mon* – depicting a swooping hawk within a circle. 'I am pleased that you have all come,' said Lord Hayato, 'It was gracious of you to answer my summons, and most polite.'

'*Hi!*' they said, the affirmative syllable uttered in a single bark. Then they smiled at the small joke because they admired and loved their Lord, and rejoiced to follow his commands. He was sixty-five years old, grey and thin, tall and clever. He was very clever: very well read, very wise. He was the fountain of ideas that tickled men's minds and made them wonder. Yet afterwards, they wondered why nobody had thought of such ideas before? Because once Lord Hayato explained, then everything was obvious! Thus some men ruled by force, some by cunning, and some by political alliance. But Lord Hayato ruled because nobody ever knew what he was going to do next.

So Lord Hayoto smiled at his sons and samurai, where they stood in this bright-lit uppermost chamber of the castle, with its translucent screens slid back on the sun-facing side, giving a view over the ocean below. Lord Hayato nodded and paused, gone into his own thoughts for a moment. He glanced round the chamber: plain, neat, and empty except for the stairs to the floor below, and a flower arrangement in front of a scroll bearing a poem. Lord Hayato looked at the poem. He had chosen it carefully. It spoke of the faraway and the strange. So he frowned, and all present stiffened in anticipation.

'Ah!' they said, knowing that he was about to speak.

'Where is my eldest son?' said Lord Hayato.

4

'Here, my Lord and father,' said Kimiya Hitamoto, the tallest of the five young men standing in front of him.

'Step forward my son,' said Lord Hayato, choosing Kimiya not just because he was the eldest, but because Kimiya could be relied upon in all matters of drilled learning and neatly packed memory.

'My son,' said Lord Hayato, 'what is the name of the island that we rule?'

'Hito Island, my Lord and Father,' said Kimiya. He showed no surprise at so facile a question. He was too disciplined for that.

'And where is Hito Island?' said Lord Hayato.

'At the most southern end of the islands of Japan, my Lord and Father,' said Kimiya. Lord Hayato nodded. The questioning continued.

'How far are we from the nearest island of Japan?'

'Twenty miles by sea, my Lord and Father.'

'What is the name of this nearest island of Japan?'

'Kyushu island, my Lord and Father.'

'So!' said Lord Hayato, 'We are Clan Hitamoto of Hito Island. Tell me, my son, how do we differ from all other clans?' This time even Kimiya wondered where this was leading. He puzzled greatly because he wanted before all else to be a good son to his beloved father, and he therefore gave a Hito traditionalist answer.

'We differ because we have kept faith with *Bushido*,' he said, 'the way of the samurai!'

'Which means?' said Lord Hayato.

'That we are trained in arms and ready for war,' said Kimiya.

'And what of other samurai?' said Lord Hayato.

'They are corrupted! Japan has been at peace for two hundred years, and other samurai have become clerks and accountants, with wooden swords.' Lord Hayato nodded.

'And who rules over Japan?'

'The Shogun rules, my Lord and father.'

'And what of the Emperor?' said Lord Hayato.

'The Son of Heaven, is honoured by all Japan.'

'But does he rule?'

'No, my Lord and Father.'

'Why not?' said Lord Hayato.

'Because The Son of Heaven lives in his palace at Kyoto and the Shogun rules from Edo Castle.'

'Why does the Shogun rule?' Kimiya began to sweat. He felt that he was being lured out onto a lake with thin ice. The questions were too easy.

'Because of the civil wars two hundred years ago,' he said, 'The Shogun leads Clan Tokugawa, and Tokugawa won the civil wars.'

'Why did they win?' said Lord Hayato, and again Kimiya gave a traditionalist answer.

'Because Tokugawa had the biggest army.'

Lord Hayato shook his head.

Tokugawa did not win by numbers,' he said, 'but by intelligent use of novel weapons: the Tanegashima firearms that we did not ourselves invent, but merely copied from the Portuguese foreigners. Then later, when armies were disbanded during the long peace, the Tokugawa Shoguns ruled by intelligent politics to divide the Clans. *Yes?*'

'*Hi!*' said everyone.

'Hi,' said Lord Hayato. 'but now their politics are failing, alliances are forming among the clans, and the present Shogun is building armies again, in order to punish those clans he does not trust.'

'*Hi!*'

Lord Hayato nodded. He paused a moment and clapped his hands. Instantly the screens hiding half of the chamber slid back. Then, having slid the screens, clan servants in plain black bowed low, and crept out of the chamber and were gone, even as Lord Hayato's sons and samurai looked into the revealed space and gasped, because they saw an array of wonders: secret, foreign and forbidden.

'Come,' said Lord Hayato, and led the company towards four low tables, laid out in line. He went to each in turn.

First there was a monstrosity of bright metals, with tubes and beams. It was three feet long by two feet high, and it breathed smoke from a tiny furnace. So when Lord Hayato pushed a tiny lever, the mechanism began to hiss and move, and a metal beam rocked to and fro to the wonderment of all present.

'Ahhh!' they said.

'This is a model of an engine driven by fire,' said Lord Hayato, 'It pumps water from the depths of a mine.'

And the next: a thick, brass disc, five inches wide, with a glass front over a dial with pointers and barbarian characters. The disc was thrown open to display fathomless complexities within.

'This is a mariner's chronometer. By means of this instrument, the barbarian navigators can find their position anywhere on the oceans.'

The two final wonders Lord Hayato explained together. One was a strange arquebus with a mechanical device instead of a match-lock, and a pointed blade fixed to the muzzle. The last of all – yet another model – displayed a cannon mounted on wheels, with a carriage for its ammunition, and harness for horses to draw the whole thing.

'This firearm is a musket,' said Lord Hayato, 'It needs no match but makes fire by flint, and the blade enables men to hold off cavalry, while this cannon serves as galloping artillery, moving at speed yet stopping in an instant to fire into the enemy from any angle that a general chooses.'

All but one of Lord Hayato's sons gazed at their master in awe for his for his ability to interpret these devices. Lord Hayato turned again to Kimiya, knowing that he would give the traditional – and wrong – answer to the next question.

'My son,' he said, 'I have gathered these foreign devices in secrecy, and now I ask you what we may learn from them?' Kimiya frowned. He thought hard.

'We learn that foreigners are cunning.'

'And?' said Lord Hayato.

'And dangerous!' he said, 'Thus Japan is closed to the world. The Shogun forbids all contact with foreigners. No ships may come and go.' He paused, looked at the devices and blinked at his father. 'And it is death to have such things without permission.'

'Well done, my son,' said Lord Hayato. Kimiya breathed deep in relief and everyone else relaxed. 'And now,' said Lord Hayato, 'where is my youngest son?' He looked down the line at Masahito Hitamoto: thirteen years old, just weeks from first shaving his brow in samurai style, and being given two swords.

'My son!' said Lord Hayato.

'My Lord and father?' said Masahito.

'If Japan is closed to the world,' said Lord Hayato, 'how did I get these foreign devices?'

'Lord and father,' said Masahito, 'Japan is not totally closed. The Shogun allows outside trade from the port of Nagasaki. We trade with China and with the Dutch, so these devices must have come from the Dutch.'

'Correct,' said Lord Hayato Hitamoto, 'But what do we learn from the devices? What do *you* learn?'

'My Lord and Father,' said Masahito, 'I learn that foreign ideas are better than Japanese ideas.' These appalling words drew a gasp of horror from the sons and samurai, and they looked at Lord Hayato to see what he would do.

'Well done, my youngest,' said Lord Hayato, then turned to the rest, 'Now listen to me,' he said, 'Listen well!'

'*Hi!*' They said.

'We must plan for the day when the Shogun comes!' said Lord Hayato, 'Assuming that when he comes, he will bring numbers vastly greater than ours, because the other clans will join him.'

'*Hi!*' They said.

'Fortunately, this will not happen for some years,' said Lord Hayato, 'because the Shogun has a list of rebellious clans to deal with, and because the invasion of Hito Island will be a colossal effort, taking years in preparation.'

'*Hi!*'

'So we have time to prepare by gathering arms and stores, and in training men.'

'*Hi!*'

'But there is something better that we shall do.' He stepped forward and bowed slightly to his youngest son. 'One of us shall leave Japan, and go among the foreigners. He shall learn their languages, and he shall become himself a foreigner.' Lord Hayato paused to study his youngest son's face, and as Lord Hayato had hoped, Masahito looked back at him and nodded. Then Lord Hayato looked at the rest, and felt the urge to laugh, because the dropped jaws and round eyes were hilarious.

'So,' said Lord Hayato, addressing everyone, 'Masahito will leave Japan aboard a Dutch ship. He will leave with a few followers and much gold. He will leave Japan, knowing that under the Shogun's law it is death to return. But he will none the less return when the time is right, bringing with him such weapons and assistance as shall enable our clan, not only to defend itself but to defeat the Shogun and dominate Japan.'

'*Hi!*'

'For this task,' said Lord Hayato, 'I have chosen my youngest son because only the young can learn new things.' He smiled. 'The old have arthritis of the mind, as well as the bones!' He laughed. Everyone laughed.

8

Later, in the private discussions that followed, Lord Hayato's other sons and the leading samurai, agreed that there was nobody like Lord Hayato in all Japan: and in this they were correct. They also agreed that Masahito as the youngest, and a concubine's son, had been chosen because he was expendable: and in this they were wrong. Lord Hayato knew his youngest far better than that.

– 1797 –

CHAPTER 2

Shortly after two bells of the forenoon watch of Tuesday May 2nd 1797, and with Bonaparte gathering men and stores all along the coast of France, hoping to invade England, my ship, the heavy frigate *Euphonides* – pride of the Fleet – was closing on Boulogne with a strong blow from the north on our larboard beam. We were dashing along at an extraordinary rate, under courses, double-reefed topsails, t'gallants, jib and driver, and laid hard over with the sea foaming white beneath the bow. The log was hove, and out went fourteen knots of line: the greatest we'd measured that commission, indicating such speed that the shore batteries had as much chance of hitting a swallow as of landing a ball on board of us.

So far so good, my jolly boys, but for the business in hand we had to go dangerously close inshore where the sand-banks lay, beckoning us onward to death and ruination. So, to make sure we didn't run ourselves aground, it was time to take in sail until we were making just five knots or less, which speed – for a frigate under way – is about the greatest that can be maintained if the lead is to be hove in order to measure the depth of water under the keel. Once again, so far so good, but nothing is perfect in this wicked world, and a speed of just five knots gave the gunners their chance in the French shore batteries, and they must have grinned and looked at us, and twirled their moustaches before setting to with handspikes, to lay their pieces on target.

But more of them later because in the meanwhile, one William Staines of 23 years old, able seaman, was lashed to the fore chains of our lee bow, heaving the lead with his right hand while the rest of the 25-fathom line was held neatly coiled in his right. His back was hard against the deadeyes of the fore-shrouds and his feet were balanced on the chain-plate. Mere landmen would have been amazed at the fearful precariousness of his position: pinned to the outside of the hull with the spray stinging into his eyes and drenching him to the skin. But Staines was used to it, and anyway, we were going in to give Mossoo another hammering and the thought of that kept him happy.

Staines had been hand-picked by our Bosun, because the work was hard, with the 7-pound lead prism flashing round on its line in a great arc, then leaping forward as Staines hurled it ahead of the plunging bow of our ship. But Staines managed it, and I marked him down for double grog: him and all his messmates if we should live so long as dinner time. Then the line paid out like a live thing, and its various knots and markers slipped rapidly through Staines's fingers: two leather strips for two fathoms, three leather strips for three fathoms, a piece of white duck for five fathoms, red bunting for seven, and a leather washer for ten, and so on. Staines could tell them at night or in fog, that's why he was there. So he watched the line go down and slacken as the lead hit bottom.

'By the deep – ten!' he cried in a sing-song, carrying voice to tell us all that there were ten fathoms of water under the bow. So we were already close in, and later it would get shallower, for the mouth of Boulogne harbour was constantly choking itself with sandbanks that shifted with wind and tide, and Staines of all people knew that a calculated risk had to be taken in running over them. Thus there was always the chance of grounding on a sand-bank that hadn't been there last time, and which would be a seriously unpleasant thing to do if it happened within range of some of the batteries infesting the coast around Boulogne.

So Staines hauled in the line and swung for another cast. He would do that for hours if he had to. The ship's safety depended on him and he knew it.

On the main-deck, 'Chalkie' White, 25 years old, and a gun captain, crouched over the breech of *Black Dick*, his starboard gun. Chalkie and his mates – a dozen in total, with a ship's boy to run cartridges up from the magazines – manned a pair of guns: one on either beam. The larboard gun was called *Mrs Dick,* although *Lady Howe* would have been more accurate, since Chalkie had named the first gun after Admiral Lord Howe under whom he'd once served and whose nick-name was Black Dick.

Like all our forty, main-deck guns, *Black Dick* and *Mrs Dick* were 24 pounders weighing 47 hundredweights and stretching nine feet six inches in the barrel. They were large and heavy pieces: especially for a frigate, and especially if the crew had to be split to man both guns at once. But that was a rare event and hadn't happened yet this commission.

At the moment, the entire main-deck battery was run out, as were the 32 pounder carronades on the quarterdeck and foc'sl. Everything was ready for action, with firelock triggers screwed to the breeches, and matches smouldering in tubs in case the locks failed. Every gun was primed, loaded and shotted, awaiting only a tug from the gun-captains on the long trigger-lanyards, coiled with over the cascables at the far inboard ends of the guns. Likewise, at the moment there was little to do as *Euphonides* bore down upon her target, but there was no slack discipline aboard my ship, and the gun crews had to stand ready, and not skylark, nor lean out of the ports to see what was happening. Otherwise they were well and truly hemmed in because in the first place, the main-deck bulwarks were too high to see over, while at the bow and stern, the main-deck was covered by the quarterdeck and foc'sl, and even in the open waist, the ships boats and spare spars were lashed on the skids that spanned the waist, blocking out most of the blue sky.

So Chalkie White, was crouched over the breech of *Black Dick* as if taking a practise sight on a target, but really he was hoping for a look at the Fort Rouge earthworks which were our destination and target.

'Whatcher see, Chalkie?' said number two, the second gun-captain, out of the side of his mouth.

'D'you see them buggerin' Froggies yet?' said number eleven, one of the hand-spike men.

'No,' whispered Chalkie White, 'Not a soddin' thing.'

'Silence on the Gun-deck!' bawled an angry voice, 'Avast there, or I'll stop the grog of every man!' Mr Rosewell, the second lieutenant, aged 28, was pacing up and down the main-deck, waiting for the order to fire. He was as anxious and excited as any man, and just as hungry for a sight of what was coming. But if he had to act stern and cool, and not see over the side, then so would the bloody hands!

So Rosewell turned his anger on the four midshipmen, stationed up and down the deck, in charge under him, of three gun-crews each.

'Cannot you young gentlemen keep your men in order?' He bellowed, 'It's like Bedlam!' and he stamped along, with his hands tight-clasped behind his back, glaring at the men looking for some unfortunate to find fault with. Someone was going to suffer if Lieutenant Rosewell couldn't see what was going on.

Up in the Maintop, Mr Pollock, master's mate, 18, and Mr Midshipman Barclay, 14, had the best view in the ship. The Maintop was a D-shaped platform, 60 feet above the deck, firmly carpentered to the mainmast, immediately above the main-yard. It was 20 feet across its flat stern and 15 feet long towards its curving bow. Astern it had a nice safety rail to stop clumsy persons falling off. On either beam it was fenced in by the four taut, tarred lines of the main topmast shrouds. But where it faced out towards *Euphonides's* bow, the maintop was quite open and a landman would have been horrified by the deadly drop from this unquiet, heaving place high up in the singing rigging.

For convenience, the top was pierced with *lubbers' holes* like hatches, whereby any man who wished to be thought a no-seaman could ascend in comfort into the top via the main shrouds. The alternative was to climb the futtock shrouds which ran outwards from *below* the top, and from an area far *smaller* than the top, such that they fanned outwards and upwards, obliging the climber to hang sickeningly on his back, scrabbling to fight gravity, while the ship's lively movement did its best to shake him off.

But Mr Pollock and Mr Barclay had gone up into the top at a run, not even conscious of the futtock shrouds. Not any more. Not aboard *Euphonides*. Even the six marines keeping company with them in the maintop, hadn't dared come through the lubber's hole. They'd come up slower with their boots and muskets and pouches, and with a lot more care and white knuckles. But they'd done it because their sergeant had them in his eye as they climbed, and his views on the matter were no secret.

Now the marines had loaded ball cartridge and stood ready to fire at such opportunities as might present. They were the pick of the ship's marksmen and for action stations they wore forage caps and seamen's blue jackets; their smart red coats being put away for more formal occasions.

Pollock and Barclay were also the pick of the ship. They had the best eyesight, they had my own best telescope, and they had my confidence as being sharp-witted enough to notice what *should* be noticed and to set in down in a note-book provided for the purpose. Thus Pollock and Barclay worked as a team, Pollock keeping the glass to his eye and calling out what he saw, for Barclay to record with his pencil. It was they who'd marked out the sites of the ever-growing number of batteries. It was their records that passed to Commodore Bollington in command of our squadron aboard the flagship *Sandromedes*, over the horizon, and eventually to their Lordships of the Admiralty in London. Even Mr Pitt the Prime Minister might see them if he chose to enquire.

So Pollock and Barclay had their own names for the batteries and knew them like friends. They knew which were smart and which were slack to open fire. They knew which were the most dangerous.

'Chasseur, firing!' said Pollock, 'Four guns, full salvo!' The French coast was much closer now, and Pollock could see white cliffs, green grass, and waves breaking on the shore. If he'd chosen to look, he'd have found the mouth of Boulogne harbour in plain sight a few miles ahead and even the low-lying works at Fort Rouge could be made out. But for the moment, Pollock was more interested to see what the batteries could do. The white balls of smoke were blown swiftly inland off the embrasures of Chasseur battery, and later came the thud-thud-thud of detonations. Pollock put down the telescope and scanned the sea immediately ahead, astern and on either beam of their ship. 'No fall of shot observed,' he said, then '*Ah!* There!' he pointed to a cluster of short-lived plumes of water where a cluster of heavy shot had plunged into the sea.

'Bah!' said Pollock, disappointed, 'Quarter of a mile off!'

'Yes,' said Barclay, 'But look at the range! Could *you* do better? And it *was* their first salvo.'

'They'll not get in many more,' said Pollock.

'Shows how keen they are even to try,' said Barclay, 'Little Boney's lit a fire under 'em ... Ah! Bombadier's firing!'

'And here's Fort Rouge,' said Pollock, turning his glass on the remarkable French earthwork that Napoleon's engineers – *Les Genies* – as the Frog army called them – were raising up out of what looked like open water out beyond the mouth of Boulogne's river: the Liane. It was yet another scheme of the French to ward off the Rosbif navy by sheer force of engineering. 'Got to credit them,' said Pollock scanning the busy works with professional approval. Look what the buggers have built! D'you think our engineers could have done it?'

Barclay shook his head, because Fort Rouge was a truly heroic concept: a battery thrown up on a sand-bank that once had barely surfaced at low tide. Hundreds of boat loads of broken rock had been dumped on the sand, and then hundreds of timber piles driven in, and a gun-platform built, and now the beginnings of a deep parapet was rising to shelter the guns that soon would be in place in a narrow crescent, ninety yards long by twenty deep, where thousands of men had laboured for months. But now their work was to be smashed in ruins as *Euphonides* ran past like the angel of death, and at last our gunners could see their target, large through their ports. From bow to stern, our guns went off in disciplined sequence, each one hurling a charge of grape and round-shot. Deafened by the appalling roar of the guns, and blinded by their smoke, Will Staines, the leadsman, steadily did his duty and found one fathom or less under the keel, as the ship thrashed onward. Fortunately, Mr O'Flaherty, our sailing master, had judged the thing to a nicety and the muzzles of the starboard battery were no more than 30 yards from the earthworks and the wretched workforce.

First to die were the gunners manning the half-dozen field pieces, which were all the defence that Fort Rouge had at present. Before they could throw themselves flat, the gunners were smashed into offal and hurled among the splinters and wreckage of their guns. Elsewhere men had taken shelter in pits and trenches dug for the purpose. Mostly they survived and some of the soldiers even returned fire with their puny muskets. But here and there a ball ploughed into a pit of human bodies and pulped and minced and smashed.

Then *Euphonides* was bearing away and the shore-batteries that had been silenced while Fort Rouge was between them and the enemy, opened fire on us again, and with a fire that grew steadily more accurate as they got the range, such that great water-spouts heaved up around us as shot plunged into the grey waters: chop-chop-chop, at lightning speed, throwing spray and dead fish all over our decks.

Up in the maintop, as the marines reloaded, Pollock yelled out the details of everything that was under way inside Boulogne harbour, and then turned his gaze on the batteries:

'Dragoon firing! Lancer firing! Hussar firing! Windmill *still not firing!*'

'What's wrong with 'em?' cried Pollock.

Down on the quarterdeck, I personally gave orders to wear ship and bring her round to give the Frogs our larboard battery, while on the main-deck, Chalkie White and his mates sponged, reloaded and ran out *Black Dick*. Then they ran across the deck to take *Mrs Dick* in charge as the ship heeled over to come about and run down on Fort Rouge again. Now facing fully alert and eager gunners in a dozen batteries, *Euphonides* came down to give her second broadside with shot and shell whistling all around her hull and through her rigging.

Again we passed close in to the sand-bank and its works. Again we poured out iron and lead, and again we came past without losing a spar. We did that twice more, until shot began to tear into our hull, at which point I judged we had done enough and it was time to spread our wings, pick up speed and haul out of range of the French batteries.

So it was an excellent reconnaissance and a useful bombardment. We brought away fresh and valuable intelligence on the Boulogne invasion flotilla. We destroyed a battery of 8-pounders. We killed some dozens of men and wounded still more. But more important by far than all this, we had continued in the vital process of hammering fear into the wretches given the job of building Fort Rouge, thus further reducing their efficiency and delaying completion of the works.

But none of this was done without cost, because it ain't the nature of warfare that you get something for nothing. Indeed it ain't the way of the world at large, and that is the reason I've told this little tale in such a way as to concentrate your attention upon others, and not your Uncle Jacob, because although only one of us was wounded, four of us were killed.

Thus William Staines was shot dead by musket fire, and found hanging by the lashings that secured him in the main-chains. Thus Chalkie White was gutted by a shell fragment, and bits of him found in various places upon and around *Black Dick*. Thus Mr Pollock was blown out of the top by the wind of a passing shot and never found at all, while Mr Rosewell lost much of his left thigh to a splinter thrown up by the enemy's shot, and he bled to death despite our surgeon's best efforts to save him.

Conversely, Commodore Bollington in command of our squadron, thought we'd done exceedingly well, and told me so at dinner aboard his ship, since only four killed in a whole ship's company was nothing to the Navy in wartime, and even I agreed with him for a while, since I thought that all the future held for me was command of *Euphonides*, the finest ship in the fleet.

So it's as well, my boys — my very jolly boys — that I didn't know what was waiting for me just around the corner.

CHAPTER 3

(Transcript of a letter written early in 1797 and known to be from Mr William Pitt, the Prime Minister, to The Earl Spencer, First Lord of the Admiralty. No date nor addresses appear on the letter, which presumably was delivered by special courier. A naïve use of capitals attempts to disguise actual names though most are easily guessed. But 'R' was Mr Philip Charles Rowland. For more of him see Chapter 4 which follows, and also 'Fletcher and the Great Raid'.)

My Lord,

As discussed yesterday, and in summary, the State has occasional need of a diplomatic agent of rare and special kind. He must display intelligence, initiative, boldness and tenacity, and be ready to kill without hesitation. He must however be of low rank, without powerful family or friends, such that we may – if need arise – deny all knowledge of him.

You already know that during recent events in France we lost the services of R who had for many years acted as above but was killed in action. But you may not know that the man who was R's choice as his replacement – indeed his ideal and outstanding choice – is now aboard a ship of the Sea Service, and is thereby under your command.

Since I – and the others – entirely endorse the choice made by R, and given the unique demands of the Indian/Japanese business, we should be infinitely obliged if you would at your most early and urgent convenience, bring ashore the chosen man, and fetch him to London where he may be instructed, since he is at this moment in command of His Majesty's ship E and is Captain JF.

I am, My Lord, etc, etc,

P.

CHAPTER 4

So much for Fort Rouge and my belief that I was safe aboard *Euphonides*. More of that later, but first you should be reminded of certain things. Thus 1797 was a bad year. The French wars were sizzling and Napoleon Bonaparte was in control of France. He had enormous armies ready to march, and enormous fleets of ships a-building in the French ship-yards: and fine ships they were too, because no man can deny that the Frogs built better ships than we did. So God help England if ever those fleets got past our blockade, and out to sea, because man-o-war business can't be learned in harbour with the crew cosy in their hammocks. It has to be learned under sail, with the ship heaving, the deck-heads dripping on the men below, and all hands piped on deck when the sea turns nasty.

Meanwhile we had to fight the Dutch fleet which, unlike the French, was indeed battle ready. We fought them at Camperdown which we won, and a sad business it was too, because we should naturally be the allies of the Dutch who are decent and seamanly folk very much like ourselves. But Napoleon forced them into French service, so it was his fault.

In further sorrows, 1797 was the year of the great mutinies at Spithead and the Nore, and it was the year when I was recovering from adventures in France which got me almost garrotted and blown up by a devious, dangerous, lying, murdering creature named Rowland whom you may recall from the previous volume of these memoirs. Rowland was a secret agent and wanted me to be one like him, but I swore over his dead body that I'd never do anything of the kind.

Finally, it was the year when I got a new name, and became known to the public. The new name was what the lower deck called me when I wasn't supposed to be listening, and it came from ships I'd served in before *Euphonides*. The name was Jacky Flash: *Jacky* from a corruption of Jacob, and *Flash* from the west-country pronunciation of Fletcher – many of the crew being west-countrymen – whereby they swallowed the 't' and sounded my name as *Flash'r*. But that was just my lower deck name, and the public got to know me as the famous nautical rascal who was reported in all the newspapers, not that I ever wanted fame. Indeed I did not. I wanted quiet. I wanted to slip away and not be noticed, to get on with the career in commerce, which would have been the love of my life if only I had been left to do it. Instead I was known as the man who had sunk ships with submarine mines, and as the *natural* – meaning bastard – heir to the enormous fortune of the Late Sir Henry Coignwood, whose witch-wife Lady Sarah was living proof that exceeding beauty can go with exceeding spite. That blasted woman wanted me dead to get her husband's money, and plotted against me for years, starting with getting me took by the Press Gang. Then later the Navy seized me by the collar, pointed to certain naughtiness on my part – a little bit of murder and mutiny – and offered absolution from hanging if I would serve in the Fleet, give up the Coignwood inheritance, and abandon my ambitions in trade.

God knows why the Navy wanted me, because I never wanted the Navy. I had no interest in the sea, and a strong dislike of hot shot, cold steel, and hideous foreign fevers. Or do I fail to make myself clear? And besides that, I was – from birth – always adept at monetary calculations and believed that trade not only increases the wealth of the individual trader, but contributes to the general wealth of mankind. So just remember, my jolly boys, that your Uncle Jacob was pressed *into* the Navy, and always wanted to get *out* of it.

[Untrue! Fletcher was immensely proud of the Royal Navy and loved the ships in which he served. He was a fine seaman, a natural leader, and a navigator to rival Cook of the Antipodes. But he persisted duplicitously in denying these truths so long as he lived. He was ambivalently dishonest in this respect. S.P.]

And so to what happened next. It began on Monday June 12th with *Euphonides* detached from Bollington's squadron, and running northeast under easy sail off De Panne on the north west coast of France. Our duty was to capture any French merchant ships, or even better a convoy, that might try sneaking along the coast, and a happy duty it was too, and the dream of any frigate captain. This, because under the Admiralty's 'Prize' system of legalised piracy, any ships that I took, would be condemned in a Court of Admiralty, then purchased on Britannia's behalf, and the proceeds distributed among my ship's company with a huge share going to me. By then we'd already caught two fat merchantmen, with cargoes of wine, brandy, grain and other desirables, and the prize money had brought happiness to every soul aboard, including Jimbo, the ship's cat.

So, just on the turn of the afternoon watch, I was busy with my calculations of the ship's position, a task that is another piece of happiness to me, either by clock or by lunar, and one of the few consolations of the sea life – that and my immunity to the sea-sickness. Then far off I heard the flat *thud* of a ship's gun – just the one detonation – and the sound of one of the midshipmen galloping down from the quarterdeck. I heard his feet hammering the woodwork all the way down the companionway and up to the door of my day cabin, just under the break of the quarterdeck on the larboard side and opposite the Master's on the starboard, where we could be close to the ship's wheel and the binnacle.

Then the boy was shouting, and I heard him clearly since the door was wedged open for the fresh air.

'Sail approaching, with signal for the Cap'n!' he said, 'For Jacky Flash! Ship coming on like a galloping horse with every stitch set! Coming on with signals flying!' I recognised the voice. It was Mr Midshipman St John, fourteen years old, though not the youngest of the six we had on board. There was one little chap of only eleven, though the eldest was older than me at twenty-five. St John was just four feet nine inches tall, his voice unbroken, the son of a merchant-service captain, and very keen. He was busting to give me his news, but there was a lobster-coat, cross-belted marine guarding my door with his musket.

'All very well mister-sinjun-sah,' says the lobster, 'But 'oo might this Jacky Flash be? I don't know none such aboard this ship, so 'oo sent you dahn here to the Cap'n's door?' It was the ancient ritual of wrinkled cynicism sneering down on youthful zeal.

'It's a sail! It's a sail!' says the mid, 'It's a signal!' I heard him hopping on the spot. He was excited.

'Oh?' says the marine, 'And 'oo might that be from?'

I got up, put on my hat, took my telescope off its hooks on the bulkhead, and abandoned my calculations. I was curious. I wondered why a ship – presumably a King's ship – was asking for me? So maybe it was premonition, or maybe my memory of that moment is clouded by what followed, but I'm damned sure I wasn't happy even when I left that cabin.

23

Then I was out of the door, the marine and the mid saluting, and I was past the men at the wheel, up the companionway to the quarterdeck where the officer of the watch was in command of the ship. He was Mr Pyne, the first lieutenant and the greatest man in the ship after me. He was a veteran, greying officer and very good in a steady, duty-doing way. He was totally reliable, totally steady, and happy to be Number One in *Euphonides*. Mind you that hadn't stopped him resenting me when first I came aboard, less than half his age. But he'd forgiven me by then, so off came his hat and all other hats on the quarterdeck, while tars without hats put touched brow and stamped deck in the ancient custom of the Service.

They did this with reverence, my jolly boys, because you have to understand that not even Julius Caesar was quite so much in command of all he surveyed, as the captain of a Sea-Service ship in King George's time. A captain could make and break, praise or damn, reward or flog, and all aboard knew it. Not that I ever ordered a flogging because I always believed it kinder to knock down insolence the instant it appeared, and precious few of the insolent ever came back for more.

[It should be noted that Fletcher was hugely big and strong and aggressively violent at fisty-cuffs. Once when he was already an old man, and because the local youth were urging him on and the ladies gazing in awe, I saw him engage a professional pugilist at a County fair, and when all was done, the pugilist was proud that he had lasted nearly a full minute before being knocked out of the ring. S.P.]

Thus all present gave honour at my appearance on the quarterdeck and there was quite a number of them. For one thing, the news of the signal had gone round the ship, and all hands were coming up to see what was going forward. For another, the midshipmen were mustered for lessons in the wielding of their quadrants.

Their instructors were Mr Tildesley, second lieutenant, and the Rev. Dr Goodsby, the ship's chaplain. Goodsby was a highly educated man who was my secretary for the various enterprises that I ran aboard ship, such as claiming wages for non-existent servants, selling off goods condemned as unfit, and the safe carriage of gold coin for bankers. All these activities were illegal, but every captain was at it in those days, whatever the Parson might tell you in church. You just believe your Uncle Jacob, they were, because it's only since Queen Victoria met the blessed Saint Albert that things got so stiff and clean.

Better still, Goodsby had strong family connections with Child's of Fleet Street: one of London's oldest and most trusted banks, which is why – long before I came aboard *Euphonides* – he'd got so splendid a posting in the first place, because he could get his captain – now myself – favoured treatment from Child's including acting as my agent, to chase prize money out of a lazy system and get it snug into my account with Child's.

Meanwhile, I record the astounding fact that also undergoing navigational instruction among the mids – and to the bafflement of the entire universe – was Mr Norton our Lieutenant of Marines, because he fancied himself as a navigator. Of course he made a foul mess of it, and by his reckonings we might as well be in St Paul's cathedral as off the coast of France. But what can you expect from a soldier? But then Mr Pyne was addressing me.

'Signal, Sir,' he said, 'two points off the bow,' and another *thud* came across the water as a gun was fired. That meant the signal was urgent. So I raised my glass and looked, which was no simple matter on the quarterdeck of a frigate, because the bulwarks on either hand were topped with nettings to hold the hammocks of the men on duty. Each hammock was a long, fat, bound-around sausage of white canvas, bearing its owner's mark, and the dozens of them leaning neatly on one another, made a nice barricade that was supposed to stop shot if the enemy was alongside – which it certainly did not – though it did hide you so they couldn't aim straight at you.

So if you wanted to see what was bearing down upon you, you had to climb on to one of the quarterdeck carronade slides. Either that or you had to get up into the main or mizzen shrouds and that has never been my fancy, since I'm too big to be easy with going aloft. So up I got on to a carronade slide, with all present standing back to give me room. But even that's not easy. Not with the ship working under you, and the wind blowing, and the spray trying to blot out the view from your glass. But it comes with practise, and after a while you don't even notice the effort.

So there was the sea: all grey and green and wallowing, with white foam on the tops of the waves, and a few gulls astern of us for whatever might go over the side that they could eat, and there – in the round field of my fine Dolland telescope – there was neat-little, sharp-little, bouncing, bounding cutter, still some miles off, and it was indeed coming on like a racing stallion. It wasn't much more than a gentleman's yacht, about a hundred tons burthen, with a billowing spread of canvas: a huge fore-and-aft mainsail bent to a gaff and boom, a square topsail above it, two staysails for'ard, and even a square spritsail under its long, out-stretching bowsprit.

Someone was driving that cutter as hard as she would go, and she was indeed a King's ship, under British colours and with a hoist of signals straining in the wind. I felt rather than saw that Midshipman St John was hopping up and down nearby, dying to tell me what the signals read, because he'd looked them up in the code book, and I don't doubt Mr Pyne felt the same. But that wouldn't have been polite now, would it? It wouldn't have been proper to tell the captain how to read signals. If I'd been older and known to be short-sighted, they'd have told me. But not me. So I looked, and stared, and did my best to remember Popham's Code.

[Popham's code was the Navy's standard definition of signal flags published by Admiral Home Popham in 1799, though unofficially in use earlier. Fletcher's claim of ignorance is affectation. He knew much of the code by heart since his memory was astonishing in all such matters. S.P.]

Finally, I worked it out. It took some effort because some of the signals can mean several things. Thus the flags signalling number 65, can mean: *Any, Anything, Anyhow* or *Anywhere* and you have to work out which by the context. So – and with a ball of powder smoke from the cutter followed by another *thud* in emphasis – the signal was saying:

'Most urgent Admiralty orders for Captain Fletcher.'

Oh dear. Oh dear indeed. Just when I was nice and snug and I thought they'd leave me alone. So I sighed, and got down off the carronade slide.

'Orders coming aboard, Mr Pyne,' I said.

'Aye-aye, Sir!' said Pyne.

'Back the main tops'l and heave-to,' I said, 'so soon as the cutter comes up with us.'

'Aye-aye, Sir!' Pyne said, and I saw how full the decks had become, and the shrouds too, and all the muttering between every man aboard ship. So I frowned.

'And get these idle buggers to their duties!' I said. I wasn't happy and didn't see why they should be either.

'Aye-aye, Sir!'

So Pyne bellowed, the boatswain and his mates bellowed, and the tars doubled to their duties, and the officers and young gentlemen pretended they'd not been nosing in the captain's business, and got back to their quadrants. But Mr O'Flaherty, the master, came and stood beside me. The master – sailing master – was the ship's expert in navigation. He had no King's Commission like the lieutenants, only a Warrant from the Navy Board, and in theory he was a hired craftsman and not a gentleman Sea Service officer. But that was rot, because any captain who ignored the master's advice on seafaring matters was in peril if things went wrong, and the master always messed in the gunroom with the lieutenants. Our master was a balding, middle-aged Irishman named O'Flaherty: a fine seaman who'd served with me on other ships. I liked him, I trusted him as a friend, and he knew more about my past than anyone else in the ship.

Cap'n!' he said, raising his hat.

'Mr O'Flaherty!' I said.

'Admiralty orders?' he said.

'Yes,' I said, and shook my head.

'Well,' he said, 'If I might say so, Cap'n, there can't be much to worry about, since you must be high in their Lordships' favour or you'd not be in command of so fine a ship as this.'

'That's what worries me,' I said, 'Any change must be for the worse.'

Then there was the inevitable wait as the cutter – *Chaser* she was called – pranced like a dancer and swept round in a most elegant fashion. Round she came into the wind, sails roaring and cracking, her gunn'ls heeled nearly under, and then with topsail thrown back into the wind, she lost way and wallowed in the ocean: rising, falling and rolling less than fifty yards from *Euphonides*.

Seen close up, His Majesty's cutter *Chaser*, was a most beautiful little vessel: some seventy feet on the keel, and twenty on the beam, bearing two six-pounder long guns, and four six-pounder carronades. There couldn't have been more than thirty-five men aboard, and every one a veteran to judge from the way her captain handled her. At once she hoist out a boat, and six hands and a coxswain tumbled aboard, and a seventh man got in with careful trepidation, going down a rope-and-plank ladder thrown over the side for him. We saw the epaulettes on his shoulders and heard the boatswain's calls as he went over the side.

27

Mr Pyne saw that, and yelled an order

'Stand by to give honours, and rig the ladder!'

'Aye-aye!' and the boatswain stood by the rail with two mates ready with their pipes, while our marines paraded, and all hands not working the ship faced the rail, ready to stand to attention. A brief pause followed as the hands in *Chaser's* boat pulled as if their souls were at risk, should they be seen as slack in the eyes of another ship's company. Then they were bumping alongside, and the wicked sea was heaving ship and boat up and down in contrary motion, in the wicked attempt to cause drownings or the breaking of limbs among those in the boat who were trying to get out of it, and up the towering sides of the ship.

But that was no more than the normal wickedness of the sea, and somehow an elderly, senior, Sea Service officer was climbing over the rail, to the screech of boatswain's pipes, and slipping, and beckoning for assistance with flapping hands and fraught features such that O'Flaherty stepped forward, being close by, and grabbed hold of the officer, heaved him on to our main deck, and stood him up straight. Or perhaps it wasn't just because O'Flaherty was near by, because a few words passed between them because they already knew each other.

'Much obliged Mr O'Flaherty,' said the officer.

'My pleasure, Sir,' said O'Flaherty, and stepped back and saluted, and the elderly officer nodded. Then having looked about the ship, he nodded again, pleased with what he saw – which was no more than he should have been, aboard *Euphonides!*

There he stood for a while, and pulled his clothes in to their proper places, and got his hat properly on his head, all the while keeping an oilskin package safe under his arm, which package doubtless contained the Most Urgent Orders, that were for me, and as I looked at him, the elderly officer spotted me for who I am: which wasn't hard given the size of me.

'Captain Fletcher!' he said, 'I am Smythe-Lewis, Sir. I am in His Majesty's Service, Sir, and proceeding under the strictest orders from Their Lordships of the Admiralty.' He paused and sniffed, and reached for his dignity but couldn't quite grasp it, since his face was soaking wet from the passage in the boat, and a large snot-drop dangled from his nose. Worse still, his voice crackled with phlegm, and he had to cough to clear his tubes: 'I am there-fore ... *cough-cough!* Come aboard, Sir ... *cough-cough-cough!*' he said, 'I am come aboard, Sir ... *cough-cough-cough-cough!* To relieve you of command.'

CHAPTER 5

'In our Hito tradition, cockerels are auspicious, and we paint them on the walls of our houses. In England the people cause them to fight. They fight in public arenas where the greatest noblemen sit beside commoners and each shouts at the other as if they were equals.'

(From the 'Foreign Journal' of Masahito Hitamoto. Entry dated Tuesday June 13th 1797.)

Inside the Royal Cockpit off Birdcage Walk, London, the noise was tremendous. Near three hundred men – and exclusively men since females were barred – were crammed-packed into three, circular rows of seating lit by tall windows running round the walls of the one-hundred foot cupola with its white dome in Portland Stone designed by Mr William Kent in the 1730s.

The company was a typical London mixture of rogues and royalty, peers and pickpockets, lumpers and lawyers, grooms and gentlemen, soldiers in scarlet, squires in wigs, plus porters, pox-doctors, clerks, clergymen, and millionaire East India nabobs. All wore hats, and most waved walking sticks or horse-whips to emphasise their opinions, as they howled and cheered, whooped and clamoured and bamboozled each other into incomprehension, since Kent's noble dome had the unintended effect of throwing back speech in booming cacophony.

Enjoying the show, in a prized position in the front row, sat two young men of very different appearance as they took restorative gulps of brandy from a silver pocket-flask. One was curly haired, fresh-faced, and pumped full of money. His clothes were excellent and he was Mr Oswald Kilbride: known to his friends as *Ozzy.* With him was his very good, though recently met, friend whom everyone addressed as *Massimo,* because someone fluent in Italian had remarked that this Italian name sounded like a condensation of the gentleman's real name which was too strange for an Englishman's tongue. Thus Massimo was Japanese, and was small and dark, most pleasing to the female sex, and with straight black hair and exotic, slanted eyes. He was dressed in style and looked every inch the young London buck. More than that, to the wonder of everyone who met him, he *spoke and acted* like a young London buck, with a flawless accent, and the manner and bearing of an Englishman.

In fact the only thing that marked out Massimo as being different from other Englishmen was the fact that he was invariably accompanied by at least two men who were as Japanese as himself, and as well-dressed as himself, but who treated him with enormous respect. They were in their thirties and when they moved, they did so as if springs were wound up within them, waiting only for the word of release. But they said nothing, and displayed the total absence of emotion that Englishmen expected of Orientals, and it was notable that when Massimo addressed these followers, then occasionally – briefly and for an instant – he let slip a very different character which was formal, authoritarian and dominant. But this character disappeared in an eye-blink, when Massimo spoke to any English man or lady, and smiled and laughed and joked.

Today, one of the stone-faced retainers sat on either side of Ozzy and Massimo. They sat with arms folded among all the howling confusion. They were silent. But Massimo was not.

'Bring 'em on!' he yelled, 'Bring 'em on, and we'll make our bets!'

'Yes! Yes!' said Ozzy.

'Yes!' said three hundred voices, and Massimo and Ozzy took another gulp each of Ozzy's flask, or at least Ozzy took a gulp, and he certainly *thought* that Massimo had done likewise, grand fellow that he was, and whom Ozzy had met at Brooke's Club only a week last Tuesday.

Then something like silence fell as two *Setters* entered the small, twenty-foot, circular arena raised up off the ground before the front row of seats. Each Setter carried a flannel bag that wriggled and squawked, one bag being red, the other green, and each man bowed to the Master of Ceremonies, sat in a high-back chair at one end of the arena, and who had been chosen for his huge voice.

'M'Lords and gennelman-all!' he roared, 'An' yer royal 'ighnesses likewise!' Much laughter greeted that, and those present – supposedly incognito – who were of blood royal, smiled graciously at those around them. 'Now best of order, and quiet – *IF* – you please,' cried the Master of Ceremonies, 'best of order for the first contest.' A brief pause, more cheers, then: 'In the red! At one hundred and twenty-five ounces: the game cock *Billy Ruffian* of Bamford!' Deafening cheers followed, but the Master of Ceremonies merely raised his voice, 'In the green! At one hundred and twenty-one ounces: the game cock *Little Arthur*, of Middleton farm!' More cheers followed, then, 'Both birds fully docked and trimmed, and armed according to house rules.' Still more cheers followed, then, 'Gentlemen Setters?'

'Here, Sir!' they said.

'You may release your birds!'

After that it was bedlam and pandemonium. The noise was incredible as bets were made, and blows exchanged among the audience, and collars scragged and curses roared, while two game cocks were dropped out onto the arena, and shoved at each other by the Setters such that the birds, ducked and weaved, leapt and darted, and finally struck with the vicious steel spurs fastened to their feet, to make more deadly the combat that nature intended to be fought with claws.

The result was blood and feathers all over the small arena, followed by death and mutilation.

It was the same for all the fights that followed, apart from one pair that would not fight and got their necks wrung. It was fine entertainment for all those who cared for it, which certainly included Ozzy Kilbride, who certainly believed that his friend Massimo had equally enjoyed it, though Ozzy's flask – a large one – had been quite full when he went into the cockpit and now it was quite empty, and Ozzy hadn't really the head for brandy, and was at the rosy stage when all the world is lovely. In any case, Massimo said that he enjoyed the fights. He said so, in the heaving queue on the way out.

'Grand fun!' he said, 'a bang-up sporting feast! Better than dog-fights.'

'Yes,' said Ozzy, 'we tried the dogs yesterday. Was it yesterday?'

'Day before,' said Massimo and laughed.

But then, as they jostled and fought for the exit, poor Massimo was bumped and almost knocked over by a very large and aggressive person who appeared to be a coal heaver, and had two friends exactly like himself. Ozzy noticed that the large person made no attempt to apologize.

'*Effin* monkey!' he said, 'Get yer *effin* arse out o' the way of an *effin* Christian!'

31

'Yeah!' said his friends.

And then Ozzy grinned, as the two Japanese followers who had come out with Massimo, closed upon the aggressive persons, and although the two Japanese followers were smaller than the aggressive persons, the aggressive persons found their right hands seized and themselves howling with the pain of dislocated thumbs, and then tripped over with all the world laughing at them. One struggled up to fight, but a Japanese gentleman spread two fingers and poked him in both eyes at once, such he howled and made no further trouble. Ozzy laughed. It was very funny.

Outside, Birdcage walk was broad, sunny, lined with trees, and full of the carriages of those cockpit patrons who had them. There was much merry shouting between lords, coachmen, urchins and beggars, and Ozzy allowed himself to be steered towards a small, maroon-painted barouche: an expensive open carriage with hood thrown back for this fine day, and set to a pair of horses with a coachman on the box. The coachman wore the livery coat and gold-laced tricorn of his trade, and he saluted Massimo with his whip because he was yet another Japanese follower in Massimo's service.

'Beg pardon, old fellow,' said Massimo, 'But I've business pressing, so d'you mind if we run you home, and perhaps meet tomorrow?'

'Oh?' said Ozzy, 'Ain't we going to Hoby of St James's for my new boots?'

'Can't be done, old fellow,' said Massimo, 'Business, don't y'know.'

'Oh,' said Ozzy, 'Yes. Suppose so. Very good of you to run me home. I'm feeling a bit tired.'

In fact Ozzy was so tired that he dozed in the comfortable carriage, and never noticed that the route to his father's London House, was not direct, but passed down Leadenhall street, where the carriage stopped opposite a vast and noble building, with huge Ionic columns topped by a pediment of classical sculptures, two tiers of great windows, and a busy traffic of humanity flowing through its doors.

Ozzy found himself nudged into consciousness.

'I say, old chap,' said Massimo, 'What building is that? I've seen Kings' palaces that are less fine!'

'Oh that?' said Ozzy, peering. That's East India House. It's where the East India Company lives.'

'Is it now?' said Massimo.

'Yes,' said Ozzy, 'My Pa's a great man in there. He does something or other.'

'Does he?' said Massimo, 'How interesting.'

'Not really,' said Ozzy, 'But Pa's good for my bills.'

'I've some business in the East India trade,' said Massimo, 'D'you think I might meet your Pa?'

'Certainly,' said Ozzy, 'Anything for a friend. Come to dinner tomorrow.' He was a kind young man, even if stupid.

Later, when Ozzy had been placed in the hands of his father's servants, the maroon barouche went to Dunelm Square, where Masahito Hitamoto had a town house. The three samurai put the carriage away and stabled the horses. Then Masahito took tea in the library. He took tea according to tradition, sitting on a cushion not a chair.

The tea ceremony was performed by Fumito Nakono, leader of the six men who had accompanied Masahito from Japan. He was a nobleman himself but considered it an honour to serve the Daimyo's son. Nakono and Masahito said nothing until the ceremony was complete. Then Masahito spoke. He spoke in homely Japanese, but he could equally well have used Dutch, Spanish, Portuguese or French, as well as the English which he had perfected as the most useful.

'I shall see the father tomorrow,' said Masahito, 'The son will arrange it. The father is precisely the kind of man we have been looking for.'

CHAPTER 6

In fact I was delighted with the angry growl that rose up from *Euphonides's* people when Smythe-Lewis said he'd come to take my ship. I was delighted because it flattered my vanity, and Smythe-Lewis looked round in alarm, and I almost felt sorry for him because it got even worse when some of the crowd on the main-deck shouted in derision.

'Smuggler!' they cried, 'Smuggler!' I didn't know what that meant but Smythe-Lewis did, and he blinked and looked round and sighed: and the men's anger turned to laughter. But I had no time to study his miserable face, because in such a moment as this a duty fell upon a captain to address his crew.

'Silence on the lower deck!' I yelled, and yelled it at my utmost force, 'Clap a hitch your bloody hatches or I'll come down among you, and God help them as I catch hold of!' You youngsters should particularly note the manner of my words, because they were exactly what the men expect when they know they are being cheeky, and they wouldn't be happy without them.

So: Silence. Shifty faces. Hidden grins. But they gave up their growling and laughing, and Smythe-Lewis addressed me with a little speech.

'I bring orders for you, Captain Fletcher,' he said, 'orders of the most powerful and secret nature, and of which I am innocently unaware. But! It has been vouchsafed unto me, that I am allowed to reveal unto you, that my taking of command of this ship, is on a purely temporary nature, and that you will resume command at …'

'HUZZAH!' cried the entire ship. Hats in the air. Delight and delirium and the noise shook the ship from main truck to keelson. They roared and yelled and drowned out Smythe-Lewis so completely that I had to give another performance. I turned on the men and lifted my voice in a mast-head bellow.

'God damn your bloody eyes for a set of impertinent buggers!' I said, stamping my foot like the Devil's hoof, and frowning like a thundercloud. All of which performance the men loved because – as I have just said – I was behaving in such a manner as the hands expect from an officer, since Jack Tar don't want soft words and sweet reason. Not him! He wants a captain who knows his mind and makes damn sure that the crew know it likewise.

Silence again, and I glowered a bit, just to make sure that there was decorum among the ship's people: *including* the lieutenants and mids, who'd had been as cheeky as the rest. Then I spoke to Smythe-Lewis.

'Welcome aboard, Sir,' I said, 'I assume you have your sea-chest in the boat?'

'Yes, Sir,' he said.

'See to it!' I said to my first lieutenant.

'Aye-aye, Sir,' Pyne said.

'Then let's you and I go below, Mr Smythe-Lewis,' I said, 'For I assume we have much to discuss.'

'We do, Sir,' he said, 'We do indeed.'

So off we went to the great cabin at the stern, with the furnishings, pictures and decorations I'd inherited from the previous captain, and which were so fine as to make Smythe-Lewis sigh with envy, since he knew they wouldn't be his very long. Meanwhile my Steward and a couple of men were waiting to make us snug, and off came Smythe-Lewis's boat cape, and our hats, while chairs were shoved under our bottoms, and drink and glasses brought out, and the door closed and ourselves left private.

'Now, Sir,' I said, with only the gulls watching us, because they were staring in through the stern windows that ran from side to side of the cabin, showing heaving grey ocean and a smudge of French coast, 'Now, Sir, may I ask what orders you bring for me?'

'Here, Sir,' he said, and shoved an oilskin package across the table, and I noticed for the first time that in fact he had two of them. One was for me, and one he kept. He put the second one on the table in front of him. He tapped it. 'Here is my commission, Sir, to be read before the ship, thereby establishing my right – however temporary – to command her before returning her even unto your own charge.' He reached out and tapped the package that lay in front of me. 'And this, Sir, contains orders for yourself, from highest authority, and the details of which I am not privy to, saving only to know that they concern your recent adventures in France – and of which adventures their Lordships have need of deep inquiry.'

He spoke like that: too many words, and hard to follow. But I fastened on the good news that peeped out through the undergrowth.

'So am I definitely to take command of this ship once more?' I said, 'After their Lordships' inquires?'

'To the best of my limited and imperfect understanding, Sir,' he said, 'That latter is indeed the most likely to be the case.'

I took that for *yes* and smiled.

'More port, Sir?' I said.

'Indeed, Sir,' he said.

After that he was quite decent. Since my orders were so profoundly secret, and since I was still captain aboard ship, he insisted that I be left alone to read my orders, and he went up on deck to meet my officers. Poor devil: I really did feel sorry for him by then. He knew the ship didn't want him, and he looked so miserable that you'd have thought he was about to take a cockle-boat into action against a three-decker. So off he went and I found a knife and slit open the sealed and sewn-up package, which – as routine for anything secret – was weighted inside with a couple of grape-shot so it could be thrown overboard to sink, if the bearer was about to be took by the enemy.

Then the package was open and out fell a leather document-folder. It held two documents on thick, expensive paper, watermarked for the Crown Stationers, and beautifully drafted by skilled clerks. The first was a letter to me, the second an inland passport with an impressive red wax seal, and I've still got them and this is what they said.

Admiralty House,
Whitehall,
London.

Thursday May 11th 1797.

Captain Jacob Fletcher,
Aboard His Majesty's Ship,
Euphonides.

Sir,
    You are hereby directed and required, at your utmost urgency,
and at your peril in case of prevarication, or delay, or lack of

diligence; to repair on board of whichever of His Majesty's ships
shall brings you this message, and to come ashore by the most
direct and proper course, and once ashore to present yourself
at Admiralty House, again by the most expeditious route, and
sparing no expense, and there to report upon all matters apper-
taining to steam propulsion of ships, as you may have acquired
during your recent sojourn in France.
Given by command of Their Lordships:
J.C. Edwards
Under Writer to the Office of the Lord High Admiral.

To Whom it shall concern.

Let it be known that it is the Will of His Majesty, our Sovereign
Lord King George III of the House of Hanover, that the bearer
shall be allowed to pass freely and shall be given every assistance
and precedence that His Majesty's subjects have within their
utmost powers to give.

The bearer:
Captain Jacob Fletcher, of His Majesty's Sea Service, lately in
command of His Majesty's ship Euphonides, being a gentlemen of
outstandingly large, muscular and forbidding appearance with the
scar of an old wound faintly to the left of his brow and forehead.
Signed for and by His Majesty's desire, this Wednesday May
11th 1797 in the Thirty-fifth year of His Majesty's Reign.
J.C. Edwards
Keeper of the Royal Cabinet,
St James's Palace,
The City of Westminster,
London.

I would point out that these papers had all the resonance of authentic
bureaucracy, such that every man must bow the knee to them. The passport looked to be a standard form, with the date and my details filled in

later, and they'd got me right. I am indeed very big and have an old scar on the brow, courtesy of an American privateer. I didn't like the word 'forbidding' though. I also noticed that despite what Smythe-Lewis had said, the letter had no mention of my being sent back into *Euphonides* and it was cold as charity and it was stuffed with threats.

Thus I dared not delay, because their Lordships of the Admiralty could break a captain as easy as snapping a carrot. I called my steward back, and gave orders for my things to be packed for a journey, at which stage the ship's own bureaucracy intervened. It stepped forward with matters that – in the ship's opinion – were themselves too important to be delayed. In the first place, all the warrant officers: purser, surgeon, gunner, carpenter, boatswain and others, wanted me to sign off their accounts as true and accurate, before falling under the power of a new captain, whose ways they did not know. This wasn't so bad, because they did know *me*, and knew what would happen to anyone who tried to get a fraud past me. So I just signed them off without looking.

More tedious was the fact that every man in the ship who could write, wanted to send letters to families ashore by the cutter that was taking me off, and which everyone knew was bound for England. And that took time. But by the end of it you wouldn't believe the size of the canvas bags that were bulging full of post.

Then finally I found that I must take someone ashore with me: Mr Midshipman Ordroyd, *Phaeton* Ordroyd to his loving family. He was a pretty-faced, lanky youth, with a silly grin who was always acting foolish: tripping the other mids down companionways, and sticking paper spills to the soles of their shoes if they dozed off in the mess then lighting the spill to cause the victim to jump madly as his foot felt the heat. So Mr Ordroyd's bum had felt the boatswain's cane more than any other bum in the ship. Beyond that I didn't know how to deal with him, since he was too skinny for me to knock down. The other usual punishment for a mid was mast-heading: sending him up to the main-mast cross-trees, to swing in the wind a hundred feet up until he was sorry, but Ordroyd liked that and would sit up aloft singing happily.

But he wasn't singing now, because he was the single one of us that was wounded in the Fort Rouge attack. A shell fragment had sliced his left arm and laid it open to the bone, which wound our surgeon sewed up. But then the wound turned nasty and started pouring out pus, and Mr

Ordroyd was confined to his hammock, and despaired of by the surgeon, Mr Davenham, who came to me in the midst of my preparations, bringing with him the chaplain for support.

'Begging your pardon, Captain,' said Davenham, 'but it's Mr Ordroyd, Sir.'

'It is indeed, Captain,' said the chaplain.

'The fact is Captain,' said Davenham, 'that if we don't get him ashore under dry conditions, with fresh fruit and vegetables, I fear that a general mortification might set in which would cost Mr Ordroyd his life.'

'Oh,' I said.

'Indeed, Sir,' says the chaplain, 'And with utmost circumspection, Sir, I would remind you – as indeed you know already – that Mr Ordroyd's father owns land that sends five members into parliament and has other influence in London, besides.'

'Never mind that, Sir,' said Davenham, 'The poor lad's not yet seventeen, and I fear for his life!' He looked at me all pleading. 'And it's easily done, Captain. The boatswain says we can rig tackles to get the young gentleman into a boat, and the cutter's people can heave him aboard, just the same.' So Mr Ordroyd had to come with me. How could I say no? He was an irritating little tick but I couldn't let him die for it. So I agreed and off went surgeon and chaplain, smiling. Then O'Flaherty came down to the Great Cabin. I heard the marine sentry stamp to attention, and tap on the door.

'Mr O'Flaherty to see you Cap'n,' he said.

'Come in,' I said, which he did with a smile on his face.

'Cap'n, Sir,' he said, 'On behalf of the ship's people, could I ask you to stay below for a while?'

'Oh?' I said, 'Why?' He just smiled and tapped a finger against his nose.

'Might I just ask, Sir, that you wait and see?' I knew him and trusted him, we'd been through dangerous times together. So I sat down and reached for the decanter that was still there.

'Will you take a glass, Mr O'Flaherty?' I said.

'A small one, Sir,' says he because bizarre as it was in an Irishman, he disliked strong drink. So we sat and he sipped, and I cocked an ear at the sound of many feet moving about ship and many shouted preparations. But O'Flaherty just chuckled, and most deliberately turned my attention elsewhere.

'Do you know about Mr Smythe-Lewis, Sir?' he said,

'Do I know what?' I said.

'About the smugglers?' he said, and I shook my head.

'Ah, I thought as much,' said O'Flaherty who was pleased at that, and told me a tale to keep me entertained. 'It was years ago,' he said, 'Smythe-Lewis was in command of *Polyphemus*, sixty-four: a small ship for the battle line, but a good 'un, with 24-pounders on the gun-deck. But she was severe short-handed of seamen.'

'Go on,' I said, 'I've never heard this.'

'Well,' says O'Flaherty,' I was aboard as master. And there was a hot press for fear of war with the Americans, and we was in Portsmouth fitting out, and the Press Tender came alongside, and the officer in command came aboard, and said he had seven fine seamen, and did we want them, and Smythe-Lewis says, by Jove yes we did!' I nodded , understanding the vital need to have a good number of trained seamen aboard ship. 'So they was brought aboard and all hands looked them over, including Captain Smythe-Lewis, and damn fine men they were too. Seamen every inch, and well-dressed too in seamanly rig, each man with his trug of goods, which is rare in pressed men who normally come aboard bare-arsed and filthy, without ...' He paused. 'Ah!' he said, 'I'm sorry Cap'n, I wasn't thinking.'

'Never mind,' I said, 'I was pressed, and everyone knows it and I don't care.'

'Aye-aye, Sir,' he said.

'Go on!' I said.

'So: Captain Smythe-Lewis, was blessing his luck, when the officer of the press tender got struck with sudden conscience, and admitted that the seven were Cornish smugglers, who were took when a frigate laid alongside and threatened to give a broadside if they didn't strike. Well: all aboard of us looked at one another, but Cap'n Smythe-Lewis was desperate for men, and he said he'd have them come what may, and he asked the smugglers if they were willing to enter the ship, at which their leader stepped forward, and swore that they were loyal hearts and true, and ready to serve King George.'

'And were they?' I said.

'You must judge that for yourself, Cap'n,' says O'Flaherty, 'Because our first lieutenant begged Smythe-Lewis not to take them, and I begged him not to, and so did the boatswain, and everyone else. But not only did he take them, but once we were at sea, he rated them crew of his launch with fancy clothes, extra pay and their leader as coxswain.'

'And?' I said.

'And,' says O'Flaherty, 'they was good as gold, all the way out to the West India Station, but then when we was anchored off St Kitts, Smythe-Lewis had to go ashore with despatches for the Governor. So! Out with the launch and the smugglers aboard, all dutiful and polite, and they pulled for the shore, and helped Smythe-Lewis up the jetty with great respect.' O'Flaherty laughed.

'And?' I said.

'That night, with Smythe-Lewis at dinner in the Governor's house, they took the launch, pulled for another harbour, boarded a ship, captured it by force, and sailed it to a French island and sold it and escaped free and were never heard of again.' Now, I laughed too.

'Is that why they call him Smuggler?' I said.

'It is, Cap'n, and it's why he'll never stay in command of *Euphonides*. Poor Mr Smythe-Lewis has friends in high places so he's constantly employed afloat, but he gets the work nobody wants: such as being put into this ship, only to be took out of her again.'

Then O'Flaherty forced himself to take a drop more, in fact quite a few drops more, which was not like him, and he chatted a bit, until Mr Pyne came down, and asked if I were ready to come on deck and leave the ship. He nodded to O'Flaherty, and O'Flaherty nodded back like a pantomime conspirator. Then up we went onto the quarterdeck, and there – to my uttermost surprise – I saw all hands of the ship's company mustered in best, shore-going rig, with the officers in full dress, Jimbo the cat in his little blue jacket and tarred hat, and the ship scrubbed fit for a Royal inspection, and the ship's band of music standing by. It was an exceptionally large and fine band, since music was a great tradition in that ship.

'One! Two!' cried the band master, waving his baton as I came on deck, and they gave Handel's '*See the Conquering Hero Comes!*' They gave it with full hearts, and all hands stood to attention.

Well, my jolly boys, you know my views on the Navy and the sea life, so you will understand that while it was very nice to see what the ship thought of me, and while I could not help but be proud, there was a longing in my innards for the world to admire me for something else than being a sailor. Where were the great manufactories that I'd have built? Where were the Fletcher Emporiums? Where were my counting houses and legions of clerks? They were only in my dreams, while here I was being celebrated as a combination of Francis Drake and Rollicking Bill the Pirate. But I must admit that tears filled my eyes and for an instant I was choked for words, because you can drive men to their duty, but you can't make them do something like that, out of their own free will.

When the music was done, I gave the speech that was expected of me, calling on them to wreck, sink, smash and burn everything afloat that belonged to the King's enemies, and to be obedient to their officers until such time as I might return. Then they gave three cheers for me, Mr Ordroyd was lowered into my launch, and I shook hands with Smythe and the ship's people were cheering and waving hats as I went over the side to the screech of the boatswain's pipes. Down I went into the launch, which was very much *not* crewed by smugglers, and which was pulled away in time to the ship's musicians giving '*Heart of Oak*' as hard as they could blow.

I suppose after that, poor Smythe-Lewis must have read his commission to all hands, to make himself legally their captain. I don't know because I wasn't there. I was climbing aboard *Chaser* with another set of boatswain's calls sounding, and Ordroyd was hauled up after me, and the ship's small company mustered to attention, though in plain, sea-going rig. The captain – Lieutenant Turnbull – was a messy creature, even younger than me, with untidy long hair spilling out from under the civilian round hat, and a shabby old service coat, sea-stained and sun-bleached, with wooden toggles for buttons. But uniform regulations were never fully observed in those days, especially aboard ships so small as this.

He gazed at me with round eyes as I'm afraid they all did aboard that ship. It was because of my reputation. I was the famous Fletcher, you see. I was Fletcher of the submarine mines and steam-boats; Fletcher who'd sunk ships; Fletcher who'd hammered the enemy and blown things up; Fletcher who'd started his sea life via the Press Gang. I'm afraid they admired me for all that, and worse still, they acted as was common in in those days, when seamen aimed to become followers of a famous patron who would get them promotion and advance their careers. Thus there were Nelson's followers, Collingwood's followers, Howe's followers and so on. So I feared that Mr Lieutenant Turnbull and his crew, wanted to become *Fletcher's* followers and look to me for advancement. If so, then they'd be disappointed, because my career in the service never did follow a normal course, but was more precarious even than Nelson's, and look at that poor devil: he suffered wounds and mutilation aplenty before finally being shot through the backbone.

But before the real trouble began, I had a voyage aboard *Chaser* which was very interesting in that I was taught the hard way, that since I'd always served on big ships, I had no idea how nasty life can be aboard a small one when the wind gets up.

CHAPTER 7

*'Most precious and adored Lady Meiko, without whose dear face I
cannot live, I am happy to say that I have thought only of the words
that you have spoken and that these words guided my own words to
my samurai after the Lord-my-Father's funeral.'*

(From a letter of Wednesday, June 21st 1797, from Kimiya
Hitamoto, Daimyo of Hito Domain, to the Lady Meiko, The
House of Flowers, Port Hito.)

The funeral of a Hito Daimyo was unlike the funerals of other Daimyo. It
was a military parade according to the scriptures of the Okobo Buddhism
native to Hito Island. Thus the auspicious number of seven hundred
soldiers was drawn up in rigid ranks, ready at dawn on the drilling field
before the great temple of the Hito *Kami* – spiritual forces of nature –
which was built on an earth mound raised in ancient times, on a site
sacred to Buddhism, Shinto, and the reverent worship of the ancestors.

The new tomb of Lord Hayato Hitamoto stood on the eastern slope of
the temple mound, where it would face the rising sun each day. It stood
within a circle of seven massive, stone grave markers splendidly carved
and polished, and the tomb itself was a stone pagoda above the burial
chamber, where the body of Lord Hayato lay in a casket *within* a casket,
of polished wood.

Outside the pagoda, waiting in dignified silence the new Daimyo stood
with his leading samurai, and with seven Buddhist monks who chanted
a holy prayer and swung bronze incense burners decorated with lucky
silver rats, to drive off impure thoughts.

The new Daimyo was Lord Kimiya Hitamoto, eldest son of the late
Lord Hayato, and he wore the gorgeous *O-yoroi* parade-armour of the
samurai, with its vast, antlered helmet, grotesque face-mask with hanging

44

moustaches; its shoulder-guards, breastplate and skirts, all of iron scales bound together with scarlet cords; and its arm-guards, gauntlets and shin-guards in blue-lacquered steel. It was further decorated with golden tassels, and marked with the swooping falcon *mon* of Clan Hitamoto. Such an O-yoroi was a year in the making for skilled craftsmen and a treasure to be handed down the generations. It was worn only by great noblemen, and never risked in battle.

Seventy samurai stood behind Lord Kimiya, likewise in parade armour, though discretely less glorious than that of their master, while as for the great mass of spearmen, arquebus men and bowmen facing the tomb: they wore plain, black-lacquered steel that was fit for combat.

As the sun rose, and light touched the tomb, the monks ceased chanting and bowed to Lord Kimiya. He bowed in return, and behind him the samurai bowed. Then he turned on his heel, the samurai ranks parted, and he marched through them, and stepped up on to a platform purified with prayers and covered in embroidered silk, so that he might give signal to the waiting host.

He stood straight, drew his war-sword and raised it high over his head. Behind him the senior samurai drew swords, and cried out in a single voice:

'*BANZAI!*'

And the host responded.

'*BANZAI!*'

Banzai – may you live ten thousand years – the traditional Hito acclaim to the new Daimyo who became the Daimyo only on completion of the funeral rites of the old Daimyo. They cried Banzai six times more to give the number seven, then the parade dismissed, and the men marched off past the platform where Lord Kimiya watched them go by. When all was done, Lord Kimiya stepped down, and beckoned to the most trusted of his samurai, who came close and bowed. Lord Kimiya was a mature man of forty-two years, he was married with children and he waited a long, long time for this moment. He had waited in great impatience.

'Now,' he said , 'to ensure that the Lord my Father shall be remembered in honour, we shall begin by destroying all those foreign books and devices that seduced him into un-wisdom.'

CHAPTER 8

My brief passage aboard His Majesty's cutter *Chaser* was even worse than it might have been, since Mr Phaeton Ordroyd had to be given the captain's cabin, which otherwise would have been mine. Not that it was much in the way of accommodation: a low and narrow box where no man of normal size could stand without stooping, and where I would have had to crawl on the floor. But the lad was quite ill by then. He was delirious and his bad arm hot to the touch and smelling rank, as he swung in his hammock cared for by the cook, who fancied himself a bit of a doctor. But having bothered to take Ordroyd with me, there was no point in denying him what comfort we might give him, and being right at the stern, at least the cabin had a couple of windows to let out the bad air, and bring in the fresh. Also, *Chaser* was a dry ship at the stern, even when she was going at the incredible rate of sixteen knots.

Nowadays, the clipper ships and steamers can beat that, but I marvelled at such speed when I saw the log hove and the knots run out. What's more, the speed seemed all the greater in a small vessel, since when you were hanging on to the steep-canted deck, trying not to go over the side as she pitched – which she did like a bloody dolphin – then you saw the white foam only a foot below you on the lee side, and it looked tremendously fast.

I'm sure that Turnbull, her commander, was driving her hard to impress me. But *Chaser* was heavy sparred for her size, and even though it's supposedly a square rig that's the best driver, her big, fore-and-aft mainsail on its booms, was a straining white cloud when *Chaser* had the wind abaft the beam, and the pressure in that sail hurled us onward till every line hummed, and the pumps had to be kept going to keep out the water she took aboard from seams forced open in the bow. So *Chaser* was a speedy ship indeed, but in addition she was a ship that knew plenty about me, because my supposedly secret orders weren't half so secret as Smythe-Lewis had let on, and Turnbull mentioned them, early in the voyage.

I was standing beside him near the tiller, hanging on to the rail and cursing the fact that after all my years at sea, I hadn't got the sea-legs for a vessel as lively as this, and I was noting the way the helmsman steered. The ship had no wheel, just a big, twenty-foot tiller which must have been too stiff for a man's strength when *Chaser* was flying at speed. So the end of the tiller was made fast to a block and tackle on either side, and the tackles secured to the rails beyond, such that heaving on the tackles to starboard or larboard, gave mechanical advantage whereby the tiller moved and the ship steered. Very neat, and not something that you saw on a big ship, unless it was a jury rig after storm or battle damage.

Then Turnbull came up and spoke to me, which meant yelling in your ear on that ship when she was under way. Turnbull had just finished bellowing at his people to get up another spritsail, to make her go all the harder, which I wouldn't have done for fear of damage, but I suppose Turnbull knew his ship. Then Turnbull touched finger to hat-brim like a foremast hand.

'Beggin' your pardon Captain Fletcher, Sir!' he said.

'What is it?' I said, looking down at the scruffy little devil with his toggle-buttons and his eager face.

'If this wind holds, we'll be in Portsmouth this time tomorrow, Sir, and in good time for your orders.'

He made me gasp, the little swab. What sort of seaman challenged the weather like that? Was he asking for us to be blown on our beam ends?

[Note Fletcher's seeming superstition, which he would unshakably insist was *not* superstition, but practical understanding by seamen, of phenomena beyond the knowledge of landmen. See later for a more profound example. S.P.]

'How long have you been at sea, Mister?' I said, and his little face fell.

'Since a boy, Sir. Went to sea with my uncle Pellew aboard *Winchelsea*, frigate.'

'And didn't your uncle Pellew tell you not to curse the bloody weather?'

'Yes, Sir. No, Sir,' he said, grasping for the best answer.

'And what do you know about my bloody orders?' I said.

'That you're ordered ashore as fast as the wind shall blow, Sir.'

'Oh?' I said, and what else might you know?'

'Steam, Cap'n Fletcher, Sir,' he said, 'You're to inform their Lordships on the French steam ships.'

'Well bugger me,' I said, 'Is there any man aboard this ship, that hasn't read my sealed orders?'

'Yes, Cap'n Fletcher, I mean no, Cap'n Fletcher, I mean …'

'And who else knows?'

'We all did, Sir?'

'*All*? What the damned Hell d'you mean *all*?'

'All of us, Sir, there was five of us sent out to find you in case …'

'Five?'

'Five, Sir. Five of the fastest of us.'

'And did they all have sealed orders for me?'

'Yes, Sir. Whichever one of us found you, was to give them to you.'

'Good God!' I said, and thought about that. Somebody must have seriously wanted me ashore. Then I looked at Turnbull's miserable face, who clearly despaired that the hero Fletcher thought ill of him. I sighed. 'Oh belay that,' I said, 'Just bring us ashore without drowning all hands of us.' That was unfair. It wasn't his fault that Smythe-Lewis had blabbed. But then I frowned. At least I *supposed* it was Smythe-Lewis? I didn't know. Anyway, I let Turnbull off the hook. 'Never mind, Captain,' I said, 'She's a grand little ship, and you manage her very well. Just hold your course.'

'Aye-aye, Sir!' he said, flattered at my calling him captain. 'Aye-aye!' he said.

After that – whether or not it was because of Turnbull's rash words – the wind blew contrary and I was three days in that bouncing little craft. Yes, she was fast, but I was in a cabin like a coffin, with room for only a hammock and chamber pot, and I never got used to *Chaser* nor got my victuals down me without spilling half on my shirt-front.

On the other hand, it was *Chaser's* motion that cured Ordroyd. It threw him out of his hammock on the first night aboard and burst open his wound. It woke him up, he yelled loudly, and the cook, Turnbull and I squeezed into the stern cabin to see what was wrong. A swinging lantern gave just enough light for us to see, and the cook got there first because he was already there. He was a bright spark who knew that Papa Ordroyd was thumping rich, and was currying favour by looking after his son. So the cook had slept in the cabin and was tending to the mid with a bucket of water, and some rags which he said he'd boiled for cleanliness though they didn't look it.

'Never you mind, Mr Ordroyd, Sir,' he said, 'Look'ee here, young sir. It's all burst out and the blood's washed away all the corruption, which is the best thing for it!'

'Ohhhhhhh,' says Ordroyd, half conscious, and laid on his back with eyes staring.

'See Cap'n?' says the Cook, 'See, Mr Fletcher, Sir?' He took a rag and wiped the deck to scoop up what had come out of Ordroyd's wound. Then he held it out, dripping, for us to see. Fortunately, the light was bad, but I caught a whiff of it.

'Well done, Mr Cook!' says Turnbull and stared hard at the rag and nodded, his stomach was stronger than mine in that respect. 'We'll help you get Mr Ordroyd into his hammock,' he said, 'and then you can bind him up again. Or shall I send for the sailmaker to stitch him?'

'Won't need that, Cap'n,' says the cook, 'Such a wound is best bound up loose and left to drain.' So that's what was done. But was me that hoist Ordroyd into his hammock. There wasn't much of him to hoist, while there's plenty of me, and it was easier for one man than three. After that, would you believe it, the little blighter perked up something wonderful. The cook was right. The wound had cleaned itself, he was young and fit, and the young heal fast. So he was awake and chuckling next morning, and galloping down his salt pork, pease-pudding and biscuit. Then the day after he was up on deck, grinning at everything and thoroughly enjoying *Chaser's* plunging and heaving. He let out whoops of delight whenever the spray drenched him, or *Chaser* rolled gunn'l under and the sea came aboard then hissed out through the scuppers. But Turnbull had the sense to order him lashed to a pin-rail for fear he'd be lost over side, being still weak, while I told Ordroyd to cease his damned whooping and grinning because I was fed up with it.

We anchored at Portsmouth early on the 15th of June where I bid farewell to Turnbull and *Chaser*. Then Ordroyd and I were rowed ashore, where I waved my documents at everyone from the Harbour Master to the Port Admiral, and very soon we were in a bang-up, cracking fine post-chaise, painted shiny green and black, and our sea-chests aboard, on the way to Admiralty House, London. It was iron hooves on stone cobbles through the postern-gate in the fortified wall that ran round the town in those days. Soldiers saluted as we passed, and we looked down from the luxury of our finely upholstered, two-seater, enclosed coach-body with glazed sashes, and drink and food stowed in the locker beneath our feet. Ordroyd let down the front sashes for the breeze, and snapped his fingers in joy at the two horses drawing us along and the liveried post-boy on the lead horse, with whip in hand.

'Goooo-on! Goooo-on!' he cried till I told him to shut up or be thrown out. After that it was torture by boredom for seventy-five miles, six changes of horses at posting inns on the London road, and eight long hours swaying in that blessed coach. But before the railroad, a post chaise was the fastest means of overland travel, averaging twelve miles in the hour including stops, and we thought it wonderful. So we sat back, gazed at rural England with its hedges and fields and trees, and Ordroyd chattered non-stop. Short of wringing his neck or actually throwing him out, I couldn't stop him, because you youngsters must understand that in those days, the discipline of a King's ship ended when her people went ashore. That was established tradition, whatever the rules might say, and if the crew thought an officer had been unfair or vicious, he was likely be beaten severely if they met him in the street. After all, that officer hadn't got marines to back him any more, nor the boatswain and the cat. He was on his own, and must either rely on his own two fists, or run like mad.

My problem in the chaise with young Phaeton, was that I certainly could not use my fists on him. I've already said he was too small for that, and worse still, while he was definitely getting better, I couldn't risk even boxing his ears for fear it might open his wound again. So I had to put up with him and his schoolboy jokes such as seven-year olds might laugh at.

'Look at the pigs, Sir!' says he as we passed a herd of them driven through some town, 'Look at the little curly tails of 'em! D'you think the tails get in the way when the old boar climbs aboard to do his business?' And 'Sir! Sir! Look at that church steeple! If the parson got up there, he could see into all the windows when the ladies undress for bed!'

Also, I suspect that he was one of those who fancied I might become his patron and get him a leg-up in promotion, and therefore he was trying to be friendly and get me to like him. So once we got into London, with the smoke of a million fires, and the dung of a million horses, he invited me to stay his father's town house.

'In Dominic Gardens off Brunswick Square, Captain Fletcher,' he said, 'Jolly fine house. all brand new, and railings and servants and everything, and dozens of rooms, and roses at the back. We'd not know what to do with ourselves if you didn't come, Sir, and we'd be so pleased if you did. Do say you will, Sir.'

I put him off a few times, out of pride. Thanks to prize money and other enterprises, I had plenty of gold in Child's bank and I could have bought a decent house. But I'd never done so, having been mostly at sea for years. So it would have to be a hotel, unless the Admiralty had some better plan. So I was faced with the unpleasant fact that there was nobody in London – or indeed all of England – who would give me a bed for the night out of friendship. It wasn't a happy thought, and when Ordroyd persevered, I gave in.

'Chef's an emigre Frenchman, Sir,' he said, 'food's an angel's dream, fires in every room when its cold, best wines in the cellar, pretty serving girls, and a carriage and horses, and accounts with all the ...'

'Mr Ordroyd,' I said, 'Yes! I thank you for your offer and I would be happy to stay at your father's house. But only on one condition.'

'Oh damn fine, Captain, and what is the condition?'

'That you clap a hitch on your jawing tackle and stay silent for a good long while.'

'Aye-aye, Sir!' he said, and he stayed silent for five minutes at least, because we were well into the city now, and he was staring at the incredible density of wheeled traffic passing by, and the incredible variety of humanity on the pavements, and the vast buildings, and the tall spires, and the shops, and statues and hawkers and colour and noise beyond belief. But then he spied an enormous brewer's dray – one of Whitbread's – with a great load of barrels on board, a uniformed driver and assistant on the box, and a pair of hairy-white-hoofed lumbering horses of enormous size.

'Oh stap me, Sir!' he said, 'Just look at those. Like damned elephants! Never seen the like.'

'Indeed,' I said, and wished I hadn't because that encouraged him and the stopper was out of his gob.

'How much hay d'you think they eat, Sir? Do you think they ...' I did my best to ignore the rest, until the post-boy turned back, saluted with his whip and spoke to us. He was a cockney, because a chaise company always put on a boy who knew the route before the vehicle navigated a difficult passage, and that went a hundred times over for London.

'This is it, Gents,' he said, 'this 'ere is White'all what we're goin' dahn, and 'orseguards Parade is orf White'all, and Admiralty 'ouse is in the 'orseguards.'

'Thank you driver,' I said, 'Take me to the Admiralty, then you can take this gentleman to …' I turned to Ordroyd.

'Fifty-five Dominic Gardens off Brunswick Square,' he said.

'Right you are Captain!' said the post-boy.

'Your masters are paid already,' I said to the post-boy, 'But this is for you to make sure you set down Mr Ordroyd carefully, with his wounded arm, and take my sea chest along with you.' I gave him half a guinea for himself. Vastly too much, but I was still feeling small compared with young Ordroyd with his family and house waiting, when I had nowhere to go. So I was boasting that I had money too.

Then I got down, Ordroyd waved and the post-boy saluted.

'Fifty-five Dominic Gardens!' cried Ordroyd.

'Off Brunswick Square!' I replied, and off they went and I was outside Admiralty house: five stories high, with its huge wide span of columns and domes, and its elegant red brick interspersed with finest white stone, and the union flags flying above, and a guard of marines at the doors, who'd already spotted my epaulettes and cocked hat and were presenting arms.

It was a strange moment. It was late afternoon and I was most uneasy. Of course I was very tired after eight hours on the road, and hardly sleeping much aboard *Chaser*. But it was only normal for a seaman to do his duty when exhausted. How else do you think men could take wooden ships to sea under sail? No, it wasn't that I was physically tired. The unease I felt had to do with the fact that I had no idea why I was there. Yes indeed, I had recently been in France on adventures recorded in an earlier volume of these memoirs. Yes indeed, I had seen the French attempt to build steam ships to cross the channel. But every scrap of knowledge that I'd brought back had already been wrung out of me as a washerwoman wrings a shirt. So what more did the Admiralty want?

As I dithered, a marine lieutenant in a show-piece version of uniform, minced towards me, and raised his hat. His coat was tailored skin-tight, his boots shone, his linen was snowy, his face was smooth, and he'd never seen a shot fired in anger. That was obvious.

'Would you be Captain Fletcher, Sir?' he said, 'The celebrated Fletcher?' He'd spotted me. People do. It comes with my being so big.

'Yes,' I said, 'I'm Fletcher.' I raised my hat. 'Jacob Fletcher, come aboard.'

'Been expecting you, Sir,' he said, 'Orders, Sir! Special orders.'

'I know,' I said, 'So lead on.'

He did. He led me deep into the building, then up a staircase, and to a nicely-furnished room, with flowers on a table, and a view of Horse Guards Parade and a comfortable armchair where I was asked to wait, and the lieutenant vanished, and a splendidly-dressed servant appeared, and brought generous refreshments and a large decanter which I thought best to leave alone. Then three high-ranking officials appeared, all civilians in smart clothes, and all with the short, white wigs that pen-pushers wore if they wished to appear learned. These gentleman checked my name and other details, then bowed to me and whispered behind their hands, and went away, and I dozed off a bit.

Then I was shaken awake by an elderly official who came with a folio note-book and most politely asked to follow him. Thus I was taken to a small office with a large window letting in the evening light, and I was sat at a desk, the note-book was opened before me – it was blank - and pen and ink were standing by.

'Captain Fletcher,' said the official, 'As a matter of vital importance to the Navy and the Nation, Their Lordships of the Admiralty would be infinitely obliged if you would – in clear handwriting – describe all that you know of the attempt by our French enemies to apply steam to the propulsion of ships.'

'But I've already done that,' I said, 'I did all that months ago.'

'Their Lordships are aware of that, Captain,' he said, 'and yet they ask you to search your memory should anything have been omitted. So please do your best, Captain, and there will be a person waiting outside, to whom you may report when you are done.' He bowed again and then left and closed the door behind him. So soon as he left, the door opened again and the same servant as before brought another tray of refreshment and another decanter. Then he bowed and he left too.

So, my jolly boys, your Uncle Jacob had to do as he was bid, because this was the Admiralty and its word was law. After all, everyone from the mincing marine to the elderly gent had been polite, and nobody had given any impression that I was in any kind of trouble. Quite the contrary: they'd bowed and scraped as if I were the Emperor of China.

So I picked up a pen, dipped it into the ink and began. Soon, and to my very great surprise I found the work interesting, and this was – without doubt – the moment in my life when I decided that I would one day write down my memoirs. So I enjoyed myself and was at it for hours. In addition, I ate all the food and drank most of the decanter, and it was nearly dark when I was done.

Then I pushed back my chair, rubbed my face with my hands, and got up and went outside into the corridor, and there indeed, and blinking to stay awake, was an old and wrinkled minion in plain, ordinary clothes, who'd been there all this time. On sight of me he stood up, stamped a foot and touched his brow.

'Ah!' I said, 'A seaman!'

'Aye-aye, Sir!' he said, and I smiled. He was a creature like me. Not like the rest of them here. I was meeting a friend in an alien land.

'Tell them I'm done,' I said, and I felt for a coin in my pocket, found another half-guinea, but changed it for a full guinea and gave it to him. It was a month's pay for an able seaman.

'Aye-aye, Sir!' he said, more than delighted, and saluted again and was off at the double.

Soon he was back with the four gentlemen I'd seen earlier, and noted that they now looked quite tired. So I hoped that I'd kept them out late, and caused them to miss their dinners and be scolded by their wives in due course.

'Have you completed your report, Captain Fletcher?' said the elderly one, who was clearly the senior.

'I have indeed,' I said.

'And may we see it?' he said.

So of course they saw it. We went back into the room, everyone looked at my report, I was obliged to initial and number every page, and to sign the final page, which I did, and then they all signed too, and everyone nodded.

'And now Captain,' said the elderly gentleman, 'We shall send you onward to fifty-five Dominic Gardens.' He smiled at my puzzlement. 'The young officer with whom you arrived,' he said, 'called out that address quite clearly.'

'Oh,' I said, 'I suppose he did.'

'We have summoned a carriage,' said the elderly gentleman, 'and if you would accompany me, Captain Fletcher, I will lead you to the main doors, where the carriage will take you up.'

'Most kind, Sir,' I said.

Soon I was outside the Admiralty, alone in the dark, with a couple of sentries looking at me, and the moon and stars above. It was about eleven o'clock with no carriage in sight, and having no further duties the tiredness came down on me. Then hoofs and wheels sounded, and an expensive closed carriage drove up and stopped. A fine pair of horses stamped and snorted, and there were two footman at the back as well as a driver in front. There was drapery fastened to the carriage doors to cover what was beneath – a gentleman's coat of arms perhaps?

One of the footman got off his perch, opened a door and, threw down the steps. The carriage was dark inside.

'Get in, Captain,' said a voice, and I knew this wasn't right, because that voice had a mighty self-confidence, and this most certainly was not any kind of Hackney carriage bound for Dominic Gardens. 'Get in!' said the voice, 'Get in at once, or not only will you never see your ship again, but you'll dangle on the end of a rope.'

CHAPTER 9

'Mr Kilbride conveyed me to Perry's Dock at Blackwall, on London's River Thames, where giant ships are built for the East India Company. I was filled with wonder to behold them and I was satisfied that in many ways Kilbride's interests coincide with ours. But I cannot fully trust him.

(From the 'Foreign Journal' of Masahito Hitamoto. Entry dated Tuesday June 26th 1797.)

Kilbride pointed with his stick. He pointed at a structure so large that it dominated the landscape for miles: an enormous, tower-like, timber shed with a pitched roof, rising a hundred and fifty feet into the air. Kilbride was a small, intense man of forty-five, with heavy eyebrows, dominating personality and a limitless dedication for work. On occasions he was swept on the flood of this dedication causing him to rant rather than converse, and this was such an occasion.

'That's the Blackwall Mast House,' he said with relish, 'Tall enough to hoist in, or hoist out, the mainmast into any ship in the world! Nothing like it in any other yard!' He pointed again, positively willing his listeners to share his passion. 'See the crane and tackles at the peak of the roof? Enormous! Prodigious! Powerful!'

His listeners contemplated the crane: Lord Masahito, who nodded politely, while his four samurai stood unmoved, and a dozen clerks from Kilbride's office nodded their very heads off in the presence of their master, and couldn't have nodded any harder

'And the dock itself!' said Kilbride, sweeping his stick to encompass the huge, deep-water basin, entirely enclosed by masonry, and the great hulls anchored within, and the masts and yards, and busy activity, and all the life of a working dock, with ship's a-building, others fitting out with a hammering and sawing, and a constant coming and going of craftsmen. 'Now, Mr Massimo,' said Kilbride, pushing through the rest, to take Lord Masahito's arm and stand so close that his breath was in Masahito's face. In that instant Kilbride was so much away his own thoughts that he never noticed the gasp from the samurai, and he never knew that had he been in Japan, his head would have been smitten from his shoulders for such an abomination of rudeness.

'Now, Mr Massimo,' said Kilbride, 'Cast your eyes on this beauty!' He pointed to the huge ship moored close by the Mast House. 'The Company's ship *Duke of Cornwallis*,' he said, 'fresh fitted out and ready for sea! Look at her! Over sixteen hundred tons! Biggest merchantman in the world! Forty guns throwing twenty-four pound shot! More cargo capacity than any other ship ever built! Man-o-war timbers! Yards rigged with …'

Masahito ignored the rest. It was technical detail. It was not important. What was important was to establish exactly what Mr Kilbride wanted to do with this enormous ship. So Masahito was patient and tolerated Kilbride's fist clinging to his arm. He'd long since learned that the western barbarians had no sense of good manners.

Later, a dinner was served aboard the new ship. The weather was fine so a table was spread with food on the highest stern deck, with a view down her enormous length, past towering masts. Masahito was given a place of honour between Kilbride and the most senior of the clerks while the samurai – to their enormous relief – were not required to sit and dine, being perceived as mere servants. They were therefore excused what would have been a sickening gluttony of meat, and a hoggish excess of wine. They were entirely content to stand behind Lord Masahito at respectful distance

But Masahito had learned barbarian ways. He had learned well, having started young. He could sit at table, wield knife and fork, swallow masses of beef, and give the impression of downing claret. He was skilled and practised and – as ever – he amazed the company with his fluent English. Then after the meal, Kilbride proposed that he take 'Mr Massimo' below decks on a personal tour of the ship … just the two of them alone.

'A pleasure, Sir,' said Masahito, and spoke swift Japanese to his men: *Koko de mattete!* he said: *wait here!*

'*Hi!*' they said sharply, and bowed in unison, and all the English smiled at their quaint behaviour.

Once below decks, Kilbride made a brief show of walking the gun deck, past the blacked-iron barrels on their carriages, and he pointed briefly to the hatchways leading to the enormous holds further below. Then he took Masahito by the arm and led him to a quiet corner, where the light came in through an open gun-port, and he looked round to make sure nobody was listening, and he stared hard into Masahito's face, and Masahito forgave him because he stared through ignorance and not intention to offend.

Kilbride opened his mouth to speak, but Masahito was quicker.

'So, Mr Kilbride,' he said, 'Why shall you go to Japan?' Kilbride was taken aback.

'Japan?' he said, 'Who says I'm going to Japan?'

'Nobody,' said Masahito, 'but it is my assumption that you will.' Kilbride laughed.

'Do you know, Mr Massimo,' he said, 'when you came to dine that night with my useless son who's as scatter-brained as his mother that I married for her beauty, do you know, Mr Massimo, I thought you were just the same as him.'

'The same as Ozzy?' said Masahito.

'Yes,' said Kilbride, 'But I saw in ten seconds that you weren't, and next day I had men ask around the town after you. Clever men. Men that I trust. And do you know what they found out?'

'Pray tell, Mr Kilbride.'

'You're a high nobleman among your own people. You've got money. You've been all over Europe. You've been out of Japan since you were a boy, you're fascinated by steam engines, manufactories and munitions of war, and you made a chum of Ozzy just to get into my house. I know that because *you've* been asking round the town about *me!*'

'Not just you, Mr Kilbride,' said Masahito, 'But I congratulate you on your research.'

'So what do you want?' said Kilbride, 'that night, Ozzy was drunk and my wife making eyes at you, but you were clever as Old Nick in getting me to show you this ship.' He tapped his stick on the wooden deck.

'It wasn't difficult,' said Masahito, 'you talked about it all night. *It* and the East India trade.'

'Did I, though?' said Kilbride.

'You did,' said Masahito, 'Then you turned the conversation to Japan.'

58

'Did I?'

'Yes.'

'So?'

'So,' said Masahito, 'Let's see if your plans for Japan run parallel to mine, so that perhaps – only perhaps Mr Kilbride – we might *just* be able to help one another.'

'Ahhhhh!' said Kilbride, and smiled.

CHAPTER 10

So who was inside that coach that could threaten a hanging? The voice gave a clue. It was the voice of one of the great ones of England. It had the same authority of command as the Duke of Wellington's voice. I met the Duke in later years, and when he spoke you felt that even the living room furniture would march in step if he gave the order.

So I looked around and wondered what to do. It was dark, I had nowhere to run – I had no idea of where Dominic Gardens might be – and I couldn't outrun a coach anyway. In fact, I was so tired that I couldn't have outrun a one-legged cripple. Meanwhile there was a nice, comfortable coach ready and waiting. What finally persuaded me was the manner of the driver and the footmen. They were servants, not bandits, and they didn't have the nervous excitement of men about to go into action. I'd seen that too many times not to recognise it, and they didn't have it so nothing nasty was going on, and I got up into the coach.

'Drive on!' said the gentleman within.

'Yes, m'Lord!' said the driver, and off we went, and the iron tyres rumbled and the iron hoofs clopped and the coach body swayed, and my eyes got used to the dark and I looked at the man sitting opposite, and who was looking straight at me. He was about forty, straight nose, heavy brows, smooth cheeks, confidant and intelligent. He'd obviously come from some formal event because his hair was powdered white and he was elaborately dressed in a dark velvet coat, with a blue sash over his shoulder, and a large, twinkling star on his breast. Looking at the star I saw a red cross and blue ribbon depicted in glittering stones. I was startled: God's Boots! He was a Knight of the Garter! I could tell at a glance, because those badges of knighthood had an absorbing fascination for Sea Service officers. We knew one star from another and dreamed of having one, because there's nothing like a knighthood to show who Britannia loves and who she does not, and the Garter was the top of the tree, and the peak of desire. It was the foremost order of knighthood which even Nelson never got: he was only a Knight of the Bath.

'You are Captain Jacob Fletcher.' said the man opposite. It was a statement, not a question but I judged it wise to respond.

'Yes, m'Lord,' I said, and you youngsters should mark well the respectful manner of my address, because it was obvious that I was in the company of enormous rank and power, and when you find yourself in such company, it is wise to tread very carefully indeed, and to avoid giving any offence which can be avoided. How right I was in this approach was revealed by the noble gentleman's next words.

'I'm Spencer,' he said, 'First Lord.'

'Ah!' I said. 'Oh!' I said. 'Aye-aye, m'Lord!' I stumbled on the words because he was – in the name of sweet, bloody Jesus and all the bloody angels – he was *First Lord of the Admiralty!* He was the Earl Spencer who sat at the right hand of the Prime Minister, the King, and in all probability Almighty God Himself if ever He wanted advice on the Navy! Spencer was the man who took the government's decisions to Admiralty House and told the Admiralty what to do with its vast fleets, its tens of thousands of guns, and its hundreds of thousands of men. A mere captain like me was an ant beneath the wheels of his chariot.

So the carriage rocked and swayed, along a dark, night-time Whitehall, with the street lamps giving pin-pricks of light in the dark, but not revealing very much, which reflected exactly the state of my mind, and Spencer looked at me to see how I would respond. At first the sweat broke out all over me. What the hell could this mean? What was I doing in a coach with the First Lord? But then I realised that this wasn't right. This wasn't the way the First Lord went about his business. If he wanted to say something to the likes of me, why hadn't he gone down the chain of command? Why hadn't he spoken to their other Lordships, and so to various officials, then to an admiral, and to the officer – Harry Bollington – in command of my squadron? That put some of the bounce back inside of me because the First Lord was acting odd, and perhaps doing something he shouldn't? Besides, I didn't think that I was in trouble. For one thing I hadn't done anything wrong recently, though believe me, my jolly boys, that don't stop those above you from punishing you! And better still I'd done things in my last adventures in France that the First Lord had cause to approve of. Indeed … and then a very, very nasty thought came unto me. It was a very nasty thought indeed.

Oh no! Oh horror! Not bloody Rowland. Please don't let it be anything to do with him. Spencer interrupted my thoughts. Perhaps he'd guessed them. He was a very clever man.

'Fletcher,' he said, 'Following your exploits in France, you have come to the notice of group – a group which I represent – that has work for you. The group is informed that you are an ideal choice for this work, and by this work you will be privileged to perform services of inestimable value to your King and Country at this time of war across the entire globe.'

I groaned with self pity, because it *was* bloody Rowland, dead these many months and now stood up in his grave pointing his bony finger at me, the devious, dangerous, lying murdering swine. They wanted me as Rowland's devious, dangerous, lying, murdering replacement. Rowland had told me all about it, and he'd explained how it worked. There was a secret group of the highest in the land – the *Shadow Men* I called them, though they had no name of their own – and they included the Prime Minister, the First Lord obviously, and others. This group had been running for generations, recruiting and replacing its members, as some died off, and the group kept a tame agent to do its dirty work. This agent could do much as he pleased, and had enormous influence, but if his doings became public knowledge, then the group would empty him out of the window like a pot-full of piss. So I said nothing, and the carriage rumbled on and went down dark streets that I didn't know.

'Well?' said Spencer, 'What do you have to say for yourself, Fletcher?' But I still said nothing. 'So!' he said, 'Do you remember Boatswain Dixon of the Impress Service? Do you remember him and the press tender *Bullfrog*?'

I did indeed, and if you've read the first volume of these memoirs, my lads, then you too will recall the sadistic, pig-faced, moron that was Boatswain Dixon, and how he terrorised me when first I was pressed, and beat me with a rope's end. His pleasure was to creep up behind and hit me when I wasn't expecting it, and he did it till I was near suicide. You may likewise recall that finally, I hit him on the head with a four-pound shot swung in the toe of a stocking, and heaved him over the bows of His Majesty's ship *Bullfrog* which good and merry ship rolled over him and drowned him dead. That's what I meant earlier about *a little bit of murder* and the Navy's held it over me for much of my life, because I was seen in the doing of it.

'Ah!' said Spencer, 'I see from the look on you that your memory is clear.'

'Yes, m'Lord,' I said, because there was no denying it.

'In that case, Fletcher,' he said, 'we shall not proceed to vulgar threats, since on the one hand we offer you noble service, and on the other a court martial, and you are far too intelligent to make the wrong choice.'

'Yes, m'Lord,' I said.

'You are also exceedingly cunning and devious,' he said, 'and a man who goes his own way. I have this on high authority!' Normally I would have denied that, and answered back. But I was very tired and I wondered where all this was going. So I said nothing. 'Huh!' he said, 'But be reassured, Commodore Fletcher, that while others might despise these latter characteristics, I willingly accept them because without them you could not be the man that I seek.' That surprised me, but it didn't surprise me half as much as the fact that he'd called me *commodore* which was the next step up from captain, though it wasn't exactly a rank because it was the title of someone placed temporarily in command of a fleet. But it was a tasty posting, bringing benefits in pay, prize money and perquisites, and which – usually – was given only to very good boys indeed, such as captains of outstanding ability and long service.

'Commodore?' I said.

'Oh yes!' he said, 'Sit back and think about it, because I shall soon have something to show you.' I would have sat quiet, but I found even he was human and was curious. 'So you're Fletcher,' he said, 'I can see it by the size of you, and I hope that we shall get on, even though you're a rogue and a villain.' I think he meant that as a compliment. Then he pursued a fresh topic, purely out of interest. 'And did you really sink a ship with an undersea mine?'

'Aye-aye, m'Lord,' I said, 'I towed the mine behind a sub-marine boat.'

'Tell me about it,' he said. So I did and the telling kept us busy until the carriage stopped, a while later.

'We're here, m'Lord!' cried the coachman.

'Good,' said Spencer, and pulled down one of the sashes, 'Look,' he said, 'Do you know what building that is?' I looked out and saw a monster stone building in the dark. It reared up like a cliff, and I almost smelt the money within it. A few lights shone through the windows, and there were liveried doormen standing at the main entrance, which was lit by big, glazed lanterns.

'No,' I said, 'It's damned big whatever it is.'

'It's East India House,' he said.

'Oh?' I said, with considerable interest because the East India Company was one of the wonders of the world, and one that I admired enormously. Familiarly known as *John Company*, it was the biggest commercial enterprise in the world, with thousands of staff, and a near monopoly of trade with the eastern world, meaning India and beyond. It was wealthy beyond counting, it had fleets of huge ships, and it brought in silks, spices, drugs, carpets, tea and all the exotic luxuries that the western world had come to think of as indispensable necessities. It made my mouth water to think of it. It was trade made not just large, but enormous and colossal!

'Ah!' said Spencer, 'I see the enthusiasm that shines from your face. I see that you think you know what John Company represents.'

'Think?' I said.

'Think, Commodore Fletcher.'

'Oh?' I said.

'You clearly understand that the company is a giant of commerce.' I nodded. 'Indeed,' he said, 'it is a giant among giants. It has no rival.' I nodded. 'But did you know, commodore, that the East India Company is something very close to being an independent sovereign state?'

'Is it?' I said.

'Yes,' he said, 'An independent sovereign state, free from the jurisdiction of His Majesty's law, and the rule of Parliament.'

'How can that be?' I said.

'Let me explain,' he said, 'John Company rules over Bengal and all else in India worth having. It has driven out its French and Dutch equivalents, and now has a locally recruited army of two hundred and sixty thousand men which is twice the size of the British army.

'Oh?' I said, 'I didn't know that.'

'Not everyone does,' he said.

'But surely they're only native troops,' I said, 'Not like proper red-coats?' He shook his head at my ignorance.

'Five years ago,' he said, 'In '92, an army of these native troops took the fortress of Seringapatam, in Mysore, which was enormous, and was equipped with modern artillery behind massive stone walls and every artifice of military engineering. It was furthermore defended by fanatics. But the Company's army took it by direct assault. They took it by night, at the point of the bayonet, and by so doing, they took control of a powerful Indian nation. Is that *proper-red-coat* enough for you?'

'Good Lord!' I said.

'Good Lord indeed,' he said, 'and in addition to this formidable army, the Company has the world's biggest fleet of the world's biggest merchant ships, all of them bearing guns, and it is building a fleet of pure men-o-war to complement them.'

'Good Lord!'

'Thus,' he said, with emotion working on his face, 'the Company makes war, it passes laws within its territories, it strikes coin, and it conducts negotiations – political negotiations – with the rulers of native Indian states.'

'But isn't it all this done under British rule?' I said.

'Of course it is,' he said, '*Supposedly*, and of course we have passed laws – numerous laws – to regulate the company's activities. But the company is cunning, Commodore Fletcher. It is as cunning as you are in finding ways to continue its trade, and it is particularly adept at finding ways around British law. Also, and before all else, the company's centre of operations is on the other side of the Earth, such that a return journey takes a year, even if a man instantly steps off the outbound ship, and on board of a homebound ship, without so much as taking a cup of Indian tea.' He stared hard at me again, and stopped talking. He was looking for some response.

'So what do you want from me, m'Lord?' I asked.

'Before I tell you, Commodore Fletcher, may I take it that you wish indeed to become a commodore? And that you will act on behalf of the Group that I represent?'

'Yes, m'Lord,' I said, 'Yes to both,' what the Hell else was I to say? He nodded.

'From what I hear of you, Fletcher,' he said, 'you are honest in matters of trade. So regard this agreement as trade, whereby you honestly provide your services for a reward, and always remembering Boatswain Dixon, and what will happen to you should you prove dishonest.' I thought that over. Then I nodded. I had little choice.

'You say *agreement*, m'Lord?' I said, 'Shall we sign a contract?' He just laughed at that. But then he produced a leather wallet full of papers.

'These are for you, commodore,' he said, 'They will give you some names and information. And unlike the papers sent out to your ship – the papers that brought you ashore – these are not false.'

65

'False?' I said.

'Of course,' he said, 'so that they can be denied. Or do you really think that there is such a person as J.C. Edwards who is both an underwriter at the Admiralty, and Keeper of the Royal Cabinet at St James's Palace?' He waved a hand as if brushing away a fly. 'These posts do not exist and neither does J.C. Edwards. He is a nonsense and a nothing.'

'I see,' I said, 'and I suppose you didn't really want to know about French steam-boats?'

'Indeed not, commodore,' he said, 'That was merely a ruse to bring you ashore.'

'So that's why all the world and its dog knew what was in my secret orders?'

'Quite. And it is why all the world and its dog does *not* know that you have had any contact with myself, despite the fact that – as we proceed to number fifty-five Dominic Gardens – I shall explain what you shall do,' he raised his voice, 'Drive on!' he cried.

'Yes, m'Lord!' said the coachman, so the coach rolled and Spencer explained and it didn't take him long.

'You are to insinuate yourself into the company of the men whose names you will find here.' He tapped the leather wallet. 'And you are to prevent them by whatsoever means may be necessary from succeeding in their proposed activities regarding Japan. I repeat, with emphasis, that you may use absolutely any means to do this and yet be saved harmless in British law, provided only that your task is completed with success.'

'Japan?' I said, 'Japan? What do they want with Japan?'

'They want to own it!' he said, 'Take it! And thereby become something bigger even than England.'

'Well why don't you stop them?' I said, 'Send the Fleet?' He sighed at my ignorance.

'In time of war, Fletcher? With the French across the channel? We need every ship and every gun, right here to face the French!'

And that was it, my jolly boys. He wouldn't say another word no matter what questions I asked. In any case, as I've said, I was very tired by then, and perhaps my mind wasn't as sharp as it should have been. Then the coachman whipped up the horses, the carriage moved at a smart trot through west London and soon found Dominic Gardens, which weren't gardens but a typical smart London square. There was a small park in the middle and a run of high-class, terraced houses all

66

around, with flat pillars and pediments, and all stuccoed over to make them look as if carved from a single block of white stone. They did indeed have neat iron railings, and areas below for the servants, and three floors rising above. They had huge windows, neatly capped with arches, and bridges of steps across the areas, leading to smart front doors with more pillars and porches to guard them. The square looked like something out of an illustrated prospectus of homes for the superlatively rich. So even Spencer was impressed.

'Very pretty, Commodore Fletcher,' he said, 'you'll find from your papers that you'll be ashore a while, so I don't doubt you'll be comfortable in such accommodation as this. Though I surely do not have to mention, that not one word must be passed to any third party of your contact with myself, nor of your orders, and I must also insist that having read your papers you will promptly burn them. Is that clear?'

'Aye-aye, m'Lord,' I said, 'but how shall I report to you?'

'Your papers will tell you,' he said, 'and I wish you good luck.' He held out his hand and I took it. Then, for the first time, he cracked his solemn face and smiled, 'Did you really navigate a sub-marine boat?' he said, 'That swam beneath the sea? Really and truly?'

'Yes, m'Lord.' He shook his head.

'Amazing,' he said, then, 'Don't worry, Fletcher, you'll get your ship back. Good night to you!'

'Good night, m'Lord,' I said, and off he went, keeping well inside so that nobody should see him.

Then I went up the steps of number fifty-five and would have knocked at the door but it was already opening, and dizzy as I was from exhaustion I felt as if fortune had opened the gates of fairy-land, because a blaze of light came out of the door, and hordes of pretty, little people burst out with wings on their back, and wispy robes and coloured tights, and faces painted, and little green caps on their heads, and all chattering and laughing and smiling.

As to their being small, I'm afraid that most folk seem tiny when you're as big as me, or at least they do when first you meet them, and then you get used to it. But the fairy look came from the costumes they had on for some entertainment that was going on within. I found that out because the leading fairy – arm in a silken sling – was Mr Midshipman Phaeton Ordroyd.

'Captain!' he said, seizing my hand, and working it like the village pump, and he grinned, all red and flushed with the drink he'd taken aboard, 'It's Perse's birthday, and I'd forgotten it, and everyone's a fairy, on Perse's birthday, and all our *best* friends are here, and it's tradition in the family.' Then he looked round. 'Perse! Perse!' he cried and the most gorgeous little creature came forward who was the image of Mr Midshipman Ordroyd, only feminine and beautiful rather than merely pretty-faced. She pushed through a crowd of other gorgeous little creatures – male, female and who knows what – and she curtseyed like a dancer in front of me, and performed wonderful expressions with downcast eyes followed by upward gaze, and the most lovely brown eyes, and round limbs and plump fresh skin on display to the limits and beyond of decency, and all smiling and merry. 'Say hallo, Perse!' said Ordroyd.

'Good evening, Captain Fletcher,' she said with the most wonderful smile. Now I know that seamen are wonderfully vulnerable to a woman's smile when coming ashore after time at sea, but by George she really was wonderful and the spine of me tingled from top to bottom. Ordroyd saw my expression and laughed. Then he turned to the rest, 'All together, everyone: say *good evening Captain Fletcher*. Are we ready? One … two …' and he waved his good arm and they all said, 'Good evening, Captain Fletcher!' and they all laughed, and I did too. Who wouldn't?

'We all stayed up for you, Captain Fletcher, Sir,' said Ordroyd, 'didn't we?'

'Yes-yes-yes- huzzah!' they all cried.

'We did indeed, Sir,' said the lovely little Perse, who looked about eighteen to me, and in the flower of youth, and she curtseyed again, giving me a view straight down her décolletage, and she smiled straight into my face. She smiled so bold and saucy that I thought:

'Hallo? What's this?' But then I realized I must go careful because the kinship between her and Ordroyd was so marked, that she was obviously his sister. Elder sister I supposed.

'Perse?' I said, 'Is that your name, ma'am?'

'Oh no,' she said, 'I'm Persephone, but everyone calls me Perse.' She turned away. 'Who am I?' she cried.

'Perse!' they cried, and she laughed and everyone laughed, and she turned and wriggled her backside at me in the most outrageous manner, to whoops and howls from the company because there wasn't one of them entirely sober. Then she looked over her shoulder at me, and worked the lashes again.

'Do come in, Captain,' she said, 'After everything I've heard about you, I truly cannot wait to become better acquainted.'

Well my jolly boys, there used to be an old joke about there being a flag signal in the Service code book – that read *Permission to lay alongside*. In fact, there never was such a signal, but if it had in all truth existed, then that's what Persephone Ordroyd had just run up the mainmast. It was a most promising beginning to my stay with the Ordroyds, and it got even better … right up until the moment that they got me into fighting a duel.

CHAPTER 11

'You weren't there, Davy, so here's my judgement of the meeting. Kilbride
spoke well. He always does. He could argue with a brick wall until
it wept. Then I put the prepared question, and he gave the prepared
answer, and if his venture succeeds we'll be ruling an empire.'

(From a letter of Monday, July 3rd 1797, from Sir Robert Valentine,
Director of the East India Company, to a friend 'Davy' whose
full name was not given but who may also have been a Director.)

'My lords and gentlemen! Directors all, of the Honourable East India
Company!' said the chairman, 'I declare this meeting to be open, and a
quorum present!'

At these words, thirteen of the wealthiest men in England solemnly
rapped the shining mahogany table with their knuckles, as their sign of
approval. They rapped the table even though they knew very well that
thirteen was the minimum for a voting quorum, and that numerous other
directors were not present, and more fool them for not keeping up with
the Company's politics.

'Thank you, my lords and gentlemen,' said the Chairman, and he
glanced up and down the committee room, with its portraits of past
directors, its plasterwork ceiling representing astrolabes, back-staffs and
quadrants, and its wall-carvings of fruit by Grinling Gibbons.

'I now call the Honourable Mr Director Kilbride.' said the Chairman,
'to present a proposal.' He smirked. 'A proposal of which we have heard
general rumours, and now await precise enunciation!'

'Hear-hear!' said the meeting, and gave another rumble of knuckles
on mahogany.

Kilbride seized his moment. His chair slid back, he shot like a terrier
to a line of artist's easels set up near the head of the table. The easels were

covered with green baize cloths. Kilbride faced the meeting and as small men do, he drew himself stiff upright with raised chin, to make best use of what height he had.

'Thank you, My Lord,' he said to the Chairman.

'My pleasure, Mr Kilbride,' said the Chairman.

'So,' said Kilbride, 'The government tries to rule us!' He paused for response. 'It does, now, don't it?' The meeting growled and rapped knuckles. 'Yes,' said Kilbride, 'It's tried with acts of parliament and with putting a Supervisory Board over us, to run their noses into our affairs.' The meeting growled again, and heads nodded. 'But none of those noses are here today,' said Kilbride, 'at the least I don't think so,' he said, then he ducked down and made a pantomime of looking under the table. The meeting laughed and rapped table once more.

Yes. Yes, you liked that, didn't you? You're with me, so far, you herd of fat arses. So Kilbride whipped off one of the green baize covers. 'Here's India,' he said, 'Where already we rule.' He uncovered the next easel. 'And here's China, where we wish to rule.' He stepped forward wrapped in ambition. 'China, my Lords and gentlemen. China! Limitless people, limitless wealth, limitless land.' The meeting nodded. 'China!' said Kilbride, 'land of dreams for trade, but too strong to be taken by the Company's forces alone.' The meeting nodded, and Kilbride threw back another cloth.

'Ah!' said the meeting, and some members nodded to each other having anticipated what was revealed.

'But,' said Kilbride, 'here's Japan, which produces everything that China does. So I've put effort into asking about Japan, and I've inquired particularly of Dutchmen, since they have always traded with Japan.' He looked round the room. 'Ain't that true, my lords and gentleman? Don't the Dutch trade at the port of Nagasaki?' Heads nodded. There was full agreement in the room. The Dutch were formidable rivals in trade and their doings were of great interest.

'So,' said Kilbride, 'Japan is full of spices, porcelain, silk and tea, all ripe for trade, if only we could get at it.' Heads nodded. 'Which was impossible, ' said Kilbride, 'because Japan was closed to the world and was full of soldiers called samurai.' Again there was a murmur of assent and Kilbride studied his audience, knowing that he'd not quite got them yet: not got them in the palm of his hand. They were listening, and their

71

greedy eyes were round, but they were cautious. '*But,* my Lords!' he said, 'Japan isn't full of soldiers any more.'

'Oh?' said a few voices.

'No!' said Kilbride, 'Because Japan has shut out the world, and has been so very peaceful for so very long, that the samurai have gone soft, and taken up poetry and flower arranging.' The meeting laughed. 'No, my Lords and gentlemen,' said Kilbride, 'this ain't a joke. This is reality. They've taken up flowers and poetry!' He smiled. 'Those two, and book-keeping for their masters.' Kilbride smiled again. 'So, my lords and gentlemen, since Japan has no military alliance with any other power, I ask you: what's to stop us wriggling free of King and Parliament, by taking Japan for ourselves? And then, with Japan in our pockets, we might look again at China!'

'Hmmm ...' said the meeting and there was no drumming of knuckles. Perhaps Kilbride had gone to far? Perhaps he was merely a dreamer?

'Mr Kilbride?' said a voice and heads turned towards Director Sir Robert Valentine, baronet, who was a sound, careful man, and definitely not a dreamer.

'Sir Robert?' said Kilbride.

'Are you proposing,' said Valentine, 'that the Company should invade and capture an entire nation? The Japanese nation?'

'I aim that we should control it,' said Kilbride, 'for purposes of trade.'

'That is the same thing, Mr Kilbride,' said Valentine, 'So have you planned this venture? Have you considered the detail? And above all ... *have you costed it?*'

'Ah-ha!' said the meeting, and 'Indeed!' said the meeting, and 'Hear-hear!' as directors turned to each other in righteous scepticism. They nudged and nodded. They winked and sneered. They drummed knuckles like thunder. But Kilbride smiled, and threw the covers off the remaining easels to reveal boards bearing an awesome parade of tables, figures and diagrams.

'Thank you, Sir Robert, for your question,' said Kilbride, 'My lords and gentlemen, we took Seringapatam with an army of twenty thousand. Here are my plans to land a similar force on the shores of Japan, and everything is costed down to the last ship, the last penny and the last grain of gunpowder.'

'Oh?' said the meeting, and the directors were profoundly impressed.

CHAPTER 12

I was two weeks in Dominic Gardens and I've seldom lived in such luxury. There wasn't a single thing I could desire that wasn't within my easy reach so long as I was there. I had a room with French furniture, silk hangings and a bed the size of a three-decker. Servants were everywhere, I didn't lift a finger other than to shave and dress myself, the food was excellent, the wine was limitless, and the company excellent. They even got me some civilian clothes, of which I had none. I had only an undress uniform that was weather-stained, and full dress that was too formal.

And of course there was the delectable little Persephone: Perse. She ran the house, and was its sun, moon and stars. All the time I was there, Papa Ordroyd was in Lancashire with his cotton mills and Mrs Ordroyd was long dead of the influenza, and remembered only by a portrait in the front hall. Judging by the portrait she was something amazing horse-faced to have given birth to Phaeton and Perse, but nature plays these tricks, and with Mama gone, Perse was in charge. She commanded the servants, chose the decorations, wrote the menus, arranged the entertainments, and kept a salon for the bright and beautiful of the town.

When I first stepped into that house I was so tired that I asked if I might go at once to bed. But the fairies wouldn't have it! They kept me up. They dragged me into the hallway, spinning round in their fancy costumes, and looking up with their dear little faces, and I grinned and grinned and grinned. I'd been at sea for months, remember, and before that I'd been in France and at war, and the whole time surrounded by men: leather-faced matelots and hairy-arsed soldiers. So when I looked at the fairies I could have eaten them up. I could have bitten lumps out of them they looked so neat and sweet.

'No! No!' they cried, 'You shan't go to bed! We've waited up for you, Captain!

'We've heard all about you!'

'There, Sir!' said Phaeton, 'Shall you disappoint the ladies?'

'Including myself?' said Perse, 'Are you not a man, Sir?'

Well, my jolly boys, who could resist? And there was music coming from the withdrawing room, and I was persuaded to take a glass or two, and so I joined in with their silly games. Thus by easy stages, and to the best of my recollection, I was at one time dancing a hornpipe to thunderous applause, at another I was blindfolded and chasing fairies round the room in time to *Cock of the North*, and finally I was running up and down stairs, with a lady on each shoulder, with my arms around two pairs of plump thighs and the ladies squealing and shrieking and hanging on to my hair.

[A favourite game of Fletcher's. In later years he became famous for it, and – to my uncomprehending disbelief – the younger element of female guests would laughingly beg to be run up stairs and would not be content until he obliged. S.P.]

Finally of all, I was in a dark cupboard somewhere in the house, deep in embrace with a lady, and neither of us wearing more than a smile.

'Oh! Oh! Oh!' she cried.

By George it was fun. I repeat the that I'd been at sea for months, and I inform you youngsters for the betterment of your education, that what I was doing was no more than usual among seafaring men lately come ashore. Furthermore, though memory struggles thanks to the claret and the exhaustion of the moment, it is possible that more than one lady, and more than one dark cupboard was involved in these manoeuvres. After that, I don't remember going to bed, but finally I did, and being utterly spent in every way it's as well that I was alone, since I'd have been of no service whatsoever for anything other than sleep.

I woke up late, feeling unwell. So I slept a bit more, then got up and a manservant appeared and I found my chest unpacked, and clothes laid out ready, and hot water for the wash basin, and everything else I needed. As I have said, it was an easy house to stay in. Since guests were always in the house, and entertainments always under way, there was always breakfast till noon, and later if you wanted it. So I went down, nodded to everyone, noted two different ladies who smiled a special smile, and noted that neither of them was Perse. She was elsewhere – running the house I supposed – and Phaeton was still in bed.

So I had breakfast, looked at the newspapers that were brought in every day, and had to explain to the company that most of them were wrong in blathering on about the mutinies of the Channel Fleet at the Nore and Spithead, and declaring that the Navy couldn't be relied upon to save us from the French.

'Rubbish!' I said, 'Those mutinies were about *pay*. The men hadn't been paid for over a year, poor devils, and they were angry. It was all about pay!' It was too. The Channel Fleet hadn't been paid, nor given shore leave for a disgraceful time, and everyone in the Service knew it.

'But what if the French should come?' said one frightened young chap: they were all of them young. They were Perse's set, the sort that she liked: young, pretty and rich.

'Bother the French!' I said, taking care with my language, 'If the French come out, the Fleet will fight! There'll be no disobeying of orders, 'cos the men won't need orders. They'll up anchor and sail all by themselves.' The little chap smiled. They all smiled and I was their hero. It was an embarrassment, but I was soon relieved of it, because Phaeton came to breakfast, with Perse leading him, and jolly fine she looked too in some sort of muslin gown with a pretend shawl over the shoulders, so that everything that was pushed up to bounce, was supposedly hidden but wasn't.

'Huzzah!' cried the company round the breakfast table, and they applauded Phaeton as their new hero, quite displacing me for the moment. But he deserved it by their standards. He had genuinely seen action, and genuinely received a wound, and now here he was, having spent good time getting himself into fashionable rig, with cravat at his neck and hair curled, and his arm still in a sling, and his lovely sister hanging on to him. But she looked straight at me.

'Captain, Fletcher, Sir!' she cried, and did the most delightful imitation of a seaman's salute, stamping her little foot and raising a small, pink finger to her brow, 'Mr Midshipman Ordroyd come aboard, Sir!' It was all very jolly and everyone laughed.

After breakfast I went up to my room and sat down at desk by a window, and went through the papers Earl Spencer had given me, and what interesting papers they were too: there wasn't one signature anywhere, nor any mention of who'd written them, nor why they'd been written, nor who they'd been written for: namely myself! The nearest to a mention of me was phrases such as: '*you will exert yourself to the utmost of your ability,*' and '*you will by all imaginable and conceivable means prevent.*'

So neither Spencer nor I was named. But there were other names. Thus the person who was to do the exerting and preventing, was told: '*you will – before the end of July – report for further instruction to Mr Arnold Knowles, who is Chief Steward of Saint's Club of George Street, London.*' Now that was clever. Saint's was a club for Sea Service officers. It was famous, and Knowles was notorious. He was notorious as a middle man for top rate London whores, and as a banker – on exorbitant terms – for officers who got themselves into debt at the gambling tables. So he was a man that any officer might approach, in furtive confidence, for a private conversation as indeed I would have to. I shook my head in surprise. Knowles was renowned as a cunning greaser who kept his mouth shut. But if he was my channel to Earl Spencer, there must be more to Knowles than anyone knew. So I'd just have to wait and see.

Finally the papers said that I was to take particular note of the future actions of Mr Stephen Kilbride, and Sir Robert Valentine, both of them directors of the East India Company: my first introduction to that pair of devious bastards, may they rot, but at the time they were just names.

Apart from that there was a lot of information about how the East India Company worked, some lists of ship names and types, details of the ranks and officers of their ships and much else besides. So I read it all a few times, then went down to the kitchens and amazed the servants by personally stuffing the papers into the fire, beside the spit-jacks, ovens and cisterns for hot water. I got smiles from the kitchen maids though, and they were all pretty, just as young Phaeton had boasted.

After that, I spent a number of choice days at fifty-five Dominic Gardens, and a few choice nights. So, once again for your education, you youngsters should note that that the fun and games I'd enjoyed in dark cupboards was not normal in the houses of gentry: not at all! That was only the way things were done among Perse's set. What was normal, and still is, was a discreet shuffling from room to room at night, after everyone's supposed to have gone to bed, and the servants aren't supposed to be sniggering behind doors, listening for all they're worth – which of course they are. That's how it was done, and if on your nightly wanderings, you passed another gentleman in his dressing gown, and under full sail with his slippers in his hand for silence, then you took care not to meet his eyes, and pretended you'd never even seen him. Also you took damn good care to get into the right bedroom, according to the invitation received, though I have it on good authority that occasional mistakes in this respect were not necessarily rebuffed with outrage.

So it was night time sailings at number fifty-five, and the first night that I crept into Perse's room, I was astounded to find that she kept costumes for these occasions. In particular she had a skin-tight rig of black silk, that turned her into a cat, complete with ears, whiskers and a tail. By Jove but I was surprised, and I wondered where she'd got such ideas, and her so young. But she'd got them all right, and she purred and hissed, and curled up and wriggled on the bed, and lashed her tail such that I damn near fired off my broadside before I'd engaged.

In addition to these entertainments, I met the most amusing people at the salon Perse kept in the afternoons. They were all light-weight, cheerful little folk, and they laughed and chattered, and tea was served in a reception room on the first floor. It had big windows, mirrors and coloured landscapes on the walls, a huge Afghan carpet on the floor, more French furniture with lashings of gold leaf, and Perse lounging on a chaise-long, and smiling at everyone. That's where I met Mr Leonard Tipstaff – a genius in my opinion – because of a most remarkable talent.

I arrived late for the salon one afternoon, came into a room full of fun, with chatter and noise, and with perfume that you could smell as you came up the stairs, never mind when the servants opened the doors. The room was full, and everyone was gathered around a table set up in the middle where a young, sandy-haired, scrawny man was sat scribbling on an artist's pad with a clutch of pencils in his left hand, from which he selected, hard or soft, and a stump of charcoal too, and was taking likenesses of the company. He had spectacles on his nose, his bent-over head showed a bald patch, and he was untidy in dress.

'Ah!' said Perse, as I came in, 'Here's the captain! Meet Lenny Tipstaff,' she said, and placed a dainty hand on his head. Then 'Get him, Lenny!' she said, and Tipstaff looked up at me – just a glance mind you – and shoved aside what he was working on, and swept a few lines across a blank sheet, and then looked at me and grinned. Everyone leaned over to see what he'd done, and gave up a communal sigh of wonderment, and shook their pretty heads awe, as they looked at the lines, then looked at me, and then the lines again.

Naturally I went forward to see, and there, by Heaven, done with just a few swift strokes of a pencil … was myself! It was amazing. He'd got me. He really had. It was me! I looked at the other drawings he'd already done, and real, live people leapt off the paper. I looked round and could recognise every single one from Tipstaff's instant, easy scribbles. Naturally they all laughed, and who wouldn't?

'Lenny's a caricaturist,' said Perse, isn't he, everyone?'

'Yes!' they all said.

'Best in London,' said Perse, and seeing my interest, she was kind enough to steer Tipstaff into a corner where I could speak to him by myself.

'Amazing gift you have, Mr Tipstaff,' I said gazing down at him. They were all tiny in that room.

'No more than your own, Captain Fletcher,' he said, 'You're a seaman, gunner and navigator and everyone who sails with you loves you.' That took me aback, I can tell you. I was lost for words. For one thing he wasn't the light-weight I'd took him for. The rest may have been but not Leonard Tipstaff.

'Very kind of you, Mr Tipstaff,' I said finally.

'I've followed your career, Captain,' he said, 'I've always wanted to go to sea, but I get sea-sick.' He smiled at me, and looked sad.

'Everyone gets sea-sick,' I said, 'but you get used to it.'

'I don't,' he said, 'I can't bear it,' and he nodded towards Phaeton, with his coat off and sleeve rolled up to show off his scar. 'Look at him,' said Tipstaff, 'mad as a monkey, brains of a snail, but he's ready to go to sea again, and I couldn't do that.'

'But you can set down an amazing likeness,' I said, feeling sorry for him and wishing to make the conversation cheerful, 'How does it work? Do you have to study a face?'

'No,' he said, and tapped his head, 'One look and it's in here. It's always been the same with me, and once it's in my head I just set it down. I never forget a face, either.'

We talked a lot more after that. I learned that Tipstaff worked for Mrs Hannah Humphrey of St James's who ran London's foremost print-shop, and together with the famous Gilray and Rowlandson – both far better known than – he turned out the hilarious, satirical caricatures that all the town laughed at and admired, and everyone waited to see who'd be the next among the politicians and royalty to be publicly mocked.

So we became friends, firm friends and I liked him a lot, because not only did he get me out of a very considerable difficulty a few days later, but he led me to something wonderful after that. The difficulty started that night, when Perse got me in a corner before dinner. I smiled because I thought she was a cat on the prowl again, but it wasn't that.

'Will you do me the most vast and enormous favour?' she asked with the brown eyes glowing.

'Anything, ma'am,' I said.

'Phaeton is going to Brooks's Club this evening,' she said.

'Is he a member?' I said because Brooks's was highly exclusive.

'A member since birth,' she said, 'thanks to his father's money.'

'I see,' I said, 'who's he going with? Not on his own, surely?'

'That's the problem,' she said, 'he's going with friends I don't trust.'

'Why?'

'Because mostly he keeps away from the card tables.'

'Mostly?'

'Yes, because he hasn't the wit to keep up with the play, and doesn't enjoy it.'

'But?'

'If he's with his friends, he'll play just to be like them,' she said, and I nodded. Brooks's was famous for gambling. Fortunes were won and lost over cards, and the games went on all night, and were the main attractions of the club.

'So you'd like me to go with him, to keep him safe?'

'Yes,' she said, 'I can't go. It's a gentleman's club.' She moved so close I could feel the warmth of her, and she whispered, 'And you may rely upon me, Captain, to show my appreciation later.'

Thus an hour later I was inside the yellow-brick, Portland stone mansion that was Brooks's. I was in the Great Room with its enormous Adam fireplace, and vaulted ceiling lit by chandeliers, while shaded lights illuminated the tops of the gambling tables. These tables were surrounded by seated gentlemen, all totally absorbed in their whist, picquet and quinze and what numbskull idiots they were, since gambling is a shameful, stupid and despicable way to waste the wealth that better men have created, in commerce and trade, and done so by their virtuous exertions, their firm determination, and their tireless diligence. So I have no words strong enough to condemn, vilify and anathematize gambling, and damn-well forbid that any of you youngsters, as have an atom of respect for your Uncle

Jacob, should ever indulge in gambling or I'm damn-well done with you, and there's a bloody-damned end of you, and serve you damn-well right!

[Note that the above paragraph is a mere abbreviated summary of Fletcher's prolonged sermon on the evils of gambling and the virtue of trade, which sermon was delivered at such volume as to alarm the entire household and shake the glasses in the window frames. S.P.]

So I took very seriously my duty of keeping Phaeton from sitting down to play, but I let him stand behind one of his blockhead friends to watch. This he did, getting steadily more bored at the game went on, and sinking glass after glass from the waiters who went to and fro with trays of drink. So he soon became merry, which I let him do, because otherwise he was sulky and bad company, and I also took a few myself because I was as bored as him. So what followed is in some degree my fault, because Phaeton became so merry that he kept talking to me, to the annoyance of the room, where silence was required so as not to disturb the players.

'Don't you play, Captain?' he said.

'No!' I said.

'Not ever?'

'No!'

'Shhhhh!' said a voice.

'Oh, sorry, sorry, sorry,' said Phaeton and grinned and stumbled and caught hold of the shoulder of one of the players to steady himself. 'Whoops, whoops, whoops!' he said, and the players frowned, and the man whose shoulder he'd grabbed turned and looked at Phaeton with a face like a snake. He was a cold, narrow, bony creature: hair slicked down, fine clothes, and bitten fingernails clutching his cards.

'You will apologise, Sir,' he said, 'You will apologise at once.' The table went quiet. The whole room went quiet and the waiters gasped. Everyone was looking at Phaeton. I read the signs, and grabbed Phaeton.

'Say sorry,' I said, 'Apologise to the gentleman.'

'What for?' said Phaeton, 'I only slipped. I think the floor's slippery.'

'Say sorry,' I said.

'Why?' he said, with his head full of drink, and he gave me his silliest, little-boy smile, 'I'm sure the gentleman don't really mind,' he said, and looked at him, 'You don't mind, do you, Sir?' He took hold of the shoulder again and shook it. This time the gasp was audible because it came from every man in the room, as the gentleman pushed away Phaeton's hand and stood up. He was as tall as me but thin, and he was a nasty creature with a nasty face, and nasty eyes that weren't right. He stared and didn't blink. He showed no emotion.

'You will apologise at once,' he said to Phaeton, 'You will acknowledge fault. Then you will leave immediately taking your friends with you.'

'What?' said Phaeton, and he laughed, drunken idiot that he was.

'I see,' said the gentleman, and reached in his pocket. I didn't like that. I didn't know what was in the pocket. So I shoved Phaeton out of the way and stood in his place, facing Mr snake-face.

'Wait, Sir,' I said, 'the boy's drunk. He's only seventeen years old, and he knows no better. Leave it to me. I'll take him home and teach him his manners there.' Everyone looked to see what snake-face would say. Some of them nodded. He did not.

'An insult has been given,' he said, 'and no apology offered.'

'Bah!' I said and shook Phaeton, 'say sorry, damn you!'

'No!' said snake-face, 'Not good enough. I demand satisfaction.'

'From him?' I said.

'No, Sir. The boy is indeed drunk. But you are not and you are in charge of him.' Then the hand came out of the pocket with a visiting card, which he offered me, 'I therefore demand satisfaction from you, and I ask for your address so that my friends may call on you.'

81

CHAPTER 13

*'Having completed the first part of my mission I ran into doubt, as a
ship runs into a rock. I was unsure that I had chosen wisely, and wished
beyond all means of expression that I could have the endorsement of
my beloved father. But then the wise Nakano spoke.'*

(From the 'Foreign Journal' of Masahito Hitamoto. Entry dated
Friday July 14th 1797.)

Fumito Nakano, knelt deferentially to one side of Lord Masahito, even
though Nakano, at fifty, was more than twice Masahito's age, and had known
Masahito since he was a little boy. Thus Nakano had gone into exile at the
command of Lord Hayato, his Daimyo, but Nakano would have gone
willingly, in order to defend Masahito against the horrors of barbarian life.

Now the two men occupied cushions in the middle of what had been
the withdrawing room of Lord Masahito's house in Dunelm square, but
the room had been altered, to Nakano's instructions to resemble as closely
as possible the interior of Japanese manor house, with plain walls, tatami
mats, and sliding screens. So they sat in silence, in surroundings as peaceful
and proper as could be contrived, while Nakano considered the question
that Lord Masahito had just asked.

After sufficient contemplation, Nakano bowed.

'My Lord,' he said, 'You ask if my Lord your Father would have approved
your choice of Kilbride, to assist in our plans to defend Clan Hitamoto?'

'I do,' said Masahito, 'Kilbride has told me that he plans to take a great
army to Japan, to break open Japan to foreign trade, and that he promises
to act together with our clan as equal allies in all things, to defeat the
armies of the Shogun.'

'Yes, my Lord,' said Nakano, 'but we cannot trust him and must rely
on means as yet unknown, to bend him to our will.'

'That is correct,' said Masahito, 'And now I need the Lord my Father's blessing that I have chosen well in Kilbride,' Masahito sighed, 'But the Lord my Father is ten thousand miles away, even if he still lives, and no message has passed between us in all these years. So how can I know that I am doing my duty as a Hito samurai, and the son of my father?'

'I understand your doubts, my Lord,' said Nakano, 'But perhaps my Lord your Father is still with us.'

'How can that be?' said Masahito.

'Because of a certain story, ' said Nakano, and bowed, 'May I tell it?'

'Of course.'

'So,' said Nakano, 'When he was ten years old, my Lord your Father was the boy Hayoto Hitamoto. He was in a class of high-rank samurai boys under instruction by a reverend monk of the Okobo Buddhism that we follow. All the boys behaved well except Hayoto, who constantly showed disrespect. So the monk warned him with a famous proverb:

"The nail that stands out, gets the hammer!" But the monk had used these words before, and Hayoto had thought about them. So he said:

"Yes master, but what if all the men of a village say a dam is safe, except one who knows it is not? Should he be silent until the village drowns?" He was beaten for those words and deserved it.' Masahito smiled.

'That sounds like my father,' he said, 'he would say that.'

'Indeed. And now we turn to you, my Lord.' Masahito nodded, and Nakano continued, 'You may remember that when you were about the same age, you were under instruction by a great philosopher of *Kyodo* – the way of the bow – who was shooting with his disciples watching, and he shot so beautifully that one of the disciples shed tears and knelt before him.

"Master," he said, "how can I become a perfect archer, when delicate judgement is needed to aim the arrow, at the same instant as heavy strength is needed to draw the bow?"

"My son," said the master, "you must become the arrow!"' Masahito smiled because he remembered what happened next.

'Everyone sighed,' he said, 'then struggled to understand.'

'But you did not struggle to understand,' said Nakano, 'You said, "A crossbow lets a man pull the string to the lock, then relax and take aim in comfort. So he can shoot *without* becoming the arrow."' Masahito laughed.

83

'I was beaten for that,' he said.

'You were beaten on the orders of my Lord your father,' said Nakano, 'You were beaten for insolence, just as he had been. But my Lord laughed when they told him what you had said to the Kyodo master, because he knew that you were like him.' Nakano bowed. 'And I say now, my Lord that you are not just *like* your father, you *are* your father. Your mind is his mind, and as long as *you* live, then *he* lives.'

'Most beloved Lady Meiko, princess of my heart, mistress of my dreams, keeper of my soul. I bow before you in thanks for your words at our last meeting, and each second that passes before we may meet again, shall seem to me a thousand years.'

(From a letter of Saturday, July 22nd 1797, from Kimiya Hitamoto, Daimyo of Hito Domain, to the Lady Meiko, The House of Flowers, Port Hito.)

The tea house of The House of Flowers was very old: built in 1581, by the immortal master of design, Sen No Rikyu. The tea house therefore represented Rikyu's three virtues: rustic simplicity, directness of approach, and honesty of self. These virtues ordained a small and simple wooden structure, with pitched roof, sliding screens, and space inside for precisely four-and-a-half tatami mats.

To foreign eyes, the tea house was plain and bare of decoration. But even a foreigner would recognise that everything was precise and pure, and that the tea house sat in a garden of immaculate beauty, with shrubs, flowers, rocks and streams in such perfect harmony that any visitor must be soothed by their tranquillity.

Inside the tea house Lord Kimiya Hitamoto, sat in the correct *seiza* position: back straight, knees folded beneath him, and with hands respectfully rested in his lap. Two samurai from the highest ranks of his retainers, sat with him, and the only decoration of the house was displayed to Lord Kimiya's right: an alcove with a hanging scroll of Fodai poetry, and a plain vase of flowers arranged to represent calm thought, and auspicious omens.

But neither Lord Kimiya, or his retainers looked at anything other than the Lady Meiko, highest and most beautiful of all the Geisha in Hito as she played the three-string *shamisen*. She too, knelt in the seiza position

84

and was radiant in multiple layers of kimono, each a masterwork of design, and she wore the white face-paint, and the high and complex hair-style of her profession. That, and a bare neck that was so slender as to rouse passions of desire in the three men who sat before her.

Sadly, this was especially so for Lord Kimiya, who longed for the Lady Meiko. To him, she was exquisite, she was matchless, she was divine. Compared with her, his wife and concubines were nothing. They provided sons and relief from lust, but nothing more, while the Lady Mieko was the love of his life. But the Lady Meiko was a Geisha, and under Hito law, no Geisha could have carnal relations with a client. This was forbidden because it was not the work of Geisha, but that of an entirely different class of professionals: the *Oiran* courtesans who were as expensive, educated and lovely as any Geisha, but who – in their turn – were not allowed to offer the spiritual ecstasy of music, poetry, and dance because that was the work of the Geisha. In this matter the law followed Okobo Buddhism which taught *one man, one job*, and it was precisely the same for women.

In addition, there was something else that only Geisha could offer, and that was informed discussion on the affairs and politics of men. A senior Geisha understood these complexities and could even give advice, though with infinite care that the self-esteem of a client was not damaged by the words of a mere woman.

So, when the music ended, and the Lady Meiko bowed, the two samurai bowed to her and left the tea house. They stood outside at a respectful distance, at the head of their Lord's ever-present bodyguard and patiently waited.

Inside, Lord Kimiya poured out words that he could say only to Lady Meiko. She listened, and waited until he was finished. Then she bowed and spoke.

'You are still grieving for your father, My Lord, and that is natural and honourable.'

'It's more than that,' said Kimiya, 'I need to know that he approves. I need his blessing.'

'May I ask why?'

'Because of my little brother. The one he sent away.'

The Lady Meiko nodded. She had heard all this before. She had heard it many times. But it was her duty to listen and give comfort.

'Masahito was sent away,' she said, 'because he was strange, and was therefore fit to live among the foreigners.'

'Yes, but my father was strange. He loved foreign ideas, and Masahito was the same. Masahito was like him.'

'A lesser man might be jealous of this, My Lord, but not you.'

'Why not?'

'Because Masahito resembled the one flaw in your noble father's character.'

'His love of the foreigners?'

'Yes, and you have purified the memory of your father by destroying all evidence of this flaw.' Kimiya nodded.

'Every trace has gone,' he said, 'I have done everything to defend his memory.'

'But there is one thing that you have not done,' said the Lady Meiko, and Kimiya closed his eyes, anticipating the grace that would come upon him with his Lady's words. 'Any other Lord than you,' she said, 'would not only have destroyed books and devices, he would have closed the mouths of the servants who knew of these things: them and all their families. He would have closed their mouths in death! But you did not do that because you are a just and merciful ruler. You trust your people, and are kind to them, and in this supreme matter you are exactly like your father: and he lives on in you.'

CHAPTER 14

Persephone looked at the visiting card. She read every line. She turned over the card as if seeking further information. Then she looked at me. 'Francis Delaine,' she said, '*Franky* Delaine!'

'Do you know him?' I said.

'I know *of* him,' she said, 'everyone does.' She put down the card on the little table in front of the sofa where we sat in her dressing room. It was late, the house was quiet, candles were burning, and almost everyone – guest or servant alike – was in bed, except for Phaeton, who I'd deposited in the flag-stoned kitchen below, so he could sick up his drink into a bucket, and not spoil the carpets if he missed.

'So who is Delaine?' I said, '*Wha*t is he, if everyone's heard of him.'

'Franky Delaine,' she said, 'He's nothing much. He has enough money to live in style, he plays cards – and usually wins – and he fights duels. Everyone knows him, and everyone avoids him, or they take care to be polite when they do meet him.' Then she gasped and suddenly threw her arms round me and kissed me. By George that was nice. It really was, she was all soft and warm. 'Thank you! Thank you!' she said, 'I knew you'd look after Phaeton, and you did and you are my champion!'

Well, my jolly boys, I thought that the drums were beating to quarters and we were going into action there and then. It was a big sofa with plenty of room to manoeuvre, and I was just getting my coat off, when she spoke again and this time her face was serious. It was very serious indeed.

'So will you fight?' she said.

'What?' I said.

'Fight!' she said, 'fight Franky Delaine!'

'I should damn well say not!' I said, 'duelling is for idiots. It's stupid at any time, but in time of war it's stupendously stupid. Aren't the French killing enough of us? Should we do their work for them, and kill one another?' So I laughed, but Perse didn't. 'What's the matter?' I said.

87

'He's fought lots of duels,' she said, 'he's killed five men, wounded more, and some others have been forced into grovelling apologies. The youngest he killed was only seventeen, just like Phaeton.'

'Well,' I said, 'that ain't right, and he needs a hanging. But I'm not going to fight him.'

'Jacob,' she said, 'if you won't fight he'll *post you up.*'

'He'll do what?'

'He'll post you up. That's what Franky does if a man won't fight.'

'And what's that?'

'He'll pay printer to run off several thousand notices and he'll have them posted on the walls up and down all the best streets and squares in town, with copies sent to all the gentlemen's clubs, and the posters will say something like: *whereas Captain Jacob Fletcher has been challenged to a duel and has refused to give satisfaction, then Captain Fletcher is a coward not worthy of the King's Commission.*'

I thought about that, and you youngsters will have to think likewise and remember that things weren't the same then as they are now. Nowadays a gentleman is supposed to behave himself – not that they do, but they're supposed to – but under good King George a gentleman could bellow and rage and roar. He could get blind drunk. He could spread his seed among the ladies of the town. He could get out of his carriage and fight a meat porter if he wanted. He could do all that and *still* be received in polite society! But he couldn't be a coward, because if he was, then every door would close in his face.

'So that's *posting up*, is it?' I said.

'Yes it is,' she said.

I think I must have groaned, because she cuddled up close, dear little thing, and I put my arms round her, but I wasn't thinking about her: I was thinking about duels. The trouble was that duels were fought with pistols, and I'm so big a target that any fool could put a ball into me, and if Delaine was a notorious duellist then I guessed he'd be a crack shot and could hit me with his eyes shut. So I was afraid, my jolly boys, I freely admit it.

Now don't mistake me: if it was a boarding action then I'd go over the side with a brace of barkers and let fly and throw 'em into the enemy's face, then out with a cutlass hacking left and right and bellowing at the top of my voice, because that's how it has to be done. I'd led boarding actions before and I'd do it again, but that's not the same as standing still for some bastard to take his own good time aiming at you. That's madness and it's against nature. But it looked as if I'd have to do it.

'Leave it to me, Perse,' I said, 'but if you'd forgive me this once, I'll need to sleep on it, and sleep by myself.' So she nodded, looked miserable, and I went off to my room with the big bed and tried to sleep. I tried but it was hard, because it wasn't just the duel that was worrying me, but whatever it was that Earl Spencer had in mind, and I even thought of giving up England entirely. I could draw money from my bank, and take ship for America which country I've always admired, and if I couldn't be British I'd most happily be American. But that wouldn't work because I was too well known now – especially in the sea ports – and too easy to spot. So I'd probably be recognised, word would get to Spencer and I'd end up facing trial for Boatswain Dixon. Added to that I'd got used to being Captain of a ship, with men saluting, and honours given, and I couldn't bear becoming a miserable fugitive chased by the law.

Then thinking of the law rubbed in the vast irony that duelling was illegal in England, but the magistrates who enforced the law were gentlemen who thought duelling was a private matter between gentlemen like themselves, and none of the Law's business! So if you complained to a magistrate that you'd been challenged, he'd most likely call you a whining coward and send you on your way.

What with one thing and another it wasn't an easy night, I didn't sleep very much, and in the morning Delaine's friends called. They came at ten o'clock They asked for me, and Perse came and found me in the garden behind the house, where I was pacing up and down trying to think of something clever to get me out of my troubles.

'Jacob,' she said, 'They're here, they are in the library, and I have been thinking. You are entirely correct. Duelling is foolish, and a man of such proven valour as yourself, should be able to refuse it, and no man will think the worse of you,' and she smiled. Those were splendid words. They were indeed, bless her heart. The only trouble was that her smile wavered and I could see that she didn't believe any of it: not really. 'So tell Delaine to go to Hades!' she said, 'and to take his posting up with him!'

'Thank you, Perse' I said, and kissed her. I kissed her hand, what with the servants watching, and as I let go her hand, then suddenly …. the Heavens were full of music. A choir of Angels was singing! Hallelujah! Hallelujah! Posting up, eh? Posting up, my jolly boys?

89

So I went into the library, and there they were: two of them, friends of Delaine, and I detested them on sight. Both were young, neither had brains, they reeked of perfume, and they had the sallow faces of creatures who were up all night and asleep all day. But that wasn't why I despised them. What turned my stomach was they were toadies to a sick-in-the-mind killer. They were flies on a turd. But I smiled merrily.

'Good day to you gentlemen,' I said, 'To whom do I have the pleasure of speaking?'

'I'm Drayton,' said one. He had a sweaty, pompous little face that was trying to be grim but only looked surly.

'And I'm Gallant,' said the other, who was even worse: having an unclean odour hiding under the scent. They never dreamed how close they were to a boot up the breech and being thrown down the front door steps. But it wasn't the day for tricks like that.

'Delighted to make your acquaintance gentlemen,' I said, 'So! Shall we proceed at once with the details? I stand ready to face your principal, Mr Delaine, whom I shall meet at any time and place of his choice, my only condition being that since my own pistols are in my ship, I would ask that we use those of Mr Delaine, provided only that I am given the feel of them before loading, so as to get their balance.'

'Very proper, Sir!' said Drayton.

'Very proper!' said Gallant.

'Our principal usually chooses Kingslake park,' said Drayton, 'at dawn, beside the boating lake pavilion, and his preferred distance is twenty paces. Would that suit you, Captain?'

Twenty paces, I would point out, meant that one of the seconds measured that distance then the two combatants stood at either end of it, facing one another with pistols in hand, and then – at a given signal – each took a shot at the other. It also meant that if both missed, then the two men stood there waiting while the seconds reloaded, so each man could have another shot. And that went on until somebody was hit, or somebody could take no more and gave humble apology to the other, who walked away victorious and boasted of it ever after.

None the less:

'Yes!' I said, and let it be tomorrow.' I smiled. 'Whenever I fight, I always insist that it should be without delay.' They blinked at that. 'It's kinder to the opponent, don't you think? And I wouldn't want Mr Delaine to suffer any nervous anticipation.' They looked at one another, severely puzzled, 'So please assure Mr Delaine of my best wishes,' I said, 'my best wishes for clear light and a good aim.' Then I saw them to the front door, and shook their hands. 'Do tell Mr Delaine to wrap up warm,' I said, 'It can be chilly at dawn!'

'Oh,' they said, and they were off, and I saw the house servants looking at each other. They'd heard what I said, and I don't doubt their report of it would go round the town to the betterment of my reputation. Servants do gossip, don't they?

After that I got my coat and hat, kissed Perse, found a cab and went to Hannah Humphrey's shop and asked for Tipstaff. I was hopping from one foot to the other in fear he'd not be there, but he was, and I was introduced to Mrs Humphreys – no beauty but a witty old trout who chattered a lot – and then, at my request, Tipstaff showed me into his studio up in the attic, with big windows in the roof for the light, and very fascinating it was too. There were prints everywhere, complete and half-done, and desks and pens, and dust and clutter, and all the paraphernalia for painting prints in colour. The place was a complete muddle, and you had to wade through papers to get across the room. But Tipstaff found a couple of chairs, and a bottle and some glasses and we sat and talked. At first he was nervous, but finally he laughed, and I smiled.

'And can you do it?' I said, and he grinned, and tapped his head.

'Once it's in there, it's there forever.'

'And there has to be two of you,' I said, 'so can you bring a friend who'll keep quiet? 'One that you trust?'

'Yes, yes,' he said, 'I'll bring Henry, Mrs Humphrey's son. He's my printer anyway, and we'd need a printer wouldn't we?'

'Of course!' I said, 'Better and better! And you'll come to Dominic gardens?'

'In our dog-cart,' he said, 'I'll drive, and I know Kingslake Park well.'

'Good!'

After that it was all plain sailing until an hour before dawn next morning, and I hadn't spent *that* night alone, believe me, because nature has the most powerful effect on women if their man is facing shot and shell the coming day. Perse came over in floods of tears, and I had to say that everything would be all right, and that I'd faced worse and would doubtless face worse

91

again, and that only brought on more tears. So I did my best to comfort her in the traditional way, which is a gentleman's duty, and he mustn't think only of himself on these occasions: indeed he mustn't, my jolly boys.

Next morning I was waiting in the dark, outside number fifty-five in my greatcoat when Tipstaff arrived. The dog cart was a small one, with one horse in the shafts, and Tipstaff and another man on the box as well, both wrapped up, and looking anxious. They weren't so sure as I was, that all would run smooth, but at least they were there.

'Morning, Mr Tipstaff,' I said.

'Morning Captain,' he said, 'This is my friend Mr Henry Humphrey.'

'Mr Humphrey, Sir!' I said, raising my hat, 'I really am very obliged.'

'That's all right, Sir,' said Humphrey, but he was more nervous than Tipstaff.

'You'll have to ride in the back,' said Tipstaff, which I did, and the cart rocked as I hauled myself aboard, and the horse snorted in alarm. But then we were off, through a quiet, just-awaking city, with only the odd watchman about, and tradesmen throwing back the shutters of their shop windows, and the sudden roar of a gleaming mail coach in-bound from Bristol, fresh off the Great West Road, and charging like the wrath of God, with four horses up, lights burning, passengers on the roof-seats, and the driver cracking his whip. But then it was gone, and only its echoes behind, and then all was quiet again.

It wasn't far to Kingslake Park, which was out to the west of London, by the turnpike, and was known for its café and large boating lake, and the little rowing skiffs that were rented out by the hour. It had woods all round and was also known as the place where blockhead morons went to exchange pistol fire over perceived insults, and now I was one of them.

The sun was just up, with a brightening sky as we rolled along the gravelled path from the park gates towards the boating pavilion. Delaine and his seconds – Drayton and Gallant – were already there, with a hired Hackney Carriage and driver. Delaine stared at me with his snake-face. He was leaning on a black walking stick, while Drayton had a case of pistols under his arm. They were all in greatcoats and hats. So Tipstaff pulled up, threw on the brake and we got down with the dog-cart creaking and swaying. The lake pavilion was right next to us, casting a long morning shadow, and the lake was shining, with a few ducks and swans at their business, and crows in the sky overhead.

'Good morning, gentlemen!' I said in a good, loud voice, because it doesn't do to be meek on such occasions.

'Good morning,' said Drayton and Gallant.

'These are my seconds, Mr Tipstaff and Mr Humphrey,' I said

'Gentlemen!' said Drayton and Gallant.

'Gentlemen!' replied Tipstaff and Humphrey.

'Mr Delaine, Sir!' I said, stepping forward and holding out my hand. Delaine stared at me and calmly turned his back. But I had time to look him over and he really was one that the Devil was waiting for, down below. He was utterly calm, not a muscle moving on his face, and pair of flat-dead eyes that looked straight into your face and out of the back of your head.

'Sir!' said Drayton to me, 'My principal cannot acknowledge you until satisfaction is given.'

'Indeed not!' said Gallant.

'Then let's get on with it,' I said, and turned to Tipstaff. 'Sir,' I said, 'can I ask you to reassure me that Mr Delaine's pistols are present, and are fit for service?'

'Yes, Captain!' said Tipstaff, and there was some fumbling and panto-mime, as Drayton opened the case, and Tipstaff – who'd never touched a firearm in his life – had a look at them and poked them a bit.

'All sound, Captain,' he said.

'In that case, Gentlemen,' I said, 'and in accordance with the agreed procedure, I ask that before the pistols are loaded, I might take them in my hand to get the feel of them.'

'You may, Sir!' said Drayton.

'Good,' I said, 'and now I would ask all present, including Mr Delaine to give close attention to my actions for fear of any impropriety.' Delaine ignored me so I let out a good masthead-hailing shout, 'Mr Delaine!' I cried, 'I shall need you particularly to witness my actions.'

'Indeed!' cried Tipstaff, and nudged Humphrey.

'Indeed!' cried Humphrey, and Delaine turned round out of curiosity to see what was going on. So I gave a little bow to Drayton, and took the pistols out of the case. They were absolutely the finest pair I had ever seen in my life. They were by Joe Manton of London, they had the very finest locks, with water-proof pans and gold-lined touchholes, and they had blued, octagonal, rifled barrels with Manton's name and address inlaid in gold on the top. The chequered walnut stocks had the most perfect fit of wood to steel, and they sat in the hand so beautifully as to line up each pistol on target entirely naturally, as the hand was raised and the eye looked over the sights. Never mind what they cost – and it must have been a very great deal indeed – because they were true works of art.

So even Delaine gasped when I took his pistols, one after the other, and hurled them out into the lake with all my might and just as far as ever I could. Splash! Splash! In they went and down they went and the ducks quacked and the swans hissed.

'Ah-Ha!' said Tipstaff.

'Oh-Ho!' said Humphrey.

'Smack!' said my fist, and Drayton was on the ground. 'Smack!' and down went Gallant, and the pair of them gulping like goldfish.

'Now then,' I said to Delaine, 'Come here, you slimy swab! Come here, you dollop of crap! If you want a fight, then put up your fists and fight like a man!' But I'd miss-judged him. He was a deal worse than I'd thought. He stepped back, clicked something in his stick and whipped out three feet of bright steel.

'I'll have your eyes!' he said and took a step forward, 'I'll have your ears first, then your nose, then your eyes.' I didn't expect that or I'd have been a lot more careful. So I did what I could under the circumstances. I hauled off my greatcoat, rolled it over my left arm and charged the blighter before he could form his attack. But he was quick as lightning, and lunged with the blade, which either by luck or judgement, I caught in the thick roll of cloth, and it bent, and snapped and then I was on him.

If he'd fought fair in the first place I'd not have battered him so hard. But he didn't. He came at me with a swordstick, and even then he tried to pull another knife from somewhere. So he got a serious hammering, and I had to haul him to his feet half-conscious afterwards, and drag him over to the Hackney Coach, where I held him by the scruff of the neck and looked up at the driver.

'You!' I said, 'Sling your hook! Now!'

'Yes, Cap'n,' he said, and he did. He ran like a greyhound.

'Bring Drayton!' I said to Tipstaff, 'And Gallant too. And get the ropes out of our cart.'

Ten minutes later, Mr snake-face, duellist Delaine and his friends were stood up in a row with their wrists tied to the wheels of the Hackney Carriage. They faced the vehicle, but each man's britches and drawers were

94

round his ankles, and their snow-white arses shone bright in the morning sun. Delaine was still dizzy, but we found a bucket and threw some of the lake over him, and he woke up and snarled at me and let loose a string of foul oaths that I won't report because they weren't even clever: just nasty.

'Mr Tipstaff,' I said, 'Have you got the print?'

'I have, Captain,' he said, 'I've just brought it from the cart,' and he handed me a nicely framed, superbly executed print, all beautifully coloured and a joy to see. In fact it wasn't actually a print, but a pen-and-ink drawing from which a print would be made. It was a drawing by Tipstaff who had once seen Delaine in a chop-house: a drawing prepared in advance, to my instructions, so that it could be brought, ready for use to the field of play. But print or drawing, it served purpose because it showed three men tied to a coach, with their bare bums facing the world and all but one looking away, and that one was the most perfect likeness of Delaine, while to one side was a perfect likeness of myself throwing a pair of pistols into a lake.

'See that, Delaine?' I said, 'Now here's the rules. You will go away and keep quiet about this affair. You will issue no more challenges to anybody in future, and you will steer clear of Mr Tipstaff and Mr Humphrey, though I advise that you should do your best to find out who they are, because that will help you understand the peril in which you stand.' Delaine just gaped at the print. He said nothing. 'Aren't you going to ask what happens if you don't follow the rules?' I said.

'God damn you,' he said.

'That's for Him to decide,' I said, ' so I'll tell you anyway because if you keep my rules, this print shall remain secret and nobody shall ever hear of what happened today. But if you break my rules, then ten thousand copies will appear all over London, and in all the Gentlemen's clubs especially Brooks's, and you will know that the print tells the truth so you can't deny it! Are you following, Mr Delaine? Because I'm no expert, but you are, so you will understand that if you don't tread careful, you won't just be posted up, you'll be *printed up!*'

95

CHAPTER 15

'Kilbride spoke of ships and men. He did so in detail. He is a master of detail. If the venture depended on detail it must succeed. He was less convincing on relations with the Hitamoto. This worries me.

(From Sir Robert Valentine's Diary. Entry of Friday July 21ˢᵗ 1797.)

Mr Stephen Kilbride and Sir Robert Valentine, sat at their port in the huge dining room of Sir Robert's house in Berkshire. Their wives were long gone to the withdrawing room, the servants had been sent away, the decanter was running low, and two men were a small company for a table that would seat two dozen in comfort. But this was an occasion when dangerous secrets were under discussion, and two was enough: two middle-aged gentlemen, in formal evening clothes and powdered wigs.

Valentine poured another glass for himself, and offered one to Kilbride, who shook his head. Kilbride didn't want port, he wanted an answer.

'Sir Robert?' he said, 'Be open with me. What's your word in the matter?' Valentine looked at the enormous Jacobean fireplace with its representation of the Plagues of Egypt, carved in age-blackened oak. He looked at the line of ancestral portraits on the wall. He looked at the large portrait of King George, that proclaimed the supposed loyalty of the House. He thought deeply. He took another glass of port, then another. His face was rosy with drink, and his speech was becoming slurred.

'I still do not understand why we need to be so obliging to a tribe of natives,' he said, 'If we can land twenty thousand men on their damned Hito Island, then we're their masters. Or do you disagree?' Kilbride listened to this nonsense. He got his fingers under his wig. He scratched his head. He cursed, and pulled off the wig and threw it along the table. It slid into a candelabrum, and the candle flames fluttered and wax spattered on to the table.

'They ain't a tribe,' he said, 'they're a nation. These people ain't savages. They're like the cleverest peoples of India, but better organised. The Dutch say ...'

'Damn the bloody Dutch!' said Valentine, 'How do you know you can trust them? Everything you know about Japan comes from Dutchmen, and they're our enemies now.'

'Only 'cos Bonaparte has hold of their country,' said Kilbride, 'otherwise they're traders just like we are.'

'*Rival* traders!'

'But still traders, and I trust them.'

Valentine emptied his glass and poured himself yet another. Kilbride frowned. Kilbride did not approve of getting drunk. He tried another approach.

'We can't land twenty thousand all in one go. You know that, don't you?'

'If you say so.'

'I do say so! I've shown you the figures. With the ships available, and the length of the voyage from Bengal, then if we are to land a balanced army of horse, foot and guns, then the most we can carry in one sailing is five thousand men, with five hundred horses, a field battery of nine-pounders. I've shown you the figures, Sir Robert, you've seen them!' Valentine muttered and growled and eventually nodded. 'I'll take that for *yes*,' said Kilbride, 'So for that reason alone we shall need local allies. Remember that the Dutch say ...'

'The Dutch say? Do they indeed?'

'Yes they do! The Dutch say that there are twenty-five million people in Japan and ...'

'Twenty-five million?' said Valentine, 'That's fantasy! That's absurd!'

'It's not!' said Kilbride, 'I keep telling you, these people – the Japanese – are organised, they are disciplined, they keep records, they take census. It's twenty-five million people. So when they go to war, any one of their big clans can field an army of a hundred thousand men, and an army that size would defeat our five thousand even if they were armed with sticks and stones, let alone muskets.'

'Matchlock muskets,' said Valentine.

'Still muskets!' said Kilbride, 'And they're damned adept in using them.'

'So why are we even bothering with Japan?'

'Because, because, because,' said Kilbride with patience, 'because we shall do the same as we did in India: We land. We build a fort. We make allies. We help them in their wars. We gain goodwill. We land more men, and then more men ... and ... and ... we slowly take over! It's a long game and it's a wining game.'

Valentine sniffed. He took still another glass. Slowly he nodded.

'I'll give you that,' he said, 'that's what we did in India.'

'Of course it was!' said Kilbride.

'But what about the rest of it?' said Valentine, 'Language and beliefs?'

'We must have allies for that too,' said Kilbride, 'we can't speak a word of their language, we don't know what's sacred to them and what's profane. If we just blunder in and don't watch out, we'll insult them every time we breathe. Look how touchy the Hindus and Moslems are with their religion!' Valentine nodded.

'Aren't they just?' he said, 'Damned heathen that they are!'

'Well there you are then,' said Kilbride, 'if we don't take care in Japan, we won't have no damned allies, and we *must* have allies, so we need someone to show us the way, and that someone is Lord Masahito and ...'

'Lord Masahito? *Lord?*'

'Yes he's a Lord. He's got more noble blood than you.'

'Oh has he indeed?'

'Yes! said Kilbride, 'Listen to me! Lord Masahito is a gift of providence. We couldn't do this without him and we must bless the day we found him.'

'You mean the day *he* found *you*,' said Valentine, 'What if he just wants to get hold of our muskets, ships and guns for his own ends? Have you thought of that?'

'Of course I have,' said Kilbride, 'but we can't do this without him, so you just leave it to me, and I'll fix him!' Kilbride took the decanter. He filled his own glass and Valentine's. 'So,' he said, 'You lead one faction on the Company's Board and I lead another. With your men and mine, we can vote through any decision we choose. So are you in or out, Sir Robert?' Valentine wriggled in his chair.

'The risk,' he said, 'what of the risk? It would be treason. We could end up in the Tower of London on a capital charge.'

'Risk, risk, risk!' said Kilbride, 'Life's a risk. You could fall and break your neck! You could be struck by lightning or dead of the apoplexy! So do you want an empire or not?' But Valentine still dithered.

'When does the convoy sail?' he asked.

'It doesn't *sail*,' said Kilbride. It gathers off the Downs, awaiting the Navy's escort and a favourable wind. You know that very well.'

'So when does it gather?'

'Middle of August. You know that too. So are you with me or not?'

There was a long pause, then Valentine smiled.

'All right,' he said, 'I'm with you ...'

'Good man!' said Kilbride and they drained their glasses.

' ... for the moment,' thought Valentine.

CHAPTER 16

After the duel, and following my glorious return to the arms of Perse, and the embarrassingly grateful Phaeton, there were a number of developments. First, the truth of Kingslake Park leaked out, so somebody had blabbed. I think Tipstaff and Humphrey kept quiet, but the Hackney carriage driver may have seen something, and Perse's servants had spread some gossip and guesswork. But my guess is that Delaine's seconds were the source. The talk around town was that they shunned Delaine after the failed duel, because he'd made idiots of them, and he wasn't the man they'd thought him to be, and so they wanted revenge. In any case, everyone seemed to know that Delaine had lost his drawers, and finally, a week after the duel, Hannah Humphreys published a print by James Gilray, who always was her favourite, and the print was a colossal success.

The print, entitled *Jacky the Giant Killer* was very simple and it showed the head and right hand of a giant who was peering down at his palm where a tiny, forlorn figure was standing dressed only in his shirt, with his knees knocking and his hands pulling the shirt to cover his tackles. The tiny figure was Delaine and the giant myself, and the likenesses were good – not so uncanny as Tipstaff's – but still good. I don't know how Gilray got them so accurate: perhaps he sneaked a look at each of us? Perhaps he got hold of Tipstaff's print of the duel? But he did it somehow, and the print sold in vast numbers and there was no club or salon that hadn't laughed over a copy.

So the print became famous and was responsible for two events of great interest to me. The first was that Delaine took to drink, he never appeared in public again, and was eventually found in an armchair with an empty brandy bottle at his side, a fowling piece between his knees, and the top of his head blown off. I won't pretend to be sorry, and if you youngsters are inclined to weep, then think of the seventeen-year old who Delaine killed in one of his stupid, pointless duels. Delaine was a murderous brute and the world was better off without him.

The second event was the most profound surprise I ever had in all my life. I was sitting in the garden with Perse, Phaeton and some of her little friends, and the birds were singing and the sun was shining, and everyone was still treating me as the Greek hero – whatever his name was – who slew the monster that had snakes for hair.

[**Perseus, who slew the Gorgon. S.P.**]

Then the butler came out and bowed to Perse.

'A lady and Gentleman have called, ma'am,' he said, 'they are asking for the captain, and they have a letter of introduction from Mr Tipstaff, who I know to be a friend of the captain's, and since they are entirely respectable persons, I have shown them into the morning room to await your pleasure.'

'Oh?' said everyone.

'A lady and Gentleman?' said Perse, 'do we know them?'

'No, ma'am,' said the butler, 'but they are most proper and correct persons.' Perse looked at me.

'Captain?' she said, 'Do you know of any lady and gentleman, who'd seek you out here?'

'None, ma'am,' I said, because I didn't.

'Then we'd best go to see them,' she said. So we did.

The morning room was on the ground floor, at the front of the house, with a view of the street outside and the little park. It was brightly lit by big windows, it was furnished in Perse's excellent taste, and a lady and gentleman were sitting on a the Frenchy-style chairs that Perse adored. I barely noticed the gentleman, because as soon as I saw the lady, I felt odd. First I felt odd, and then dizzy.

As for the lady, she shot to her feet as Perse and I entered the room. She stared at me, her hand want to her mouth in a great gasp, and she swayed on her feet. She was in her thirties, smooth-skinned and pretty, with curly hair showing out of her bonnet. She was very well dressed but not in the sort of fashion that Perse and her friends wore. She was a sensible woman who wore sensible clothes.

But she made me dizzy. A hot, thick haze came over my head, and I would have reached out to Perse for balance, only the lady was far worse than me, and would have fallen if I hadn't stepped forward and grabbed

101

her, as did the gentleman. Then as we lowered her into her chair again, the oddest feeling came over me because she *smelt* familiar, which is strange because men aren't supposed to recognise folk by their smell. That's for dogs to do. But none the less there was a waft of something that stirred the profoundest feelings inside of me.

Then Perse was ringing for the servants and I was kneeling by the lady, and holding her hand, because I couldn't bring myself to let go of it, and there was that scent again, and I was dizzy again, then Perse was offering a glass of water, and the lady was drinking, and looking at me.

'I'm sorry,' she said, 'I was overcome by the resemblance.'

'What resemblance?' I said.

'To our father,' she said, 'I'm your sister Mary, and you're my little brother Jacky.'

So then it was my turn. The room went round. The floor came up and hit me. Everything went black. Then I woke up on a chaise longue with my boots off and cravat undone. Heaven knows how they heaved me up and got me on board of it, considering my size. But somehow they'd done it. And then it was all very pleasant, with Perse and the servant girls fussing round, and the strange lady was now holding *my* hand.

'Oh Jacky,' she said, 'see how you've grown, and I used to hold you in the crook of my arm,' and she wept tears and Perse threw her arms around her, and the gentleman put a hand on her shoulder.

'There, there, my dear,' he said, and the lady – my sister – poured out words as if they'd been brewing in her mind for years, as I suppose they had.

'Our mother died not long after giving birth to you,' she said, 'and I was only thirteen but I raised you till you were nearly one, and then our father took you away for your own good, and it broke my heart, but it was for fear of your stepmother who'd have killed you for sure, but he did love you, Jacky, our Pa did really love you, and I did too …'

There were a lot more tears after that, and in the middle of them, my sister produced a gold locket on a chain, and it clicked open to show a neat, sharp miniature portrait of a lady: a pretty young lady.

'This is your Ma, Jacky,' she said, and she raised a hand to her hair, and tried to smile, 'Everyone says I look like her.' I nearly went over again, and I had to hang on to the chaise longue, because I'd thought at first that the portrait *was* of Mary, but suddenly I knew why the scent of Mary had disturbed me so much. It was my mother's. The two of them were identical in that too. 'See?' said Mary, 'I'm like her, and you're like our Pa. You're the very image of him,' she said, 'isn't it amazing?'

It was indeed amazing, though if you youngsters have read this far of my memoirs you will already know that I am like my father, Sir Henry Coignwood in every way including his talent for business. You will also know that my stepmother Lady Sarah Coignwood tried to kill me when my father died. She tried again and again, out of pure spite and to get hold of my father's millions, and if you don't remember the details, then go back and read the early volumes again, because this isn't the place for them, not when I want to get on to the things Mary told me that I'd never known before, and you don't know either.

'You see, Jacky,' said Mary, 'Our Ma was Daddy's true love, and he kept her in a beautiful cottage, with all found and servants. And she never wanted for anything, and neither did I, and your stepmother never found out. And then you were born, and Ma died, and I cared for you until your stepmother *did* find out. And you were sent away to be raised in secret, for fear of your life. And I was too, until I was sixteen, when your Pa found me this lovely man.' She looked up at the gentleman who was standing behind her, and for the first time I took a good look at him.

He had the air of a prosperous tradesman. He was large, a red-faced countryman, and well dressed in plain and decent clothes. He smiled at me.

'Good day to you, Captain,' he said, 'I'm Hyde – Josiah Hyde – and I suppose that I am your brother-in-law.' He held out his hand, and I decided it was time to give up having the vapours so I stood and shook his hand.

'Very pleased to meet you, Sir,' I said, 'Very pleased indeed.'

Then Perse spoke: she spoke to Mary's husband.

'Sir? Did you say *Josiah* Hyde?'

'I did indeed, Ma'am.'

'Josiah Hyde the coach-builder?'

'Yes, Ma'am!' he said that with pride.

'Well, Sir,' said Perse, 'We've a barouche by Hyde, and it's the best vehicle in our stables.'

'Thank you, most kindly, Ma'am,' said Hyde, and patted Mary's shoulder, 'and I owe it all to this lady's father.'

'Yes,' said Mary, 'Pa brought us together, and we were married away from London to be safe, and Pa helped Josiah in his trade.'

'I was just a harness-maker,' said Hyde, 'But Sir Henry, he set me up, and he gave advice which I followed. He had the golden touch, did Sir Henry, and now I'm carriage builder to the nobility!' He shook his head and looked at me. 'I do declare, Captain, that it's like looking at Sir Henry to see you standing there. You've even got his voice!'

'Have I?' I said.

'Yes!' said Mary, 'and then we saw the print of you and the duelling man, and I knew it was you, though I'd read about Jacob Fletcher in the newspapers. But the print was so like our Pa, that I knew it was you, so we came to London to find you, and we thought of going to the Admiralty, but Mr Hyde had a better idea.' She looked at him.

'Yes,' he said, 'We asked at Mrs Humphrey's shop, since she'd published the print, and a young gentleman by the name of Tipstaff, was kind enough to give us your address and a letter of introduction.'

'And now, Captain,' said Hyde, 'with the permission of this lady,' he bowed to Perse, 'We're resolved to insist that you come down into Kent to stay at our house, just so soon as ever you may.' He smiled, and I stood in some confusion. I looked at Perse.

'Ma'am?' I said, 'this is all very new to me. I've found a family, but I've never been made so welcome as in your house. I really don't know what course to steer.' She thought a bit, looked at me, and gave a little gesture with her hands, as if accepting the inevitable

'Mr Ordroyd will return, quite soon,' she said, 'I had a letter from him this morning. And that may influence your decision.'

'Ah!' I said, 'Yes,' because unless the servants at number fifty-five were quite impossibly discreet, then it would not be comfortable for me to be under the same roof as Mr Ordroyd, should he learn of my nightly exercises with Perse. She saw that I understood, and gave a shrug and a smile.

'Fortunes de la Guerre,' she said, probably the only piece of French that I understand. Mind you, that's all I understood in that moment because there was something else that I'd missed entirely. Thus we decided that I'd leave there and then, with my sister and brother-in-law, who not surprisingly – considering their trade – had a top-class travelling chaise outside, with a pair of fine horses. So the servants were set packing my things, Josiah and Mary's address in Kent was given to Perse in case of letters to me, and I took Phaeton aside for a discreet word. I took him out into the garden as far from the house as possible.

'See here, Mr Ordroyd,' I said, all seaman-style, 'I've something to say.'

'Aye-aye, Sir,' said he, grinning.

'Now you must surely know, Mr Ordroyd, that your sister and I have become very close. But I promise not to breathe one word of this to the world – and especially not one word aboard ship – since your sister is a most splendid lady, what with running the house and servants, and I have the greatest respect for her. So nobody shall hear a word from me. Is that clear?'

He said nothing. He just stood there looking puzzled. He worried and worried and then spoke.

'My sister, Sir? What sister?'

'Perse!' I said, 'Who else?'

'Perse?' he said and laughed aloud.

'What's funny?' I said, not pleased in the least.

'Perse isn't my sister,' he said, 'She's my mother.'

'*WHAT?*' I said, 'But she can't be! She's not much older than you.'

'Oh but she is, Sir. She was seventeen when she had me, and now she's thirty-four.'

'But, but,' I said, 'isn't she *Mrs* Ordroyd?'

'Oh no, Sir, that was Papa's wife. When she died he wanted some fun so he got Perse.'

'He *got* her?'

'Yes, Sir, she's his mistress. Didn't you know? Everyone knows.'

He came out with it just like that! He came out with it and certain things became clear that had been foggy: Perse's cat-suit, for instance, and some of her other antics. Also the raucous fun of the house, and the behaviour of her set. Also why Phaeton had grown up quite so silly-headed, and empty of responsibility. Also the fact that nobody had told me what everyone thought everyone already knew! Everyone but me, and now I was something awfully confused on the matter of mothers and I had a lot to sort out in my mind.

I did some of that on the journey, which took six changes of horses and most of the day by easy stages, stopping at the best posting inns on the way. The chaise was superb: a bigger and more splendid version – a gentleman's version – of the post-chaise that had brought Phaeton and me to London. It had a big, glossy body mounted on springs, a driver on the box and two servants on seats behind, so it was obvious that Mr

Hyde had indeed prospered in trade. There was plenty of room inside, on the single, forward-facing seat, for two large men and a small lady to sit in comfort, and we passed most of the journey with the glazed sashes let down, since the weather was fine. And so, and roughly in order I went over the following facts.

My sea-chest had been packed and hauled aboard the chaise. I'd said goodbye to Perse, all proper and formal, kissing her hand on the steps of number fifty-five, and her looking a bit sour, but who could blame her? I'd also said goodbye to Phaeton, promising that so soon as I was at sea then he'd be with me: I thought I owed Perse that, at the very least. What I didn't tell Phaeton was that he had as much chance of advancement in the Sea Service, as a cannon ball has of swimming, and he'd have to be satisfied with that.

Afterwards I fixed my mind on being at Saint's Club before the end of July, I amused myself going over the events of Kingslake Park, I tried not to worry too much about Earl Spencer, and I fixed on his promise that I'd get back aboard *Euphonides*.

I thought over all that, and most of all the astonishing fact that I wasn't alone in the world any more. I had a family. I even had a birthday. My first guardian, Dr Woods had timed my age from the day he got me, which was December 12th, because he couldn't be bothered to find out the day I was born. But Mary told me – it was June 24th – and I was therefore five months older than I thought I was. She also told me about her own children: my nephews and nieces.

'Yes,' she said, 'Mr Hyde and I have four children.' She smiled. 'There's Jacob – who's named for you, Jacky – and he's ten, then John who's eight, Sally who's six, and our baby Sophia who's three.'

That was all very jolly, but other things were not.

'Fine building, there,' said Hyde, as the chaise sped through a village with a big stone church, capped with a lead-sheathed spire, 'Do you attend divine service, Jacob?'

'Er, yes,' I said, fearing the worst, 'aboard ship, we muster all hands for Church on Sundays. It's in King's regulations.'

'Good, good,' said Hyde, 'Mrs Hyde, the children and I: we all attend both morning and evening service without fail.'

'Splendid,' I said, with my heart sinking.

'And we love a fine church,' he said, and took a careful look at me, 'even though we are Dissenters.' He paused. 'Dissenters! I hope that doesn't shock you, Jacob?'

'Er, no,' I said.

'Wesleyans,' he said, 'we are Eastern Wesleyans, and we taste no spirituous liquor unless prescribed by a physician.' At this, I thought it best to change the subject for fear of hearing worse.

'Mary, Josiah,' I said, 'I have a duty – a Service duty – in London in July. So do you think, that I might have use of this carriage to get me back to my appointment?'

'Of course,' said Mary, and I managed to keep the conversation away from the soul-saving Mr John Wesley for the rest of the journey.

We arrived in Canterbury – our destination – late in the afternoon with the sun setting. In fact we were just out of the town, where my sister and brother in law had a house in its own grounds, with a deer park and railings and a gate-house with a keeper. The address was simple: Hyde House, London Road, Canterbury, and Hyde House wasn't a nobleman's mansion, but it was a big, new, stone building on two floors, all bright and cheerful, with flowers in tubs by the door, and inside there was fresh paintwork, and Chinese wall paper in the bedrooms. There was also a considerable number of big, timber sheds within easy walking distance of the house, these being the manufactory where Hyde's carriages were built. It was closed when we arrived, but Hyde was keen to show me something of it, once he'd given the servants their orders.

'See the mistress inside, and bags unpacked,' he said, and there were curtseys, bows and 'yessirs,' and Mary smiled at me and went into the house.

'I'll see you later, *Jacky*,' she said, and may the Lord forgive me that I was getting fed up with being called that. 'The children will be in bed,' she said, 'but you'll meet them tomorrow.'

'Here, Jacob,' said Hyde, 'come this way,' and he pointed out each shed in turn, 'This is the carpentry shop, the iron-works is over there, and the wheelwright shop is there, and the harness shop there, and the paint shop last of all. You can have a good look tomorrow.' I nodded cheerfully because I love commerce, I love trade and I love manufacture. So I was impressed.

'Tomorrow,' I said, and then a man in a leather apron came round the corner of one of the sheds, with a bunch of keys in his hand. He raised his hat to Hyde.

'Good evening, Mr Hyde,' he said, 'and to you, Sir,' he said to me, 'May I make so bold as to ask if tha' might be Captain Fletcher?'

'That's me,' I said.

'So tha' found him, Mr Hyde, Sir?' said the man with the keys.

'I did indeed,' said Hyde, and turned to me, 'this is Mr Barnsley, my works foreman.'

'Mr Barnsley,' I said and shook his hand.

'Eee,' he said, 'but tha's a big bugger!' His voice was slow and deep and sounded strange, because he was from the north, and I was used to seaman speech, which meant that of south-west England, or the sea-colliers from Newcastle who sounded entirely different from Barnsley. In those days we southerners didn't know the north of our own country, and the accent of Yorkshire – which was where Barnsley grew up – was almost unknown to us. But Barnsley was a man I grew to like, and he spoke so cheerfully, in his strange accent with *thee* and *thou*, that I took no offence at his words.

I didn't but Hyde did. He frowned.

'Mr Barnsley,' said Hyde, 'shame on your obscenity, in front of Captain Fletcher!'

'Oh, don't mind me, Sir,' I said to Hyde, 'I've heard worse than that aboard ship.' By Jove I had too. Just you believe me. So we chatted a bit, then Barnsley excused himself to complete his locking up for the night.

'I must apologise for Barnsley,' said Hyde, 'He's vulgar in speech, even though he can be amusing,' and even Hyde had to smile, 'very amusing! And he's a fine craftsman, totally honest, and I couldn't do without him in managing the works.'

Then we went into the house, where we had a late supper which was excellent, and only tea to drink which was not, and prayers before bedtime which was worse. At least the bed was comfortable, though I missed Perse, and in the morning things got better. I liked the children, and Barnsley made me laugh more than any other man I'd ever met, and he kept a bottle of salvation hidden under his bench.

CHAPTER 17

'The Tokugawa cavalry came on with ignorant confidence. They believed that the rain was their ally because their Samurai are poets who have forgotten how to make war.'

(From a letter of Wednesday, August 2nd 1797, from Kimiya Hitamoto, Daimyo of Hito Province, to the Lady Meiko, The House of Flowers, Port Hito.)

The rain was steady, heavy and ceaseless. There was little wind, and the soaking downpour ran river-like all on to the helmets, armour and *Sashimono* banners that the Tokugawa officers wore, fixed to the back of their war-harnesses. The banners hung limp and heavy, but still they displayed the Tokugawa *mon*: three hollyhock leaves within a circle. The horses tossed their heads, and fought for solid ground among the damp turf, as they came up over the hill, and rumbled forward, two hundred strong, as the elite vanguard of the army behind. They came on in discipline and in excellent formation, since their leader kept the pace slow, being more concern with dressing the lines, than speed. And this was a wise precaution, since the rain was so heavy, that it was impossible to see far ahead, and it would be easy to ride into such traps as pitfalls or hidden trenches.

This cavalry formation was led by Lord Shinobu Tokugawa in the red-lacquered armour of a high-rank samurai. He was a veteran horseman and a kinsman to the Shogun, but he had never seen military action. He was followed a horse-length behind by his five chief subordinates, and behind them a line of signallers, and then the main body, in black, battle-lacquer and bearing lances. The mass of horsemen made just enough noise that Lord Shinobu could hear them even over the rain, even as it battered and splashed on this helmet, and cascaded onto his shoulders and ran down inside his armour, soaking everything that it met.

Lord Shinobu ignored these discomforts. His mind was entirely concentrated on seeking out what defences Clan Hitamoto might have prepared in front of him. The advance had been easy so far. Hitamoto forces had not opposed the Shogun's army as it marched to the seaport facing Hito Island, and spies had reported that there were no entrenchments on the road. But spies could never be trusted, and there was a vital need to advance with care.

Lord Shinobu raised a hand.

'Halt!' cried the Chief Signaller.

'Halt!' cried the rest, and two hundred men reined in and stopped.

Lord Shinobu beckoned to his five subordinates, who rode up level with him and faced him in a half circle as he wheeled around. The rain was very bad now. It was hard to see, hard to speak, and the horses were nervous.

'Who knows this road?' cried Lord Shinobu. One man raised a hand.

'Come forward!' cried Lord Shinobu. The samurai came close. He bowed his head. Lord Shinobu acknowledged him and the two men held a shouted conversation.

'Have we reached the narrow place?' said Lord Shinobu.

'No, my Lord, it is a few hundred yards ahead.'

'Is there cover there? Cover from the rain for arquebus men?'

'No, my Lord. There is a precipice on one side, and rocks on the other, but no cover.'

'Then you may resume your place. We go forward.'

Lord Shinobu wheeled his horse round. He raised a hand and pointed forward.

'Advance!' cried the signallers.

Lord Shinobu rode forward in confidence. Even if the Hitamoto had the will and the men to block the narrow way, there could be neither archers nor arquebus men in rain such as this. The rain was a blessing because it would slacken the bow-strings, soak the arrow-feathers, and extinguish the match-cords. So at worst there would be spearmen, and they would be easily visible, and Lord Shinobu's orders were to find the enemy, to ride them down if they were weak, and to fall back and report if they were strong.

So Lord Shinobu went forward in confidence. He was even confidant at the narrow place, where – at last – banners were raised, displaying the swooping falcon mon of Clan Hitamoto. The banners were raised over lines of soaking-wet, glistening-wet Hitamoto infantry who had not even fortified the road in front of them! There was no hedge of spearmen, no bamboo fences, no entrenchments. Lord Shinobu frowned. This was not right. This was too easy. But there was honour to consider. The banners of Tokugawa flew over the force that he led. He could not order retreat, and he *would not* order men forward where he dared not go himself. So he drew his sword and held it high for his followers to see.

'Banzai!' they cried, and raised lances. There was even the instinctive quickening of pace that follows any sighting of the enemy by horsemen. But Lord Shinobu left that to his signallers.

'Steady!' they cried, and the two hundred men pulled back, and resumed their slow advance.

As Lord Shinobu approached the Hitamoto line, the roadway narrowed. There was only thirty yards from impassable rocks on the left to a sheer drop on the right. Lord Shinobu frowned again as he saw that he was facing a column of Tanegashima arquebus men. They stood in silent ranks, shoulder to shoulder with their useless, soaking wet firearms held at waist height, and pointing towards the oncoming Tokugawa cavalry. The ground in front of them was strewn with large rocks, so horses could not advance at a gallop. But a careful trot was entirely possible. Lord Shinobu frowned again. This was wrong. Something was wrong. It could never be so easy. He went forward. His men followed behind.

Lord Shinobu was less than twenty-five yards from the foremost Hitamoto line, when he saw for himself what was wrong. He saw what an experienced commander would already have guessed – a row of glowing red lights beneath the neat, water-proof covers fixed over the locks of the Hitamoto arquebuses. He saw all this as a Hitamoto officer gave an order, and the arquebuses came up to the shoulders of the first rank, and delivered a bellowing volley right into the Tokugawa cavalry, striking Lord Shinobu dead and mowing down men behind him.

'*Hi!*' cried the Hitamoto officer.

'*Hi!*' cried the Hitamoto front rank, as they turned sideways and retreated through the ranks to the rear.

'*Hi!*' cried the second rank, as they stepped forward and gave their volley.

All the other ranks, did the same: fifteen of them. Then the arquebus men took up the spears that were their secondary weapons, advanced over the ruins in front of them, and efficiently dispatched every man or horse that was not dead, or had not run.

'Well done,' said Lord Kimiya, who rode forward with his staff when the work was complete. 'Now take their heads, and place them on bamboo sticks in this place, facing the way they came. Also, bring me the sword of their leader but ensure that his armour is displayed beneath his head.'

It was the first battle of the war between Hitamoto and Tokugawa. It was also the first time that Lord Kimiya Hitamoto saw heads taken and placed on bamboo sticks, and even though he knew that this was the correct and proper thing to do, he was sickened by the sight of it.

CHAPTER 18

This wasn't the first time I'd met children. Years ago, my sea-daddy Sammy Bone – the man who taught me my trade as a seaman took me to the home of his brother who had children, and I was much charmed by them. But Jacob, John, Sally and Sophia were my own flesh and blood, and when they called me Uncle Jacob – not Uncle *Jacky*, thank the Lord – and I found that I liked it very much indeed.

When I met them at breakfast the first day in my sister's house, they were nervous at first, which isn't surprising, because I was a giant to them. So they sat like good boys and girls and looked at me over their porridge and whispered to one another.

'None of that!' said their mother.

'Indeed not!' said their father at the head of the table, 'we've not even said Grace!'

It was a long Grace, I'm sorry to say, and the children looked at me while their father delivered it, and I winked and smiled. Then later, in the garden I had them crawling all over me and laughing, and then I ran them up and down in a wheelbarrow yelling out commands.

'Allllll-hands! Allllll-hands!'

'Allllll-hands!' they cried, and they shrieked and giggled, as I weaved the barrow to starboard and larboard. Then:

'Stand by to go about!' I cried, 'Hands to the braces! Beat to quarters!' and so on, and so on. I think they liked me, and sister Mary and brother-in-law Josiah looked on and beamed. It was good and I was happy, though I'm not so sure that Mary and Josiah approved when Jacob, John and Sally too, all declared that they wanted to go to sea.

'Uncle Jacob will take us, won't you Uncle?' said little Jacob.

'And I'll be a pirate!' said John.

'And me!' said Sally.

Well at least Sophia didn't want to go, so their Ma and Pa would still have their youngest.

Later I was properly shown round the carriage works, which was interesting, with dozens of men at work who treated Hyde with great respect, and goggled at me because they'd all heard about Delaine and Kingslake park. Then after the tour I was left in company with Mr Barnsley, since Josiah had to go and do his accounts.

'I do them each day, Captain,' he said, 'to keep up. I have to, otherwise there'd be a reckoning with your sister,' and he laughed.

'Aye,' said Barnsley, 'She's one for the accounts is Mrs Hyde. Never known a lady with such an eye for figures.'

'You see, Captain?' said Hyde, 'everything has to be right and tight,' and although he smiled, he knew that a sharper brain than his would be looking over his shoulder, and I realized that it wasn't only me that had inherited our father's talents. So off went Josiah, and Barnsley smiled.

'Well, Captain,' he said, 'It's just past noon, and from what I hear you sailors take a drop at that time.'

'Indeed we do, Mr Barnsley,' I said.

'Then if tha'd follow me,' he said, 'We can have a look at my tack room.' He winked and I smiled.

'Lead on, Sir,' I said.

The tack room was up in the rafters of one of the big sheds. It was an office and workshop, and was extremely tidy, with tools in rows on pegs in the wall, and a desk for ledgers, and a work bench. There were a couple of chairs and a table too, all placed neat and square. I thought of Lenny Tipstaff's muddle of a workplace and smiled at the neatness here. But best of all:

'Here we are then, Captain,' said Barnsley, opening a cupboard under his work bench, 'What's tha' pleasure? I've got brandy, rum and Scottish spirit.'

'Rum will do nicely!' I said, 'watered one to three, if the water's safe here?'

'Oh yes,' he said, and took a jug from a shelf nearby.

'Doesn't Mr Hyde disapprove?' I said, as he poured me a good measure.

'Not him, Captain,' said Barnsley, adding water, 'Since he don't know.'

'Ah,' I said, 'Your good health, Mr Barnsley!'

So we had a most pleasant talk, Barnsley being interested in the sea life, and myself constantly amused by the things he said, always delivered straight-faced, and slow as if he were serious. The first time he made me laugh, was when I was cursing the stupidity of duelling. He listened, and nodded, and then looked at me and shook his head.

'Only too true, Captain,' he said, and he seemed to think a bit, and leaned forward as if in confidence and said, 'but all the world's weird, 'cept thee and me lad,' then he paused, as if reflecting deeply and added, 'and even tha's a bit weird.' I think I must have choked with laughter over that, because I was trying to drink as he said it. So I liked Barnsley a lot, and the children too, and Mary and Josiah certainly made me welcome. But I had to go to chapel on Sundays. There was no getting round that, and I went with dread the first time, expecting the very worst.

The chapel was plain and square, with no tower, no bells, and no altar inside, and everything plain and whitewashed. But the place was cram full, and everyone in their best clothes, and all smiling at Mr and Mrs Hyde, and gazing at me such that I realized I was on show, and they'd come to see me! There was music too, with a band, and Wesley's hymns that had damn fine tunes, so I lifted up my voice and bellowed along with the rest, and hoped not to deafen them.

[Fletcher is uncharacteristically modest. He had a fine bass voice and kept a tune well, His only fault lay in the lewd nature of the nautical ditties that he would deliver after dinner. S.P.]

Of course the sermon was dreary. It was all about SIN and every bit as bad as I'd expected, and if a ship's chaplain had delivered it there'd have been mutiny on the lower deck. But chaplains know that you can't keep seamen from sin, so they preach about something cheerful.

In general I have to say that I liked being with my family, I was glad I'd got one, and if Mary and Josiah were odd about drink, then at least there was Mr Barnsley. So I took early opportunity to ride into Canterbury with him on a wagon, when he went to Josiah Hyde's Bank to get coin to pay the hands. Supposedly I was there as a guard, ready to wield a pair of pistols and a blunderbuss that Barnsley kept under the seat for the defence of his master's silver, but in truth I wanted to buy some bottles for Barnsley's store, because you can't drink from a shipmate's pot without paying your share.

Canterbury is a fine town with a famous cathedral, and with shops and squares and busy folk, but what stands out in memory was Barnsley's comments on the folk we saw in the street, especially those whom he knew. He'd wave to them as we passed, and smile, and then he'd deliver a few words to me, in his slow, dry, northern voice.

'Look!' he said, pointing out the first, 'There's Mr Franks, the Alderman,' then he raised his voice, '*Good day to you, Mr Franks!*' And to me, 'he's a fat bugger, ain't he? Lives on pork pies.' And later, 'There's Wilson the bookseller. *Good day, Mr Wilson!*' he cried, then, 'see the sporting gun under his arm, Captain? He's off after rabbits, cross-eyed sod that he is. He'll most likely shoot the tits off the Parson.' Then later: 'Ah!' said Barnsley, 'Bless my soul if that ain't the Parson himself , our good Mr Sylvester. *Good day to your reverence!*' said Barnsley. He raised his hat in respect, and the Parson tipped his in return. 'There he goes, Captain Fletcher,' said Barnsley, 'A very holy gentleman indeed. See the manner and bearing of him? Even when he farts, he blows the air of sanctity out of his arse.'

But best of all we passed a fine, large woman in good clothes, and a fashionable hat with ostrich feathers, as she cruised down High Street smiling at all the men.

'Hallo Nell!' said Barnsley.

'Mr Barnsley!' she said, 'G'day to ye, Sir!'

And good day to thee, Ma'am!' and he saluted with his whip and we drove on.

'Who was that?' I asked.

'That was big Nell,' he said, 'She's famous, Captain. A very generous lady that gives instruction to boys and satisfaction to men.'

'I see,' I said, and grinned.

'She does a very nice *sixpenny stand-up* behind the lending library after dark,' he said, 'There's always a line a-waiting, and she could easily charge more, but she don't because she loves her work,' and he whispered solemnly, 'You see, Captain ...'

[In this moment, as he remembered what was said by Mr Barnsley, Fletcher was consumed with such paroxysms of laughter that he was unable to articulate speech. But then, recovering himself, he uttered words so gross that I threw down my pen and refused to transcribe. At this, his laughter became rage, and after words had been exchanged, he leapt from his chair and with a strength beyond belief in so old a

man, he threw me over his shoulder and stormed out of the house, with family and servants hopelessly attempting to restrain him. He then marched to the Lilly Pond where he promised to throw me to the fishes if I did not repent. On my firmly insisting that I would drown rather than be dishonoured, and with the entire household pleading my case, he fell once more to laughter, and set me on my feet, saying: 'So there *is* a man inside you after all. In that case I'll write it myself.' The which he did, though I have now struck it out. S.P.]

… her XXXXX XX XXXXXX XX XXXXX XXX XXXX

I was a little over two weeks at Hyde House, and I was happy there and have been welcomed back many times over the years. What with a family, and a birthday, I was sorry to leave which I did on Friday July 21st to get back to London in time for my meeting before the end of July, with Mr Knowles of Saint's Club. So Josiah most kindly leant me his travelling chaise, and a driver and servants for the style of it, and this time I did stay in a London hotel – one that Josiah recommended – all arranged in advance by post. I thought that was better than turning up at 55 Dominic Gardens for a meeting with Mr Ordroyd senior.

Thus, on the morning of July 24th, I was in service dress and going up the steps of Saint's club in George Street, having spent a couple of days admiring London for its diversity of population, its fabulous wealth, its armadas of shipping, its wondrous beauty of architecture, and its murderous street traffic that was determined to run you down unless you watched out, as you tip-toed across streets mired ankle-deep with the dung of a million horses. This was a skill that Londoners were bred up to, and which I didn't have. But the kindly Londoners were ready with helpful advice.

'Ged-out-of-it you bugger!' screamed a Hackney carriage driver.

'Bloody sailor! Whatcher bloody doin'?' said a butcher's delivery boy.

'Ain't you got no bleedin' eyes?' said a carter, hauling on his brake, with horses rearing and stamping, 'Didn't you bleedin' see me comin'?' The answer to that, was *no I didn't* because I was looking down at the shite, trying to keep it off my nice, shiny top-boots.

God knows how I managed to get across George Street still alive, and it was a vast relief to be going up the stairs, through the stone portico on to clean ground. So I went up to the doorman in his livery coat. He was an old seaman in a wonderfully choice and juicy berth. This beauty didn't quite stand in my way and hold out his hand, but he clearly had that plan in his head, even as he saluted. He needn't have worried. I'd never been to Saint's but I knew the drill: everyone did in the Service. Thus the house was free to Sea Service officers in uniform, but the accepted tip on first entry was a whole Spanish Dollar, and I was ready with one of those big, silver coins. I also knew that it was custom to give a name on first entry, and that the name would be passed, so all the staff knew it, and would forever remember it.

'Fletcher,' I said, 'lately of His Majesty's Ship *Euphonides.*'

'Aye-aye, Captain,' said the minion, who stared at me, and his lips formed a silent circle of surprise.

'Would that Captain Fletcher the duellist?' he said, and the swab had the cheek to grin.

'Fletcher of the *Euphonides!*' I said, and frowned because I'd had enough of duels.

'Aye-aye, Cap'n Sir!' he said.

'I'm here to parlay with Mr Knowles,' I said, 'Where might I find him?'

'In his private room, Captain Fletcher,' he said, and snapped fingers and a slightly lesser minion appeared, tricked out like a footman in knee-britches, laced coat and wig. So I was led down corridors and past big, cheery rooms to Mr Knowles's door and found the club to be very pleasing, and very full of Sea Service officers, and smartly furnished without trying to imitate a royal palace as Brooks's did. I liked it and have stayed there since, because there were always rooms available, and everything was free including food – but not drink – provided you were there a week or less, and which was all because it was founded in 1748 by Admiral Lord Saint, God bless him, who took a Spanish treasure ship and wanted to spread the benefit to his brother officers.

Then the minion was rapping on Knowles's door.

'Come!' said a voice, and I was inside, and Knowles was standing, behind a massive desk, in an office with nice bright windows, and paintings of ships hung all round, displaying powder-smoke, French colours being struck, landings on foreign shores, and heroes dying in battle with weeping angels above.

'Captain Fletcher of *Euphonides!*' announced the minion and left closing the door behind him.

'Captain Fletcher,' said Knowles, 'do sit down, Sir,' and he did, and I did and I looked at him. He was a tiny man, thin and shrivelled, and smiling, and dressed the expensive, heavily embroidered, en-suite clothes of a past generation, with his own hair worked into side-curls and a long queue at the back with a silk bow at the nape of the neck. This was the man who everyone said was a *cunning greaser*, but I saw none of that in his character. All that I saw was the most amazing cheerfulness, and sly winks, as if everything were a joke between friends. Not that it was, my lads, because jolly little Mr Knowles was a sharp 'un and no mistake. So I can only conclude that he could adopt one manner if you were after whores or a loan, and quite another manner if – like myself – you were merely trying to get yourself horribly killed as a secret agent. So he was cheerfully direct.

'You are Fletcher,' he said, 'Rowland's replacement,' and he put his head on one side like a blackbird looking at a snail. 'Did you kill him?' he said, and laughed.

That made me jump, it really did, because the question came out of nowhere, totally unexpected and it was dangerously close to the truth, because I *would* have done for Rowland given the chance, but fact it was Rowland who'd tried to kill me.

'No,' I said, 'he died of the apoplexy … all by himself.'

'I see,' he said, and never mentioned Rowland again, but I'm damn sure he'd known the swab and known him well. He looked at me for a while, perhaps thinking of Rowland, and then he spoke. 'Your body looks fit for our work Captain Fletcher,' he said, 'and if you really did throw pistols into the lake and contrive that clever print – then your mind is equally fit.' That was a surprise. He obviously knew about the print we'd kept hidden. I wondered how he knew that, but never found out. Then he produced a canvas bag that had been sitting on the floor on his side of the desk. He took out four packages in brown paper and pushed them towards me. Two were thin and flat, one was obviously a rolled-up chart, and the last was fist-sized, lumpish and heavy. 'These are for you,' he said, 'and do not ask what they contain, because I have taken great care not to know.'

He said that as if challenging me to disbelieve him, and he was right to do so because he'd just spoken of *our* work, as if he were one of the Shadow Men who owned it. So I didn't think for a moment that he was only the message-passer that he pretended to be. But that's espionage for you, my jolly boys, and why I detest it and cannot urge you strongly enough to avoid it yourselves. But I took the packages, and the bag, and then he gave me a sealed letter from another drawer.

'In case of your being asked to account for your being here,' he said, 'you will note that this letter is addressed to Miss Nunn of 16 Compton Street. Miss Nunn is a great beauty. She entertains gentlemen, and charges a great deal of money to do so,' he gave a very thin smile, 'which you will pay me now.'

'What?' I said, 'Pay you?'

'Of course!' he said, 'You are known to be wealthy, and you are known to despise gambling, so the world will know that you did not come seeking a loan.' He spread hands in emphasis. 'You therefore came seeking a lady, Captain Fletcher! That is what the world will conclude, and in that case the procedure is as follows: I am paid by a gentleman. I write a letter to a lady introducing him, and the lady entertains him in a private house, avoiding the need for him to repair unto sordid premises or to handle money when he meets the lady.'

'But I actually have to pay you?' I said, 'Now?'

'Yes. You pay by bill of hand to your bank. Then my own bill of hand goes to the lady for the bulk of the sum. That way everything is documented and can be proven.'

'And do I actually have to meet Miss Nunn?' I said, and he smiled again.

'My dear Captain Fletcher,' he said with the most cheerful grin, 'I leave that entirely to your own judgement.' I thought about that.

'Do you choose these ladies?' I asked, 'Choose them yourself?'

'Yes. I choose them for beauty.'

'And you say Miss Nunn is a beauty?'

'Yes. A very great beauty. How else could she charge such a sum as this?' He slid yet another paper across the desk. It was a bill of hand already drawn up for a very large amount, and awaiting only my signature and the date. So I gulped at the cost, remembered that I could afford it now, and signed. 'Good,' said Knowles, 'then we are done,' and he offered me a monkey-like hand to shake, then he got up and showed me out, chattering about nothing all the while. He was a puzzler and no mistake. I liked him and he made me laugh, but I knew it would be a serious mistake to take him for a clown.

After that I would have left Saint's at once but outside Knowles's office I met an officer that recognised me and he wanted to ask about that bloody duel, and he was an Admiral so I couldn't refuse him, and he was in company with other senior officers, so I was there a while.

As for Miss Nunn, while I've never had need to pay for such services, it has never been my practise to waste money, and the sum had already been paid and was a jolly sight more than Big Nell's sixpence. So I took a Hackney to Compton Street, and Miss Nunn turned out to be a very lovely lady indeed: by Jove, what a smasher! And to prove it, she hooked a client a year later and ended up the Marchioness of a place I won't mention. So these days she's a rich dowager in her carriage, looking down her nose on the common herd. But she remembers me and gives a little smile if we meet in the park.

So it was late before I got back to my hotel, feeling very considerably tired after some remarkable and vigorous exertions, and opened the packages that Knowles had given me. I started with the lumpy one because I know gold when I feel it, and it was indeed full of guineas: just the guineas and no word of explanation. But that didn't surprise me, because I already knew that Spencer and his chums were awash with money – the State's money, England's money – and to them it was just grease to make the wheels turn smooth.

The second was indeed a chart. It was a Dutch chart of the Islands of Japan, the Dutch being the only seafaring nation allowed to trade with the Japanese. So their charts were by far the best and somebody – Spencer I suppose – had gone to the trouble of making sure that I had one, and it was a good one too, by Van Keulen of Amsterdam, cartographers to the Dutch East India Company.

The third was the best, because – all drawn up in Admiralty style and with signatures and seals, on a crackling sheet of finest paper – it was my commission as a commodore, just as Spencer had promised, and I was commanded to:

'… go aboard and take command of His Majesty's Ship Euphonides, now lying at Portsmouth, and further, to take command of such others of His Majesty's ships assembled there, which shall be given unto your command in the task of escorting to Bombay – or to such other ports within the administration of the Honourable East India

*Company as may be necessary – to convey safely to their destination,
the ships of the Company which shall assemble off the Downs from
August of this year'*

So I was as good as aboard *Euphonides* again, and I'd gone up the promotion ladder like a sky-rocket. That was the good part, and it could hardly have been better. The bad part was the fourth package, which contained a document, on which my name did not appear, and neither did anybody else's excepting only Mr Stephen Kilbride, and Sir Robert Valentine, whose names I'd already been given. Since I was ordered to burn this paper – and that's all it was, just a scrap of cheap writing paper – I did burn it, and what follows is only memory, but I have a good memory and the original won't have been much different. Note how it started straight off without preamble and stopped dead when it was done.

*Kilbride and Valentine have persuaded the EIC to land Company troops
in Japan with the aim of subjugating that nation under Company rule.
The Company has some ships for this enterprise ready in India, and
more will be provided by the Company's convoy departing the Downs
by late August. You will prevent the landing in Japan by all possible
and imaginable means including direct action against the Company's
ships including firing into them, boarding them, sinking or burning
them. It is furthermore necessary that Kilbride and Valentine should
not return from this venture and you will act at discretion to prevent
their return. An extraordinary document of command has been sent
to Portsmouth for you to take with you aboard your ship, requiring
that all Officers of HM's Diplomatic Service, Sea Service, and Land
Service shall render you every proper and legal support as may be
required. Also HM's Government will render you every proper and
legal support, so long as your publicly known and proven activities
are proper and legal.*

Burn this when you have read it.

So there it was, my jolly boys. Your Uncle Jacob was ordered to take all the risks, which presumably included murdering Kilbride and Valentine, while the precious, gilded gents who gave the orders, had made clear without saying so, that if I got caught doing anything that was not 'proper and legal' then they'd vanish like a fart on the breeze, and I'd be left to hang. The irony of it was that the aforesaid precious ones must surely have known that the only sort of lunatic who'd willingly act under such orders was a one-in-a-million freak like Rowland who actually *relished* walking a tightrope over a river full of crocodiles. So I damned Rowland ten times over to Hell because he'd told them I was exactly like him and they wouldn't believe that I wasn't!

The trouble is, that anyone looking at me would think that I truly was like Rowland. Look at the size of me! Look what happens when I go forward with a cutlass! Likewise anyone would think that I truly was a cunning, crafty bastard like Rowland, because sometimes I truly am a cunning, crafty bastard. Look at that stupid duel. But if I'm crafty and cunning it's *only in my own interest* and not King George's, and above all nobody will ever believe that my heart is in trade, and I never wanted to be a man of action. So I hope you believe me, my jolly boys, because nobody else does.

Well, at least I had Rowland to blame, and I wish it had been me that killed him, but it wasn't. Ah well, ah well, I took comfort in the fact that I was going to sea again, because there were decent folk there, and perhaps a bit of trade might come my way while going out east?

CHAPTER 19

'Kilbride and Valentine are men without honour who will betray their own nation, and Valentine cannot control his love of drink. But I am forced to work with them even if I cannot trust them, because no Englishmen with honour is prepared to take soldiers into Japan.'

(From the 'Foreign Journal' of Masahito Hitamoto. Entry dated Friday July 28th 1797.)

'I'll tell you now, my Lord,' said Kilbride, 'I'll tell you something I wouldn't tell anyone else.' Kilbride nodded. He looked at Sir Robert Valentine, and he too nodded. Then both men looked at Masahito, who smiled, and at Nakano, his chief servant, who did not smile.

'And what might that be, gentlemen,' said Masahito, 'what further secrets might be hidden in this enormous ship?' The four men stood on the windward side of *Duke of Cornwallis's* poop deck, close to the taffrail with its three huge stern lanterns. The ship stretched out in front of them: masts and yards, stays and shrouds, with boats on skids in the waist, and huge anchors visible on either side of the bow, and a massive bow-sprit jutting forward. The ship was silent: still at Blackwall, with sails furled and rolling gently at anchor. But she had her full crew on board: nearly four hundred men, and all prime seamen because the East India Company paid well. Many of the hands were on deck, to see the strange phenomenon of a Japanese Lord, whom they'd been strictly ordered to treat as if he were a real, English Lord.

The ship's officers were also present, standing in a clump, by the mizzen-mast, politely keeping clear of the Japanese Lord and Mr Kilbride and Sir Robert. They stood in their Company version of Sea Service dress: cocked hats, blue coats, shiny buttons, and they whispered and muttered. Some way apart, five samurai stood and studied the foreigners who could not be patient, not even for an instant, but must chatter among themselves.

'Well, *My Lord*,' said Kilbride, and Masahito smiled to himself. Kilbride had only recently adopted this reverential form of address. 'For one thing,' said Kilbride, 'this ship's a damn site bigger than she's supposed to be.' Kilbride nodded. Valentine nodded.

'Is she?' said Masahito.

'She is, My Lord,' said Kilbride, 'She's bigger than a seventy-four gun two-decker, and close to a ninety-gun second rate.'

'So that would mean a ship of some two thousand tons,' said Masahito, 'and is she planked and timbered like a warship of that size?' Kilbride gave a small bow.

'You've studied the matter,' he said, 'I can see that, your Lordship.' He turned to Valentine. 'Don't you agree, Sir Robert?'

'Oh indeed,' said Valentine, 'I do congratulate you ... *Lord* Masahito.' Kilbride was pleased. It had taken long and hard persuasion to get Valentine to give proper respect. Of course it was a pity he'd paused before saying the vital word, thereby spoiling the effect to some degree. But he'd got the words out of his mouth.

'Yes, My Lord,' said Kilbride, 'She has man-o-war timbers: three foot of oak at the waterline. So she's fit to carry her guns and resist the enemy's shot.'

'And what guns will she carry?' said Masahito.

'Forty, twenty-four pounders on the gun deck,' said Kilbride, and forty, thirty-two pounders on the lower gun deck.'

'I see,' said Masahito, 'but is it not the case, Mr Kilbride, that Company ships have real gun-ports on the upper gun deck, but only *painted* gun-ports on the lower deck,' he smiled, 'in order to strike terror into those who confuse pretence with reality.' He laughed. Kilbride laughed. Valentine laughed. Valentine laughed even as he cursed the bloody Jappo for knowing too much. But Kilbride was more urbane.

'I think your Lordship already knows the truth,' said Kilbride, 'This ship has two tiers of working gun-ports.'

'Then where are the extra guns?' said Masahito, 'The twenty-four pounders are already aboard, but where are the thirty-two pounders?'

'Out in India,' said Kilbride, 'To be taken aboard where the Admiralty and the Navy can't see.'

'And what of the hands to man those guns?' said Masahito, 'I hear that this ship has four hundred hands, and that is not enough to man a battery of eighty guns.' Even Kilbride was surprised now. He was surprised, and he was worried that Masahito knew too much. But fortunately he was ready with an answer.

'You're right, My Lord, and we'll take aboard another four hundred men, once we're out in India. Then we'll have the Company's very own, top-rate man-o-war to be the flagship of our fleet, and able to batter any ship east of the Cape of Good Hope.'

'And what enemies will she batter?' said Masahito.

'Yours and mine, My Lord,' said Kilbride, 'because we shall, in all things, act together.'

'So much for enemies at sea,' said Masahito, 'what about enemies on land?'

'Ah!' said Kilbride, 'I've been waiting to show you, My Lord. So if you'd follow me below?' Masahito gave a small bow to Kilbride.

'Please lead the way, Sir!' he said, and Kilbride indicated a companionway leading below, and the clump of Company officers, seeing the motion, instantly stood straight, raised hats and bowed to the Japanese lord, just as they'd been told to do.

Down in the depths of the huge hold, there was only lantern light, and dim illumination from what sunshine could penetrate the gratings of one deck after another. Everything smelt of tar, timber and dampness, and Kilbride led the way down narrow planked paths through a tight-packed, lashed-down jumble of equipment and gear, that had never been designed for easy stowage aboard ship.

'Here you are, My Lord,' said Kilbride, 'Other ships in the fleet are carrying muskets and ammunition, and men. But they will mostly carry the usual cargoes that we send out east, and it's the same aboard *Duke of Cornwallis*, because this has to be a sound commercial voyage. But we're also carrying three dozen nine-pounder, horse-artillery guns. That's guns, plus limbers, caissons, tools, and shot of every kind: round-shot, grape, canister and shells.

'Well enough,' said Masahito, seeming to show no great interest, 'I suppose these guns may be of some service.' He smiled and kept to himself his matured opinion that of all the weapons invented by the foreigners, these mobile artillery pieces would be of the most powerful and useful, since nothing like them existed in Japan, and their impact on the battlefield would be devastating. 'But,' he said, 'where are the horses to draw these guns?'

'Out in India, My Lord,' said Kilbride, 'That way we spare them being shipped half way round the world. We'll take on horses and gunners, in India. We've got plenty of both out there, fully trained and as good as any in the world.'

'Good,' said Masahito, 'and have you anything else to say? Now that we are alone in this quiet place?' Masahito had stopped smiling. Kilbride saw that, and he worried again that Masahito was too damn clever. So he glanced briefly at Valentine, who nodded.

'Go on,' said Valentine.

So it was time for a little speech.

'My Lord,' said Kilbride.

'Sir?' said Masahito.

'I know … and you know …' said Kilbride, 'that we can't entirely trust each other,' and Valentine nearly choked in amazement at so direct a statement. He coughed and spluttered in his own spittle. 'Yes, yes, yes,' said Kilbride and thumped his back, and turned again to Masahito.

'My Lord,' he said, 'Don't tell me you're surprised by what I said.'

'I am not,' said Masahito, 'and it is best to be honest. So please continue. Please tell me how we may manage our distrust.'

'Easily, Mr Lord,' said Kilbride, 'Because neither of us has all the power, and I'll prove it by telling you another truth, which is that we can't land twenty-thousand men all in one go.' Valentine spluttered and choked again but Kilbride ignored him, as did Masahito who looked only at Kilbride.

'Then how many men can you land: *all in one go?*'

'Five thousand.'

'Which means?'

'Which means that we'll be in your power,' said Kilbride, 'in Clan Hitamoto's power. And it's not just numbers. It's: where do we land? How do we take shelter? How do we live in a land we don't know? Where do we get our daily bread? We will vitally depend on you.'

'Until you land the next five thousand,' said Masahito.

'But by then we'll know each other,' said Kilbride, 'we'll have fought as comrades against your enemies, and we'll know that we can trust each other, and that's the best I can offer right now, 'cos we can't have perfect trust right now, but we need one another right now, and neither can go forward without the other.' He held out his hand. 'So is that agreed, Lord Masahito Hitamoto? Or do we stop everything here and now?'

Masahito thought very carefully.

Kilbride and Valentine looked to him for his answer.

Nakano looked to him for his answer.

Then Masahito took Kilbride's hand.

'It is agreed,' he said.

CHAPTER 20

The next couple of weeks were busy. They were very busy indeed. First I had to get myself to Portsmouth, and introduce myself to the Commander in Chief Portsmouth, a post of vast importance, usually filled by an admiral of vast experience who'd gone to sea before Noah built the Ark and served in every conflict since. In 1797 this was Sir Peter Parker, then over seventy and with the usual reputation of his kind: cantankerous, opinionated and capable of downing enough drink to float a three-decker.

'Fletcher?' he said, when I was shown into his office in Admiralty House, 'Would that be Fletcher of the submarine boat?' He sat at a desk with clerks and aides on either side, and my commission in front of him. He had a thin nose, a small mouth and a red face, and he was another one who wore the styles of his youth, complete with a heavy, square wig. 'Huh!' he said, 'Don't bother answering, Commodore, I can see who you are, and you've a lot to learn on convoy drill, and on the Company's ships you will protect, and His Majesty's ships that will fall under your command.' He set me to work at once, sending me off with a greying, elderly post captain who was a mere book-carrier here, and for the rest of the day I was burdened with a great deal of technical information.

In addition Parker himself gave me the most thundering document signed and sealed by a formidable body of officials: those of the Court of St James, the Prime Minister, the Secretary of War, and the First Lord. It was for me to present to all persons ...

'... of whatsoever degree, requiring and commanding them in His Majesty's name that they deliver all assistance within their power to Commodore Jacob Fletcher of His Majesty's Sea Service.'

After that I was lodged for the night at Admiralty House, and entertained to a formal dinner by Parker and his wife, and with other Portsmouth dignitaries in attendance. To my surprise, I was treated most remarkably odd. Everyone was in full dress and the silverware and candles were on display, servants stood behind, and course after course was served. All very nice, and I was given a place of honour at the table, right opposite Lady Parker. She was a hard-looking woman in her forties, or at least she looked hard when talking to others, but she smiled at me, and carefully agreed with everything that I said.

'Indeed, Sir, my own view precisely,' and 'quite so, Sir.' Later, when the ladies left us to our port, we gentlemen discussed the war, damned the French, and finally Parker proposed the loyal toast, as we did in the Service before joining the ladies.

'The King, God bless him!'

'The King!' we all said. Then blow me down if Parker didn't turn to me!

'And may fortune favour your duties, Commodore Fletcher,' he added.

'Indeed, indeed,' they said and raised glasses.

I didn't know what to make of that, and it was only as I was going to sleep that night, that I guessed, and I sat right up in bed. Parker knew! He knew what I was doing, and I don't mean convoying merchantmen out to India. He knew that I was doing something secret for the First Lord and his chums. I suppose the *thundering document* would have given a clue, but I think that First Lord Earl Spencer had whispered in Parker's ear, because the first thing Parker mentioned when he saw me was my submarine adventure, and Spencer had been fascinated by that. Either that, or Parker was himself one of the Shadow Men?

I thought about that, sitting up in my bed, with the distant tramp of marines' boots outside, and some yelling in the dark

'Halt! Who goes there?'

'The new guard!'

'Advance new guard and be recognised!'

Tramp! Tramp! Tramp!

How was anyone supposed to sleep?

Then the second wave of realisation hit me. Admiral Sir Peter Parker was treating me so nice and polite because there was an aura shining about me, of a greater power than his, because I was the First Lord's bulldog and the Prime minister's wolf-hound! Then the third wave struck as it occurred to me that this aura was exactly what the swab Rowland had described when he tried to lure me in. He'd said that men would bow and women would curtsey, and that I'd get away with murder, assuming that I was so warped in mind as to *do* murder, which Rowland certainly was and I certainly wasn't … leaving aside Boatswain Dixon of course. It all came in a jumble and it was a long time before I fell asleep.

There were a few more days like that, and I was even allowed out to see my flotilla anchored at Spithead. You youngsters should remember that warships seldom came to anchor at a quayside in those days, because you'd lose half your crew if they were pressed men, and anyway we had too many warships and too few quaysides. So normal practise was to drop anchor in some sheltered place, and Spithead was one such, and a very great one too. Spithead was the few square miles of water between the Isle of Wight to the south west, the mainland to the north, and various sandbanks to the east, and was thereby sheltered from the violence of the sea. So if King George's Navy had a home, then Spithead was it.

I was let off my instructions and taken for a walk down Broad Street, to Portsmouth Point, because Portsmouth Point looked straight out into the Spithead anchorage. The Point had a fine sandy beach for boats to land and was always full of noise and clamour. There were taverns, inns, buttocking shops, old clothes dealers, and money-lenders for anyone seeking to get themselves into serious debt. In time of war, with ships coming and going, you could never go down Portsmouth point without falling over drunken seamen staggering to and from the boats, and then there were officers bidding farewells to wives and children, sea-chests being heaved along by porters, barrels being rolled, customers arguing with tarts, and one-legged fiddlers scraping out a tune for a few pence in a hat. I loved it. I always did and always will. It was the sea life made real, with the smell of the salt sea and folk laughing and weeping and the gulls calling. By Jove it was wonderful.

[Note again Fletcher's love of the sea, despite all his protestations regarding trade. When he described Portsmouth Point he would laugh and joke, rousing all the company to merriment. Even I laughed on occasions. S.P.]

Then it got even better. I was in company with the elderly officer – Captain Challenger was his name – who I'd met earlier in Admiralty House. He liked Portsmouth Point as much as I did, and we took a drop in one of the better inns later on. But first we went down to the water's edge among the boats, and he pointed out among the dozens of ships anchored, what I had in fact already spotted for myself.

'There's *Euphonides*, Commodore,' he said, and I was prickled with the oddity that I now outranked a man like him who'd been afloat since before my father was born. But I didn't dwell on that. I had my Dolland three-draw telescope and was looking over *Euphonides* from stem to stern, and learning again what a glorious beauty she was, and better in some ways – though not all, my jolly boys – than even the lovely Miss Nunn. 'And if you'd turn your glass this way, Sir,' said Challenger, 'you'll see the Frigates *Syrillian* and *Phoraos*, both mounting thirty-two eighteen pounders. Then – over there, Sir – you will see the sloops *Warrell* and *Dunford* mounting twelve eighteen pounders, and finally the topsail schooner *Spicer* bearing eight twelve-pounder carronades. And I really do congratulate you, Sir, on taking to sea such a fine squadron, because every one of them is recently coppered, recently rigged and fitted out overall, and each has been stored with extra powder and shot, since you are known to be a gunnery specialist who insists on live-firing practise.'

'Oh?' I said, 'I didn't know that was common knowledge.'

'It is common knowledge aboard *Euphonides*, Sir,' he said, 'and when asked what stores they needed, the First Lieutenant and the Master asked for extra powder and shot, insisting that it would be the very thing you would ask for.' Well that was something. I would have too. Live firing practice was a drill I'd copied from my first Captain – Sir Henry Bollington, famous for the battle of Les Aiguilles – and he was a gunnery master.

'I see,' I said, 'And what's happened to my replacement? To Smythe-Lewis?'

'Ah!' said Challenger, and he didn't quite utter the nick-name *Smuggler*, but I could see that it was in his mind. 'Captain Smythe-Lewis,' he said, 'is long since gone ashore. He has been placed in charge of the Impress Service – the Press Gangs – in Cornwall, Devon and Somerset,' and Challenger's face was expressionless. 'It is a well-paid position,' he added.

'Of course,' I said. 'Poor old Smuggler,' I thought, because everyone sneered at the Impress Service. At least he wouldn't starve.

Three days later I was back on Portsmouth Point, with my sea chest packed, and the ever-grinning Mr Midshipman Phaeton Ordroyd, also with his box packed – himself summoned by urgent express mail – but managing to keep his trap shut because now that his arm was fully and totally healed, and now that we were going aboard ship again, I'd promised to kick his arse black and blue if he didn't shut up, and after one or two demonstrations that I meant it, he learned the lesson. Anyway, he looked so much like Perse that I forgave him a little.

Then joy of joys, *Euphonides's* launch was grounding, and the launch fresh-painted and shining and the hands in their smart, uniformed rig, and a smiling lieutenant in command, not just a mid, and I was on the boat, and all made shipshape and we were pulling out to the ship.

What a moment! It was one that I cherish. It was like coming home. I could still barely believe I'd got six ships under my command, and just for the moment, my worries over Spencer and the Shadow Men were out of my mind. But then I got a surprise. We bumped alongside *Euphonides*, I went up the ladder that was rigged and ready, the boatswain and his mates shrilled a welcome on their calls, and I tried to look every way at once to take in all the delights of the finest ship in the Fleet.

'Good day, Sir!' said Pyne, the first lieutenant.

'Good day, Sir!' said Mr O'Flaherty, the master.

'Good day, Sir!' said Tildesley, the second lieutenant.

The other quarterdeck officers followed. They pressed forward. I shook hands. Then I looked at the ship's people, all drawn up by divisions on the main deck, and was surprised to see that they were all in everyday working rig, as were the officers. That was a puzzle. I could see that they liked me, but considering the send-off they'd given me when I handed over to Smythe-Lewis, this was disappointing. I supposed that they didn't actually regard me as a *new* captain, but a *returning* one, having got rid of poor old Smuggler. But I was wrong.

Meanwhile I went through the formality of reading out my commission, without which I was not legally in command. Then when I was done, Pyne stepped forward.

'Captain, may I speak?'

'Go ahead Mr Pyne,' I said.

'We have something to show you, Sir,' he said, and took out a pocket watch, 'We remember when first you came aboard, Sir, you had us beat to quarters to see how fast it could be done?' I smiled. I'd guessed what was coming, and why the men were in working clothes. I could see that the watch was no ordinary instrument, it was a stopwatch. 'You may remember, Sir,' said Pyne, 'that we cleared for action and ran out the guns in one minute and thirty-five seconds?'

'I do remember Mr Pyne,' I said.

'Then with your permission, Sir?'

'Aye-aye, Mr Pyne, you may beat to quarters!'

So he nodded to the marine drummer boys and the drums rolled and the people leapt every way at once, like a set of demented goblins, and never any one of them got in any other's way, and guns were cast off of their sea-going tackles, and hauled in, and rammers plied, and flintlock triggers mounted, and cartridges made ready, and marine sharpshooters to the fo'c'sle and tops, and the decks cleared below, and sanded for grip, and the guns went rumbling out.

Then, when it was all done, and the hands stood gasping at their stations, Pyne clicked his stopwatch and showed it to me.

'A second under one minute, Sir,' he said and I shook my head in pretended dismay.

'Dear me, Mr Pyne,' I said, 'It'll have to be faster next time,' which I said because such jokes – feeble as they are – are expected on such occasions as a tradition of the Service, and you youngsters should never forget it if you are in command. So everyone laughed.

'Aye-aye, Sir!' said Pyne, then 'three cheers for Captain Fletcher!'

Which they gave with a will, and hats in the air, then it was business as usual over many days, and you wouldn't believe the amount of book work and paper work that goes with taking command of one of His Majesty's ships. Fortunately, I could leave most of it to Goodsby, my secretary, but I still had to check his summaries and sign off accounts. Then I had to meet my captains – *my* captains! – and entertain them aboard the flagship, and get to know them, and draw up plans for convoy formation, and signalling, and standard procedures in case we met French cruisers. Once again I could rely for much of this, on Pyne, the first lieutenant, and especially on O'Flaherty, the master, who was a seaman of vast experience, but I had to have a grasp of it all, and I blessed the good fortune that I have so good a memory for detail.

Then I went aboard each ship in my flotilla, to get a look at the vessels and the state of their gear, and also the state of their crews. You will remember that this was the year of the great mutinies – especially at Spithead – and although it was all due to stupidity in the Admiralty, and was all over by mid-June I wanted to test the mood of the men in the five ships under my command. And 'going aboard' didn't mean a quick tour, a fat dinner, a gallon of wine, and straight back to *Euphonides*. It meant that I had every captain show what he could do: beat to quarters, strike the topmasts then send them aloft again, check that the shot wasn't rusting, poke around in the sail lockers looking for mould, and most important of all, meeting the boatswains, pursers, coxswains, gun-captains, top-men and the rest, of every ship, to search for any signs of sulking or disobedience, which are the warning signs of trouble aboard ship, and which I always looked for with a careful eye.

Fortunately there was no sulking, and I had plenty of time for all this, because I went aboard *Euphonides* on July 29th, while the East India Convoy was supposed to be assembled in the Downs by mid-August, and I'd been firmly assured – even ordered – that the Navy mustn't arrive first. Admiral Sir Peter Parker himself had told me that, over that formal dinner on the first night we met. He told me between courses, with dishes being cleared and glasses filled, and even the servants nodded furiously at what Parker said.

'Mr Fletcher, you must make John Company wait!'

'Indeed!' said every officer present, and their ladies too.

'You must take care to do that, Mr Fletcher,' said Parker, 'because John Company has far too grand an opinion of himself.'

'Indeed!' said everyone, and they nodded to each other, and poked those who'd taken too much drink, so that they should not miss this important passage of conversation. Parker was duly encouraged and developed his theme.

'John Company thinks he's King George,' he declared, 'D'you know he's even got his own little navy? With so-called officers.' He shook his head in disbelief. '*Officers*, Sir! Officers in blue coats and buttons! And d'you you know, Mr Fletcher,' he said, thumping the table in disgust, ' John Company's ships *don't even fly British colours!*'

'Shameful!' said the company.

'Aye!' said Parker, 'He's got his own damn – forgive me ladies – his own damn wretched rag instead? And d'you know …'

He went on at length, and it was made un-blinkingly clear to me that the Navy did *not* wait upon the East India Company, but rather that it was *the other way around*, and that it would be very good for this latest convoy to lie at anchor awaiting the Navy's pleasure. So it wasn't until August 15th that I gave the order for my flotilla to up-anchor and sail, when – as with all other things in the King's Sea Service – there were formalities and ceremonies to observe. In this case, I was to take *Euphonides* alongside Parker's flagship, the massive first rate *Queen Charlotte*, which I'd served aboard at the battle of the Glorious First of June, and which – since then – had been a main focus of the mutiny earlier in the year. But her crew were now shriven, forgiven and purified, and all was well again. So if I'd been sure that my flotilla could manoeuvre properly, I'd have led them in procession past the flagship, to give honour. But I didn't know how they'd behave under sail, so I took *Euphonides* alongside, alone.

For such a purpose the ship was holystoned, polished and gleaming, the officers in Full Dress, the people in best shore-going rig, and of course Jimbo in his jacket and hat. We came to within hailing distance, all nice and smart, with the yards manned, the band mustered, and at a command from our First Lieutenant, the people gave three cheers, the band gave *God Save Great George Our King* and all aboard raised hats to the Flagship, and to Admiral Parker who was himself aboard. Note that well, my jolly boys, because Parker wasn't normally to be found on his Flagship but ashore in Admiralty House, where his work was done. So I think that his presence aboard was further evidence that he knew plenty more about myself and Earl Spencer, than ever he admitted.

'Good day to you, *Euphonides!*' he cried, looking down upon us from the great ship.

'Good day you, Sir Peter!' I cried, 'Permission to proceed to sea, Sir?'

'Permission granted, and may God speed your endeavours!'

At this, and without further commands because we'd rehearsed it, Euphonides made sail, we hoisted the signal to form line astern of us, my flotilla followed, and we proceeded out of Spithead with our band playing *Rule Britannia! Heart of Oak! Britons Strike Home!* and all the rest of the sea-faring repertoire, together with *The Lincolnshire Poacher* which has nothing to do with the sea, but I had them play it anyway because it was my favourite tune, being so exceedingly cheerful and merry. So it was a fine beginning to the voyage, whatever horrors came after.

CHAPTER 21

'My father's wisdom was proved yet again. Beyond Hito Island, the only Hitamoto soil is Port Kagominato which we traditionally fought to hold, and my father's excellent preparations at Kagominato brought further disaster upon the forces of Tokugawa.'

(From a letter of Friday, September 29th from Kimiya Hitamoto, Daimyo of Hito Province, to the Lady Meiko, The House of Flowers, Port Hito.)

Port Kagominato was the best and nearest port for the voyage from Kyushu Island to Hito Island. It was the obvious launching place for any invasion of Hito Island, since it gave the shortest possible transit of the ocean, and had a huge harbour where fleets could assemble. But unfortunately for the Shogun and Clan Tokugawa, Port Kagominato was still held by Daimyo Kimiya Hitamoto, who stood with his staff respectfully behind him, all of them in gorgeous samurai armour of scarlet, gold, and vermillion, and helmets ferociously crested with antlers and horns.

These noblemen stood behind their master on the timber observation platform that rose over the Hitamoto defences – high walls behind a deep moat – that enclosed Port Kagominato, and kept it free of the Shogun. The moat was crossed only by timber bridges heavily defended by gatehouses where they met the city walls. Now, Lord Kimiya studied the fortifications with immense satisfaction because they were the result of decades of patient engineering by his father, grandfather and great grandfather before him. They had been prepared for such a day as this, and were the product of Hitamoto tradition.

'See!' he said, and pointed out over the observation tower's rail, 'here they come! Here comes the retreat of the broken men!'

'Hi!' said the high-rank samurai that stood behind him, and everyone looked down over the fortifications as a roaring, howling mob of men, came down the road that led down out of the Kyushu mountains, on to the coastal plain, through rice-fields and villages towards Port Kagominato. Some hundreds of men, in plain battle-armour were retreating down the road in seeming confusion towards the Hitamoto lines, and heavily pursued by Tokugawa infantry and cavalry.

'Careful now,' said Lord Kimiya, thinking aloud, 'Careful, careful,' and his followers could not help stepping to the rail and gripping it with armoured hands in this intensely vital moment. They saw the Swooping Hawk banners waving in the dust that was beaten up by the sandals of men clumped into a rough circle, with long spears jutting out like the spines of a hedgehog. Among them, and without proper command, some few fired arquebuses in seeming panic, without taking proper aim. But mostly the men in the circle, simply faced out towards the Tokugawa forces that beat against the Hitamoto spears, and seemed constantly on the point of breaking the defensive circle. But the Hitamoto circle did not break. Instead it continued in its shuffling, scampering retreat, with its men crying out as if in despair.

Meanwhile the main mass of the Tokugawa army came on behind at a quick march, with the smoke of countless arquebus matches rising over the packed ranks of spearmen, arquebus men, bowmen and cavalry. They came in great numbers. They came in thousands. The tramp of their march was heavy, the beating of their drums rose over everything. They were led by high-rank samurai in multi-colour armour, riding splendid horses. They were a newly formed army, raised out of a nation that had been at peace for two hundred years. But Clan Tokugawa had re-discovered the arts of war, such that military discipline had been kicked, flogged and beaten into men who had been rice-farming peasants six months ago.

Meanwhile Lord Kimiya judged distance. The retreating Hitamoto force was only two hundred yards from the wide moat.

'Now!' said Lord Kimiya, 'let them in!'

'Hi!' said a samurai, who leaned over the rail and waved a hand. Instantly, a booming of huge *Taiko* drums came from the signallers waiting at the foot of the observation tower, causing soldiers to heave open the gates in the great wall. This seemed to cause panic among the men of the retreating Hitamoto force, who promptly gave up all pretence of formation, and ran at full speed towards the safety of the open gates. The timber bridges rumbled under their onrush and some few were cut down by the pursuing Tokugawa cavalry, but mostly they ran like cowards. They ran so fast that nothing Tokugawa could catch them.

Then the gates were thumping shut, and some few of the Tokugawa horsemen got in after the Hitamoto cowards, and some few of the cowards were shut outside, and were speared, shot and stabbed, and only a weak and small firing came from the Hitamoto ramparts to resist the advancing Tokugawa guard that now densely filled the bridges. The Tokugawa bowman and arquebus men shot at the Hitamoto loopholes and ramparts, while the main Tokugawa army came on in splendid step, with drums beating and colours flying.

If the Tokugawa commanders had been able to see inside the Hitamoto wall, they would have received a warning, because once the gates were shut the Hitamoto cowards – who were in fact the hand-picked elite of the Hitamoto army – stopped, wheeled about and turned on the Tokugawa cavalrymen with levelled spears, and swiftly killed every one of them. But all this was hidden, and the main Tokugawa force marched steadily forward until just out of range of a Hitamoto bow or arquebus. Then their commander raised a hand and the whole, huge force of thousands, stamped and stopped and fell silent awaiting orders.

'Good!' said Lord Kimiya, 'they have stopped exactly where my father's wisdom predicted.'

'Now, my Lord?' said the most senior samurai.

'No,' said Kimiya, 'Let us enjoy the moment a little longer.' He smiled and looked at the massed Tokugawa ranks, drawn up on either side of the road leading into Port Kagominato.

'How many are there?' said Lord Kimiya to the samurai.

'Five thousand at least, my Lord. Perhaps more?'

'Yes,' said Lord Kimiya, 'and again I say it: they are exactly where my father predicted.'

'Hi!' said all the samurai.

'Give the signal,' said Lord Kimiya.

'Hi!'

Taiko drums boomed again, and men ran with lighted torches out along tunnels dug beneath the wall and deep beneath the moat. There were many tunnels, and the men had trained long and hard for this moment. The tunnels led to safe places where fuses could be lit, leaving time for the men who lit them to get clear, because an astonishing quantity of gunpowder had been carefully placed outside the walls of Kagominato, in a variety of different quantities, in a variety of prepared, waterproof locations. Some of the powder barrels had been waiting for years: very many years, because they were there by long-anticipated planning.

Lord Kimiya and his samurai gasped as the first explosions bellowed and flashed, throwing up water, splintered timbers, and flesh, blood, bone and white smoke. But that was only the charges laid under the bridges, destroying the timberwork and throwing men into the moat, where those not killed outright, would be drowned by the weight of their armour. The bridge explosions were large, but when the main powder-mines blew, the concussions were so enormous that the observation tower shook violently: beams split, joints parted and the structure nearly went over, throwing Lord Kimiya and his samurai into a heap on one side. But they were up on the instant and scrambling for sight of what was happening in front of the fortifications.

When they saw it, even they were horrified at the appalling result of many tons of black powder going off under the feet of their enemies: lurid light, colossal white smoke, thunderclap sound, ears ringing and deafened. Out beyond the ramparts men and horses were ripped, rent and hurled upwards to fall back in fragments: some blacked and charred, some still on fire, and some men miraculously alive but left blinded, bleeding and naked by the appalling shockwave of the explosions.

When the last of the powder was fired, and the last of the smoke cleared, the cratered land beyond the moat was hideous with human mutilation and the moaning of the wounded. Lord Kimiya himself could hardly bear the sight of it, because like all his followers, while he had planned for war, and had been bred up to war: he had never actually seen it. But now he had, and he was wounded in the mind. As a samurai he could never admit this, especially to himself. But the wound was there and it never healed.

Meanwhile the remnants of the Tokugawa army fled in panic.

The battle of Port Kagominato was won by Hitamoto tradition.

It was Tokugawa's greatest disgrace.

It was Hitamoto's greatest victory.

But the war did not proceed so well after that.

Not for Clan Hitamoto.

CHAPTER 22

We left Spithead on August 15th and I took the flotilla out onto the deep blue water, for squadron manoeuvres to make sure that my six ships could act together and not like a set of prima donnas, and which is by no means as easy as it sounds. British men-o-war were supposed to sail in lines as straight as a ruler, then come about on the opposite tack as neat as clockwork, and the gaps between ships as exact as if measured with a chain. Well, it can be done and I'd seen it done, especially by the Channel Fleet under such a commander as 'Black Dick' Howe. So all I had to do now, my very jolly boys, is get the ships of my squadron to do the same.

I gave two weeks to the task. That was two weeks of frustration and temper. Two weeks of signals going up and down, and guns fired for emphasis, and bringing my captains aboard for yet another meeting, and banging of the table with my fist, because I couldn't bang heads.

'And you, Lieutenant Tishell,' I said to the young man – even younger than me – in command of *Spicer*, the smallest ship in our flotilla, 'Yours isn't the worst-signally ship among us,' I said, and looked round the table. It was packed. There were many officers to cram in, and elbows were close as they looked at me clutching glasses of my best Spanish wine, and the vessel rolled and the lamps swung above. 'I'll say that again,' I said, '*Spicer* isn't the worst at signalling, nor the worst at obeying,' I looked up and down the table, and noted which of them didn't meet my eye. 'But *Spicer* will tomorrow act as flagship, and will give a series of commands, by signal, which every ship will obey, including this one, and ...'

I'll spare you the rest. You have to say these things. You have to say them in this way. It's the same in trade, or in any other enterprise. No team ever drills itself. But it's tedious, my jolly boys, it truly is, and if you're in charge of it, your bowels twist in pain when, later on, the rogues attempt to carry out your instructions in practise, and get it wrong for the tenth time.

So next day, *Spicer* was flagship, with Tishell working through the list of orders I'd given him, and making the most appalling mess of giving incorrect signals, and giving them too late, and then giving contradictory commands. I suppose he was nervous, because he was a decent seaman or he'd never have been in command of such a neat little ship.

'Oh bloody hell fire,' said Mr O'Flaherty, with his glass on the latest flags that *Spicer* had run up, 'that's not right!' and every man aboard *Euphonides* that had a glass, studied Spicer's signal and shook his head. We were at the far end of the line, where I could easily see how the squadron behaved, and I was up on a carronade slide for a better view.

'Signal the flagship!' I said, 'Make: *Signal not understood.*'

'Aye-aye, Sir!' said the signals mid, and up went the flags.

That went on for day after day, until finally even *Spicer* got her signals right, and the six of us managed to manoeuvre something like together. I suppose I shouldn't complain. It takes far more than weeks to get a squadron of big square-rigged warships to work in company. It's the work of months and years, because even so fine a ship as *Euphonides* didn't change course simply at the turn of a wheel as a steamer does. She came about only by the disciplined teamwork of dozens of men hauling on lines to heave the massive yards around, and by the highly skilled top-men trimming her sails aloft, with bare feet gripping the foot-ropes a hundred feet above the deck, and every top-man not only heeding his officer, but taking the initiative to act contrariwise if necessary.

Even steering wasn't simply a matter of hauling the wheel around, and the quartermasters who steered, were the lower-deck's elite, working by experience and by *feel*. They had to because the wheel was fastened to a timber drum, with rawhide cables bound around it leading below to transmit the wheel's commands to the great beam of the tiller. The tiller was thereby hauled to larboard or starboard as the wheel turned, and the tiller turned the rudder itself. All this was done by lines running through blocks, and there was always tension and stretch in the lines, and it was therefore a matter of fine judgment by the quartermaster to know just how much turn of the wheel should be applied for a given effect, while always and always he must be constantly wary of the wind in the topmost sails – those that reacted first to a change of wind – for fear of acting too quick or too slow on the wheel, and throwing the vessel all aback, with sails flapping and the ship left rolling and helpless.

And that, my jolly boys, was what it was like in *good* weather. If the sea turned nasty it was very much harder indeed.

At the same time as this, and since I had my reputation to protect, of being a gunnery enthusiast, I insisted on a live-firing gun drill, with ship competing with ship for speed in running out, speed in delivering repeated broadsides, and in aimed fire at floating targets rigged for the purpose: empty casks with flags on staffs. This inevitably put myself in the centre of the stage, because all hands in the squadron were nursing their blisters and wounded pride from all my drills, so all hands wanted to see if Commodore bloody Fletcher and his precious bloody *Euphonides* really were so good at gunnery as they were supposed to be! So it was their chance to get up in the shrouds or on the guns to turn their glasses on myself.

Fortunately, this particular task wasn't so hard as it might have been. I already knew that Euphonides could clear the decks and run out guns faster than any other ship in the squadron. Also, it was almost certain that we'd be best at aimed fire because not one other ship in the squadron had ever practised it before! If that sounds unbelievable, then I quote no lesser an expert than Nelson himself who said: *'no captain can do very wrong if he places his ship alongside that of the enemy.'* That was advice to captains who might not see what Nelson was signalling in the smoke of battle, but it expressed the fundamental British idea that sea battles were won not by long range aimed fire, but by rapid fire at close range when you couldn't miss. Well, rapid fire is indeed important in a fleet action, but in a single ship action as you close with a distant enemy, it's long range fire that starts the battle, and might even end it.

So, I had *Euphonides* beat to quarters and I had the larboard main-deck battery run out. That was twenty, long twenty-four pounders each throwing a round iron ball five and a half inches in diameter. Each gun was, of course, smooth bored, since rifled artillery was far in the future. But under ideal conditions: with a good crew, with clean and un-rusted shot, and firing from a steady platform on land, then within the point blank range of the gun – say two hundred yards – each shot from smooth bore artillery would strike within a few feet of the last. But that is the ideal, and firing from a rolling, plunging ship is something else, and on this occasion it wasn't even myself who was in charge of the guns.

It had to be the second lieutenant, Mr Tildesley, because he was gunnery lieutenant, and if I'd taken the job from him it would have been humiliation, and Tildesley didn't deserve that. So I stayed on the quarterdeck, with Pyne, O'Flaherty and everyone else who had any right to be there, for a good view down the gun deck, with twenty guns, each served by a twelve-man crew and a boy to run cartridges. We had a stiff blow coming from abaft the beam, and that at least was ideal, so the ship was steady, and her motion mild, and we were bearing down a target-cask, bobbing in the grey waves with a scrap of red rag flapping from a ten-foot shaft. This had been dropped over the side on a previous run, and now we'd come about, and were returning with deadly intent as far as the target was concerned.

'Steady, steady,' said Tildesley, walking the deck with hands clasped behind in the approved manner, 'Wait till your target presents. Are you with me gun-captains?'

'Aye-aye!' they cried: twenty men stood safely back behind their guns, each holding the lanyard that would fire the flintlock trigger screwed over the touchhole of the long black barrel: that was nine-and-a-half feet of cast-iron barrel; two-and-a-half tons of it. Then I smiled because Tildesley delivered my own words that he'd learned from me, just as I'd learned them from my sea-daddy Sammy Bone, who truly was a master gunner aboard the old *Phiandra* years ago.

'It's the ship that aims the gun,' said Tildesley, 'they're laid point blank and trained on the beam, so the guns don't move, and you captains must sight down the barrels, and see how the ship points them as she rolls, and you must judge your time and you must give fire only when the gun is ....'

'Boom!' the first gun fired, drowning Tildesly's speech, as the gun-captain, crouching for a good view over the sights, judged that it was *bearing on target* as Tildesley had been about to say. So the gun-captain jerked the lanyard, the gun fired, it leapt back, it was checked by its breeching tackles and the crew darted in to reload. Then boom- boom! Two more guns fired, then all the rest, in the time of their gun captains. It was a good drill. Well done, Tildesley, and well done for the tight grouping of the shot that fell all around the target, throwing up columns of water higher than our main mast.

But the cask survived. Its red flag mocked us. It waved merrily. At two hundred yards it was too small a target for smooth bore guns on a rolling ship. None the less, with every shot placed within a few square yards of ocean, that was about as good as could be expected. So the gunners had done well, and in all truth, actually hitting the cask was a matter of luck.

'Bring her around, Mr Pyne,' I said, 'bring her round and give it the starboard battery.' So we ran on then Pyne brought her around with the squadron looking on, and every man aboard *Euphonides* praying that nothing should go wrong with our manoeuvring that would bring us into disgrace. But nothing did, and now the gun crews were manning the starboard battery, since each crew was responsible for two guns: one larboard, one starboard, and in the rare eventuality of the ship being engaged on both sides, then each of the pair was served by half a crew.

'Now, lads!' said Tildesley, 'It's double grog for the crew that hits the target, so take your time and don't waste your fire.'

Boom! Boom! Boom! Twenty guns again. Nobody won double grog because nobody hit the cask. But we'd shown the squadron some neat action in coming about so fast and in battering the sea so close to the target. In any case, the honour of our ship was more than saved by the poor performance of every other ship in the squadron. Yes, they could clear and run out at speed. Yes, they would have been deadly to any enemy alongside of them. But they'd never practised shooting at a target and their performance was hopeless. Some fired too late on the downward roll, and their shot plunged into the sea close alongside their own ship. Some fired too late on the upward roll, and pierced the blue sky with a shot that fell God-knows-where a mile or two away. Worse still, on some of the ships – despite my telling them not to – the gun-crews tried to heave their guns round to bear on target, rather than allowing the ship to do the job, and that doesn't work because you can't heave them fast enough.

Part of me was pleased that *Euphonides* had shown the squadron she was indeed best at aimed fire, but I couldn't accept a poor performance from the others, so I dealt with that over the next days by bringing the squadron's gunnery officers aboard *Euphonides* for training, and sending Mr Tildesley, Mr Pyne and myself into the ships of the squadron so that we might bellow into the ears of their gun crews. It was a busy time for the ships' boats, and all the better in the training of them too.

Finally, starting with *Euphonides* herself, I had the carpenters of the squadron fit a pair of gun-ports in the stern of every vessel. In those days the guns of a ship-of-war were mainly on the broadside, but when chasing an enemy a ship must fire on the bow, and it was normal to have a gun or two mounted to do so. What was less common was to have ports astern.

145

This was because ships were weak at the stern, where timbers did not close in around the vessel as they did at the bow, and space was allocated to windows. Thus there were fewer heavy beams to which gun tackles might be secured to absorb the heavy recoil, and it was difficult to mount guns at the stern. It was difficult but not impossible, and it was a useful drill to insist that my captains found a way to do it.

But the drills couldn't go on for ever. Despite what Sir Peter Parker had said, I was obliged eventually to take my squadron to the great anchorage of the Downs where the East India Company's ships had been kept waiting. The Downs was an offshore anchorage like Spithead. It lay off the east coast of Kent, near the town of Deal, between the Straits of Dover and the Thames Estuary. Thus the Downs was convenient for shipping coming out of London, and was protected from the prevailing westerlies by the land, and from easterlies by the great crescent of the Goodwin sands which rose out of the sea, in sand islands, and could be a deadly hazard to navigation if you ran on to them unawares.

The Downs was every bit as important to merchant shipping as Spithead was to the Navy, and once again I must instruct you youngsters on the reason why, which is the fact that the wind blows as it chooses, and not as we wish. Likewise, I can never stress too much the utter dependence on the wind, of shipping before the age of steam. For very short distances, and by tedious manoeuvring, ships could tack to and fro across the wind, and make some way against it. But no ship under sail, could make decent progress for very long without the wind being in a favourable direction, which meant coming from astern or on either beam.

In the case of vessels outbound from London, what they wanted was a steady blow from the east or thereabouts, to take them north up the coast of England, or south into the Atlantic or beyond. So it was a practical convenience of merchant navigation, to get a ship out to sea, provisioned and equipped in respects for a voyage, and then if a favourable wind did not blow, to drop anchor somewhere safe and wait for one.

That's the way it was, my jolly boys, and there wasn't no getting around it other than by patience, and I've seen ships in their hundreds anchored in the Downs, in easy sight of land, with bells ringing the hours, lights burning at night, and close enough to hail one another or to laugh at the sound of some idiot falling down a companionway through too much grog, which happened plenty enough times that you knew it when you heard it.

146

So I led my squadron to anchor in the Downs on Wednesday August 23rd, and had no trouble finding the nine East Indiaman we were to escort to Bombay. We had just sounded two bells of the first watch – say nine p.m. shore time – the sun was sinking and the shadows forming, but the East Indiamen, nine of them, stood out as easily the biggest and finest of the ships present. In those days, three hundred tons was a good size for a merchant ship, but all these East Indiamen were over one thousand tons, and their flagship was an absolute monster, the size of a first-rate three-decker. Also, they all had what appeared to be two rows of gun ports like line-of-battle ships, though only one row was real and the other merely painted, because these were merchantmen before all else, and designed to defend themselves not against warships but only pirates and the like.

Thus the major structural difference between an East Indiaman and a King's ship of similar size was the absence of warship 'tumble-home', which meant upper decks narrower than lower decks, and the ship's sides sloping inwards. This was necessary to keep the weight of the uppermost guns as far inboard as possible, to prevent excessive rolling at sea. But Indiamen didn't have upper guns, just one battery on the gun deck, and therefore the upper decks could be nice and wide for cargo storage.

At least that was the supposition, but I noticed that the very big ship, *The Duke of Cornwallis,* had a distinct tumble-home, and when I examined her with my glass I could see two rows of working gun-ports, which was interesting. I could also see that the East India ships did indeed fly the company's flag, not normal British Colours. The company's flag looked strongly like the American flag with its red and white stripes, but instead of having *stars-on-blue*, in the top left, the Company's flag had a Union Jack. On first sight, I thought Sir Peter Parker had been excessively prejudiced against John Company's flag, because it did show the British colours. But later, the time came when I would cheerfully have cut up the East India flag into handy squares for use in the bog house.

Having found the nine ships we were to convoy out to India, I signalled for my squadron to anchor astern of the flagship, and took station in *Euphonides* a short pull from *The Duke of Cornwallis,* where we dropped anchor. Then I sent the hands to dinner, and sat down and waited for John Company to make the first move because enough of Sir Peter's prejudices had crept into my own mind that I wasn't going to do that so myself. Sure enough a boat was lowered from Duke of Cornwallis, and a Company officer came aboard with a letter for me.

I was in the Great Cabin, taking a glass with my some of my officers, to demonstrate that I was not specially expecting anyone, and the Company's man was brought below, and shown in by the officer of the watch, Mr Allen, our third lieutenant.

'Captain Stacey come aboard, Sir!' said Allen, 'Captain Stacey of *Duke of Cornwallis.*'

'Ah,' I said, rising and holding out my hand, 'Welcome aboard, Captain. These gentlemen are Mr Pyne, my first officer, Mr O'Flaherty my Master, and Dr Goodsby our chaplain.'

'Sir! Sir! Sir!' said Stacey and he shook hands, and sat down where I indicated and was given a glass. He was in his forties and had the speech and manners of an educated man. His uniform – the Company's uniform – was clearly based on the King's uniform, right down to epaulettes and a cocked hat. The buttons were different of course, and he held no commission from the King but only the Company's warrant, and his ship's officers would be his first mate, second mate, third mate, and so on, not lieutenants. But he looked like a seaman, he had the air of command, an exceedingly fine ship in his trust, and I suppose we had much in common. I liked him.

'I bring a letter of invitation, for you, Sir,' said Stacey, 'for yourself and your first officer to dine aboard *Duke of Cornwallis*, tomorrow, at one bell of the noon watch. My Ship's Husband sends his best wishes, and hopes that you will take this opportunity to attend, and to meet the officers of the Company's ships anchored here.'

'Husband?' I said, 'Ship's Husband?' I'd never heard anything so bizarre. Stacey laughed at my reaction. I imagine he'd been expecting it.

'Indeed, Captain. The Ship's Husband! He is Mr Kilbride and a very senior servant of the Company.' He smiled. 'Let me explain. The title *Ship's Husband* means that Mr Kilbride has the right to replace a ship worn out in the Company's service. He may build a new ship and sell it to the Company, and then another to replace the new ship when *that* is worn out, which may be in only a few years, given the hard knocks an Indiaman suffers.' He smiled again and took a sip from his glass. 'As you may imagine, Sir, it is most profitable to be a Ship's Husband. Also Mr Kilbride is a director of the Company, as is his colleague Sir Robert Valentine, who accompanies us to India on business of his own.'

'Mr Kilbride and Sir Robert Valentine?' I said, 'Well, Captain Stacey, I accept their kind invitation on behalf of my first officer and myself, and we should be most interested to come on board of your ship to meet them,' and that was exact truth because Kilbride and Valentine were the men I was supposed to kill.

CHAPTER 23

'There can be no duty worse than being the second to a man who performs the honourable despatch. If the second strikes well, he merely does what is commonplace and gains no credit. But if his stroke fails, then he is deeply dishonoured.'

(From a letter of Thursday, October 19th from Kaito Watanabe to his father Lord Gakuto Watanabe, in Edo Province.)

Kaito Watanabe took the swords from his servant Hinatu, who bowed with reverence as he passed them to his master: the long katana, the short wakizsashi, the pair of them mounted in matching scabbards and grips.

'Are they sharp?' said Kaito, betraying his nervousness, because the world would end before Hinatu allowed any sword to be blunt, let alone that of his master.

'Hi!' said Hinatu and bowed again. Then he smiled. Hinatu was very old and Kaito was very young, and Kaito had never wielded a sword except in practise or in drill. 'They are sharp,' said Hinatu, 'as sharp as the master-sharpener can make them.'

'Hi,' said Kaito and put the pair of swords into his girdle. He slid them in place with neat, smooth motions. At least he could do that. Then he walked out on the terrace among the elegant displays of potted plants, so very harmonious and serene. The plants were serene but Kaito was not. He went right up to the balustrade and looked down from one of the upper stories of Hiraoka castle. It was one of the biggest in Japan. A thousand samurai stood in arms to defend it. It was planted in the middle of a lake, and it rose over a plain of pines and rivers. Kaito looked at the birds above, and the sentries on the bridges below. It was not his home castle: not the stronghold of Clan Watanabe. It was the castle of Clan Hiraoka – close and traditional allies of Clan Watanabe – but it was still a castle, and Kaito was seeking calm in familiar things like sentries, bridges and birds.

'Master?' said Hinatu, and the old man stepped forward and placed a hand on the boy's arm. In some families, with some young masters and some old servants, the touch of a servant would have been unthinkable impertinence. But not for Hinatu, and not for Kaito, who would one day be Lord Watanabe.

'Hinatu?' said Kaito, and looked down on the wrinkled, spindly creature with his nearly bald head, and brown-specked hands that were like bird claws, and who was so very dear to him as the servant who had picked him up when he fell down as a little boy, and told him to be a man and never cry, and taught him silly songs and saucy rhymes.

'Master,' said Hinatu, 'It's like this. You raise your blade, you don't even think about it, and then you strike. That's all, master. That's all you do.'

'But why Lord Hiraoka?' said Kaito, 'It's not his fault. He's never been anywhere near Hito Island, and he hasn't been involved in any of the battles!' Hinatu bowed and explained.

'It's him because he is the Shogun's supreme commander, and all the others have to do what he says.'

'But he's never done anything,' said Kaito, 'He's never said anything! Everyone knows that. He didn't tell the generals what to do in the battles and he was a thousand miles away when they blew up our army at Kagominato!'

'Yes, master,' said Hinatu, 'but someone has to take responsibility. Someone has to atone, and all the generals are dead. The Hitamoto saw to that. Our generals led the attacks, and they were killed in action, and with honour.' That made Kaito angry. He stamped his foot.

'But the Hitamoto acted *without* honour! They never came out to fight. They just waited in ambush. There's no honour in that!' Hinatu shrugged.

'If you're fighting for the homeland then you have to win,' he said, 'and the Hitamoto were fighting for their homeland, so anything they did was honourable. The only dishonour is to lose if you're fighting for the homeland.'

'What?' said Kaito, 'Are you on their side?'

'Of course not, master, but you have to stand in your enemy's sandals to know how he's thinking. You have to see it *his* way.'

'And what about *our* way?'

'Ah!' said Hinatu, 'That comes next. The Shogun will appoint a new supreme commander, and it will be up to him to find a better way of dealing with the Hitamoto.'

'And what's that?' Hinatu shook his head.

'That's up to the new supreme commander!' he said, 'It's not for an old man like me to say.' Then Hinatu looked over Kaito's shoulder. Four samurai stood behind Kaito. They wore formal robes. They bowed respectfully.

'It's time,' said Hinatu, 'Remember, master, strike without thinking.'

'Hi,' said Kaito.

'The Shogun will be chief witness,' said Hinatu, 'It is a great honour. Lord Hiraoka will preserve his own honour, and the honour of all those who fell.'

'Hi.'

'It is also an honour on Clan Watanabe that Lord Hiraoka asked you to be his second.'

'Hi.'

Kaito Watanabe turned and bowed to the four samurai. They bowed to him. They led him down many stairs, and out into a garden in the castle grounds. It was an exceedingly beautiful garden, and a quiet place had been set aside and screened from view by white, hemp *Jinmaku* curtains, six feet high and stretched between posts. Armed guards stood at the entrance to this quiet place, and a folding screen immediately behind the entrance hid the inside from view. Kaito Watanabe could feel his heart thump as he followed the samurai into the quiet place and around the screen. The whole of the interior had been perfectly levelled, and covered with tatami mats in green – the Hiraoka Clan colour – and the Shogun himself and a dozen of his most noble retainers sat in a row on stools: straight-backed, and magnificently dressed in court robes. Kaito and the samurai bowed, and Kaito was led to a place facing the Shogun, where a large white cloth was laid on the mats, before another screen. The samurai showed Kaito where to stand. They bowed. He bowed. All of them bowed to the Shogun.

There was a long silence then Lord Hiraoka entered the quiet place with seven followers, all dressed in funeral white. Lord Hiraoka was a man in his sixties, fat and heavy in the body. He advanced with steady paces and bowed to the Shogun. He showed no fear. He bowed to the Shogun who bowed in return. He bowed to Kaito. Kaito bowed in return. Then Lord Hiraoka was led to the white square. He knelt, facing the Shogun.

His name and rank were proclaimed by one of his followers. The Shogun bowed. Lord Hiraoka drew his arms from his sleeves, pushed his upper garments aside, and bared the bulge of his abdomen.

One of the samurai gently nudged Kaito into the best possible place, immediately behind the kneeling Lord Hiraoka, and nodded to Kaito, causing Kaito's heart to pound with such force that Kaito's body shook and his hands trembled. The nod was the sign for Kaito to draw and make ready. He did so. The katana shone in the sunshine.

In complete silence, a samurai handed Lord Hiraoka a wakizsashi blade, shorn of its hilt and decorations, but folded in thick paper to give a good grip, leaving just the tip and a hand's breadth of blade exposed. Kaito stared down at the back of Lord Hiraoka's neck. Kaito thought that everyone could surely *hear* his heart thumping.

Lord Hiraoka took the blade in both hands. He drew breath. He placed the tip of the blade to the left side of his abdomen. 'Ugh!' he said. He stabbed the blade into his middle and drew it to the right. Skin was sliced, yellow fat peeled open, red muscle parted and grey viscera bulged out of the wound.

Kaito waited to ensure that Lord Hiraoka's cut had been fully and properly made. Then he struck. He was either more skilful than he knew, or was exceedingly fortunate. Lord Hiraoka's head rolled forward, but a strip of skin was left un-cut beneath the chin, such that the head sagged down upon the torso and did not fall clumsily to the ground. Kaito's stroke was therefore perfect. It could not possibly have been bettered and honour was preserved most excellently on all sides.

The Shogun appointed a new supreme commander at once. His name was Emon Yoshida, a man whose lineage could not be compared with that of the late Lord Hiraoka since the Yoshida Clan's honour had been stained when – thirty years ago – Emon Yoshida's father had been banished to China for political offences. But the Shogun was entirely pragmatic in the appointment, because the result of the banishment had been that the young Emon Yoshida chose soldiering as a profession and had spent twenty years campaigning as an officer in the Chinese Army of Mongolia.

CHAPTER 24

I don't know even to this day whether it made things easier, regarding my orders to become a murderer, or more difficult in that respect that I took against Mr Stephen Kilbride on sight. I didn't like him. He was too damn bloody intense. He took hold of a room-full of company like a man grabbing a spaniel by the scruff of its neck. He was a skinny little creature in his late forties, but he seized my hand when we met and squeezed it hard, as some idiots will do when trying to prove manhood, as if trying to crush the bones, and he looked me in the eye as if he owned me.

His chum, Sir Robert Valentine, was a lesser man, by which I mean lesser only than Kilbride. He was clearly in Kilbride's pocket and followed the little bugger in every way, but Valentine wasn't some fluffy duckling that waddled after its mama. Indeed he wasn't. He was a round, comfortable sort: well-dined, deep-drinking, and very rich. He came with servants in tow, and was no fool. I marked him as one of the calculating sort, who takes great care to work out which interests will rise and which will fall, and then gets on the winning side. But the mere fact that he was a director of the East India Company meant that he was a formidable man of business, as all such are, and that he was committed to trade and profit. Which of course should have made me like him. But in the present business, Valentine was a disciple and Kilbride was the messiah and I didn't like what Kilbride was preaching.

I met them aboard *Duke of Cornwallis* when Pyne, my first lieutenant, and I went across for dinner as invited. The ship was something extraordinary, and Pyne and I were fascinated.

'What's the size of her supposed to be?' said Pyne as our boat's crew pulled in steady towards the huge ship.

'She's supposed to be sixteen hundred tons burden,' I said, 'but she looks even bigger than that.'

'Yes, Sir,' he said, 'She's massive, and look at that lower tier of gun-ports. She's rigged and ready to take aboard a lower-deck battery.'

'She is indeed,' I said, 'D'you think John Company's building a real navy?'

'Looks damned like it, Sir!'

So we grumbled and sneered as Sea Service officers did, when discussing East India ships, and never guessed how close to the truth our guesses were. But then we were going aboard, and sheer professional curiosity overwhelmed all else. Yes, they had a proper ladder rigged. Yes, they piped the side, man-o-war fashion. Yes, the ships officers were lined up in their version of full dress, and yes, their full dress was passing smart and a very close imitation of the real thing. And yes, the ship was neat and clean overall, and all lines secured and ship-shape, and riding to anchor most smartly for a merchant vessel. But nothing about her could be compared with *Euphonides*.

[Note that never in all his years would Fletcher admit to any ship being as smart as one under his own command. It was another vanity, and the foregoing is in fact high praise for *Duke of Cornwallis*. S.P.]

Captain Stacey, master of *Duke of Cornwallis*, was waiting to receive us as we came aboard.

'Good day to you, Captain Fletcher!' he said, 'And Mr Pyne!' He turned round to wave a hand at his ship. 'Now gentlemen,' he said, 'How d'you like *the Duke*? Because I'd value your opinion.' He smiled. 'Though of course, I realise that nothing that compares with King George's ships.' I laughed. He was a decent sort, and he'd hit square on what I'd just been thinking. Pyne laughed too, which was something remarkable for that dour blighter, and after we'd met Stacey's officers, we actually fell into conversation of *Duke of Cornwallis* and we discussed her copper plating, the great size of her yards, her best point of sailing, and other matters. Then finally:

'I see she has man-o-war tumble-home,' I said, 'I've not seen that before on a merchant vessel.'

'Ah!' said Stacey, 'that's Mr Kilbride for you. He plans to get a voyage out of her to the Indies, and then sell her to the Navy as a ship of the line.'

'Can he do that?' I said, 'With a ship already sold to the Company?' Stacey just laughed at that.

'Trust me, Captain Fletcher,' he said, 'Mr Kilbride has his ways. He's up to every trick that man can imagine.' That was interesting because it showed that Stacey didn't much care for Kilbride. But that might have been Company politics. Meanwhile, Kilbride himself wasn't on deck to receive us and that was the first point against him in my opinion. He was down below in the Great Cabin, which we were taken down into, and which was very like that of a major warship, and which was set for dinner with lavish opulence of silver, and of linen, cut glass, patent lamps, paintings, and even pots of fresh flowers that must have been plucked that morning.

And of course there was Kilbride with Sir Robert Valentine just astern of him on his larboard beam. They were both done out in fancy dining clothes and they both looked like money. There was also, and much to my surprise, a young gentleman of the oriental persuasion sitting in the place of honour at the head of the table. He was something wonderfully smart in his clothes, he was completely at his ease, and it was obvious that Kilbride and Valentine regarded him as an equal, or perhaps even more. But all three of them got up as Pyne, Stacey and I entered and they came forward with smiles, led by Kilbride.

'Ah! Captain Fletcher!' said Kilbride and grabbed my hand in both of his and scrunched it as I've already mentioned. That was the second and third points against him all in one go, because I don't like a man taking my hand in both of his as if I were a choirboy and he the parson, and I sneer at the bone-crushing because God help any man's hand if I gave it my full strength in return! Then came a further surprise, or rather several of them, as Kilbride made the introductions:

'Captain Fletcher, and Lieutenant Pyne,' he said, 'may I introduce my colleague Sir Robert Valentine?' We all nodded, and then Kilbride turned and actually gave a bow towards the oriental gentlemen. 'And of course,' said Kilbride, 'I present you to Lord Masahito Hitamoto, one of the greatest noblemen of Japan, who is pre-eminent in rank aboard this ship, and who is travelling the world with his companions, and whom we have the honour to carry – part way - on his journey home.'

Well, my jolly boys, what sort of a mouthful was that? And how was your uncle Jacob to react to it? It was like being presented to the King of the Cannibal Islands, and a cushion shoved in front of you, so you could get down on your knees. But while I wondered just what might be the precise etiquette, the Japanese gentleman himself came forward. He was a small chap compared with me, but most men are, and he was good looking, fit to please the ladies, with dark hair, dark eyes and neat features. And then he spoke.

'My dear Captain Fletcher,' he said, 'What a pleasure it is to meet you. I have heard so much of your exploits afloat, and only the finest of officers would be entrusted with such a ship as *Euphonides.* So I greet you with much pleasure.'

God stap my vitals! He spoke like a bloody Englishmen! Not a trace of foreign accent, not a hesitation, not a blink! It took me aback, I can tell you. Meanwhile he shook my hand with a man's grip not an idiot's like Kilbride. But in those first moments of meeting, what astounded me was his English and I couldn't help but remark on it, especially as I've never learned any foreign language and can't understand how anyone can, because it's all gobble-gobble to me.

'You speak English amazingly well, Sir,' said I, and seeing the pain on Kilbride's face, I corrected myself, 'I mean, *my Lord,*' I said, and Kilbride gulped with relief as I continued. 'However did you get it so perfect … my Lord?'

'I came to England a boy,' said Masahito, 'and languages are easy to the young.'

'Not for me, m'Lord!' I said, and he smiled in the most friendly fashion.

'Ah,' he said, 'but you have other talents, Captain Fletcher. Many of them!' and Kilbride and Valentine nodded like puppets, toadies that they were. But so did Pyne and Stacey, and I appreciated that.

After that, and having been sat in the place of honour between Kilbride and Masahito, and with Stacey and his officers round the table, they served a superb dinner of many courses, with fresh bread and vegetables, excellent wine by the bucket, and servants behind every man of us so we hardly had to move to grab our victuals.

Lord Masahito proved to be a most charming fellow and was so educated in his knowledge of England and Europe in general that I was impressed, and I couldn't help but wonder what he was doing in company with swabs like Kilbride and Valentine? Then eventually the dinner was spoiled by Kilbride, who got himself worked up to enthusiasm by the passions inside of him. He was an absolute little Napoleon Bonaparte in his ambitions and he lectured us non-stop about the undeveloped opportunities for trade out East.

'India, Gentlemen,' he said, 'Great kingdoms still not under British rule! Fathomless wealth of gold, precious stones and rare minerals. And beyond India: Persia! Afghanistan! China! And even Japan!' He raised a glass to Lord Masahito, who smiled and toasted him in return, so I wondered what was going on there?

But to give Kilbride his due, the subject was a good one and he knew it well, and I must admit that he caught my interest. But then he spoiled even that. 'Now you, Sir,' he said, fastening his eyes on me, 'You're not just a man-o-war's man! Not you, Sir! Isn't that right, Sir? You're a man of business,' and he winked and chuckled, 'or you would be, if given the chance!' and the wretched little sod had the cheek to poke me in the ribs.

I didn't like that one bit. You youngsters who've read my memoirs will know very well that I never chose the Navy, and always wanted to get out of it and into trade. But I'd learned by then that to say such a thing in the company of Sea Service officers is like pissing on the drawing room carpet. So I kept all such thoughts to myself and it certainly wasn't generally known aboard *Euphonides*, so Kilbride must have done some deep digging.

Later, when dinner was done, and all toasts drunk, Kilbride declared that I must tour *Duke of Cornwallis* to see what a fine ship she was.

'Nothing like her is afloat in this world or the next!' he declared, to loud applause from all of *Duke of Cornwallis's* people who were around us, and all of whom had taken a drop or more. 'Biggest merchant ship in the world!' said Kilbride, 'Three cheers for the ship!' which they gave with a will, then up he got, and staggered with all the wine he'd got under hatches, 'but see how she rolls, boys!' he cried, and everyone laughed since we were at anchor and barely moving. 'You come with me, Sir!' he cried, hauling me out of my chair, and linking and arm in mine, and leading the way, 'Captain Stacey'll take care of Mr Pyne and his Lordship. You come with me, Sir, and we'll tour the ship!'

Since I couldn't knock him down, much as I'd have preferred, I had to go with him, and off we went to see the cargo holds, through hatchways and down ladders, with the crew saluting and making way, and him staggering like a drunkard until the moment we were clear of everyone else, and surrounded by great bales of woollen cloth in waterproof wrappings. I remember the manufacturer's name, stencilled on them: *Bolten's Mill, Bradford, Yorkshire.* That stuck in my mind because Bradford was famous for its great, five-floor manufactories powered by steam or water-wheels, with gears turning, drive-belts humming, and machines clacking and thrashing in the pursuit of wealth. It made my mouth water, it really did.

158

But then, the instant we were properly alone, the drink seemed to drain out of Kilbride. We were on a timber walk-way lit dimly by lanterns, oppressive with the smell of fabric, and all sound deadened.

'Now then, Jacob Fletcher, of Polmouth in Cornwall,' he said, 'Jacob Fletcher who never wanted to be in the Navy, and who press-ganged into it, and who heaved Boatswain Dixon over the side, and was pursued almost to death by Lady Sarah Coignwood.' He grinned and stared at me hard, 'Or am I talking to the wrong Jacob Fletcher?'

Little bastard. Little swine. He made an enemy in that instant. Previously, I'd merely disliked him. But not now. Not now, because he thought he'd got hold of me. He thought he'd got me helpless. Clever little swab. He'd made some inquiries, hadn't he? I could see that. It was obvious. He'd asked about. He'd spent some money. So he'd got me square in his sights. Or so he thought, and it did cross my mind to twist in return: to twist his damned neck till it snapped. 'Woah!' he said, and stepped back, as he saw the look on my face. 'Stand easy, Sir!' he said, 'and ask yourself just how big your ambitions might be? Trade, Sir? I can offer you that! Manufacture? I can offer you that! How much do you want? How big can you be? How free do you want to be? How much do you want to be yourself, Sir? Your own entire self, and not the Navy's nor King George's nor anybody else's?'

The worst of it was that he'd touched on a melodious chord. He was a very clever man indeed. He was a very powerful man besides. Just think of the ship we were in. Just think of the power of the East India Company, which was close to becoming an independent sovereign state. I was wondering who wielded the greater power: little Mr Kilbride or the Shadow Men as represented by Earl Spencer? I didn't like Kilbride, but I didn't like the Shadow Men either, and Kilbride had gone to great trouble to find out about me, and he obviously wanted something from me.

'What's your game, Kilbride?' I said, 'Why are you telling me this?'

'Ah,' he said, and lowered his voice, and came close, 'Are you ready to trade, Jacob Fletcher? Jacob Fletcher that can deal with the Devil and come out on top? Are you ready to make a bargain?'

'For what?' I said.

'For you keeping out of my way,' he said.

'Depends where you're going!'

'I'm going East,' he said, 'I'm going far to the east. To Japan and beyond, and I don't want anyone getting in my way.'

'Why should I get in your way?' I said, 'My duty is to get you safe out to India. You and your fleet.'

'Is that all?' he said, 'and what about Japan? Aren't you supposed to stop me going there?'

'Bollocks!' I said. 'What do I care about Japan? You can go to Hell as far as I'm concerned, and I won't stop you.' He winced at that, and serve him right, because I wasn't admitting anything to him. But he recovered in an eye-blink and laughed and came so close he was almost touching me.

'Listen to me, Jacob Fletcher, and I'll tell you a great truth, which is that given enough money in ready gold, it's amazing what men will tell you: men who are supposed to keep secrets. Even Admiralty secrets, even Government secrets. So I know just what your orders are, and now I'm asking you if you are *with* me or *against* me, because if you're with me, I can give you your heart's desire.'

And now, my lovely lads, since I've never told you anything than the truth in these memoirs, I have to admit that I was tempted. I was very tempted indeed. Even though I detested the little swab, the little swab was offering me exactly what I'd always wanted.

'Let me think on this, Kilbride,' I said, 'I'll need a good long think, so don't come pestering for a quick answer.' He grinned. He raised a finger to poke me in the ribs again, but he saw my frown, and laughed, then stood back and nodded to himself.

'You're a man to beware of, Jacob Fletcher,' he said, 'I can see that. But you just think on what I've said. Have your long think, and let me know. You've got plenty of time, but you let me know when we reach India.' So he stuck out his hand, and I took it. I admit that we shook hands, just as I admit that I was sorely tempted. Then we went and joined the rest and said nothing to anyone.

After that, we had to be patient. The wind decided that it would not blow the way we needed, and the whole squadron of us – my ships and John Company's – lay at anchor for day after day, and the weather was dark and cloudy, and it was wet and damp besides, and the shrouds and rigging dripped on our heads, and all hands went about muffled in foul weather gear, and the nights especially were miserable. It's hard to believe that the sea was so unkind in August and September, but that's how it was. That's what the Downs were like that year, and we had to get on with it.

Which was the beginning of the strangest events I ever witnessed at sea, and strange because ordinary perils, bad as they are, at least can be understood, whether they be storms and rocks, lee shores, or the violence of the enemy. But there's a dark world of other seafaring wonders: nasty wonders that nobody wants to know about, that go beyond what we can understand and that landmen never know. So although I don't like Shakespeare 'cos I can't understand it and the jokes aren't funny, I'm telling you, my jolly boys, that Shakespeare's man spoke plain truth when he said there were more things under the sun than we know of.

[**'There are more things in heaven and earth, Horatio, than are dreamt of in your philosophy'** *Hamlet* **Act 1, Scene 5, lines 167-8, S.P.**]

And to prove it, one of these *things* once fell upon me. It was only once in all my life, but it fell right heavily, and it fell on board of *Euphonides*. Though first you have to understand what it was like to lie anchored in the Downs, because I think that was the beginning of it, in the dark of a miserable night and with the Goodwin sands waiting patiently to the west, ready to ruin any ship that ran foul of them.

To begin with, any ship anchored in the Downs was surrounded by other ships, all of them miserably waiting, all of them with cables creaking and groaning, and all gently wallowing in a motion that can bring up the dinners even of hardened seamen. Some captains will abandon the usual two-watches for the ship's people, when larboard and starboard alternate their duties, and shift to harbour watches which give the people all night in their hammocks. I never did that, preferring to keep man-o-war duties and discipline, but still there was nothing to do at night other than look out at the black sea, and the ghostly ships with lights burning, and bells sounding the watches, and all sounding them at slightly different times, so that on occasions, the clanging went on for minutes at a time, first from one, and then another vessel, all echoing sad and distant across the anchorage.

'Hark to that, my lads,' said Mr O'Flaherty one dripping-wet night, standing by the wheel as the widespread choir of ships gave six bells of the first watch, and gave it each in its own ship's time. Several of the midshipmen were up on deck, and the hands were huddled in corners, dark-wrapped shapes, trying to keep dry. I couldn't sleep for worrying about Kilbride so I was there too, and we all turned to listen. 'Wait for it, lads,' said O'Flaherty, as one ship sounded late, 'Wait for it …' We all listened, then long after the previous ship, six clangs came from somewhere far distant. 'Ah,' said O'Flaherty, 'That'll be the bell of some poor ship, long since lost on the Goodwins, and all hands aboard of her dead from starvation and thirst, which is a terrible way to die, my lads, and only the withered bones of a skeleton's hand are left to strike the hours.'

I smiled as most of his listeners did, to this ancient and white-haired old tale, because there always had to be one ship that sounded last. But Mr Midshipman Phaeton Ordroyd didn't smile, or at least I don't think he did, because I couldn't see his face in the dark. But I recognised the shape of him and his voice.

'Is it really a lost ship, Mr O'Flaherty?' he said.

'Aye, Mr Ordroyd,' said O'Flaherty, 'And it's the dead hand of a lost soul that just struck that bell, and a warning to all of us of what might befall even a good ship, by the mysteries of the sea, since the Goodwin Sands ain't even the worst of it, for there's horrors that even the Church don't know of.' There were some sniggers at that.

'Garn,' said a voice, 'get away with you!'

'Who said that?' said O'Flaherty, sharply, and got no reply.

'What did you mean, Mr O'Flaherty?' said Ordroyd, and O'Flaherty filled his sails and set forth, having an audience listening and Ordroyd believing.

'Well, my lads,' said O'Flaherty, 'There's the true fact that when the watch comes on deck at night, the first man to see the full moon, will go mad.'

'Truly?' said Ordroyd.

''Tis well known,' said O'Flaherty.

'Aye,' said a voice in the dark, ''Tis true an' all.'

'And then there's looking down over the side, in the dead of night,' said O'Flaherty.

'Oh …' said a voice with a tremble in it, 'you don't want to do that.'

'Indeed not!' said O'Flaherty, 'Not for fear you might see the ghastly face of Davy Jones, fiend of the Devil, who grins up through the water and beckons you to go over the side into his arms.' That brought such dead silence among the hands that we could hear voices on other ships, and men coughing. This because Davy Jones was a most particularly feared monster to seamen. 'Then there's the sea-serpent,' said O'Flaherty, 'which is the length of a ship's cable, and its body has the breadth of a barrel, and its teeth are a yard long. And then there's the massive, enormous, hungry Kraken that wraps its long and slimy arms – of which it has dozens of 'em – around the hulls of whaling ships, and drags them under. And then there's ...'

'Mr O'Flaherty?' I said, 'Could we not have something more jolly? I'm bound for my hammock in a while, and I'd rather be jolly than fearful.' That made everyone laugh, and the fear of the occult went away. But later it came back.

CHAPTER 25

'I thank you, my wise and honoured father, for your powerful influence in gaining me a high rank in the Shogun's army. Thus I am in daily attendance upon his honour our leader, whose military skills are formidable. Each day brings further evidence of his excellence.'

(From a letter of Wednesday, December 13th from Kaito Watanabe to his father Lord Gakuto Watanabe, in Edo Province.)

The climate of Kyushu Island is mild in December, so Supreme General Yoshida ordered that the final briefing should be given in the open air, on the parade ground in front of his timber campaign lodge. The parade ground was lined on two sides by the tents of his senior commanders, and entirely enclosed by Jinmaku curtains bearing the mon of Clan Tokugawa.

A mixed force of nearly ten thousand men was camped in formal rows outside the curtained space, together with seven hundred horses, two hundred oxen, a hundred baggage waggons, a vast store of military arms, and a busy murmur of soldiers drilling, smiths clanging, carpenters hammering, and clerks taking note of everything that came and went, to ensure the smooth running of the expedition. All this thanks to the detailed discipline imposed on the army by its new commander, Supreme General Yoshida – known in the ranks as Chinese Yoshida - who emerged from his lodge, with seven staff officers behind him, and marched into the centre of the curtained space, between two lines of the army's officer corps – one hundred on each side – who had been seated on stools patiently waiting, and who now sprang to their feet.

'Banzai! Banzai! Banzai!' they cried, and raised arms in salute. All were dressed in plain battle armour because Yoshida was practical in all things, and favoured teamwork before all else. He therefore forbad both needless decoration, and the personal vanity that went with coloured armour, red silk bindings, and fancy helmet-crests. The only variation in this discipline was the fact that Yoshida's own armour was Chinese, but that was because it was his veteran harness of many hard-fought battles. Five of his staff likewise wore Chinese armour since they were Chinese themselves. They were followers of Yoshida, who had earned their places by merit, as compared with the two young Japanese noblemen, who were on Yoshida's staff as a gesture to Japanese pride. One of these young men was Colonel Kaito Watanabe, renowned for his part in the honourable suicide of the army's previous Supreme General.

Now, Yoshida marched to the far end of the curtained space, and wheeled around to climb a timber platform raised ten feet above the ground, with room for himself and six staff officers, and from which he could address the officers assembled below. But Colonel Kaito Watanabe did not mount the platform with the rest. He stood to attention by the steps, and took up a long white rod that had been placed there for his use.

Yoshida stood forward, he raised his voice.

'Come forward!' he cried, 'Come forward and make good look.' He was a broad, strong man of thirty-nine years. He had lost part of an ear, and a piece of his chin to Mongol arrows, and other scars were on his body. He had lived in China so long that his speech was not quite right. But his reputation was colossal.

So the officers stepped forward and clustered around a most beautiful and detailed model of the walled city of Kagominato: the city still held against the Shogun by Clan Hitamoto, still the best port from which to launch an invasion of Hito Island, and still the site of the shameful defeat that Clan Hitamoto had inflicted on Clan Tokugawa. The model was big: some thirty feet across, and forty feet wide. It showed the walls, gates and bridges. It showed the holes blown in the bridges by Hitamoto mines. It showed the moat – filled with real water in the model – and it showed the gunpowder craters beyond. It showed the buildings behind the walls. It showed the heavily-fortified harbour and piers that were protected within the walls, and safe from the sea. Everyone nodded particularly at the harbour and piers, because everyone knew how much the Shogun wanted them in order to assemble his invasion fleet.

'Make very good look!' cried Yoshida, 'Know your enemy better than know yourself! Know what can be done. Bring together all means to know the enemy. Use eyes! Use interrogation! Use spies! Use books! Use

165

anything and bring together!' The officers nodded. Yoshida was famous for his intense determination to know the enemy. 'Now!' cried Yoshida, 'See where the enemy is strong!'

Hearing this, Colonel Watanabe ran forward with his white rod and pointed to a section of the town walls.

'Forty feet high, twenty feet thick!' cried Yoshida. Watanabe moved the rod. He pointed to the gates, 'Thick timber, narrow way,' said Yoshida, 'heavily defended with many guns.' Watanabe pointed to the moat, 'Twenty feet deep,' cried General Yoshida 'one hundred feet wide!' He waved an arm towards the model. 'In all this, enemy thinks he is strong.' He paused. 'But see where enemy is weak!'

Now Watanabe pointed with his rod towards ten men who had been waiting for his order. They ran forward, knelt down, grasped tatami mats that had been laid on the ground, and whisked them away, to show the model of a deep trench running at right angles to the moat of the model city. Finally Watanabe himself walked forward, put his rod against a small lever half-buried in the ground, pushed hard, and a wooden partition opened, causing the moat to empty into the entrenchment until the moat was dry.

'Ahhhh!' said the officers and looked to Yoshida.

'Ten thousand men are gathered here,' he said, 'Ten times that number are farmers of nearby land. One hundred and ten thousand will dig. The work will be done in thirty days. The moat will be dry. Our engineers will build a ramp. We shall take the city by the ramp.'

'Ahhhh!' they said and nodded.

'The moat is not strength.' said General Yoshida, 'It is weakness.'

CHAPTER 26

We were twenty-seven dreary days anchored in the Downs. Some ships and some captains have fared worse, so I won't complain and what difference would it make if I did? I used the time as best as I could with more drills for the squadron, and with an endless round of visits between ships to get to know my own captains better, and to make acquaintance with the East India captains. In addition I did my best to knock some convoy sense into them, with standing orders on keeping station, and what do to in the event of French cruisers appearing, or fire on board, or running out of water, or plague, pestilence, mutiny and whatever else I could think of. My chaplain and secretary, Dr Goodsby, suggested that we put all my standing orders into writing for the benefit of the East Indiaman, which was some task for him and his helpers, so while I doubted that all the Indiamen would read what he wrote, I let him do it in order to emphasise to all concerned that I was serious.

I placed more reliance on some quiet words I had with those of the East India captains who showed signs of being surly. I give the example of one Ephraim Clinch, master of *Countess of Harwich*, thirteen-hundred tons, and the second biggest of them after only *Duke of Cornwallis*. He was another one I took against for the insolence of not being on deck when I came aboard. Also his ship was nowhere near so neat and tidy as it should have been even by East India standards, and his First Mate didn't show respect for the King's Uniform, and he'll never know how close he came to being knocked down on the spot. But some of these innocent pleasures you just have to forgo when you're commodore of a fleet.

'Mr Clinch, Sir?' says he, with his men grinning behind him, 'Don't rightly know where he might be about the ship. But tell you what? I'll ask around,' and he made a pretence of looking up and down the deck, then, 'Mr Boatswain?' he said, is the Old Man down below?'

'Aye, Sir!' said the boatswain and gave me a decent salute so there was one seaman among them at least. Eventually I was led below by the first mate, and it's strange how things turn out, because somehow the first mate managed to trip heavily going down a ladder, almost as if someone had pushed him, and in my eagerness to help him to his feet, what with him laid out on his back, I accidentally trod all my weight square on his nuts and raisins so that he yelped something pitiful in his pain. But these accidents happen at sea, and when he got up, I think he guessed what he'd get if he made trouble, so he didn't.

In the stern cabin, I got no dinner out of Captain Ephraim, only a miserable glass of port, and he was as rude as his first mate, and he was all prim and proper with lips like an old prune, a patronising smile, and the manner of a man being driven beyond reason.

'Standing orders?' he said, 'I can't answer to that,' said he, 'what if the wind get's up? What if I lose a spar? Oh dear me no, Sir. I'll not be given no standing orders but will shift for myself and my ship!' There was quite a bit of that between us until finally I raised a hand for silence.

'A word, Sir,' I said.

'What word?' he said.

'This,' I said, 'I hereby make you a solemn promise, Captain Clinch.'

'A promise in what regard?'

'A promise that if I signal your ship with an order, and you don't promptly obey …' I paused for effect.

'Then what shall happen?' he said.

'Then by God and all His little angels, I'll send one of my command alongside of you with orders to fire into you until you obey!' He went quiet at that, and he stared at me and I stared back, and he blinked first because he could see that I meant it, which indeed I did, knowing full well that I wouldn't be the first Sea Service officer who'd used such means to enforce discipline.

One specific discipline that I inflicted on the squadron – the whole squadron of King's ships and Indiamen together – was to beat to quarters and run out the guns at least once every week, whether in harbour or under way, and without warning given in advance. The Indiamen hated that. It disturbed their nice routine, and sometimes roused even officers out of their sleep – *oh dear me: when I was just dropping off!* They hated it even more when I made them burn powder in live-firing practise – *oh dear me: the expense and the mess!* But serve 'em right. What if the French fell on us and the Indiamen weren't ready to fight?

But finally, on Thursday, September 21ˢᵗ, the day came, with the sun high, the sky blue, and all miseries blown away by a stiff easterly, and the whole great sprawling fleet of us could smile with relief and get our anchors aboard and make sail on our chosen courses. But first I had a gun fired aboard *Euphonides* for attention, and then the signal for the convoy to make sail went aloft, and the rest of the lesser fry merchantmen all knew that they must hold back, and wait their turn until King George's ships were on their way, with John Company's astern of them.

I should stress, however that getting the anchor aboard was a heavy task needing the united efforts of every seaman aboard. An anchor aboard *Euphonides* was a massive work of twisted hemp, eight inches in diameter, one hundred fathoms long, and weighing over twelve tons. Add to that, something over two tons for the best bower anchor, and you have over fourteen tons weight to lift. The power for that was provided by the capstan which was on the gun deck, and poked up through the quarterdeck. Thus there were two levels at which the hands could heave the bars around, and heave means *push* in case you didn't know because you didn't step backwards at the capstan! Since each capstan had twelve bars, and each bar took six men, that was supposedly one hundred and forty-four men, but the more the better if you could cram them in, and I've had near two hundred at the bars in my time.

Of course, a ship's cable was too fat to be bent around the capstan, so a smaller rope called the messenger went round the capstan in a continuous loop running to pulleys on the fo'c'sle then back to the capstan, and the cable was bound – temporarily – to the messenger by six-foot lengths of rope called *nippers*. The nippers were clapped on smartly at the bow as the cable came aboard, then the seamen who'd clapped on the nipper walked beside it, as messenger and cable were hauled towards the capstan, then they smartly took off the nipper, so the cable could make its way past the capstan, for storage down below. Then the men doubled back to the bow to put on the nippers again: and so on, and so on.

All of which, incidentally, is *not* the reason why young boys are called nippers. In any ship under my command the work was done by the lower deck's elite: the nimble top-men, who worked the most lofty rigging, and were the smartest men in the ship, and who could show initiative when needed. It had to be them, because getting the nippers on and off was tricky work, and nervous too, because not one man aboard was pleased if it went wrong, with the capstan jammed, or fingers torn off, or tackles ruined. They weren't pleased at all, my jolly boys, and your Uncle Jacob certainly wasn't, so it was never a job that I gave to little boys.

Then, when the cable came up off the sea-bed, and made its way through the hawse-holes in the bow, it came in stinking and slimy, with mud, weeds and oysters attached, so there had to be a team of men scrubbing and cleaning and others working the elm-tree pumps, forcing water through canvas hoses, to wash off the foulness before the cable went below. Finally, down in the cable tier on the orlop, there were forty or fifty men, sat on their haunches handling the great, wet weight of the cable, and coiling it nice and neat, over the gratings that allowed water to drip down into the bilges, so the cable could dry out, and all of this was careful teamwork every bit as much as it was heavy hauling.

Last of all, it was the responsibility of the boatswain and his mates, to get the dead weight of the anchor *catted and fished*: meaning properly secured so the sea couldn't sweep it off when we got under way. So, with a lieutenant in charge with mids to run his orders, it was a task for three hundred men aboard a big ship, and that's *if* you were lucky enough to have that number. And of course, with ships in company it was a race, because no captain wanted to be the poor lubber whose people were last to get the anchor up. So there was singing of chanties, and boatswain's mates bellowing, and the rope's end working in ships that needed it, which no ship of mine ever did. Instead, aboard *Euphonides* I always had a fiddler sat on the capstan head to give time to the men, while the other musicians heaved with the rest, since they had to be seamen first and last.

So I would ask you to think on all that, my lads and lassies, next time you are aboard a modern ship, and the chain cable comes rattling aboard all by itself, under steam power and because someone has pulled a lever.

But once all was complete, and the squadron under way and keeping station, I sent the men to their dinners, it being the end of the forenoon watch. As ever they shovelled down their food, and took their grog and all was merry. They'd done a seamanly job of getting under way and were rightly proud of it. Then a few days later, when ship and squadron had settled down to a sea-going routing, I gave a formal dinner for my officers to celebrate our being free of the Downs and the Goodwin Sands. It was good dinner, but I learned something that wasn't good. Something that was going on among the foremast hands.

I'd had a pig slaughtered from those I took aboard, my cook had done his best, there were still some fresh greens and potatoes in store, and all the wine that a seaman needed to make merry, and the motion was steady enough that nothing got itself off the cloth and on to the deck. With myself at the head of the table, there were nine of us: four Sea Service lieutenants, the master, the Lieutenant of Marines, the chaplain, purser, and surgeon. It was a captain's duty to entertain his officers lavishly, and I had the money for it, the dinner was a good one, and the drink went down. My only problem was having Pyne, the first lieutenant on my right, who I always found a dull man. But that evening he had something to say. He said it first to O'Flaherty, the master, who was sitting opposite.

'Have you heard about the bald man, Mr O'Flaherty?'

'Meaning myself?' said O'Flaherty and laughed.

'No,' said Pyne, who could never spot a joke, 'I mean the bald man that the people are talking about.'

'Oh,' said Pyne, and he looked at me and shrugged.

'What's this, Mr Pyne?' I asked, and the chatter round the table fell silent, and I noticed that the servants – lower deck hands in white gloves – had stopped going round with the drink, and were looking shifty at one another. 'Go on, Mr Pyne,' I said, 'I've been below with my papers and haven't gone round the decks this watch.' At least that's what I told him. The truth was that I'd spent so much time worrying about Kilbride and Japan, that other things had been shoved out of my mind.

'Well, Sir,' said Pyne, 'It's just that the gossip on the lower deck, is that there was a bald man among the hands in the cable tier when we got up anchor, and ...' He sniffed and wondered how to go on.

'And?' I said,

'And the hands are saying, Sir, that nobody knows who he is or when he came aboard.'

'Nonsense,' I said, 'We've been at sea these many weeks past and no more crewmen have come aboard.'

'Yes, Sir,' said Pyne, 'But the people are still saying they saw him.' He looked at O'Flaherty for support. O'Flaherty nodded.

'I've heard the same,' he said, and looked along the table.

'So have I,' said Tildesley, the second lieutenant, 'the men in my division are talking about him.'

'Mine too,' said Allen, the third lieutenant, and all the rest nodded, except the purser, the surgeon and the chaplain, and the cabin was now so quiet, we could hear the timbers working and the rudder creaking.

'So who is he?' I said.

'Nobody knows,' said Pyne.

'But they say he keeps coming back,' said Tildesley, 'the top-men see him out at the end of a yard when they go aloft.'

'That's right,' said Pyne, 'he's never alongside, he's always at the far end, and then when you look back … he's not there. But mostly he's in the cable tier.'

'One of my men said the same, said Norton, the Lieutenant of Marines, 'My sergeant saw the bald man from behind – just a glance – the sergeant was going below himself, but when he got down the companionway, there was nobody there.

'Perhaps he'd gone to the cable tier,' I said, 'at the double.'

'Yes, Sir,' said Norton but he didn't believe me. Then, perhaps because of my preoccupation with Kilbride, I let the matter slip. After all there was plenty else to do in keeping nine East Indiamen and six warships in proper formation, which meant the Indiamen in a great square of ranks of three abreast, and with a frigate and a sloop on either side of the square, with fast little *Spicer* ahead, and *Euphonides* astern and downwind, where she could bring heavyweight support to any part of the fleet if need be. This meant a formation over a mile long and wide, if safe distance were to be maintained between ships, which in turn meant each ship was out of hailing distance of the others, and signalling had to be smart, and smartly obeyed.

Our course was southward down the Bay of Biscay, past France, Spain and Gibraltar, then down the coast of Africa where it would get stinking hot and the pitch would bubble in the seams. Then we would round the Cape of Good hope and enter the Indian Ocean. But that was many weeks ahead, and at first we sailed in what was comfortable summer weather for the northern latitudes, and I have to admit that despite the less than perfect relations between the Sea Service and John Company, the nine Indiamen maintained decent station and gave me no troubles thus far. After all, each one of the nine was a magnificent and vastly expensive, triumph of the ship-builders art, and contained vastly precious cargoes.

So John Company wasn't going to put such ships under the command of fools, and the captains understood the need for convoy discipline even if they pretended they didn't.

So the days went on, the convoy sailed steadily south, we passed other vessels: mostly British men-o-war and a few neutrals, no French cruisers appeared, we had fair weather and everything should have been happy aboard *Euphonides*. But it wasn't because the crew were beginning to sulk, and that is a very bad sign, my lads, and you must always watch out for it as a captain. You must watch out for the people not smiling. You must watch for them not wanting to dance the hornpipe to the ship's band of an evening, and especially you must watch out for a grumble or a frown when an order is given.

I freely admit that I didn't spot the signs as early as I should have. For one thing I'd never commanded a ship whose people got sulky. Always before I'd had a happy ship. That's how it was for me, and I suppose I was fortunate in that respect.

[Fletcher was not fortunate. He was idolised by the ships crews that he commanded. I have heard this from too many sources to doubt the fact. The men were happy because they were proud to serve under him. S.P.]

Finally it was Mr O'Flaherty that told me how things were. I think Pyne and the other lieutenants were embarrassed by it. So O'Flaherty had a word one morning as I came on deck. He was the oldest man aboard, he'd been my shipmate a long time and I trusted him.

'Morning, Sir!' he said, touching his hat, 'Can we have a word?'

'Of course,' I said.

'Quietly?' he said, and I saw his expression and nodded. So we went right aft, away from the quartermasters at the wheel, and the mids, and the lieutenant of the watch, and the ship's people. We went right up to the taffrail at the stern, and I could see that something was up, because just about every man on deck was glancing back at us, and then pretending not to.

'What is it then?' I said.

'It's the bald man,' he said.

'That's bloody nonsense,' I said.

'No it ain't, Jacob,' he said. I blinked at that. If he'd called me Jacob then it was serious. And it was.

'They're frightened. The people are frightened, and they're resentful that you ain't listening.'

'But nobody's said anything to me.' I said.

'Yes, we have,' he said, 'Pyne's told you, I've told you, and some of the other officers too. I winced at that. They *had* told me, but I'd not paid attention.

'So tell me again,' I said, 'and this time I'm listening.' O'Flaherty nodded and explained.

'They're seeing him all the time. The bald man. They see him below decks. They see him aloft. Anyone on his own will see him: catch sight of the bald man going round a corner, or ducking down a hatchway. And they see him especially at night, and when they look again and he's gone, and even the bloody officers are frightened to go into the cable tier alone, 'cos that's where he mostly is.'

'Well who is he?' I said, 'What is he?' O'Flaherty said nothing at first. Then he crossed himself.

'I'd rather not speak the word,' he said. I thought about that for a while.

'Do you believe all this?' I said.

'Yes,' he said, 'I've seen him myself.'

'What?'

'Yes. In the cable tier in a corner. Just a shadow of a sight as I was inspecting the cable with the boatswain. But when I looked again he was gone.'

'What did he look like?' O'Flaherty crossed himself again.

'Small. Small and bald, and not in seaman's clothes.'

'What then? What clothes?

'Landman's clothes. Shirt, vest, britches and shoes. But sort of tight and shiny.'

'What do you mean by *shiny?*'

'Sort of grey, and shiny.'

'Did the boatswain see him?'

'No.'

'Then are you really sure you saw him.' O'Flaherty nodded.

'As sure as I'm seeing you now. I saw him and you've got to do something about him, or we'll have a mutiny on this ship.'

'What?

174

'Mutiny, Jacob. The lower deck is talking about abandoning ship, and taking to the boats, to beg passage on the other ships of the fleet.'

'Good God!' I said.

'Aye,' said O'Flaherty, 'Think of God! Think of The Almighty! And perhaps you could start by talking to the chaplain?' So I did. I spoke to Dr Goodsby. I sent for him to come to my day cabin where we could talk in private, and got another surprise.

'Do sit down, Dr Goodsby,' I said as he entered. The cabin was small with just a table, cupboards and pigeon-holes for charts, a couple of chairs, and my quadrant and glass hung on hooks.

'Is this about the bald man, Sir?' he said, 'The gentlemen of the gun-room are talking of little else, so I do hope that I shall not let you down.' That was a puzzler. He was straight to the point without being told. I looked at him. He was clever and highly-educated man, quite young for a ship's chaplain, with very black hair, a high brow and a large, thin nose. He looked steadily at me with a regretful, pained expression.

'Let you down?' I said, 'What do you mean?'

'Well, Sir,' he said, 'the gentlemen of the gun-room, keep asking me to conduct a service of exorcism within the cable-tier.'

'Do they?' I said, because it was news to me, and further evidence of how deep I'd sunk in my own worries, to the detriment of keeping aware of ship's business.

'They do indeed, Sir.' He gave a thin smile. 'But of course I can do no such thing, because exorcism is particularly a rite of the Roman church, and as such is not encouraged within the Anglican Community.'

'Isn't it though?' I said.

'Indeed it is not, Sir,' he said, 'and the rite may not be performed by an Anglican priest without the permission of the Diocesan Bishop, though of course no such rank applies in this case, and I suppose that we should need to apply to the Chaplain General of the Admiralty, who is at this moment in London.'

'Oh,' I said, 'Well can't you hold some sort of other service? Preach a bit? Tell the ship's people that it's all damned – Sorry Dr Goodsby – I mean *absolute* nonsense?' He came over very awkward at that, and wrung his hands and searched for words.

'With regret, Sir, I doubt that I can. I have not the charisma of a preacher.' He paused and lowered his voice. 'Nor quite the conviction.'

'Conviction?' I said, 'Conviction? What do you mean by that?' His voice went even softer and he avoided my eyes.

'Well, Sir, consider such concepts as the immaculate conception, transubstantiation and the Holy Trinity.'

'What about them?'

'Well, Sir, while they may be noble concepts, who can believe them as fact?'

'What?' I said, '*What?*' I couldn't have been more surprised if he'd declared loyalty to France and sung the Marseillaise. 'What's the matter with you?' I said, 'You're Ship's Chaplain! Don't you believe in God and the Devil and all that?'

'*Ahem,*' he said. Just that and nothing more.

'Then what are you doing here?'

'Well, Sir, you see, my eldest brother was sent into the army, my next eldest was sent to read law, and there were three of us and that left the Church for me.' I was amazed: astounded.

'Are you telling me you never wanted to be a bloody angel-maker in the first place?' I said, 'Don't you fellows have a calling? A word in the ear from God?'

'Not in my case, captain,' he said, 'and I must confess to you now, something that you might not comprehend. The truth is, Sir, that I have always had a natural talent for financial calculation, and always believed that commerce enhances the general wealth of mankind, and therefore I would have chosen …' His voice nearly died away in shame, ' … I would have chosen a career … a career which my father would not permit … and which you, as a man of action, would surely disdain … a career in *trade.*'

Well, my jolly boys, I nearly died of strangulation, covering up the laughter at that one! But it was the end of my seeking help from the Church, and I learned the lesson that we all think we are unique. We think we are the only one, and we're not, because we're all one of a kind in one way or another. None the less, the bald man had to be dealt with, and I was obliged to do the best that I could, all by myself. So I did, and I hope that none of you, who read this, will ever suffer the terror that consumed me in the doing of it.

CHAPTER 27

'General Yoshida continues to amaze the army. He is a student of the Chinese master Sun Tzu who wrote a book on the art of warfare, thirteen hundred years ago. Thus Yoshida's orders are not those of a Japanese General, and yet they are profoundly wise'

(From a letter of Tuesday, January 16th 1798, from Kaito Watanabe to his father Lord Gakuto Watanabe, in Edo Province.)

Supreme General Yoshida rode forward with his staff officers – the five Chinese and the two Japanese – accompanied by a cavalry troop of his personal escort. Iron hooves rumbled on the main bridge into the city of Kagominato. Only days ago the bridge had been in ruins, destroyed by Hitamoto explosions that blew planks and beams into splinters. But not now: now the engineers of the Tokugawa expeditionary force had spliced in fresh timber and laid a new roadway, just as they had built the assault ramp that spanned the empty moat. The ramp was immediately to the right of Yoshida and his men as they rode across the bridge, and they gazed in admiration at so impressive a work of fascines, sand-bags and rammed earth. Its construction had cost the lives of hundreds of peasants and soldiers, but finally it had reared up so perfectly over the walls of the city, that the very first wave of Tokugawa infantry had gone over, in one great push, despite the deadly response of the Hitamoto defenders, with arrows, gunfire and hand-to-hand combat.

'Banzai! Banzai! Banzai!' The Tokugawa sentries raised arms and cheered as their general passed through the heavily fortified main gate-way, under the fighting top with its crenelations and arquebus-loops. Then rumbling hoof-beats changed to a clatter, as Yoshida and his men rode into the paved streets of the town, and looked at the utter ruin that the Hitamoto had made of every single building before withdrawing: houses torched, livestock slaughtered, pottery smashed, plants trampled. And of course, there were corpses everywhere. There were corpses of men, of women and of children. But these were disappearing fast: bourne away by the thousands of peasants who did the army's digging and heavy lifting. These humble workers stripped the dead of armour and weapons, stacked these valuables for the clerks to note, then carried away the human wreckage on stretchers at a swift trot, to fill two mass graves outside the city: one for the honourably fallen Tokugawa, and one for the Hitamoto traitors.

Of course, they stopped and bowed as General Yoshida and his staff rode by, but then they moved on again with the stoic discipline of peasants. They had been ordered to clear the town of dead within two days, and they would do it. They would do it very thoroughly, and very promptly, because they very well knew the penalties for failure.

Meanwhile the engineers were busy putting out the fires still raging in parts of the town, causing clouds of smoke to sting the eyes and make men cough. Their work was too important for interruption, but that still left thousands of Tokugawa infantrymen, in their black armour, to line the broken streets to cheer their commander as he entered in triumph.

General Yoshida received a formal greeting in the Great Plaza of Kagominato in front of the Okobo Buddhist temple, the Temple of the Ancestors, and the Palace of the Daimyo's Regent. The greeting was given by the senior surviving officer – the *only* surviving officer – of the assault team that had taken the city. He was Major Akinari Igarishi, just eighteen years old, who stood with a chosen company of those of his men who had been first over the wall behind him. The square had once been beautified with carvings, ceramics, paintings and statues since Kagominato had been very rich. But now everything was black with smoke, every building had lost its roof, devastation was everywhere, and all of it caused by the fixed determination of Clan Hitamoto to leave nothing behind for Clan Tokugawa.

Yoshida ignored all this. He dismounted, and before any other man could move, Supreme General Yoshida bowed to Major Igarishi! It was a colossal honour which brought tears to that young man's eyes, and huge cheers from the men standing behind Igarishi, and nobody who witnessed this gracious moment, ever forgot it. Neither did they forget the conversation which followed.

'You did well Akinari Igarishi!' said Yoshida, 'Your bravery will be remembered.'

'You are too kind, Lord Yoshida,' said Igarishi, 'I merely followed my superior officers, all of whom fell bravely in the first rank of the assault.'

'They too will be of good memory,' said Yoshida, in his awkward, Chinese-accented speech, 'but celebrated later. Now there is much work. Give your report, Akinari Igarishi!' Igarishi bowed low, then beckoned to a follower – a clerk – who came forward with a scroll, bowing repeatedly, before falling to his knees and offering it to Yoshida,

'The names of our honoured dead are written here, Lord Yoshida. Nine hundred and seventy-five were lost in the battle, and others wounded.' Yoshida took the scroll, unrolled it and spent a full and proper moment in reverent contemplation. Then he bowed again.

'I salute them,' he said and gave the scroll to one of his own followers, who took it and bowed as Igarishi continued.

'Six hundred and twenty-four Hitamoto soldiers were killed,' said Igarishi, 'together with numerous civilians and peasants. Also, two thousand five hundred and ten prisoners were taken, including those wounded. All these prisoners are still alive, as are many civilians who were captured, and all of these – whether soldiers or civilians – have been fed and protected.' Igarishi paused. He was very unsure of himself. He sought reassurance.

'I hope I did right, my Lord. My honoured superiors told me that it was your order that any Hitamoto soldier who was taken alive was to be spared. My honoured superiors told me that, and I followed the command of my honoured superiors, all of whom are now dead.'

'Ah!' said Yoshida, and Igarishi stood in great fear because he knew very well that it was not the samurai way to allow traitors to live, let alone feed them and care for them.

'Good!' said Yoshida, and Igarishi nearly fainted with relief, 'That is good because the teaching of Sun Tzu is that no prisoner must be killed, since this would cause the rest to fight to the last, while best victory is won by persuading the enemy to surrender. This is cheapest way to win a battle. This is the word of Sun Tzu!'

'Yes, my Lord,' said Igarishi and bowed again.

'Now, Akinari Igarishi,' said Yoshida, 'Show me the famous harbour and the ships.'

'Hi!' said Igarishi.

So a horse was found for Igarishi, and he was commanded to ride alongside Yoshida, and the whole troop of mounted men passed through the miserable, smoking ruins, until they reached the great lagoon of the harbour, where the sea breeze blew away the smoke. Yoshida looked at everything and nodded in satisfaction. The air was fresh, the sky was clear, seagulls called, the view over the harbour was beautiful. It was a happy moment. The harbour was indeed magnificent. It was formed by two broad and high headlands capped with pine forest, that stretched out, then narrowed enclosing a vast body of calm waters where countless ships could rest at anchor in safety from the anger of the sea. But today there were few ships in the harbour. Most had been burned and sunk by the Hitamoto, and others had fled. Yoshida nodded again, while horses stamped, harness jingled, and cavalrymen shifted in their saddles, straining to keep formation.

'Huh!' said Yoshida, finally. 'Tell me, Akinari Igarishi, how many ships got away?'

'Five,' said Igarishi, and suffered another moment of doubt because even now he could not entirely believe that what he had done was correct. 'I held back my men, and we let the ships sail. Five ships sailed, my Lord, each one full of Hitamoto soldiers.' Igarishi swallowed, paused and continued, 'I did this because my honoured superiors told me that you, my Lord and General, had ordered that any defeated Hitamoto who ran to the ships, should be allowed to escape.'

'Good!' said Yoshida, 'You did well. It is the teaching of Sun Tzu that enemy should never be surrounded. Surrounded enemy fights hard. If enemy has path of escape he will take it, and not fight to desperate last.' Yoshida looked at Igarishi's astounded face and said, 'How many escaped, Akinari Igarishi? Tell me that?'

'Perhaps five hundred,' said Igarishi, 'we could not count them.'

'No matter,' said Yoshida, 'we have won a Sun Tzu victory!' He waved a hand at the harbour. 'And what matter five hundred, when our Lord Shogun will send a hundred thousand men from here.'

CHAPTER 28

It was a Saturday when I discovered that our chaplain was an atheist so at least I didn't have to wait long for a suitable occasion to address all hands in the matter of the Bald Man. That occasion was Sunday Service, routinely held every week aboard ship, since Article one of King George's *Articles of War* – the very first one, mind you – required that:

> *'All Commanders, Captains, and Officers in, or belonging to any of His Majesty's Ships or Vessels of war, shall cause the public worship of Almighty God, according to the Liturgy of the church of England established by law, to be solemnly, orderly and reverently performed in their respective ships.'*

If the weather was kind, and the enemy not actually alongside and firing, Sunday Service always followed the other major ceremony of the week, which was Captain's Inspection, when the ship's mighty ruler went round with his first lieutenant, to study the ship's gear and people, with the aforesaid gear and people having first been scrubbed to special perfection. That meant myself and Mr Pyne going round the ship, though with Pyne as first lieutenant the inspection was a formality. The man was a dull shipmate but he was dedicated to his duties. He bore down hard on any sign of slackness, and I'd seen him with my own eyes bending down to look *under* the gun carriages in search of dirtiness.

This was especially so as regards the underneath of Number 5 gun on the larboard main-deck, because that was the chosen dining room of Jimbo the cat, where he took fresh-caught rats for immediate consumption of the tasty bits, leaving blood-dripping remains for later, thereby inflicting nasty stains on the snow-white deck for the gun-crew to make snow-white again.

None the less, I went round with Pyne, because it enabled me to see the men in their stations and judge their mood, looking always for sulking as I have said before. So, on that Sunday I realised how slack I had been myself, in not noticing before that the ship's crew were not happy, and that included officers and warrant officers and even such redoubtables as the boatswain, gunner and carpenter. They weren't happy because they were troubled in mind, and it *wasn't* that they were sulking, which I would have dealt with easily by knocking down the first one who displayed any sign of it. I'd have knocked him down there and then, and that would have been the end of it and I recommend it to all you youngsters as the kindest and gentlest way to manage a ship's crew, and better by far than such cruelties as flogging or stopping a man's grog.

No, it wasn't sulking. Instead it was glum faces, and men not looking at me straightforward and shuffling their feet and giving out sighs, which just ain't natural in seafaring men. Worse still I heard mutterings from those not directly in my eye. Indeed the sound followed me round the ship like a ghostly dog. Thus as soon as I and Pyne, left one station – the foc's'le sick-bay, or wherever, I heard a murmuring behind me such as I'd never heard before, and which shook me because I'd always believed ship's discipline was an easy matter for me to maintain, and the hands willing and cheerful. So finally, while inspecting the light room of the magazine, and the Gunner and his mates outside, I spoke to Pyne.

'What's going on?' I said, keeping my voice down, 'What's wrong with 'em?' He looked at me all miserable, giving a sigh of his own, and then said nothing. He just stood looking at me and deep embarrassed. 'Well?' I said, 'What is it? Damn-well tell me?'

'Sir,' he said, 'It's difficult.'

'Look here, Pyne,' I said, 'spit it out! There's nobody here but us two. Tell me!'

'Well, Sir,' he said, 'the men are disappointed.'

'Disappointed in bloody what?'

'In you, Sir.'

'In me? What'd you damn-well mean *in me*?'

'It's the Bald Man, Sir. The men think you aren't listening to them, and with all due respect, Sir, you aren't,' he got properly under way after that, 'We've tried to tell you, Sir. I've tried, Mr O'Flaherty has tried, the others have tried. The man are coming to us and telling us, and you aren't listening. The men like you, Sir, you know that. They always did, and they'd follow you anywhere. But now they're disappointed in you.'

182

That was a blow, I can tell you. It hit hard. It hit very hard indeed because Pyne was right. I'd been away in my own worries and I'd not taken the Bald Man seriously, even when O'Flaherty warned me. In fact, by then, having found out that Dr Goodsby the chaplain was no use, I'd already decided to do something myself. But I hadn't told anybody, had I? Nobody knew that I was going to try my best, and all hands aboard *Euphonides* thought that I just didn't care. It was a nasty moment because guilt is a painful thing when you're forced to admit it in yourself.

But the sea life breeds action in the face of troubles and teaches there's no use in dwelling on past sorrows. So:

'Right, Mr Pyne,' I said, 'That's enough of the inspection. I'll have all hands aft for Sunday Service, with hats off, the people mustered by divisions, and the band stood ready.' Pyne liked that. He stood up straight, and smiled and saluted, poor devil, because he thought that Jumping Jack Fletcher was going to put everything right. Oh dear. Oh dear me indeed. So there was a bellowing of orders and a great rushing and a pounding of feet, as the crew gathered, and I took my sedate time in getting up on the quarterdeck, where the ship's gentlemen were paraded in their dress uniforms, and Dr Goodsby, in his clerical robes and a bible in his hands, and a Union Flag draped over the quarterdeck rail as an altar. The ship's band were there too, and the marines with their muskets, and I got myself to the rail, looked down on the eager faces on the main-deck, and I saw that the word had gone round that I was going to step up to the mark. Oh dear, again.

So I put my faith in music to begin with, since music was a cherished part of life aboard *Euphonides*, and Sunday Service always began with a hymn.

'Bandmaster?' I cried.

'Sir?' he said.

'*All Creatures of our God and King!*'

'Aye-aye, Sir!' and he waved his baton and the band thumped and blew and the crew lifted up their voices in the old hymn that was one of their favourites, because it had a deep and rousing melody and the words were most fitting for seamen, especially the bit about *Thou rushing wind that art so strong, and ye clouds that sail in Heaven along.* It was all fine and proper.

[Fletcher stopped dictating at this point and burst into song, giving

183

the hymn in question, obliging me to join in, and giving it with such volume that others of the household came into the room and sang with us. S.P.]

When the singing finished everyone looked at me, because everyone was waiting to hear what I had to say. I'd already half decided, and I think a part of my mind must have been pondering while the rest of me was singing. So I had no trouble in turning out a speech, and if it wasn't as good as those of the Honourable Members who knock seven bells out of each other in the House of Commons, at least it served.

'Now then,' I cried in my best hail-the-masthead shout, 'I hear there's trouble on the lower deck.' That was met with silence. Surly silence. This time it *was* surliness because they didn't like it. But you have to construct a speech that way. Lead 'em into the dark before you bring 'em into the light. So I went on, 'I hear there's trouble on the lower deck, and dissatisfaction with the lawful command of this ship, as authorised by King George and Their Lordships.' Perhaps I pushed it too far, because there were growls of anger from the people, and even the mids and officers were scowling. So now for the turn. 'I hear that this ship's crew are not happy,' I cried, 'They ain't happy with someone that is recently come aboard.'

'Oh?' said their faces, 'What does he mean by that?' and the growls and surliness began to fade.

'I hear that a man is come aboard,' I said, 'who hasn't the courage to step out and face this ship's company, since he knows that every man aboard is a true British Tar, that loves Old England, and damns King George's enemies!' Note well the manner of my speech, my jolly boys, because you should always imitate it under similar circumstances. Thus the men think 'Old England' means their homes and mothers, and you should always end by directing their anger at the French or whoever else we might be fighting at that moment, which usually does mean the French.

With that I was anchored safe in port. They cheered and nudged one another, and their dear little faces beamed with joy, because Jacky Flash was Jacky Flash again. Or so they thought, and now it was my job to clinch the deal in such a way as would please the aforesaid true British Tars.

'I'm speaking of the Bald Man,' I said, and their mood shifted again, because outright mention of the Bald Man frightened them. I could see lips trembling and messmates glancing at each other for support. 'Yes, lads,' I said, 'The Bald Man! The man in shiny grey! The man who won't show his face and who lives in the cable tier.' I'd got them now. There was silence and wondering, and I felt how an actor feels when he's on stage, and his audience is listening hard. 'So, my lads, this is what I'm going to do. I'm going to sling my hammock in the cable tier this night and every other night, until either the Bald Man gets out of our ship, or he comes to see me … in which case I shall take him by the arse of his britches and heave him over the side!'

Well, the cheers I got at that, must have been heard from one end of the squadron to the other. Then afterwards we had the rest of Sunday Service, with Goodsby preaching his usual short and light sermon, then a few more hymns and concluded with all hands merry and bright, including myself until six bells of the first watch – that's eleven p.m. shore time – when it was dark, and I was tired, and I would have normally have gone to my cot in the stern cabin. But I couldn't do that because everyone was waiting for me to go down to the cable tier, where a hammock had been slung for me, all nice and cosy, with a wash-stand and chamber pot alongside of it, and a table to put my clothes and gear upon.

It was an easy-sailing night, we were off the southern coast of Spain, it was comfortably warm, the ship rolled along steadily, the squadron rolled on ahead of us, with even the East Indiamen keeping station. The masts and yards stretched up above, the stars were above them, and we were making eight knots under topsails, t'gallants and stay-sails. All was neat and tight, and the ship should have been quiet, but wasn't because the decks were alive with all hands present in the gloom, waiting to see me go below where not one single one of them would go alone, at night. Not even the officers would do that, except Dr Goodsby perhaps, who was true to his lack of beliefs and assured me repeatedly that there was nothing waiting down below. Indeed he made point of coming to see me so that he could pass on his detailed opinion in the matter.

'There is nothing there, Sir,' he said. 'There is nothing there, because nothing of that kind exists at all.' He gazed at me full of earnest conviction, 'I am convinced of this because I support the contentions of the ancient Greek Epicurus, as modified by the modern philosopher Hume, who insists that there is probably no god and definitely no afterlife.'

'Well, Dr Goodsby,' I said, 'thank you for that cheerful statement, but in that case can you tell me why the hands keep seeing the Bald Man?

And since you *are* ship's Chaplain, whatever contentions you support, I wonder if you wouldn't mind going down to the cable tier in my place?' He said nothing, so I prompted him, 'Wouldn't you just like to do that for me? Since there's nothing down there?'

'Ah!' he said, 'Ah!' and cleared his throat and looked away.

So there was your Uncle Jacob, my jolly boys, tucked up in the cable tier, in the dark, among the rats that squeaked and scampered because, even Jimbo the cat wouldn't go down there just now.

But first a word about the cable tier itself. Aboard a frigate like *Euphonides,* the uppermost decks were the forecastle at the bow, which was level with the quarterdeck at the stern, leaving a gap amidships. Next came the main-deck, running bow to stern with the ship's main battery of guns. Next was the lower deck where the crew had their messes and, below that was the orlop deck, lit by lanterns and too low for a man to stand fully upright. It was mainly a storage place, but the surgeon worked down there, and the mids had their messes. Below even that was the bilge space, with its ballast and the heaviest of the ship's stores including the massive barrels of drinking water.

So let's go back to the orlop: the home of the ship's cables. *Euphonides* had eight of these 100-fathom monsters, plus a family of smaller hawsers and ropes, which weighed fifty tons in total when dry, and a great deal more when wet. Thus the cable tier was large: about sixty feet long by ten feet wide. It was in the centre of the ship, and its deck wasn't a deck at all, because it wasn't planked over. This left the cables resting on timbers running athwart-ships, with gaps between, so that wet cables could drip into the ballast, adding to the bilge water that came in through the count-less tiny leaks of a wooden ship, and which drained into the ship's well to be pumped out every day.

The cables were thereby encouraged to get dry, or what passed for dry aboard ship, which meant permanently, stinking damp. For the same reason, the cable tier was never enclosed by complete bulkheads, but by panels with big holes cut in them, to encourage the damp to get out. But it never completely did, and while the ship's rats liked the cable tier, nobody else did, and you wouldn't choose to sleep in it, even if there was nothing nasty down there with you.

So I admit that I had the horrors when I finally get into my hammock with the ship's noises all around, and things shifting as the ship rolled, convincing me that something was creeping up in the dark, with deadly intent. But I didn't dare give up because a greater fear kept me down there: fear of failure and humiliation. So I stayed, and it wasn't nice, and it wasn't comfortable, and I was a long time getting to sleep. But I did in the end, at least for a while.

Then in the middle of the night, my heart nearly burst out of my chest, as something touched me, and I jerked awake, and lashed out as if boarders were coming at me with cold steel, and I rolled out of the hammock onto damp cable, and lay there soaked in fright, with one dim lantern swinging somewhere above me, and myself peering into the depths of the cable tier which was more shadows than light, and I looked for the Bald Man or something even worse, and I reached out for my sword and pistols that I'd brought with me in case there was nothing supernatural down there at all, but merely , something physical and relatively harmless, like a demented ape with the rabies.

But nothing happened. Nothing came forward. Nothing appeared. And then – oh hell-fire and damnation – *there was a pair of little eyes shining in the lantern light not six feet away.* My heart nearly burst itself in fright until I realised that it was a bloody damned rat that was so cheeky as to sit up on its hind legs staring at me! By God it gave me a fright. I threw one of my shoes at it, and missed, and it ran away and I tried to laugh but couldn't. At least I realised what had touched me. My hammock was slung so low as to brush against the coils of hemp, and one of the little blighters must have climbed up and run across me.

Then I fell asleep again. I fell asleep until four bells of the Morning Watch – six a.m. shore time, and I found that I was still alive, nothing had grabbed me, nothing had appeared, nothing happened at all. So I dressed, and washed in cold water and went up on deck, to be received as a hero by all hands aboard.

'Good morning, Sir!'
'Good morning, Sir!'
'Good morning, Sir!'

The weather was fine, and there were smiles left right and centre. And so to another day, and another run of one hundred and fifty miles due south, and the squadron behaving, and no sign of the enemy, and all the usual routine, of watches, breakfast, dinner and tea, and the noon observation, and the finding of our position by clock, lunar and spherical trigonometry, until the ship's bell once again struck six bells of the First Watch, and down I went again to the cable tier.

I wish I could say that it wasn't so bad the second time. But it was, and it was just as bad for each of the five more times I went down there again, because every single time I got into that hammock, the marrow of my bones told me that *this* was the moment when *it* would come because *it* had merely been waiting its time. But nothing happened other than the undeniable fact that the ship's crew were bouncing with delight, and I was their hero because here hadn't been one single sighting of the Bald Man, since your Uncle Jacob took up residence in the cable tier.

So finally I decided that enough was enough. A full week had gone round, it was Captain's Inspection and Sunday Service again. The crew were mustered in their best. We sang hymns, Goodsby preached, and I spoke. I gave them details of our position, and course – which was always my custom – and told them that they'd all been loyal hearts and true, this commission, and I cursed the French a bit more for good measure as a captain always should, then I ended with:

'Well, lads,' I said, 'as for our good friend the Bald Man, I've given him every chance to present himself to me, seeking duties aboard ship, and he's not come. So! Has anyone else seen him?' I point out here that I'd take damn good care to check with my officers that nobody *had* seen him or I'd never have asked that question.

'No! No! No!' they cried, then 'three cheers for the captain!' and they chanted 'Jacky Flash! Jacky Flash! Jacky Flash!'

'Thank you, lads,' I said, 'And the offer stands, to the Bald Man, wherever he may be, that I am here, ready and waiting, and at his disposal, but he's to come and see me and not bother anyone else!' By Jove but I got some cheers for that, and it was all very jolly, my jolly boys. Very jolly indeed. It was most incredibly jolly until six bells of the First Watch, when I went back to my cabin and my comfortable cot. But what happened then wasn't jolly at all, because I didn't get into my cot that night, believe me I didn't.

Now a sea-cot such as mine was not something for infants, but a light-weight box with low, canvas sides and the bedding enclosed, and which was slung from the deck-head by lines. It was slung fore-and-aft so that when the ship rolled, the cot didn't because it swung like a pendulum, which was all very neat and soothing. So when I'd done washing my face and scrubbing my teeth, I undressed and put on a flannel night-shirt, and got alongside of the cot, and seized hold of the sides, and prepared to swing myself aboard, which has to be done in one sure go, or everything slips away and you fall on the cruel hard deck.

But this time I didn't swing myself up. Instead I stood still and listened. As yet I wasn't alarmed, but I felt the urge to listen. So I did, and heard the familiar sounds of the ship, and a boatswain's mate yelling at someone for being a no-seaman swab … and then I got the feeling that I wasn't alone. So I listened harder because nobody had come into the cabin, and as ever there was a marine on guard outside my door. So nobody could have got past him. Yet I still felt I wasn't alone.

That wasn't nice. It wasn't nice at all. I was now sure I wasn't alone, and I should have turned to see who was there. But I didn't turn. I couldn't turn. I couldn't turn because a most dreadful fear had come over me. The horrors I'd felt down on the cable tier were nothing compared with this, and I was paralysed with fear such as I'd never felt in all life before. It was far, far worse than a boarding action or being under fire, because then you don't have time to be afraid. But I did then, and a vast, deep fear grabbed hold of me and sunk me in such agony that I felt I couldn't bear it, and it all stemmed from my certain conviction that something was in the cabin with me. It was in there with me and was coming closer every second, and the deep down soul of me believed that if the something touched me, then that would be the end of everything and myself damned and lost.

Then the thought came over me even as I sweated and trembled, that my only hope was to turn around and see what was coming after me. I knew that for plain truth – don't ask why because I have no answer – I only knew that I had to turn. But I couldn't do it! I simply couldn't, even though every hair on my body was standing straight up, and the flesh of my back was creeping. It was like the dreams when you have to run but your legs are lead: like that but worse because of the fear.

So I tried again. I tried but couldn't do it. I tried with clenched teeth and strained muscles. But I couldn't do it. I tried and tried. I still couldn't do it. Then I felt something on the back of my neck. Something was breathing on me. I was done for. It had got me. So I screamed and roared and yelled in my terror … and something snapped. It was like a ship's cable parting under load. Something snapped, and the fear went, and I was hanging on to the side of my cot and the cabin door was bursting open and O'Flaherty and Pyne were grabbing hold of me, with the marine sentry in tow, and my steward behind him, and various others of the ship's people behind them. I blinked and blinked and looked round and I saw there was nothing there other than them, and they were all speaking at once. 'What is it, Sir?' said Pyne.

'Jacob? Jacob?' said O'Flaherty.

'What is it Cap'n,' said the marine, 'Where's the bugger gone?'

I seized on that.

'What bugger?' I said.

'Him as you was shoutin' at, Sir!' said the marine.

'Jacob?' said O'Flaherty, 'listen to me! Are you all right, lad?'

'Yes, yes,' I said, 'I'm all right. It's gone.'

'What's gone?' said Pyne, and they all looked at one another. Then:

'No, no, no,' said O'Flaherty, 'we don't want none of that. Least said, soonest mended.'

'Yes,' said Pyne, 'you're right,' and he snapped his fingers at my steward, 'Get a bottle of brandy and some glasses. At the double! And everyone else, out of here and to your duties.'

'Aye-aye!' they all said.

Soon I was sat with O'Flaherty and the brandy, and Pyne had the sense to recognise my friendship with O'Flaherty and leave us alone. He went out with a nod to O'Flaherty, who nodded back. Then the brandy definitely helped. It calmed me down, and so did O'Flaherty who spoke to me like an old uncle.

'What was it, lad?' he said, 'who were you shouting at?'

'Was I shouting?' I said.

'By Jesus, you were!' he said, 'You said *get off my ship you bloody damned bugger!* You said that and worse. Very much worse. We could all hear you. We could hear you from stem to stern, and keel to main-truck.' So we talked a while. We talked a long while. We talked about our time as shipmates because that was good, and we didn't talk about what had just happened because that was bad. We didn't talk about it then, nor ever after, and neither did any man aboard ship, at least not in public. They didn't because seamen know by hard practical experience that there are some things that you must never speak about.

So when folks say that *worse things happen at sea*, then believe it because they do. Worse things happen, and strange things, and there were a couple more besides. The first concerned myself. Over the next days, looking in the shaving mirror, I saw some lines on my face that hadn't been there before, and that was no bad thing since previously I'd looked a shade too young for a ship's captain, let alone a commodore. O'Flaherty said I looked ten years older, which would have made me thirty-two. Then over the next weeks, a grey streak appeared in my hair. It was – and is – about half an inch wide, and it ran from just above my brow. It appeared slowly, as the colour went from the roots, and the hair grew out, and I never worried about that either because the ladies always liked it. But I mention it as a matter of fact.

After that, we had a whole world of troubles in India and beyond, but the other strange thing was something that *didn't* trouble us, and that was the Bald Man, who was never seen again.

CHAPTER 29

*'Most beloved Lady Meiko, I turn to you for advice. Should I keep
faith with the purity of ancient tradition, or should I defend ancient
tradition by means which are powerful, but which would offend against
that very tradition?'*

(From a letter of Monday, January 22nd 1798, from Kimiya
Hitamoto, Daimyo of Hito Domain, to the Lady Meiko, The
House of Flowers, Port Hito.)

Lord Kimiya looked at the vessel moored alongside the principal quay of Port
Hito. It was a turtle-ship: a warship. It was a full-sized copy of a model that
had been preserved in an Okobo temple during the two hundred years when
neither Clan Hitamoto, nor any other Clan had built warships nor needed
them. But now there was such a great need that turtle-ships were under
construction in every port of Hito Island, and this was first of them, and
Lord Kimiya was here to give judgement before the others were completed.

He was here with his most senior samurai, and a great company of
soldiers who stood to attention, with only their banners stirring. Even
the hundreds of fisher-folk were silent, as they stood with their families,
with heads bowed respectfully but gazing awestruck at their Lord, whom
they had never seen so close before.

But nobody gazed harder than Lord Kimiya himself. Like all samurai he
was a creature of the land. He knew little of ships and cared less. He fully
supported the Shogun in one respect at least: that Japan should be closed
to the world, and that sea-going ships were for foreigners and should be
strictly regulated, while Japanese ships should be small, unfit for ocean
voyaging, and suitable only for inshore fishing and coastal trade. Thus –
for Lord Kimiya – there was not even the possibility of copying foreign
ships of any kind. Not fishing boats, not merchantmen, not warships.

So what was this seafaring *thing* that he had approved in principle, and was now asked to give blessing upon as the pattern for a new fleet? At least it was Japanese! He took comfort in that and looked at it from end to end. It was a hundred feet long, thirty feet wide, and had no masts or sails. It was propelled only by oarsmen deep within, working their oars through round holes cut low in the hull. Most bizarre of all, the upper hull had armoured fighting towers rising at bow and stern, but otherwise it was entirely covered with a thick, timber dome bristling with iron spikes. Hence the name turtle-ship: but Lord Kimiya thought it looked more like a hedgehog. It was a pure warship, that no enemy could take by boarding, but which could attack the enemy via the towers and loop-holes that pierced the hull for arquebus fire … and also with gun-ports for cannon fire. Lord Kimiya sighed at the thought of cannons.

Then he stood straight and looked at the ship's crew, twenty yards away, lined up on the quayside by the ship's gangplank: the captain, the oar-master, the steersman, the rowers and the gunners.

'Hi!' cried the captain as he saw Lord Kimiya look towards his crew, and every one of them bowed low. Lord Kimiya nodded in acknowledgment and beckoned one of his samurai.

'My Lord?' said the samurai.

'The captain? Is that Kazuki Tomoko?'

'Yes, my Lord. The Tomoko family is loyal. The father of Kazuki Tomoko gave his entire life to the service of my Lord Hayato, your noble father.' Lord Kimiya nodded. He knew all that. He pointed at the turtle-ship.

'And he built this ship?'

'Yes, my Lord,' said the samurai. 'He supervised the entire process: the study of the model, the design, the works in the shipyard. He did all this. He is a very able and talented man. He is expert in all matters of making and building.' Lord Kimiya nodded and waved a hand for the samurai to retire. Lord Kimiya knew very well that the Tomoko family was honourable. They were honourable, loyal samurai, but – incredibly – they were also expert seamen since their lands were coastal, and full of fishermen, and even though samurai were not supposed to take an interest in the sea, the Tomoko family had done so, and in the present time of crisis, they had become very useful.

So Lord Kimiya now beckoned Kazuki Tomoko, who bowed, and

ran towards Lord Kimiya and stood before him and bowed again. He was young man, smooth-faced, pleasing of appearance and honourably dressed in plain, black battle-armour bearing the mon of Clan Hitamoto.

'My Lord?' he said, 'I am ever at your service.'

'I will go aboard your ship,' said Lord Kimiya, 'Show me everything and explain everything.'

'Hi!' said Tomoko.

So Lord Kimiya toured the ship and hated it from the first instant, since even going aboard proved to be most unpleasant, as he realised when he stepped off the stone quayside and put his foot on the gangplank. He looked down and saw the water just twenty feet below and knew that one wrong step would drop him in his heavy armour, straight down to the muddy bottom and certain death by drowning. But he could not hesitate or show fear, so he did not, even when the gangplank moved under his feet as the ship rolled slightly. Lord Kimiya shuddered.

It was just as bad inside the great oaken turtle, because protocol required that Lord Kimiya must lead the way, even though he didn't know where he was going, and everything was dark and gloomy. There were only stabs of light coming in through the loop-holes, and the closed interior smelt of tar and damp and rope. Worst of all everything was full of a most un-Japanese clutter. There were benches and hatchways and sudden drops, and coamings and beams that seemed deliberately designed to trip the unwary. Some of the samurai who followed Lord Kimiya did indeed manage to trip and fall, or bump their helmets on the timbers, and the ship moved unpleasantly with their weight. But at least nobody fell into the harbour, and Kazuki Tomoko did his best to keep at Lord Kimiya's elbow, pointing the way, and giving warnings of obstructions until at last, and inevitably, Lord Kimiya was shown the turtle-ship's firearms.

The Tanegashima arquebuses were exactly the same as those used to defend a castle ashore, except that they were stored in waterproof cases with their matches, powder and shot, rather than hanging in racks. All this was reassuringly normal. The problem was the cannon which the warship carried as its main armament.

Tomoko explained this very carefully. 'Honoured Lord,' he said, 'I believe that we must expect an invasion of hundreds of ships?'

'Yes,' said Lord Kimiya, 'Our spies report plans for three hundred ships, and a hundred thousand men delivered in several waves.'

'Then we must break their ships,' said Tomoko, 'We don't have the numbers to board and capture. We must break as many of their ships as possible, especially those carrying soldiers.'

'Yes,' said Lord Kimiya in fear of what must follow.

'This must be done with cannon, my Lord,' said Tomoko, 'and our cannon are not good enough.' Lord Kimiya said nothing. 'May I continue, my Lord?' said Tomoko.

'Continue,' said Lord Kimiya.

'See here, my Lord,' said Tomoko, pointing to a row of six cannons bedded down against the ship's side, where gun-ports could be opened for them to fire through. He laid a hand on the nearest one, kneeling to do so because the black barrel was laid in a wooden trough at deck level. Lord Kimiya and his samurai moved close for a better look. 'This is a Japanese gun, my Lord,' said Tomoko. It is a weak gun that fires a small shot of only four pounds weight, and it is held in its carriage only with ropes,' Tomoko stood up and moved to the next gun which was of a type entirely unlike the rest. It was huge. It was long and thick, and sat high on a four-wheeled carriage, and was undeniably foreign. 'This is a Dutch gun,' said Tomoko, 'it is very powerful. It fires a shot of eighteen pounds. It has projections to each side for a strong fit to the gun-carriage. The foreigners call these projections *trunnions* and they are most clever devices and are one of many reasons why these foreign guns are better than Japanese guns.'

Tomoko paused. He was highly intelligent. Given the chance, he would have copied the Dutch warships that he had studied in detail and knew to be superior to anything Japanese. But he had asked questions and learned that Lord Kimiya would forbid anything foreign. Likewise Tomoko saw that the samurai were also looking to their master, fearing his displeasure, because his opinions were well known to them. But the threat from Tokugawa was so great that Tomoko gathered his courage and knelt before Lord Kimiya.

'My most honoured and noble Lord,' he said, 'We have very few foreign guns, all taken from ships wrecked long ago. But I have arranged for new guns to be cast as exact copies of the foreign guns. We have the craftsmen, we have the iron, we have the furnaces, and we can make the moulds. If we have these guns, then our turtle-ships – which are Japanese and traditional – can come close alongside the Tokugawa ships and smash their timbers! Thus I most humbly beg, my Lord, and as a matter of greatest urgency, for permission to begin the casting of foreign guns.'

CHAPTER 30

No ship sailed direct from England to India since you had to assume six months of sea time, and His Majesty's ships couldn't be provisioned for more than three or four months, even with the decks full of livestock as you upped anchor, and the fullest load you could cram in of clean drinking water. So the usual plan was to call in – especially for watering – at ports along the way including Cape Town, near the southernmost tip of the African continent, to take on supplies, and make repair such ship-damage as had been suffered on the way. Cape Town, meant anchoring in Table Bay, off the settlement which was on the north-facing shore, with its streets and houses on a grid like those of ancient Rome or modern America.

Given the importance of Cape Town for the East India trade, it isn't surprising that it had been much fought over since the Dutch first settled it in the 1650s. But by the time we got there it was British, with a fort and flag and a garrison, and your Uncle Jacob's squadron lay at anchor for two weeks, to fill our holds, and give the most trusted of the men a run ashore, to get properly drunk and to exercise themselves in the bawdy houses.

But I run ahead of myself. I have to report a strange omission in my career as a sea-farer which was revealed on our southward voyage in the sweltering heat where the pitch really does bubble in the seams. That omission was the fact that I'd never crossed the equator! That's because mostly my seafaring had been in northern latitudes, though I once sailed to the Bight of Benin on African business when our next destination was the Carolinas, which meant a southerly course *towards* the equator to catch the westerly winds. But we found them north of the line, never crossed it, and passed on to America.

[by 'African Business' Fletcher means the Slave Trade in which detestable interest he once sailed. It was, however, only that once and he never returned to slaving despite the enormous profits to be made. In later years, while he never expressed overt disapproval of the trade, he commented often on the pervading stench of excrement aboard slavers, with their dense-packed human cargoes, and he declared them to be *'full of filthiness, and unfit to serve on board of.'* S.P.]

Therefore, my jolly boys, in seamanly parlance your Uncle Jacob was still a *pollywog* and not a *shellback*. I was an innocent to be baptised by one of the roughest traditions of the sea life.

It began as our latitude dropped lower and lower, and each day at noon observation, the hands would grin, then most politely ask their officers when we might be crossing the line? They also began making things their officers weren't supposed to know about, down on the lower deck: things such as costumes, that the officers knew all about but grinned right along with the men and looked other way. O'Flaherty warned me what was coming and offered me the way out.

'Traditions of the Service, Sir,' he said and smiled. Everyone smiled because it was noon observation time, and the officers and mids were wielding their quadrants and taking their sights, while the hands edged closer and closer. 'But it needn't trouble you, Sir,' said O'Flaherty, because the accepted penalty is a bottle of rum to King Neptune and each of his attendants.'

'Quite so, Sir,' said Pyne, and for once he smiled. He looked at O'Flaherty and both of them laughed. Some of the other officers laughed too, but not the mids.

'King Neptune?' I said, 'And his attendants?' I asked that even though I knew very well what he meant, just as every seamen did.

'Aye-aye, Sir,' said O'Flaherty, 'and honoured we shall be, to receive them!'

'Indeed, Sir,' said Pyne, and if the wind holds, they should be coming aboard at about this time tomorrow.'

'And what will they do, once aboard?' I said.

'Well, Sir, God bless all hands of us,' said O'Flaherty, 'It's shaving and ducking and such. But only for them as has never crossed the line before. Just a bit of fun.'

'Just a bit?' said Pyne, 'It's that and more!' and all the shellbacks laughed and all the pollywogs trembled.

'But you say that I may be excused,' I said, 'even though I've never crossed the line?'

'Of course, Sir,' said O'Flaherty, 'but only if you pay the penalty.'

As he said that I could see the looks on the faces of those of the hands, who'd crept up and were following the conversation with mighty interest. They looked at O'Flaherty and they looked at me, and it wasn't hard to see what response they wanted from Jacky Flash. Ah well. Worse things happen at sea as I've explained in some detail.

'Mr O'Flaherty!' I said in a good loud voice, 'since it's King Neptune himself, and it's a tradition of the Service … I'll pay no penalty, and put myself at his mercy.'

That got cheers. It got loud cheers and wicked grins. It got them because Naval discipline was never so sharp as the Articles of War proclaimed, what with its floggings and hangings. I've told you before that discipline vanishes ashore at the end of a commission, such that a brutal officer might be beaten by the lower deck. Likewise there's no discipline when the whores come aboard in port, and even mutiny had its rules such that provided nobody got killed, then once the men returned to their duties everything was forgotten. In short, my jolly boys, we officers never ruled by force alone, but by consent of the hands who knew that there must be discipline aboard ship, against the time when the sea gets angry and the wind blows hard.

So the business began next day, when we finally crossed the line, with signals having gone round the squadron to permit heaving-to for the ceremonies which would take place in every ship. Aboard *Euphonides*, this began with the lowering of a boat on one side of ship, which everyone pretended not to know about, and which boat would pull round to the other side, arriving as if from nowhere.

Bang! Bang! Bang! On the door of the great cabin, where I sat with my officers and the grog already going round. The door burst open. The boatswain stamped, saluted and roared.

'King Neptune and his suite beg permission to come aboard, Sir!'

'Proceed, Mr Boatswain,' I said, 'I shall come up directly to receive him!'

'Aye-aye, Sir!'

So up we went on to the main-deck, and I would point out that I was wearing my oldest and shabbiest uniform coat, and no hat, and no sword, and nothing in my pockets. On deck the ship's people raised a great cheer because they'd got some drink from somewhere and were all festooned and painted in bizarre costumes. So were the boatswain and his mates, who were lined up with their silver pipes to give honour as if an admiral were coming aboard. Meanwhile an enormous tub of water was laid out between the guns, by the main mast, with men lowering buckets over the side, to be brought up brimming and emptied into the tub, and the wash-deck pump rigged and the hose sloshing still more water into the tub. Beside the tub was a great throne, built out of old barrels, all bright-painted, and decorated with green rags to look like seaweed.

'King Neptune is alongside and begs to come aboard!' cried the boatswain.

'Permission granted!' I cried, which was the last order I gave, as King Neptune and his suite came over the side from their boat down below, piped aboard, and greeted with thunderous cheers. There were half a dozen of them: the lower deck's finest, most of them half-naked with their chests, backs and limbs garishly painted with anchors, fishes – anything nautical – and stripes and zig-zags of colour besides. What costume they wore was lovingly made by the typically inventive genius of seaman. The wigs and beards were made of ship's mops, but God knows where they got the grease-paint, the bright rags and the hats and baubles, but the London stage couldn't have managed it better. King Neptune himself had a crown on his head, a trident in his hand, and a beard over his chest. With him came his 'wife' in the voluminous mockery of a woman's dress with huge, padded, stand-out breasts. She had hair down to her knees, garish red lips, monstrous eyebrows, and clutched one of the ship's boys with only a rag round his loins, as her precious infant. Next came King Neptune's barber, with his apron and giant razor, and men to carry his soap-bucket and a shaving brush the size of a household broom. Then there were tritons, and a perfectly hideous mermaid with golden hair, and a fishy tail so that 'she' couldn't walk but must be carried by the men.

'Where's my throne?' cried King Neptune, 'for I'm here on serious business.'

'Aye-aye!' cried the hands, and King Neptune was led to his throne, and sat in splendour, with his wife and infant beside him, his trident in his hand, and his court around him.

'Now then!' cried King Neptune, 'I hear as there's hands aboard of this ship, which is pollywogs as ain't never been in these parts of my domain before.'

'Aye-aye!' cried the hands, as they jostled and cheered, and pushed forward for a better view, or climbed the shrouds to look down on it.

'So if there's pollywogs aboard,' said King Neptune, 'will they step forward like men? Or will they be dragged?' and every soul aboard looked at me, and I thought it best not to be dragged, and stepped forward.

'Welcome aboard, your majesty,' I said, 'because I have not yet been baptised for crossing the line.'

'Then you'll be the first!' said King Neptune, 'and you may take a tot to ease you along.'

I was handed a horn mug with a very generous tot indeed, but there was no choice other than to drink it, so I did. And after that, everything was riotous, and water-soaked, and a lot more rum went down. I was stood in front of the tub, blindfolded, then forced to sit on a plank stretched over it, while the barber's mates covered my face in soapy foam. It was rubbed in hard with the brush, and I was shaved with the great – and thankfully wooden –razor, then:

'Wash him off!' cried King Neptune, and the plank was heaved out beneath me, and I was ducked most mercilessly, till I fought my way out, and was washed off one final time by the hose and pump. Then the hands were clapping me on the back.

'Jacky Flash! Jacky Flash! Jacky Flash!'

I could barely catch my breath, but I saw how wise I'd been to come forward and not be dragged, because the next pollywog was Mr Norton our Lieutenant of Marines. He must have held back, or worse still tried to hide, and he was now being carried aloft, kicking and struggling, by four seamen who had already blindfolded him, and even his own men cheering them on. He went straight into the tub with a great splash, complete with scarlet coat, epaulettes, gorget and lace, and more water was poured over him from the buckets and the hose. Then they got him up on the plank, hanging on with white knuckles and gritted teeth, and they soaped and shaved him, and then ducked him again for good measure.

The hands were kinder to the mids, at least the younger ones, who were let off with a moderate treatment, but Mr Phaeton Ordroyd was well and truly baptised, because the men saw him as a bold young fellow who played tricks on others, and who'd doubtless appreciate the joke. They ducked him so thoroughly that I had to intervene, and with the utmost goodwill and only gentle use of my fists, I persuaded them to desist, and hauled him out of the tub before they quite entirely drowned him. I had to do that for the times I'd shared with his mother, as you'll understand, my jolly boys, when you're older.

After that, it was usual ship's routine down to Cape Town, and we did moderately well in covering over seven thousand miles from the Downs to Table Bay in three and a half months. The squadron anchored, I went ashore for the usual formalities, opposite the governor and officialdom, I waved my certificates plenipotentiary that Spencer had given me, and the business of provisioning and watering, was got under way. This was also the time for social visits between the ships of our squadron, because there can't be any boat traffic within a squadron under way, since the boat's crews would exhaust themselves pulling against the speed of the moving ships. So any ships that absolutely must communicate by boat work, must back their topsails, and heave-to, and fall behind the fleet with the hope of catching up afterwards. Either that, or the whole squadron must heave-to as we did for King Neptune, but that was special and exceptional.

So our time – and it was two weeks – in Table Bay was marked with a great coming and going between our ships, and Cape Town itself. The weather was pleasantly warm, not hot, the town was still very Dutch indeed, the scenery was magnificent with the great mass of Table Mountain looking down on the bay, and there were the usual receptions and hops that the people of a sea-faring town love to give when a fleet puts in.

But I didn't enjoy my time in Table Bay, because I had to spend so much of it getting my ships provisioned, ever chasing the shore-side people, and still more in chasing the East India captains to do their part in moving everything forward. Besides that, there was a vast amount to do merely in keeping up to date with the condition of the ships under my command. The Sea Service ships – two frigates, two sloops and a schooner – that belonged to King George, were at least under my direct command and I could order their captains to come aboard *Euphonides* to report. But that left nine Indiamen who detested the Navy, and were loyal only to the East India Company, and whose captains I had to cajole politely to get anything out of, because left to themselves they'd have kept everything secret, out of spite.

I except Captain Stacey of *Duke of Cornwallis*, from this judgement. He was as good a seaman as any officer in the King's Service, and he acted like one in every way. I am pleased to say that I liked him and he liked me, and that fact became the saving of me in due course, as you will see.

But for the rest, it was heavy work getting them to report on the state of their ships. Was there any rot in their timbers? Any salt pork uneatable? Any sea-damage or cargoes shifted? Any plague, pestilence, ruptures, boils, fires or mutinies? I had to screw this out of them by going aboard their ships rather than making them come to me, which at least meant I could look them over. But it all took time, and I had to do it because where would I be if we were intercepted by the French, and I suddenly found that half the Indiamen crews were down with the scurvy, and all their powder spoiled? So yes, my lads, it is a fine thing to be a commodore, enjoying high rank and good pay, but by George you suffer for it in the responsibility it heaves upon you. No wonder I was looking older.

And then there was Mr Kilbride, Director of the East India Company, and his chum, fellow-Director Sir Robert Valentine. They invited me and my officers on board of *Duke of Cornwallis* for another dinner, soon after the squadron was settled in Table Bay and they had got some fresh food aboard. So I went with Pyne, O'Flaherty, and others including Lieutenant Norton of the marines now fully dried out and in need of a treat. There were eight of us officers, with six hands and a coxswain, and I blame what followed on the fact that there were enough of them to generate their own little piece of *Euphonides* aboard *Duke of Cornwallis*, once they'd had a drop to drink and they were encouraging one another.

The dinner was excellent, the stern cabin of the big ship was cool and shady, and the wine flowed. Kilbride was on one side of me, with Valentine on the other, and Masahito – Lord Masahito as they constantly called him – facing opposite. Captain Stacey was a few chairs down, opposite Mr Pyne, but he raised a glass in toast to me and I toasted him back. I'd much preferred to have talked to Stacey, but Kilbride was what I'd got and from the very first moments he made cryptic remarks.

'Have you had any thoughts during the voyage?' he said to me, and he tucked into a chicken breast and fresh vegetables, with a gulp of wine as if nothing important was under way. But he looked at me sideways with his small, sharp face with the large, sharp brain behind it. Then he leaned towards me in emphasis, with Valentine staring hard. 'Any thoughts beyond Bombay?' he said.

'Any thoughts?' said Valentine.

'Of what kind?' I said. But he just smiled, and had another go at the chicken.

'Let's talk later,' he said.

'Later,' said Valentine like a bloody echo. I disliked the pair of them. Greasy bastards.

But Lord Masahito was very good company. He was a charming fellow, interested in everything and especially crossing the equator.

'I am told that you are now a shellback, Commodore Fletcher,' he said in his perfect English.

'That I am, my Lord,' I said, 'And with the bruises and scars to prove it!' Everyone laughed, and some of my officers who'd drunk deep whispered, 'Jacky Flash.'

'I am a shellback myself,' he said, 'I crossed the line aboard a Dutch ship on the way out from Japan,' and he nodded towards me in respect, 'but I was not baptised as you were. I was persuaded to pay the penalty, rather than tarnish my dignity.' He glanced at his bodyguards standing behind him. 'My followers insisted. So it was six bottles of rum to preserve the name of Hitamoto,' he said that and he laughed, though I could see that he was genuinely sorry that he'd not been ducked, and gone through the process like a man. He seemed a straight and decent fellow.

'Jacky Flash!' said my officers, and this time not so quietly, so I scowled at them, but I'd had a drop myself by then, and I might have been just a little proud of the name, and that was my undoing because after dinner, Lord Masahito put on an entertainment for us.

It was most fascinating entertainment, but first Kilbride caught me as I was coming out of the officer's privy in the stern quarter, having unloaded some of my drink. Valentine was with him, we were in a quiet passageway, and nobody else was there.

'D'you recall our previous meeting?' he said, 'Because there's ways you could oblige *me*, and ways I could oblige *you*.'

'Indeed there is,' said Valentine, and off went Kilbride again, pouring out words and standing far too close, jabbing me in the chest with his finger and getting carried off with his own passion, nasty little bugger that he was, and all intense and fierce and staring. He was battering with words as a prize fighter batters with fists.

'Get away,' I said finally, 'I don't know. I need more time.'

'Ah!' he said, and winked at Valentine, who winked back. Then Kilbride turned to me again, and came very close and almost whispered. 'Fletcher' he said, 'listen! Have you any idea of the wealth to be made in the East? Do you know how much trade there is – still untouched and awaiting – to be screwed out of India? And out of China and Japan too?' I said nothing, because I didn't know the answer, but I think that he did, and that the opportunities truly were enormous. So I did make a bit of a promise when he made me a bit of an offer, and I was precious close to going over to him right then and there. But I didn't, and the only reason was that I detested Kilbride as a man. It was as personal a matter as that. So I said nothing, and pushed past the pair of them and went up on deck.

And weren't we all just merry and bright, up on the quarterdeck? What with the drink and the food, in beautiful sunshine, with a blue sky, and the calm of Table Bay around us, and the mountain above. What's more, something had been arranged for us as entertainment, so Stacey and his officers, ushered us to the quarterdeck rail, where Kilbride slid alongside me, and we all gazed down on the main-deck, and saw a large square marked out in chalk, and the ship's crew – hundreds of them – turned out in their best rigs, standing round the square all chuckling as if they knew what was coming.

'Captain Stacey?' said Masahito, 'With your permission?'

'Go ahead, my Lord!' said Stacey, with a bow.

'Gentlemen,' said Masahito, and we turned to face him, 'you are all fighting men, in the service of your King.'

'God bless him!' said some of us.

'Aye,' said the rest.

'Then permit me to display one of the fighting arts of Japan: the art of Jiu Jitsu.'

Kilbride nudged me,

'You'll like this,' he said. I ignored him.

'It is the gentle art of combat,' said Masahito, 'with no blows struck, and the opponent defeated by tripping, throwing.' He smiled. 'And by choking,' he said, 'So perhaps it is not entirely gentle,' and we all laughed.

'I've seen this before,' said Kilbride, determined on conversation, 'It's good!' I ignored him again. Then Masahito clapped his hands and his four bodyguards emerged from under the break of the quarterdeck and stepped out on to the main-deck, having quietly slipped away and changed out of their normal English clothes, into shapeless Japanese garments. They were barefoot in loose trousers, and jackets that didn't fasten with buttons but were held closed by belts of stout cloth. They were men in their thirties I'd guess, and they were led by another man I'd not seen before. He was older, and wore similar clothes, except that his belt had coloured ends. I took this to be some badge of rank, which indeed it was. The five of them stood to one side of the chalk square, unmoving and impassive. I learned later that these men, like Lord Masahito himself, were what the Japanese call samurai, which means soldier, or warrior. Kilbride told me that.

At the same time, there came a cheer from *Duke of Cornwallis's* crew and a dozen of very large and ugly men came forward to meet the Japanese. They were stripped as if for a bout of boxing: wearing just britches and pumps, and a fine collection of broken-nosed hard cases they were too, and all with shaven skulls to prove it. At a word from *Duke of Cornwallis's* first mate, the bully-boys stopped in a line, facing the samurai across the chalk square, and jigged about, feinting and ducking and swinging. Even the smallest of them was bigger than the largest of the Japanese, and every one was a much-battered thug. But Kilbride whispered to me.

'None of these beauties has seen Jiu Jitsu before,' he said, 'They're all from other ships.'

'Gentlemen,' said Masahito, and swept a hand at the shaven skulls, 'You see before you the picked volunteers of the East India Fleet,' this brought more cheers from the crew, 'Each man has received a Spanish Dollar for turning out, and the promise of a golden guinea should he cause any of my followers to fall to the deck.' More cheers followed and much laughter. So Masahito raised a hand for silence.

'The rules are,' he said, 'that any man may fight in any manner of his choice, and may signal his own defeat either by stepping out of the square, or by striking the flat of his hand on the ground or his opponent, at which time the opponent will cease fighting and step back.' He paused to make sure everyone understood, looking particularly at the bullies, and when they nodded, he added, 'There are no other rules! Now go to it, as your officer commands!'

The first mate took charge, and set the bullies to fight the Japanese samurai, by turns with one man facing another, and there was yelling and stamping and betting among the crew. The mate picked out the biggest bully-boy for the first bout, and the bully grinned and stepped forward, and the senior man among the samurai said something, and the smallest of them said something back. He then bowed to the senior man, bowed to the bully and stepped forward, to enormous cheers.

The way the Japanese stood was very strange. He didn't clench fists, he didn't raise arms, he didn't scowl or leer, but stood with knees slightly bent, arms flexed at the elbow, hands at waist level and not a drop of emotion on his face. But the bully-boy roared and growled, and charged with a mighty swing of the right fist in a mighty blow ... and his opponent ducked, twinkled feet like a dancer, and the bully went over like a falling tree to roars of laughter. But up got the bully, in fury, and charged again, arms reaching out to grapple ... and his opponent let him close, then *himself* fell over backwards, caught the bully with his feet and threw him in the air to land with a seriously almighty crash, that left the bully stunned and unable to get up until a bucket of water was thrown over him. The whole thing was over in seconds. It took less time than you have spent in reading this. It was astounding.

The other bouts were the same, except that they got steadily nastier, because the bully-boys were veteran pugilists and wrestlers. They had quick movements, hard muscles and stoic indifference to pain, and each one learned from the man before and avoided his mistakes. But that only meant that the Jiu Jitsu men used progressively harsher means to put them down. Thus fingers were broken, two men knocked unconscious, one choked unconscious, and another one's shoulder wrenched from its socket.

This turned the mood of the crew, who became fed up with seeing Britannia's finest overthrown by a parcel of foreigners. So first they fell silent, and then – bless their dear hearts because I wish they'd kept quiet – one or more of my officers called out a name, and the boat's crew and coxswain of *Euphonides* took it up. At first it was just them, but finally the packed mass of *Duke of Cornwallis's* people were giving it to the skies, in a voice of thunder.

'Jacky Flash! Jacky Flash! Jacky Flash!

207

CHAPTER 31

'My distrust of Kilbride grows, and my personal dislike of him. Yet I am faced with dilemma because Clan Hitamoto needs Kilbride and his western soldiers and weapons, in order to face the Shogun. Also I am dismayed that circumstances will force us to deceive Commodore Fletcher for whom I have great sympathy.'

(From the 'Foreign Journal' of Masahito Hitamoto. Entry dated Tuesday January 10th 1789.)

On the day after the Jiu Jitsu demonstration, Lord Masahito took breakfast in the great cabin of *Duke of Cornwallis*. The table was cleared of yesterday's banquet, flowers had been brought out from the shore and set in vases, and a clean table cloth had been laid. Now, and since he was dining alone, Masahito ate decent Japanese food as prepared by his followers, and he ate from a bowl with chop-sticks. Even so, and as a necessary compromise he sat in a chair, at table, because it was vital to maintain the respect of these Englishmen, and he knew them very well: he knew how their strange minds worked and that they would never understand if he sat on the floor to eat.

But Masahito's remarkable understanding of the English did not replace his Japanese upbringing: it was merely a foreign veneer on stout, Japanese timber, and he smiled as he reflected on a piece of foreign wisdom which was directly relevant. Thus the Catholic Jesuits proclaimed: *'give me the child till he is seven, and I will give you the man'* and Masahito had had been nearly twice that age when he left his homeland. So when he finished his meal, Masahito sat in contemplation of the magnificent view through the stern windows of the ship: the blue sky and luminous waters of Table Bay. He sat silent with hands folded in his lap, while his followers cleared the table. He sat enjoying the moment because he was well aware – and was pleased to note – that as the voyage continued and Japan came closer, he was becoming fully Japanese again. He was also aware that he was becoming increasingly impatient with the rudeness of the Englishmen, and he knew that this irritation must be controlled. Indeed, and as a precise example of this problem, he was irritated in that very instant, because he although he was obviously in deep thought he was noisily interrupted by Kilbride and Valentine.

'Ah!' said Kilbride, entering with Valentine at his elbow, 'Good morning, my Lord!' They slammed the door, scraped chairs noisily, sat with a thump, and took their place opposite Masahito. They had no grace of movement, no dignity of bearing. Servants instantly came forward and offered them plates of steaming meat that turned the stomachs of Masahito's followers. 'Did you sleep well, my Lord?' said Kilbride.

'Indeed, Mr Kilbride,' said Masahito, 'and yourself?'

'Yes, my Lord,' said Kilbride and he launched straight into affairs of business, without respect for the beauty of the bay, which would have caused any Japanese gentleman to pause for reflection and thought. But not these Englishmen, who seized their knives and forks, and attacked their food, breathing out the smell of hot flesh, while Kilbride waved to his servants to go away, even with his mouth full and jaws working. Then he looked at Masahito's attendants and raised eyebrows. Masahito understood.

'*O makase kudasai!*' he said, 'leave us!'

'Hi!' said the four samurai and bowed and went out.

'Well, my Lord,' said Kilbride, as the door closed, 'I've got good news. Fletcher's hooked and landed.'

'Hooked and landed?' said Masahito, 'Please explain.' Kilbride grinned at Valentine and Valentine grinned back.

'Did you know that Fletcher doesn't want to be a sailor?' said Kilbride.

'No,' said Masahito.

'Do you know he wants to get out of the King's navy and become a merchant?'

Masahito considered this fact, and had to balance English and Japanese thinking, because in Japan the merchants were the lowest class. First came the Emperor, then the samurai, then the farmers, then the craftsmen, and last the merchants who were perceived as dishonourable because they made nothing, yet profited from passing on goods that virtuous persons had created. But in England, while the King and the nobles were above the rest, merchants could be very powerful and were not viewed with contempt. Indeed, the East India Company was stronger than many nation states! So there was nothing *necessarily* dishonourable in an Englishman wanting to be a merchant, but it was obvious that the English thought it strange in a naval officer.

'No,' said Masahito finally, 'I did not know that.'

'Well, it's what he wants, and he'll do anything to get it,' said Kilbride.

'That's right,' said Valentine.

'So he's going to help us in the most useful way that can be imagined,' said Kilbride.

'And what is that?' said Masahito. Kilbride and Valentine looked at one another in delight.

'I spoke to him yesterday,' said Kilbride, 'after the dinner and before the Joo-Jingle.'

'Jiu Jitsu,' said Masahito.

'Yes, yes, yes,' said Kilbride, 'that! I spoke to him and persuaded him to do something that is in our very best interest: yours and mine, my Lord.' Kilbride laughed. Valentine laughed. Masahito merely smiled. The smile was necessary to sustain working relations with Kilbride and Valentine, even though Masahito regarded their behaviour as boorish. It was obvious that they were planning to deceive Fletcher, who was himself a cunning user of deception since deception was a necessary part of conflict. But deception should be employed as a working tool, and not made the subject of immature laughter. So Masahito smiled, keeping his own thoughts contained.

'And how was Fletcher persuaded?' he said.

'By offering him his heart's desire!' said Kilbride, 'he thinks he's going to be a *nabob* in India: a merchant prince,' and he and Valentine laughed again.

'So,' said Masahito, 'what has he been persuaded to do?'

'Well!' said Kilbride, 'When we get to Bombay, he's not going to anchor his ships off the main wharves where *we* shall go. He's going to drop anchor in the harbour of Kilbride Island which is nearby, and which is entirely mine, and which is a very fine anchorage indeed, with every imaginable convenience for the supply and fitting-out of ships.'

'But?' said Masahito.

'But which is very much easier to get *in to* than *out of*,' said Kilbride, 'as Fletcher will find out in due course.'

CHAPTER 32

On the day of the Jiu Jitsu demonstration there was nothing I could do to get out of it. I knew that because the same thing has happened to me on other occasions, especially when joining a new ship when the hands are clamouring for me to do what everyone says I can do, which is to seek out the reigning bruiser and knock him down as warning to the rest that they must behave. That's the trouble with reputation, my lads: you have to live up to it.

So I did my best. I took off my uniform coat – especially as it was my full-dress – and I took off my weskit, cravat and shirt, and shoes and stockings too, for a barefoot grip. That still left a pair of expensive britches made of finest-woven wool with napped finish and gold buckles at the knee. But I wasn't going to fight naked, so the britches had to stay. So everyone got a look at me with my shirt off, and I got cheers for being the gorilla that I am, since I'm full of muscle and don't have any fat: not that there's any virtue in it, because that's the way I'm made. It's just luck.

All aboard *Duke of Cornwallis Cheered* except the samurai, who stood silent without the least expression on their faces. They just stood still while their senior man – whose name was Nakano – said something to them, and they all bowed, and stood back, and he bowed to me as I came down the companionway on to the main-deck, and then he himself stepped into the chalk square to face me. It was a bit smeared round the edges by now, what with bully-boys falling on it and being hauled off it. But it was still there, and the cheers were deafening as I stepped in.

Then Nakano bowed to me again, and stood waiting, and then he was off! He took up that same, odd, fighting stance that the rest had, and stared me hard in the eye, with complete patience and confidence. It was very strange because he was nowhere near as big as me. I had the weight, the strength and the reach, and had he been anything else than what he was, I'd have knocked him down and never raised sweat. But he *was* what he

211

was: the man who'd looked at me and told his lads to fall back and leave it to him. So I raised fists, and shuffled forward, keeping my feet apart for balance, and waiting to see what he'd do, and all the noise of the audience faded into a blur of sound, because in such a moment you've got no mind for them, and every atom of you is looking at your opponent.

So I was thinking hard on what I'd seen in the earlier bouts. I knew I mustn't charge him, or he'd throw me over, and I knew not to swing punches, or he'd grab my arm, and pull my shoulder out. Indeed I was most especially careful because he was obviously something special at this Jiu Jitsu, and even more dangerous than the rest. So I tried wrestling, not boxing. I tried going forward with arms outstretched to grab him. I thought once I'd got hold of him, then strength would win, since a good big 'un beats a good little 'un.

But it didn't work like that. In India there are thieves called *greasy wallahs* who go naked and covered in grease. They pick your pocket and you can't catch them because they slip out of your hand. It was the same with my Japanese opponent, but with Jiu Jitsu instead of grease. However hard I tried, I couldn't catch hold of him and he just wriggled free, and tripped me, and down I went with a thump. That happened, over and over again until it began to hurt. It really hurt, and my size was against me since a small man takes less harm and gets up faster than a big man, and it was frightening too, because if you go down in a fight you're done for.

Worse still, after he'd let me get good and tired, he started fighting back. He'd only been defending before, but now he went into the attack. He played the most ingenious tricks of tweaking my thumbs and fingers at un-natural angles, trying to break them or lever them from their sockets, and all with no seeming effort from him. Then he began doing the same, only bigger, to my knee-joints and elbows, and it was agony. Then he switched to jabbing his heel at the back of my knee which hurt something fierce. It was hard to bear and it went on a long time: far longer than any of the other fights, until my legs were beginning to wobble and I knew it couldn't go on much longer or I'd fall over with exhaustion. Either that, or he really would break some part of me. So it was time to give up brute strength and try something different. I took the hint from Lord Masahito's statement that we could fight in any way we chose, and that's just what I did.

'Belay there!' I cried, dropping my hands, and staring over my opponent's shoulder, 'Get out of it, you swab!' I said that as if warning off an intruder. Nakano frowned. 'Look!' I said to him, carrying on with my act, and I pointed at nothing. I pointed with my left hand, turning left shoulder forward and right shoulder back. I acted indignant, as if someone was being very naughty, and bless me but it worked! He turned his head to look, and that was my chance. I swung a right-hander at his head with all my might, and it would have knocked a horse unconscious had it landed. But he was superbly fast, and jumped away like lightning such I didn't fully connect. I caught him a clout, but he twisted with the blow, so it wasn't the paralyser that I'd hoped. Then he dropped back into his fighting stance, to carry on as before, except that he delivered a trick of his own to match mine. I think he was annoyed, which he hadn't been before.

Just as he seemed to relax in his stance, he yelled out something in his own language and leapt at me, tripped me, got me down, and put a strangle hold on my neck. I'd seen his mates do the same: getting on a bully-boy's back where they couldn't be reached, then throttling away in perfect safety. But I hadn't entirely missed with my punch and he must have been dizzy. So even though he'd got a grip on me that pressed one half of my windpipe against the other, he hadn't got himself out of my reach. I could just about curl an arm around him, so I did, and I heaved with heart, soul, mind and strength and hauled him round to meet the other arm. It was a vast effort, and nobody could have done it who hadn't my strength. But I did it, and then, my jolly boys, with arms linked together, your Uncle Jacob had Mr Nakano in a bear hug, and I squeezed with all my might.

Placed like that, we could easily have killed one other: him by choking me, and me by crushing his tripes, liver and lights. But this wasn't war to the death. This was supposed to be sport. So we both saw sense, and one of us – I don't remember which since I was near unconscious at the time – one of us eased up, and gave a brief pat of the hand as if inviting response, and the other replied with the same. We did that a few times, to be sure, and then we fully acknowledged a draw by slapping the other hard on the back. Then we rolled away from each other and stood up, which took great effort from each of us, considering the state of us, and the formidable will of each one not to be beaten. So it was effort of the mind as well as the body. But we did it. We got up gasping and heaving for breath, and dripping streams of sweat on to the planks. Then Nakano stood with a straight back, and bowed to me, and this time I bowed right back in respect, because I never fought a more deadly man in all my life.

There was a great deal of shouting and jollification after that, and the main-brace was spliced and grog all round, and Lord Masahito came up and paid me a fine compliment, or at least I think he did because I was barely able to stand, and my head was going round with utter exhaustion. So I do remember Nakano bowing – they were always bloody bowing, were the Japanese – I remember him bowing to Masahito, and saying something, and then bowing at me, and Masahito smiling then turning to me.

'Well done, Commodore Fletcher!' he said, 'Fumito Nakano, says you are the most formidable man he has ever faced. He says that you have true fighting spirit, and that if you learned Jiu Jitsu and did not pour out your strength in the wasteful way that you do, then you would be a great master.'

'Really?' I said, still wiping the sweat out of my eyes, and not properly paying heed.

'And Fumito Nakano is himself a great master of Jiu Jitsu,' said Masahito, 'who has never been defeated.'

'Very nice,' I said, 'good for him.'

'Yes!' said Masahito, 'his skill is so great that when another man faces him, it is as if the other were empty-handed and facing a swordsman.' Then there were a lot more words all round, including from Kilbride who was determined to talk to me until I told him plainly to bugger off, which he did with a grin and a wink, and a knowing look.

After that things returned to normal in the squadron. I insisted that there would be no more jolly dinners and boat trips between ships, and that all effort should be put into completing our preparations for getting our anchors up, and setting set course for Bombay. Finally, we sailed on Saturday, Jan 20th 1798, with full holds and water-butts, and the squadron in formation, heading down around the Cape of Good Hope, then northwest up the eastward side of the African continent, to pass between it and Madagascar. Then it was another two-and-a-half months voyaging to Bombay. It was all routine sea-faring, and we had good fortune with the wind and weather, and the only event of note was an attempt by Arab pirates to cut out one of our Indiamen.

This happened as we were making the passage through the Straits of Madagascar, a huge sea area a thousand miles long, two hundred and fifty miles wide at the narrowest point, and dangerous from end to end. To the west, the limitless African coast was inhabited by savage and unknown tribes. To the east, the island of Madagascar had twice the land area of the British Isles, and was ruled by local kings. It was another place to avoid since the Malagasy folk had muskets and cannon, and were too strong for foreign invasion as the French proved when they tried it in the 1700s and got kicked out. Also the people had names no decent man can pronounce.

[This is no mere prejudice. The king of Madagascar at this time was named Andrianampoinimerina. S.P.]

Worst of all, the Straits of Madagascar was a nest of pirates with ships operating from little ports held either by bribery of the local peoples or by force of arms, and the pirates were Arabs, or at least they were pirates who sailed in Arab dhows. We got sight of some of them, the second day into the Straits, when little *Spicer*, our topsail schooner out in front of the squadron, hoisted the most dramatic of all signals: *Enemy In Sight!* That stirred the blood, my jolly boys, believe me it did, because everyone assumed that this must mean a dozen of French cruisers. So I was called up on deck from my noon calculations, and Pyne instantly beat to quarters without orders – as very properly he should – and he ordered the signal hoist for the fleet to come to action stations. Meanwhile the drummer boys were beating a long roll, the hands were loading the main battery and running out, and the marine sharpshooters were going aloft into the fighting-tops with their muskets, and the Gunner was hanging wet flannel curtains at the magazine entrance to keep out sparks. It was all very smart and showed the value of practise. But best of all, I'm pleased to say, is that all aboard including Jimbo the cat were looking forward to a fight. By George it was exciting.

Then we all had a long wait, with the mids and gentlemen peering through their telescopes as the enemy came up over the horizon where we could *all* see him, and not just the look-outs on *Spicer's* main-top. But then:

'Ohhhh!' said the gentlemen and the mids, in deep disappointment, and they laughed in contempt of what came up from the deep blue, because it wasn't the topmasts of a French squadron. It wasn't even proper warships. It was a squadron of Arab dhows, a dozen or more: low-lying ships, with a pair of huge lateen sails on masts raked sharply forward. They were bearing down at terrific speed with the white water under their bows, and sails bulging and every line taut.

'Belay that!' said Mr O'Flaherty the master, infuriated at the laughter. Then he recollected protocol and apologised to me. 'Beggin' of your pardon, Cap'n,' he said, touching his hat, 'But I've seen the likes of these before,' and he pointed to the dhows, 'They're faster and handier than us with the wind abaft the beam, and to windward they'd leave us for dead! And they're cram-full of men. So they'll hope draw fire at a distance, then fall on board of a merchantman and take him! And if they do, then it's no quarter and every throat cut, except them as they keep back to play with, and God help them most of all!'

'D'you hear that?' I cried for all to hear, 'Stand to your bloody guns or I'll come among you!' There was profound silence and everyone avoided my eye. 'And hoist a fleet signal to keep better station!' I cried, 'I'll have no slackers among us anywhere: not in the Indiamen, and especially not in this bloody ship!'

After that it was cat-and-mouse. We couldn't match the dhows for speed, and they dared not close with us for fear of our guns. In theory, and on paper, we were safe because the dhows had only swivels aboard: light pieces firing two-pound shot or less. We could see them through our telescopes, just as we could see that the dhows really were heavily crewed, with many hundreds of fighting men between them, and every one hoping to grapple and board and capture. So yes, they had swivels on their gunwales, but no battering guns that could dismast a ship or beat in its timbers, while any of my squadron including the Indiamen could smash a dhow with a single broadside. That's why the Indiamen carried guns. But that was in theory, and the reality was less comforting.

'They don't give up,' said O'Flaherty that night, on the quarterdeck, with the dhows somewhere out in the hot dark. 'They're like crows round a sick sheep, waiting their chance: waiting for someone to lose a spar if the sea gets up. That or anything else that might make a ship to fall behind the rest. And the worst time is at night, when they'll try to get alongside quick-sharp, if a ship's not keeping watch. Then, in they go! Over the side, screaming and yelling.' He shook his head. 'They don't give up. They're very patient.'

So forgive me now, my lads, if I boast. I boast because your Uncle Jacob had long since been advised by the Admiralty of what to do, when faced with Arab pirates, and I had the answer ready and my squadron drilled in the doing of it. Thus during the day we were fairly safe, in our squadron formation with the Indiamen inside a screen of warships, and the Indiamen themselves with guns run out. But at night, when the dhows pressed in close, the drill aboard each ship was to make a good show of being ready for anything. Thus I had each ship's company muster three teams of men with loud voices: one astern, one amidships and one in the forecastle. And it went like this.

A great shout from the forecastle:

'All alert amidships?' Then from amidships:

'*Aye-aye!* All alert astern?' Then from astern:

'*Aye-aye!* All alert on the forecastle?' Then from the forecastle:

'*Aye-aye!*'

Then there was a quarter-hour pause, timed by the sand-glass, and the whole thing was repeated. It was repeated all night aboard each ship throughout the squadron, which meant nobody got much sleep. But we could make that up, by watches, during the day and the pirates knew that there was no chance catching a ship asleep in the night. Also I'd ordered the captains of my warships to take any opportunity for long-range fire – steady and careful fire and not just burning powder – at any dhow that came anywhere nearly in range during daylight. Thus the pirates would hear the thud of a gun, and see the smoke, and then the water-spout thrown aloft by a plunging shot. It didn't matter if the shot missed. What mattered was that they knew that we were seriously ready to do them harm.

They gave up after three days. We saw them suddenly come about, all together and as smart as the Channel Fleet. They came about and vanished back where they'd come from. Who knows where? Tribal Africa probably because they headed westward. But that might just have been a ploy to hide their true destination.

'That'll be the end of them,' said O'Flaherty as we watched them dip under the horizon. 'They're not provisioned for a long cruise. They can't carry the food and drink for so many men. But there might be others, so this mayn't be the entire end of it.' Fortunately, it was the end of it, and we had no more adventures during the entire voyage to Bombay, which we sighted on Wednesday, April 4th 1798.

Bombay lies on the north-west coast of the Indian subcontinent, and is famous enough today. But in the late nineties it was fabulously exotic, and not just to stay-at-home landmen who never saw it, but to seamen besides. It was place of wonder, a dazzling other-world. It was the capital city of all John Company's posessions inIndia. It was a dense-populated city of civilised native folk, that raised intricate stone architecture, that had strange religions, two thousand years of written history, and more languages than there are stars in the sky. Besides that, and what made my mouth water, Bombay was the centre of the Indian trade in everything wonderful that came out of the east: from jewels to spices, from silk to cotton, from dyes to drugs, and from Afghan carpets to elephant ivory.

Bombay was also strange in a physical sense, because in those days it was just at the beginning of a vast programme of engineering, whereby we British profoundly changed its geography. This, because nature formed Bombay as an anchorage at the tip of a peninsula reaching down into an enormous bay, among eight, hilly islands set in marshland. In later years, we took the tops off the hills, threw the spoil into the marshes, and filled everything in to make one land-mass. But in 1798, the town itself and its wharves and piers, lay on the east-facing side of the peninsula, looking towards the mainland. It was heavily fortified with walls, bastions, heavy guns and a powerful castle, and there were islands, still there, rising out of the marshes and sea channels.

We parted company with the East Indiamen at sea, and off Bombay, since by previous agreement, the nine big Indiamen dropped anchor off the Company's wharves in the town proper, while I took my warships to anchor in the harbour of one of the islands – Kilbride Island – a few miles off. This was a practical arrangement, as the Company's wharves would be fully occupied dealing with the nine big Indiamen, and port Kilbride was a miniature Bombay in its storehouses, wharves and workmen.

[Whether or not it was a practical arrangement for Fletcher's warships to anchor at Kilbride Island, there remains the strong possibility, that he took them there, by agreement with Kilbride. Note his comment above that he made 'a bit of a promise following a bit of an offer'. S.P.]

But before we anchored there had to be the usual pleasantries between ships, that marked the end of a great voyage in company. Had we all been in the same anchorage it would have taken place there, but since we were to part, I ordered the whole squadron hove to, so the boats could work among us. This was no more than seamanly good nature, since we'd been

218

so long together that we were almost shipmates. So toasts were drunk, promises made of meetings and celebrations ashore, and we shared all the relief and thankfulness of having sailed some thirteen thousand miles, to the far side of the world.

Added to that, there was eagerness among the King's ships to see what gratitude might flow from John Company towards themselves, because it was accepted tradition that merchant captains gave presents to their protectors on these occasions, and usually in the form of domestic silver. So there was busy boat work in that respect too, with John Company launches alongside, and chests hoist aboard and smiling faces, because the Company was very generous. Every captain and first lieutenant in the squadron received a heavy silver tankard of a quart measure, and engraved with his name, and every tankard contained enough gold coin for the whole ship's crew to be entertained to a rolling, roaring dinner.

I got a truly huge piece of plate: the first fine silver I ever owned, and I've kept it to this very day: an enormous tray by the silversmith Paul Storr. It was struck with London hallmarks: including a capital B for the year 1797. Being so heavy it was for display rather than serving up the afternoon tea, and it was engraved in beautiful flowing script:

With gratitude to Commodore Jacob Fletcher
From Mr Stephen Kilbride and Sir Robert Valentine, Baronet,
Given upon arrival in Bombay April 4th 1798,
In hopeful anticipation
Of greater things to come.

It was yet another attempt by him to pull me into his service, but you had to admire his thoroughness in getting it engraved with the date of our arrival in Bombay, because no man could predict that: not in those days, my jolly boys, and not under sail. You never knew when – or even if – you might come safe into port! He must have hauled along a skilled engraver for the purpose, because we'd not touched land and the job must have been done aboard ship. So, what with that, and the lavish silver and gold for my officers, Kilbride wasn't just showing me how rich he was, *and how rich I might become*, but he was demonstrating how clever he was, which indeed he was, the cunning little bastard.

With all the coming and going, it wasn't until the next day that I led my squadron – now consisting only of King's ships, the few miles into the anchorage of Kilbride Island. It was a fine broad seaway, with a narrow entrance defended by a stone-built fort, and which fort we saluted with blank charges, as we came past in line astern with colours flying, and a local pilot to guide us down the narrow channel into the harbour, and which needed some careful steering with sand-banks on either side. Then, inside the anchorage, Port Kilbride had every imaginable convenience for supplying and re-fitting our ships for the home-bound voyage, and there was the usual joy aboard all of us to be in port after so long at sea. So we looked forward to the delights of a run ashore, with balls, dinners, grogshops and the exotic women of the Indies who – by seamanly repute – knew such tricks as the whores of England never dreamed of.

All hands aboard *Euphonides* cheered when the anchor was let go. My officers came forward to congratulate me on so successful a voyage, and Jimbo the cat was brought out for me to make a fuss of. So I did, and he purred when I stroked him, which was all very cosy. In fact everything was cosy except for just one thing. With the Indiamen safe-delivered to Bombay the *supposed* objective of my orders was achieved. So after all the jolly comradeship with the East India crews, and gifts given, and my crews cheering, and Jimbo giving a purr, I had to face what I'd been avoiding for months past. I had to decide what I was going to do, as regards Kilbride's plans for Japan. What about the God-almighty Earl Spencer, First Lord of the Admiralty? What about his threats and commands on behalf of the Shadow Men? Could I be a mighty figure of mystery and power by doing their bidding? Or – if I played them false – could they reach out and grab me from the other side of the earth? Could they? I thought they might find that hard when I was in the realm of another power, equal to theirs.

Contrariwise, what about Kilbride and his offers of a new life for me in the East? Could I trust him? Should I trust him? Indeed, should I not only look the other way, and not interfere with his plans, but *should I actually go with him to Japan*? Was this the greatest chance I'd ever get to break free of the Navy and get safe into trade?

In short, my jolly boys, who was I to serve: the Shadow Men or John Company?

CHAPTER 33

'Be assured, honoured lady and my beloved sons, that I am not blinded as was widely reported. I have perfect sight in my left eye, and my wound is healing well.'

(From the a letter of Tuesday, February 15th 1798 from Ship-Master Kazuki Tomoko, to his wife.)

Captain Tomoko staggered as something struck his face with a dull blow. It was not even a very hard blow, and not greatly painful: not yet. None the less, something was sticking into his right eye. It had come in under the brim of the helmet. It had just cleared the cheek-guard and found its way in. It was a long war-arrow, almost spent in its flight but not quite. He reached up with two hands, seized the shaft and snapped it, close up against his face. That hurt. That really hurt and blood flowed in a stream and dripped from his chin on to the deck below as he threw away the feathered shaft.

'Captain! Captain!' The men around him in the stern fighting-tower, turned from their shooting with crossbows and arquebuses, and clustered round him in horror. 'Surgeon!' they yelled, 'The captain's been hit!'

There were twenty men, armoured and armed, in the narrow, timbered space, raised up over the turtle's hull, where they could shoot down, through loop-holes in the roofed-over tower, on to the decks of ships alongside. Tomoko saw their anxious faces and their gaping mouths. 'Captain?' they cried, 'Are you all right, honoured Sir?' But he barely heard them. The sea battle was deafening with gunfire, shouts and screams. Oarsmen chanted, drums boomed. Ships rumbled against each other, and oars splintered and smashed. Tokugawa soldiers, cheered and bellowed their war cries, and leaped like fearless wolves, constantly trying – and failing – to get aboard the Hitamoto turtles. They never gave up, and each man stepped into the

221

place of a fallen comrade, only to be shot down, or fall into the sea in his turn. Dozens of ships were packed together, as Hitamoto and Tokugawa tried to best each another, with bullets, stones, arrows, grenades, smoke bombs and flame-pots. And now Captain Tomoko could not see very well, because there was blood in his right eye.

'Get back to your duties!' he cried.

'Hi!' they said, and turned to renew their fire on the Tokugawa soldiers and seamen below. Then everyone grabbed for a hold as there came an enormous detonation from the gun-deck below, and the turtle rolled in recoil.

'There!' cried Tomoko, 'There's our big gun! Hark at him!' and everyone cheered as the Dutch cannon roared. It was the only one of its kind, and the biggest by far among all the ships engaged in this first battle of the Kyushu straights, where Kyushu Island was only twenty miles from Hito Island.

'Honoured Sir! Honoured Sir!' The surgeon was climbing up through the trapdoor, in the floor of the fighting-tower.

'Here! Here!' said some of the men, 'See to the captain!'

'I'm here too, honoured Sir!' said a voice. It was the first officer come from the forward fighting-tower.

'Let me see, honoured Sir,' said the surgeon, 'I'll have to take off your helmet, honoured Sir!'

'Do so!' said Tomoko to the surgeon, 'and you take command!' he said to the first officer.

'Hi!' said the two men.

'Keep at it!' said Tomoko, 'No letting up. Clear their decks of everything that moves!'

'Hi!'

'Now,' said the surgeon, and Tomoko's helmet came off, and was dropped on the deck. 'It's not in deep,' said the surgeon, fingering the wound. 'but the eye is destroyed.'

'Pull it!' said Tomoko, 'get it out of my face!' The surgeon fumbled in his box of instruments and found a pair of pincers. 'Two men hold his honour's shoulders!' he cried, 'and someone hold his head! He mustn't move!' then, 'Hmmm …' said the surgeon, and frowned, and put down the pincers and fingered the wound some more. He took his time. It was tricky work. The flesh had closed over the arrow point. 'It's barbed!' he said, finally. 'Honoured Sir, will you come below? I can't do this here. Not with so many men and so much movement.'

'Yes,' said Tomoko, 'I'm no use like this.' But nobody heard him because the Dutch cannon fired again, with thundering noise and clouds of smoke. Everyone cheered as a Tokugawa ship close by, was hit bow-on, and was split down its entire length by the eighteen pound ball. The ship rolled heavily and began to fill, and a desperate howling came from everyone aboard.

'What's happening?' said Tomoko who could see nothing.

'We've sunk that one!' said the first officer, 'It's going over. It's going down!'

'We'd have sunk them all with proper cannon,' said Tomoko, and then kept silent. He was ashamed of himself. Such disloyal thoughts were not for the men to hear. None the less, Tomoko knew how different it *could* have been. As it was, fifty turtles were just about holding off a similar number of Tokugawa ships that were only the first feelers of the invasion to come. They were small ships, single-masted Japanese ships, of the type that the Shogun would use for his invasion, and they would *all* have been smashed and sunk if Tomoko had been allowed to build western warships with western guns. But Lord Kimiya had forbidden that.

Fortunately, Captain Tomoko's profound concentration on this disappointment, proved a merciful distraction when the surgeon set to work, because the removal of a barbed arrowhead from an eye-socket, was not an enjoyable process.

Unfortunately, and even less enjoyable was the fact that Captain Tomoko was proved completely correct in his warnings that turtle ships were unfit for purpose in the present crisis. He was proved accurate a month later, when a fleet of some hundreds of Tokugawa ships landed their main invasion force on the flat, sandy beaches of eastern Hito Island.

CHAPTER 34

Mr Rawson Charles Hornsby was Governor of the Presidency of Bombay. That was his formal title and he was one of the biggest panjandrums who ever lived. I doubt that even the Emperor Nero lived in such splendour. So pay attention all you youngsters, because once again in these memoirs, your Uncle Jacob is going to take the back off the clock of world affairs, to show you how the gear-wheels turn.

Charley Hornsby went out to India as a *'writer'* in the East India Company's service in 1748 at the age of seventeen, and I only wish such an opportunity had been given to me, because a writer was a thunderingly-glorified clerk who supervised the paperwork of the Company's business, while remaining in eternal superiority over the native peoples who did all the work. His post also offered such great opportunities for private trade that there was enormous competition for each vacancy, and a young man in England had no chance of filling one without heavy bribes or family influence. But once he'd got in, provided he was half-way diligent, the lucky lad must end up rolling in riches.

So consider the young Charley Hornsby who was very diligent indeed. He worked hard, and he worked long, and he rose to the very top. He ended up Governor of Bombay receiving a colossal salary, living in a palace full of servants, sleeping in silk, riding in a gilded carriage, and commanding a bigger army than King George. He was himself a king in all but name, except that he answered to the East India Company. But he didn't mind that because he was loyal to the Company, and hadn't been in England for fifty years. So he wasn't really an Englishman any more. He didn't look like one, he didn't sound like one, and he didn't act like one.

That was Charley, and I met him at Government House, about a week after we'd anchored in Port Kilbride. It was easy to get to the town since it was less than an hour's pull in a launch, or faster under sail if the wind was kind. So off we went, in our full dress again, myself and my officers, to attend a levee which was our formal welcome by the Governor and his minions. Bombay in those days, ran about three miles in extent from North to South along an east-facing bay-side, and as we approached from Kilbride Island, we had a fine view of the whole town, with its massive fortifications, high buildings, and wharves and cranes and anchorages.

'There's our Indiamen,' said Mr Pyne, pointing to the north of the great port, 'Looks like there's busy work on board of them. Now what would that be? Unloading cargo? Taking on supplies?'

'Yes,' we all said, because the closer we came, the more it was obvious that the big ships were swarming with men.

'And they've not even started on us!' said O'Flaherty and looked at me. 'The swabs are giving their own ships precedence over us, when we need re-provisioning for the homebound voyage!' We all frowned at that. But it was only to be expected from John Company, and we weren't especially worried: not yet. Meanwhile, it grew stinking hot and stinking humid the closer we came inshore, and our boat finally made fast to a long quay by the Custom House, a mile or more south of where the Indiamen were anchored. I left a boat-watch aboard, and unleashed the rest of the crew with the boatswain himself to watch over them, so they should be sober for the return pull. Then out we got, among swarms of native people, and officials and uniforms, and our first sight of the Company's native troops: the Sepoys.

'Look there,' said O'Flaherty as we went up the steps, 'Those is Rajputs. Big men chosen for looks. They're one of the martial races of India: warriors born and bred.' I looked and saw a company of red-coats under a white officer, standing guard over some chests. They were indeed tall, and wore an approximation of British uniform, but with bare legs, odd head-dresses, dark faces, and long, twirling moustaches. They looked fine men, and carried Brown Bess muskets, as good as our own marines aboard ship. Then there was some shouting, and natives in Company service – superior men with bright-coloured native clothes – were bowing and making us welcome since we were obviously expected. But as for ourselves, the sweat was running down our faces, into the collars of our shirts, and we were looking to get out of the sun and into the shade.

'Welcome, Sahib! Welcome, Commodore Sahib!' they said, and turned and shouted in their own language, and people were staring at us, and folk were bustling about on shipyard business, shoving barrows and bearing loads, and chattering to one another, and women in long native costumes – *sarees* – were sweeping up rubbish. That's India, my jolly boys: the only place in the world where the dung gets cleared away by women dressed as fairy-book princesses. Then an army officer – a white man – came out of a door nearby and saluted.

'Commodore Fletcher?' he said, 'I'm to take you to Government House, Sir. You and your fellow officers.' Once again, the uniform was so close to King George's as to make no difference: red coat, silver frogging, gorgette and a bicorne hat. But what I noticed was his odd accent, one which I later heard from all the long-stay English who picked it up from the Indian peoples who speak our language. It was an up-and-down tone, a bit like a Welsh accent, and with it came an odder-still habit of jigging the head from side to side. It's the sort of thing you notice only at first in foreign parts, and then you get used to it.

Well, my jolly boys, Charley Hornsby had these tricks to excess. We met him in the huge, high meeting room of Government House. It was all worked and decorated with carvings and mosaics, and it was marble-slab floored, and cooled by huge fans like carpets – *punkhas* – hung from the ceiling, with servants hauling on lines to swing them to and fro.

'Commodore, Sir!' said Hornsby, 'You are most welcome to Bombay, and I share with my Company colleagues in thanking you for the protection you have given to our ships!' He really did have that Indian accent, and he really did jig-head from side to side, and his face was darkened by decades of fierce sunshine. He was brown and leathery and wrinkled, and very fat, and he looked even older than his sixty-seven years. He was so weather-beaten that he looked more like a seaman than a landman. He wore the company's version of court dress: a silver-laced coat of black velvet, over britches and white silk stockings. He was draped in a sash and loaded with the stars of Eastern orders that no man of my party recognised. He had an ostrich-feathered hat in his hand, a Mameluke sword at his side, and he was seated on a massive chair, carved in Indian style, and placed on a stone platform about a foot high. He sat with a cloud of minions around him: Kilbride and Valentine at his very elbow, then various Company officials, and then the captains of the nine Indiamen. Kilbride and Valentine grinned at me like monkeys, but I got a genuine smile from Captain Stacey of *Duke of Cornwallis*, and some of the others too.

I said something polite in return, and there were some introductions to persons I had not met, and then we were taken in to a lavish dinner of many courses, and Indian servants in white turbans, and everything was – once again – very odd. To begin with, there were no ladies present which was a huge disappointment, because the first thing a seaman does when attending a welcoming banquet is to spy out which of the ladies is seeking entertainment away from her husband. Then there was the food, which was formidably spiced and Indian, and then – from my point of view – there was the strain of being placed between Hornsby, and Kilbride and Valentine who still wouldn't give up.

'Have you made up your mind, Sir?' Kilbride kept whispering, 'We'll do so well together.'

'No,' I kept saying, because I hadn't made up my mind. I still hated Kilbride, but all the wealth around me was swinging my mind towards his offer. Also he didn't get much chance to pester me because his honour Charley Hornsby, was the most tremendous bore and determined to explain to me precisely how – and mainly by his own exertions, as he told it – the East India Company had taken advantage of the disintegration of the old Mughal Empire, to conquer the fragments and take them under control. So I was very bored, but Kilbride and Valentine loved it: or pretended to.

'Then there's the recent siege of Seringapatam!' said Charley, which was a great triumph of the Company's arms!'

'How was it done, Governor?' said Kilbride, laying down knife and fork, and gazing with admiration, 'I know none of the details.'

'Indeed, Governor,' said Valentine, gulping wine, then dabbing his mouth with a napkin, 'I should be honoured to hear the tale.'

The pair of them greased like the bootlickers they were, and I was surprised to see that Hornsby greased right back! He greased and greased, with his sweaty brown face all leering. They owned one another, the three of them. I could smell it. I could see it. So whatever Kilbride had planned, Mr Governor Charley Hornsby was alongside of him, and that was something profound for me to consider in making my own decision.

Eventually we got away, and pulled for Kilbride Island over blessedly cool waters as the sun went down. The mood in the boat was dull. None of the officers had enjoyed the dinner, and all were grumbling about the absence of women, until O'Flaherty laughed.

'You'll have to wait your turn for that, me lads,' he said, 'but don't worry, because – by all the saints – it's worth the wait!'

'Oh?' we all said, including myself, and clank-clank went the oars and the water bubbled under the bow and officers and men together listened hard.

'Huh!' said O'Flaherty, 'Look at the dear little faces on you!' and he lowered his voice as if telling a secret, 'The thing is, me lads, there's no white women hardly, in the whole of India. The journey's too long and the climate's too hard.' He paused and winked. 'But there's plenty of Indian women, and you wait till you see the loveliness of 'em, with brown skin, gorgeous eyes, silky tresses of hair, round limbs, and figures like a sand-glass, and none of the modesty of Christian women, since there's no Ten Commandments out here: never has been, never will be!'

'*Oh?*' we said, because by George he had us now. He had us by the throat and we were gulping for more.

'So every one of them swabs back there,' said O'Flaherty, jabbing a thumb at Bombay, 'every one, from the Governor down to the lowest clerk, he has a woman like that at home, and some of them even marry them and raise children. But they don't bring them into society. They keep it private, except to their friends who they trust, and that's not us. Not yet.'

'Oh,' we all said, disappointed.

'But don't worry, me lads, because after a little while, asking the right questions of the right people, and with a sum of money that will amaze you with its smallness … you can each be set up ashore with a girl or two like that.' So we became a very thoughtful company: indeed we did, in very deed. We were a quiet and thoughtful company, and each of us doing sums in our heads as to how much ready money we had.

Next morning I began the long battle to get my ships repaired and provisioned for the voyage back to England, or to wherever else we might be bound. I did this even though normally, after so enormous a voyage, nobody expected to turn around and go straight back home! There was a practical need for a good stay in port because, no ship could be so long at sea without damage such as leaks below, sprung spars, seams in need of caulking, and worn-out rigging replaced. Also, a decent run ashore was necessary for the health and strength of the crew. But I didn't know what Kilbride would do next, and his ships were certainly being made ready, and if mine were to embark on adventures, there was the need to take on many tons of victuals: salt-pork, salt-beef, biscuit and sauerkraut, and endless gallons of lime-juice, rum and brandy. The list was endless and that was the merest glimpse, and I've not even mentioned spare cable, iron nails, round-shot, sheet lead, and ship's tar.

So I was in the Company's offices in Port Kilbride every day, banging the table, demanding action, and getting the same replies from the Indian clerks who worked there. They were a bright set of men, who should have been capable of their jobs. But they just made excuses.

'A holy week begins tomorrow, Commodore Sir,' said the head clerk on one occasion.

'A holy week,' said the rest, in the shady, cool office, wafted by the punkha in the ceiling, while the poor damned punkha-wallah sat outside in the sun, hauling his line. 'And no man may work in a holy week,' said the chief clerk, and all the rest looked at me, and nodded in unison, with hands resting on their stand-up desks. Another time it was: 'The problem is not here, Commodore Sir. The problem is failure of supply from the interior.' Or: 'The spars were rotten when supplied, Commodore Sir.' Or: 'The cart with the rum turned over on the road, and dishonest fellows stole the whole cargo.'

They were unfailingly polite and respectful, and always gave me their full attention, and looked me straight in the eye. So I never did work out whether they were telling lies themselves or passing on the lies of those above them. I suspect it was the latter, under fear for their jobs because they were always nervous in my presence. But at the time, I assumed that this was the reasonable reaction of a poor little pen-driver when someone like me leans into his face and shouts. Even O'Flaherty thought so.

'Look at you!' he said when we came out from the office together, 'you're fit to frighten the French. No wonder their knees are knocking. Give the poor devils another day.'

So we did. We gave them a lot more days. In the meanwhile, we got fresh food, and soft bread, and I gave my crews shore leave, and there was boat-traffic to and from Bombay, and some of the other Islands. Also, we took advantage of O'Flaherty's suggestion regarding the local girls. So life was very pleasant indeed on Kilbride Island, until things turned very nasty indeed.

CHAPTER 35

'Arrangements for the voyage to Japan are moving forward, though with some uncertainty. The Honourable Hornsby, Governor of Bombay, has proved a willing ally and is deep in Kilbride's confidence. We met him today and he seemed entirely on our side. But as with all these foreigners, there is the eternal problem of trust.'

(From the 'Foreign Journal' of Masahito Hitamoto. Entry dated Saturday, May 26th 1798.)

'Mr Kilbride?' said Masahito, 'Will Fletcher join us in our plans?' Kilbride sighed.

'No, my Lord,' he said, 'or at least, he can't make up his mind, which is just as bad.'

'Can't he be persuaded?' said Governor Hornsby.

'Not by me,' said Kilbride, 'I've tried my utmost and got nowhere. I don't think he likes me very much.'

'You did your best,' said Sir Robert Valentine, 'I was there, I saw you.'

The four men fell silent. There were just the four of them present. All lower-ranking persons were excluded from this highly confidential meeting in an upper room of Government house. It was a cool, shaded, private room, and the punkha-wallah, sat on his haunches outside the door, had been chosen for his profound deafness. The room was furnished in teak, and the slatted windows looked out on the town, the walls, the bastions and the harbour.

'In that case,' said Masahito, and addressed Hornsby, 'If it comes to it, will your gunners fire into British ships?'

'Yes!' said Hornsby, 'They're under my orders and they know damn-well better than to disobey.'

'Orders?' said Masahito, 'Spoken orders or written orders?' Hornsby

230

sighed, he eased his bulk back into his chair and away from the table. He turned to Kilbride.

'Will you explain to this Japanese gentleman?' he said, 'He knows you and I assume he relies on you.' Kilbride nodded, and gathered his thoughts. As he did so, Sir Robert Valentine reached for the decanter, and offered wine to Masahito.

'No, thank you,' said Masahito and bowed politely. Valentine filled Hornby's glass, then Kilbride's, and then his own, unconsciously giving himself *just* a little more than the others, *just* to make sure that enough went down his own throat.

'My Lord,' said Kilbride, 'I ask you to understand that the officers and men of the fort are natives born and bred.'

'Not quite,' said Masahito, 'the officers are of mixed blood.'

'Yes,' said Kilbride, 'but the officers were born here and don't know any other land than India, and their fathers left England years ago.'

'Quite right,' said Hornsby, 'Look at me! I left England in '48 and don't hardly remember it any more. And as for the Sepoys and the officers, it's John Company that feeds them and pays wages that make them princes among their own folk. So it's John Company's flag they salute and not King George's.'

Masahito looked at each of the three foreigners. He studied their faces and chose the one least able to conceal dishonesty.

'Sir Robert?' he said, and Valentine blinked, 'Let us imagine that Commodore Fletcher discovers our plans and attempts to take his ships out of Port Kilbride, past the fort which guards the entrance.' Valentine gulped and looked at Kilbride and Hornsby in alarm. 'In that case, Sir Robert, do you believe that the officers and men of the battery, will fire on ships flying the British flag?' Valentine dithered. He dithered but finally nodded.

'Yes.' said Valentine, 'I suppose so.'

'They'll fire,' said Hornsby, totally confidant, 'They'll fire because they'll do as I tell 'em.' He smiled. 'And afterwards? Why, we'll declare it was all a dreadful mistake! Then we'll cashier the officer in command, and that'll be the end of it, and which is why, my Lord, that there can't be any *written* orders.'

'Again, I am satisfied,' said Masahito, 'but we must consider actions beyond Commodore Fletcher's ships coming under fire.'

'What actions?' said Hornsby.

'What indeed?' said Kilbride.

'That is precisely what we must consider,' said Masahito, 'because I have asked questions about Commodore Fletcher. I did so before we embarked in England, and later on board *Duke of Cornwallis.*'

'And?' said Kilbride.

'I learned that he is an officer of the utmost intelligence and energy, and I therefore wonder what he might do, if he finds himself trapped in Port Kilbride and unable to get past the fort, but still in possession of some hundreds of men, and dozens of heavy guns.'

'It doesn't matter!' said Kilbride, 'He can do what he damn-well likes, because we'll be long gone and he won't know where. We just need him shut up in Port Kilbride for a day or so while we get under the horizon. After that, he can whistle up the leg of his drawers!'

'Good,' said Masahito, 'because while you, Honoured Governor,' he bowed towards Hornsby, 'Might get away with an accidental firing on British ships ...'

'When it was never my fault in the first place,' said Hornsby and smiled, 'just some fool of a half-breed native officer!' Masahito nodded and continued.

'So, while you might be excused distant cannon fire, you will not be excused a face-to-face battle on land, between your sepoys and King George's seamen and marines. That could never be explained as accidental, it would cause the British to retaliate, and their retaliation would be severe. They could seize your company's assets in England. Their navy could close down your trade. They could send a fleet to Bombay with an army!'

Masahito stared closely at Hornsby. He saw Hornsby wriggle uncomfortably and lick his lips.

'There'll be no need for any of that,' said Kilbride, 'because there'll no need for action against Fletcher and his men. Once we're gone, they can be let out of the bottle with enormous apologies, and all made right.' He turned to Hornsby. 'Ain't that so, Governor?'

'Of course it is!' said Hornsby, 'We won't touch them. We dare not touch them, and there's no need to touch them.'

'Because we'll be gone!' said Kilbride, 'Gone to Japan!'

'And when we go,' said Masahito, 'what strength shall we take with us?' Kilbride smiled. That was an easy question. One with an easy answer! It was nice plain figures with no more guessing and wondering, and Kilbride reeled off the details from memory.

'Three regiments of foot, one regiment of horse, a dozen of 9-pounder horse artillery pieces, two 24-pounder siege guns, and a company of military engineers, all complete with powder, shot, wads cartridges and spares. That's just under five thousand men, in eight of our big Indiamen and four smaller ships.'

'Good,' said Masahito, 'but you said eight Indiamen and we have nine.'

'Indeed, my Lord,' said Kilbride, 'But that's because *Duke of Cornwallis* is to be our flagship with two tiers of heavy guns and a full crew to man them, which means nearly eight hundred men, which leaves no room for more. The other ships can be converted for trooping, and filled with sepoys and horses. but we can't do that to our *Duke* if she's to be a fighting warship.'

'And why do we need a fighting warship?' said Masahito.

'Because we'd be mad to set sail without one!' said Kilbride, 'Such a fleet? Loaded with men and stores? And not a man-o-war to guard them? And more than that, my Lord, haven't you said that your enemies must cross the water to reach your homeland?'

'Yes,' said Masahito, 'The Shogun's forces must cross the Straits of Kyushu to reach Hito Island.'

'Well, there you are then,' said Kilbride, 'They won't do that with *Duke of Cornwallis* in the way! And more than that, the ship will be proof positive to your people that you've brought back something powerful.' Kilbride leaned forward in the flood of enthusiasm. 'And wasn't that what you were sent out to get, my Lord? Wasn't that why you were sent you out from Japan in the first place? There'll be nothing afloat east of India, that can equal our *Duke*: your *Duke,* my Lord! She'll be a moving castle. She'll be immune to attack, she'll command the seas, control trade, open or shut any port she chooses, and make it impossible for your enemies to invade your homeland. So when they see her … *your folk will know you've done your duty!'*

Masahito nodded in respect of Kilbride's insight. He did not recall revealing so much of his own motivation. Perhaps he had been careless in conversation? Who could tell? But Kilbride was speaking the truth with exquisite precision.

'Good,' said Masahito, 'Very good. But there is one more matter to discuss.'

'Which is, my Lord?' said Kilbride.

233

'I hear that there is trouble among the captains of the fleet: the captains who came out with us from England. I refer to Captain Stacey in particular.' Kilbride and Valentine looked at each other.

'What's this?' said Hornsby, 'I haven't heard of any trouble.'

'Oh it's nothing,' said Kilbride. He smiled outwardly and cursed inwardly.

'None the less,' said Masahito, 'some of the captains are worried. They are worried about the possibility of trouble with the British Government: the sort of trouble we discussed earlier.' Kilbride breathed deeply and managed to control his emotions.

'Perhaps,' he said, keeping calm, 'but with the utmost respect, my Lord, why don't you leave the captains to me? There's some as can be bought, some as can be persuaded, and others as can be replaced. If you'll just leave that to me, my Lord, everything'll come out right.'

'I do hope so, Mr Kilbride,' said Masahito, 'I hope so very much indeed.'

CHAPTER 36

We got the warning during the evening of June 6th, which was a Wednesday, and a wet one, with the Monsoon beginning, though it was an unusually mild monsoon that year. Thus a boat pulled into the harbour of Port Kilbride, after dark. It came alongside *Euphonides* and I was called for, and I wasn't aboard because I was ashore in a cosy little house with a local girl called Shamita, who had all the virtues that Mr O'Flaherty had described. Thus I record the sad instance of my taking the last sight – by lamplight of her delectable naked bum as she turned out of bed to answer the servant who was knocking on our door. It was my last sight of any part of her because everything happened so fast and furious, that there wasn't even time to say goodbye properly. I just hauled on my clothes, kissed her once, then ran. But I did make sure she was left well provided.

I suppose the rush and tumble served me right for falling into such joyful sloth. But before you think ill of your Uncle Jacob, just you wait till you're grown up, my jolly boys, and let's see if you can resist such delights when they're in easy reach.

Pyne was outside the house, with a boat-load of seamen and lanterns raised. He was officer of the watch that night: that night and many others, since he hadn't got himself a lady ashore. He was unusual in that way too, as well as being miserable company.

'Sir!' he cried, as soon as I was out in the night with the beastly insects buzzing and the stars above and the night breeze in our faces, 'Terrible news, Sir! We've been betrayed, and I've taken the liberty of rousing out all hands, throughout the squadron, and summoning captains and senior officers aboard *Euphonides* for your orders!' He stood to attention and saluted. 'Sir!' he said, 'I thought that best!' The seamen around him nodded in agreement, and they all touched hats in respect.

'What's happened?' I said, 'What's going on?'

'Captain Stacey has come aboard, Sir,' said Pyne, 'he's come aboard, and is in the hands of the surgeon's mates, what with the surgeon himself being ashore. He's sore wounded and is despaired of, and there's others of the East India crews with him, and some likewise wounded. It's bad, Sir, there's been bloodshed, and it's treachery!'

'What?'

'It's Kilbride, Sir. It's him and the Japanese milord. They're sailing on the morning tide, the whole squadron of them with four other ships, and we're trapped in this bay.'

'Trapped?' I said, 'How can that be?'

'Don't know, Sir,' said Pyne, 'Best come away, Sir, and repair on board of *Euphonides* for further words from Captain Stacey, should he still be alive.' So that's what we did, and did it at the gallop: ourselves and everyone else belonging to the squadron who'd been tucked up warm that night. It was like Portsmouth Point, only hot and wet and dark. There were officers everywhere, saying their goodbyes, and buckling on swords, and Indian women hanging on their arms and weeping, and the boats of all the squadron waiting where the sand met the sea, and coxswains calling the oar-strokes, and oars clanking as the boats pulled away.

There was no time to think. Pyne was right to do what he'd done in alerting the squadron, and there was a thrill of excitement among all hands. Yes, we'd been deceived, but it wasn't as if it was a French squadron of the Line, that had done so. If it came to a fight against the nine Indiamen, then Heaven help them. So the oarsmen pulled fit to bust, the boats surged on across the dark water, heading for the lights of their ships: our boat to *Euphonides*, and the rest to collect those officers who hadn't been ashore, to answer Pyne's summons and join us. Meanwhile Pyne had little more to say than he'd already said, and I had to wait for more news until I was going up the ladder on board of *Euphonides*, and the boatswain's calls sounding, and all hands stood with by, together with a small group of East India sea officer – captains and mates in their uniforms – who saluted along with my own people. One of these officers stepped forward.

'Commodore Fletcher, Sir,' he said, 'Begging your pardon to be so forward, aboard of your ship, but none of this was our doing!'

'Aye!' said his companions.

'We're John Company's men, but we're loyal hearts and true, and God save the King!'

'Aye!' said the others.

'And we're here to warn you, fairly, commodore, so there shall be no war between the Company and the King!'

'Aye!' said the rest.

'And we're no part of them that *did* go along with it!'

'No!' they cried.

'Where's Captain Stacey?' I said, 'I hear he's the leading man among you.'

'He's below, Sir,' said Pyne.

'Aye,' said almost everyone.

'On the orlop, Sir,' said Pyne, 'there were five wounded that came aboard and the surgeon's mates made ready as if to receive those fallen in battle.' I nodded.

'All hands stand fast,' I said, 'Send the surgeon below so soon as he's aboard, and Mr Pyne, you come with me.'

'Aye-aye!'

Down we went, in the gloom and the lantern-light, with dark shadows and a low deck-head. The surgeon's mates had done well: planks laid over chests to form operating tables, and sailcloth laid over the planks for comfort and to soak up the blood. They were still working on one man, whose bleeding would not stop, and he cried out a lot, so I had to lean over Captain Stacey, where he lay half-conscious, to hear what he was trying to tell me. He was naked under a blanket, with his clothes cut off to get at his wounds: bayonet stabs to the chest and limbs, and himself shot through with musket balls. It was bad and he was dying.

'Fletcher,' he said, 'It's that bastard Kilbride. He never told us everything about Japan. He had every pair of hands in Bombay working on our ships. The Governor's in it with Kilbride and Valentine! They took aboard 32-pounders and the crews to man them, and all of them native seamen, and more of them than my own lads that came out from England, so she ain't barely British no more.'

'D'you mean *Duke of Cornwallis*?'

'Yes! She's bearing eighty guns. She's strong as a First Rate. Thick timbers and a huge crew. She could smash any ship in the Indies.' Then he gasped and panted. 'Drink,' he said, 'water.'

'Get him some water!' I cried, and one of the surgeon's mates would have brought it, but Mr Davenham, our surgeon, came rumbling down a companionway in that instant. He heard what I said, and himself found a pan of water and raised Stacey's head and gave him a drink.

'Sorry I'm late, Sir,' said Davenham.

'Stacey,' I said, 'What happened? How were you wounded? Why are you here?'

'Ah!' said Davenham, 'excuse me, Sir!' and he was gone off, and shoving his mates aside, and attending to the man who was crying out and bleeding.

'Bloody swab!' said Stacey, 'He wanted us to go to Japan, and we might have gone, but I asked what about you and your ships, and Valentine blabbed,'

'What do you mean?' I said.

'He'd been at the bottle again,' said Stacey, 'and I asked at the meeting ...' He paused. 'Did I say there was a meeting?'

'No,' I said,

'Well. There was a meeting,' he said, 'Kilbride brought us all to a private meeting. Him, Valentine and all the captains and mates, in a warehouse by the docks,' Stacey reached out and took my arm, 'didn't I say that?' he said.

'Never mind,' I said, 'go on.'

'Well. We didn't trust him. We knew he had some plans for Japan, but we was loading native troops and stores fit for a war! And I wondered what Parliament would think of that, and what Parliament might do to the Company? So I asked what about you. I said what about Commodore Fletcher's squadron? I asked what would Fletcher do if we sailed for Japan?'

'And?' I said.

'And Kilbride, he said you'd been bought off, and wouldn't stand in our way!' He looked at me. 'Were you? Were you bought off?'

'No!' I said, and said it with some guilt considering how nearly I had been.

'I thought not,' he said, 'and then that swab Valentine, who was full of drink, just laughed and said the Port Kilbride battery would sink you if you tried to get out! Sink you!'

'What? *What?*' I said, 'Fire on the Royal Navy? Fire on the British flag? God bugger me blind! Are they gone raving bloody mad?'

'Yes, yes!' said Stacey, 'It'd be plain treason against England! I said as much, and Kilbride started yelling at Valentine, and some of us was yelling at him, and Kilbride lost his temper, and said all those of us who won't sail were dismissed the from Company's service and would be replaced. And he called out again, and some sepoys came who he'd had waiting outside, and there was a fight.'

'You fought them?'

'That we did! There'd been gossip round the squadron, we'd half guessed

238

what was afoot even before the meeting, so we went in with barkers under our coats and cutlasses on our belts. And when the native troops came in, we were shipmates together who wouldn't take no sauce from them!'

'What happened?' I said.

'Powder and shot, and cold steel! Some of us went down, some of them went down and the rest ran for reinforcements, and Kilbride and Valentine ran with 'em, and those of us that were left, knew the only safe place for us was aboard of your ships. So we took a boat and came here, and I was carried by my comrades, God bless 'em!' His eyelids fluttered shut and his breathing slowed.

'Stacey?' I said, 'Captain Stacey?' He opened his eyes. He gathered strength. 'Listen,' he said.

'I'm listening!'

'They'll sail on tomorrow's tide. They're bound for Port Hito, which is on the south-west tip of Hito Island which is south west of Kyushu Island. It's on the Dutch charts if you've got one?' I nodded. 'Good,' he said, 'so that's where they're headed and they've embarked a whole army: horse, foot and guns. They're going to make war in Japan: a war outside India, which the Company ain't allowed to do. And you can't stop them, because the Kilbride harbour fort will fire if you try to take your ships out through the narrows.' He looked at me and his eyes closed again. 'Drink,' he said, 'drink.' I reached down for the pan, which surgeon Davenham had left on the floor. But Stacey was gone when I looked up. He'd hung on until he could give his warning, then passed over. It's like that sometimes, with folk near death: they cling to life till their duty's done. He was a good man and a brave man: a seaman through and through. He'd have been a true friend if he'd lived, and I miss him still, even after so short a time of knowing him and so long ago.

'Sir?' said Pyne. He'd been beside me the whole time, but I'd hardly noticed. 'Sir?' he said, 'I can hear boats. That'll be the officers of the squadron. Those I sent for, Sir.'

'Well done, Mr Pyne,' I said, 'I hear them,' and indeed I did. The rumbling bumping of timbers against timbers as the squadron's boats came alongside *Euphonides*.

'You receive them, Mr Pyne,' I said, 'bring them to the great cabin, tell them everything you know, have my steward serve refreshments. Then give me time to think. I'll be on the quarterdeck. I need to be quiet a while, but you come and get me after fifteen minutes of the sand-glass!'

'Aye-aye, Sir!'

So, my jolly boys, I was left on my own. But that's the way it was for a captain in King George's Navy. A captain was master unquestioned, but he was on his own. He even ate alone. He didn't dine with anybody unless he invited them special, or they invited him. Then, when it came to hard times and hard decisions, a captain made them on his own, and he carried the entire responsibility for what he did. So remember that, when you hear that captains lived in luxury, got most of the prize money, and got knighted when the ship won a victory.

Fifteen minutes was just about enough for me, pacing up and down in the steaming tropical night, ignoring everything and thinking hard. It was the moment when, with sorrow, I had to admit to myself that I couldn't follow Kilbride. I couldn't follow him even if he could be trusted to make me a merchant prince of the East, which he couldn't because he was a twisting little rat that couldn't be trusted in anything, and who'd placed myself and my ship where I could be sunk by the guns of a fort. It was only my hunger for the life of a merchant, that had kept me dithering for so long, but it's hard to deny your own nature. So, if was a choice between Kilbride, and Earl Spencer's Shadow Men, then for the moment it was Spencer. At least it was a relief to make the decision. After that the solution to problems of seamanly action came relatively easy, and if that seems boastful then it is not, because as with my great size and strength, the gift of seeing round corners and inventing ways out, isn't something clever but just the way I was born. There's no more merit in it than there is in the fact that my eyes are blue.

So, the first problem was the fort, and I'd seen forts taken during recent adventures in France. I'd seen what can be done with powder charges and surprise attacks, so I didn't even have to invent anything new ... if only I knew the layout of the fort, which of course I did not! The second problem was lack of supplies for a long voyage, but the answer to that was also obvious, if at some considerable sacrifice. That left the problem of *Duke of Cornwallis* with her 32-pounders and ship-of-the-line timbers. But that would have to wait.

Finally, when Pyne came for me, I entered the great cabin and found it full of navy blue, with a few red coats. Nearly two dozen officers were present, with seamen in white gloves stood behind, to serve the drink, and the lamps swinging overhead, and the table-top gleaming.

'Be seated, gentlemen,' I said, 'and the servants may leave,' so down we sat. 'First, gentlemen,' I said, 'has anyone anything to add to what Mr Pyne has told you?' Silence. They did not. My heart was bumping now, with all of them looking at me. I was Jacky Flash wasn't I? I was the boy that hammered the French and blew things up. Oh dear me. Dear me indeed. But on these occasions you have to make a show, and you have to say things in a certain way, because even the most senior and educated Sea Officers are exactly like the lower-deck tars: they love tradition, they hate change, and they need their captain to stand up straight under fire, and not duck when the round-shot whistles overhead.

So I waited few seconds for effect, and delivered my speech, and all you youngsters should note of the manner of it, that you might do likewise in the same situation.

'Gentlemen!' I said, 'An outrageous insult has been given our King and our Service, and I am resolved to inflict severe retribution on those responsible, which retribution I have not the slightest doubt lies easily within the talents of our squadron!'

'Ahhhh,' they growled. They liked that, and were nodding to one another because that's how you have to speak to them.

'But before turning to the details of how we shall proceed,' I said, 'I am now able to reveal that in pursuing Mr Kilbride and Sir Robert Valentine, who are the principal criminals in this affair, we act on orders delivered to me personally, by no less than Earl Spencer himself: First Lord of the Admiralty!'

'Oooooh!' they said, and their eyes went round. And why shouldn't they? And why shouldn't I have said it? It was bloody well true, and it made them swell with pride. They'd be all the better for that. 'So now we now face two problems,' I said, 'of which, I shall deal with the more serious first: the matter of supplies so that a prolonged pursuit – all the way to Japan if need be – may be carried out.'

'Hmmm,' they said, and I continued:

'Since we can expect no further assistance from the authorities of Bombay, we must supply ourselves. The solution is therefore to combine all available supplies, whether from the holds of our squadron, or whatever may be in the storehouses of Port Kilbride, in order that some – or one – of our squadron may go forth provisioned for a long voyage.

'Oh?' That was a disappointment! They didn't like that. They sat up in their chairs and groaned. They looked at Mr Pyne for support.

'Does that mean some of us will be left behind, Sir?' he said, 'Here on Kilbride Island?'

'I'm afraid it does, Mr Pyne,' I said, 'but there is no other way.'

'What will they live on?' he said, 'Those left behind?'

'They will take a share of the fresh food brought daily into the Island by boats,' I said, 'to feed the native people.'

'What about the fort?' said Pyne, 'won't it close down the harbour?'

'No,' I said, and smiled, 'because it is up to ourselves, to make sure that the Fort is unable to do that.'

'Oh!' they said, and grinned at one another.

'But what about the Governor and the Company's forces in Bombay?' said Pyne, 'Won't they make trouble for those of us left behind?'

'Hmmm,' they all said.

'That we must set aside, for the moment,' I said, 'though I doubt the Governor would dare to send Sepoys against us, because that would be outright war against England.' They weren't sure about that, and neither was I. 'But I shall not leave Kilbride Island,' I said, 'until the Governor is made to see reason.' They nodded, but I could see they weren't happy.

'But the Fort, Sir?' said Pyne, 'What are we going to do about that?'

'The fort?' I said, and gave my best play-acting smile, 'That is the least of our problems! Thus you and I, Mr Pyne, shall pay it a visit tomorrow morning.'

'Oh?' he said.

'Oh!' they all said, blue coats and red coats together.

'Tomorrow morning, Mr Pyne,' I said, 'bright and early before the sun gets too hot, because we wouldn't want to be uncomfortable, would we?'

CHAPTER 37

'I was obliged to receive into my lines, a giant Englishman of awesome size and bearing, who was Fletcher, the commodore of the English ships in port Kilbride. But you will be proud, dear mother, that your son stood firm, and sent away this ignorant giant, with downcast eyes and chastened demeanour.'

(From a letter of Thursday, June 7th 1798, from Major William Frobisher, 2nd Bombay Regiment of Artillery, Commander of Fort Kilbride, to his mother Mrs Shivani Frobisher.)

The nine East Indiamen, led by *Duke of Cornwallis,* and with smaller ships astern, were already warped out into the sea-way, and they spread their sails and proceeded in line astern, southward and westward, heading for the open seas of the Indian Ocean. They went out in great style, with crowds waving from the quaysides, and music and drums aboard the ships, and thousands of sepoys cheering, and the banners of the East India Company flying beside new flags, made for this expedition, bearing the swooping hawk of Clan Hitamoto.

The monsoon rains being late, the ships were a grand sight, as seen from the battlements of Fort Kilbride, four miles across the bay, where the Fort's officers looked through their telescopes: Major Frobisher, Captain Thompson, Lieutenant Horace and Lieutenant Middlewich. Being artillerymen, they were all veteran, East India Company officers, highly trained in their complex craft. Equally, and despite their English names, they all had Indian mothers, and had never been within ten thousand miles of England.

Standing respectfully apart from their officers, the sergeants –*Havildars* – and the gunners and boys: no less than one hundred and eighty of them, also looked across the water at the great fleet that, by popular rumour, was bound for adventures in China and beyond. These men were pure

Rajputs, proud of their Company Service, and esteemed by their families for their high wages, splendid uniforms, and the huge guns that they commanded in their powerful fortress.

But enjoyment of the spectacle was interrupted.

'Sir?' said Captain Thompson, to Major Frobisher, 'Look, Sir, there's a boat coming out from the English squadron.' Thompson turned, looked back into the harbour, and saw the boat: a big launch, full of English seamen, pulling steadily away from the anchored ships, or to be precise, pulling away from their flagship, the heavy frigate *Euphonides*: a huge vessel, almost the size of a line-of-battle ship. Thompson focussed his glass on the boat. There were two officers in the stern. The epaulettes and cocked hats proclaimed their rank.

'This is only to be expected,' said Frobisher, 'They'll have seen our ships go by. They'll have seen that from their mastheads, and they'll be curious,' then he frowned as the gunners pointed at the boat and raised a great chatter of excitement.

'Be silent!' cried Frobisher, 'Havildars, take charge of your men!'

'Sahib!' said the Havildars and bellowed until all was quiet.

'Make ready to receive them,' said Frobisher to Captain Thompson, 'But gently! It's possible that don't know our orders. So if they don't know, there is no reason to expect trouble, and if they do know, we need not worry because there are very few of them.'

'Yes, Sir!' said Thompson, and he and the lieutenants did some more bellowing, to muster a company of gunners with carbines and fixed bayonets, both as a guard of honour and to remind the Englishmen to behave. The rest of the gunners stood by and waited, as curious as their officers, to see what the English boat wanted.

Frobisher and his officers looked down as the boat came closer and closer. Soon the oars could be heard working and splashing. Then the boat grounded in the sand at the foot of the fat, grey, thirty-foot high wall of the fort. The seamen leapt out, and hauled the boat's nose out of the water. The two officers got out, dry-footed.

'Huh!' said Frobisher, 'Look at that one!'

'Huge!' said Thompson.

'He must be the commodore,' said Frobisher.

'Fletcher?'

'Yes.'

'Everyone talks about him.'

'And now he's come here.'

'See! He's looking up.'

'Ahoy there!' cried the big Englishmen, 'We need to parlay. How may I come aboard?'

Frobisher leaned out through an embrasure. He pointed.

'Go that way,' he called, 'follow the wall where it curves, and you will come to a dry-moat, with a causeway and a postern gate. You gentlemen will be received, but your men must stay on the beach.' The two Englishmen looked at one another. They looked at the fort's wall, and being members of a fighting service, they took professional note of the fact that the wall was provided with bastions, and the bastions provided with loop-holes, and the loop-holes provided with swivel guns, to pour canister on any persons standing on the beach, who might be hostile to the fort.

'Aye-aye!' said the big Englishmen, and gave orders to his boat's crew, then trudged off, with the other officer behind him, upward from the beach, to where soil began, then grass and scrubby bushes, and they followed the wall round, to find the promised ditch, and causeway and a gateway, all lavishly provided with loopholes for gunfire on attackers.

Major Frobisher and Captain Thompson were waiting for the Englishmen as the gate – small, thick and iron-bound – was swung open, and the two Englishmen were seen waiting on the far side of the ditch.

'Come in gentlemen!' cried Frobisher, and the guard of gunners presented arms with their carbines as the huge officer and the smaller officer came in through the gateway. The four men met in an outer courtyard, where nothing could be seen of the fort beyond. There, they exchanged salutes, the two Englishmen raising their hats, and the two Company men bowing.

'Do I have the honour to meet Commodore Fletcher?' said Major Frobisher, and smiled, aiming at least to *begin* in a civilised fashion. But he got a great, dark frown in reply from Fletcher, who was even more intimidating a creature at close range than he'd seemed at a distance. Frobisher was reminded of a massive, angry bear.

'Yes,' said the bear, finally, 'I'm Fletcher, and with me I bring my first officer, Mr Pyne.'

'You are both welcome,' said Frobisher, and still tried to smile.

'Sir!' said Fletcher, 'We must talk. I've just seen the East India Squadron go out on unknown business, and without a word to myself, and I have to tell you, Sir, that I have heard unbelievable rumours concerning this fort.'

'What rumours, Sir?' said Frobisher.

'That someone has had the bloody, damned, block-head stupidity to order you to fire on my ships should I attempt to leave harbour.' Frobisher said nothing, but checked that the guard of honour, had a good grip of their carbines. 'Oh?' said Fletcher, 'So you don't deny it?' and he took a step forward, and Frobisher instinctively stepped back.

'Guard!' yelled the Havildar, in Hindi, 'Present!' and a line of carbines was levelled at Commodore Fletcher.

'A-hah?' said Fletcher, 'It's like that, is it?' he turned on Frobisher, 'and myself and my officer invited inside with your welcome?'

'No, no, no,' said Frobisher to the Havildar, 'stand them down.'

'Sahib!' said the Havildar, and 'Stand easy!' in Hindi.

'Major Frobisher, if that's your name,' said Fletcher.

'It is, Sir.'

'Then I have to tell you, Major, that I don't believe a word of this nonsense of your firing on my ships.' Frobisher blinked.

What's this? Nonsense? What does he mean? He glanced at Thompson who was thinking the same. But Fletcher persisted.

'I don't believe any of it,' he said, 'I don't believe it, 'cos you damned Company men haven't the guns, nor the men, to stop my ships. So I'm warning you now – in all decency and to save you from harm – that I am determined to come past, and if you try to stop me, I'll blow your little fort in to ruins and smash your guns to atoms: such of them as you've actually got, that are in any condition to be fired.' He turned to the English lieutenant beside him. 'Ain't that so, Pyne?'

'Indeed, Sir,' he said, 'they can't face British gunnery.'

Frobisher and Thompson were so surprised, that neither of them spoke. Fletcher noted that and smiled at Pyne.

'There,' he said, 'what did I tell you, Mr Pyne? This fort's like all the others in John Company's service: carriages rotten, guns cracked, shot rusted, and not a man in the house trained up to point them.' He folded his arms and looked down on Frobisher in contempt. 'I can see it in your face, you miserable swab. So good day to you, and be warned that I'm coming out within the hour, and God help those in that try to stop me.' He turned to go. 'Come on Pyne, we've got no more business here. These are toy soldiers.'

'How dare you, Sir!' said Frobisher, and stamped his foot, 'I condemn your rudeness, Sir, just as I pity ignorance.'

'Ignorance be damned,' said Fletcher, 'I doubt you've got powder for your guns. I doubt you've got shot that will fit, and I doubt you've even got paper in the bog-house!' He waved a hand at the fort. 'This is all a sham, isn't it? Be honest now! It's fit to frighten the natives but it don't frighten me! So just open up that bloody gate and let me out. Me and Mr Pyne.' With that, Fletcher turned and walked towards the gate with Pyne following behind.

For a moment nothing happened. Frobisher and Thompson were so amazed that they just stood gaping. Then Frobisher lost his temper and uttered a curse in the Hindi he'd learned before ever he spoke English, and he ran forward and grabbed Fletcher by one of his huge arms.

'Toy soldiers?' he said, 'A sham? You come with me, Sir, and I'll show you what you'll get if you try to pass my fort!'

CHAPTER 38

'By George, Sir,' said Pyne, 'I thought you'd overdone it when you walked to that gate. What if they'd just let us out?'

'But they didn't, did they? I said, 'they showed us everything.'

'Even the paper in the privy!' said Pyne. Being Pyne, he didn't mean that as a joke, but everybody laughed. I was back in the great cabin with my captains and senior officers: them and Mr Unwin, *Euphonides's* gunner. He had black fingernails, white stubble, and he sat at the back, embarrassed to be in such elevated company because he was middle-aged tar who'd worked his way up from a powder-monkey. So he didn't even pretend to be a gentleman, but he knew his trade and was vitally needed.

It was late in the day that Kilbride's fleet had gone out, and Pyne and I had returned from the Fort, and had a good long talk with Dr Goodsby, who might not have been a very good chaplain but was a damn fine draftsman who'd made a large diagram of Fort Kilbride, based on what Pyne and I had seen: everything from the magazine below, to the battlements above. So now everyone – especially the marines – were studying the diagram closely where it sat on an easel in front of them.

'Gentlemen,' I said, 'Major Frobisher, the commander of the fort, said it was designed by a renegade Frenchman in John Company's service.' I paused. 'And everyone knows the Frogs are the best at designing forts, because they have to be … for fear of the Navy!' That *was* a joke and a weak one, but it got a good laugh. 'So look here,' I said, and everyone leaned forward, and I pointed with a stick.

'The Fort is placed deliberately at the narrowest part of the sea-way into the harbour. The navigable channel is narrow, with sand-banks on either hand, so we'd have to go slow and careful, and the channel's just fifty yards from the muzzles of the Fort's guns. And that's ten heavy guns, also taken from the French, and firing thirty-six pound balls, each one six-and-a-half inches in diameter. The guns fire out of embrasures six feet

248

above the high-tide level, and ships in the channel are so close that shot flies flat over the water, all the way to the target. So there's no need to judge the range. They just point the guns, and with whole ship to aim at, they can't miss. So it's a death trap, gentlemen, and we could never get past it.' Everyone nodded. It was true. 'Now,' I said, 'before I go on, has anybody got a question? Anything at all?'

O'Flaherty raised his hand.

'Sir?' he said, 'Are the gunners trained in their work? Would we have a chance of taking their first fire, and then getting a ship past before they reload?' I shook my head.

'I'm afraid they're very well trained. Isn't that so, Mr Pyne?'

'They are, Sir,' said Pyne, and looked at the other officers. 'Major Frobisher had them run out and dry-fire, in order to demonstrate precisely that. They know their business well. They'd score deadly hits with the first salvo and be ready to fire again with great promptness.'

'What about running past at night?' said O'Flaherty.

'No,' I said, 'can't be done. Major Frobisher took great pains to warn me not to try! Because where the Fort looks out over the channel, there's only flat marshes or sea all the way to the horizon. We'd go past with our masts and sails showing black against the stars, and we'd have to go fearful slow for fear of running aground on the sand-banks. In fact I'd never attempt it at night without a boat going before, with a lead-line sounding the way. And they'd just love that in the Fort because it would give them their best chance to aim and fire.'

'I see,' said O'Flaherty.

'Any more questions?' I said, and there were none. So I turned to Dr Goodsby, who had a pile of notes in front of him.

'Doctor!' I said, 'How many marines are there in our squadron?' Goodsby looked at his notes, and put a finger on one sheet.

'Including officers, sergeants and private men,' he said, 'Within the six ships of our squadron, we have one hundred and twenty marines.'

'And how may seamen are trained in musketry, besides them?' I said.

'Another hundred, Sir, and possibly more at a pinch.'

'Good,' I said, 'with the marines leading, that will be enough.' They all stirred with excitement at that, but I had some practicalities to deal with first. 'And now, gentlemen, before we discuss Major Frobisher's, dear-little, precious-little fort,' – that was another joke to make them laugh, because you should always make your men laugh, my jolly boys, when you're leading them to face death. It releases their nerves and helps them find courage, and it does the same for you – 'there's the matter of supplies, which I shall put into the hands of Dr Goodsby, who will act in my name and under my authority.' They all nodded and Goodsby blushed. 'He will muster on this ship, all specialists within the squadron who are responsible for stores: the boatswains for rigging and gear, the gunners for powder and shot, the pursers for consumables, and the carpenters, sailmakers, and all others according to their duties.' I paused to let that sink in. 'And all these men will cooperate to their best endeavours,' I looked squarely at each of the five captains, 'because you gentlemen will particularly ensure that that they do so,' – each captain nodded – 'in order that Dr Goodsby may compile a list of what we have, and where it lies.'

I'll spare you the rest, but it was detailed and thorough. It had to be because every specialist aboard every ship that ever floated, guards his stores and doesn't want to share them, and if you take his stores away it's like taking babies from their mothers.

After that, I set Pyne to organising working parties to move the stores from ship to ship, and Norton – my marine lieutenant – to organising a landing party of marines and seamen, each with musket and bayonet, sixty rounds, and food for three days. There was much else besides, in settling who does what, and all you youngsters take note that this is how it has to be. You can't do everything yourself. You have to delegate. You have to give your subordinates responsibility. After that, you can kick arses and bang heads, but in the end you have to trust them, because as I started out with saying: you can't do it all yourself.

Finally we discussed the Fort, and Mr Unwin – my Gunner – beamed with delight at what I asked him to do.

CHAPTER 39

'The cunning of the English was despicable. They are a cruel and deceitful people whose delight is to strike treacherously from behind, while pretending to attack honestly from the front.'

(From a letter of Saturday, June 16th 1798, from Major William Frobisher, 2nd Bombay Regiment of Artillery, Commander of Fort Kilbride, to his mother Mrs Shivani Frobisher.)

Kilbride Fort was quiet in the early hours of Friday, June 15th. The night was clear, the stars were shining, insects twittered in the dark, and there was silence apart from the flapping of a halyard against the Fort's flagpole in the sea breeze. So the fort was quiet but it was very alert. On the battlements, sentries were peering through telescopes. Buglers and drummers stood ready to sound the alert, and Havildars went their rounds to make sure that every man was at his post. Moreover, by order of Major Frobisher the Fort Commander, the Havildars went round at *irregular* intervals to make sure that the slackers – who are to be found in every military unit that ever was – did not take advantage of the fixed times when their superiors were absent.

Furthermore, all the Fort's guns – from the massive 36-pounders to the smallest swivels – were ready for action: loaded and primed, with each gun guarded by a watchman, while the rest of the crew were allowed some relaxation in their quarters. They were allowed relaxation and they'd had their dinners, but all leave was cancelled, alcohol was forbidden, sleep could be taken only in watches, and every man must be fully dressed and ready for action at all times.

The fort had been in this excellent state of readiness ever since Commodore Fletcher had been sent away downcast and educated by Major Frobisher's tour of inspection. The Fort was acutely and professionally ready because Major Frobisher was an acute and professional officer who would not slip into the lazy belief that Fletcher had given up trying to get his ships past the battery.

'Fletcher is full of pride,' Frobisher said to his officers. They were standing in a group on the battlements because Frobisher simply could not sleep, and the others followed his example. 'Fletcher is a bully who's used to getting his own way,' said Frobisher, 'and he might get angry and make some attempt to get past us, even if it is foolish. So we must be ready.' The other three nodded. The need for readiness was obvious.

'What about all the boat work that has been going on?' said Captain Thompson, 'carrying casks and bundles between their ships?' Frobisher frowned.

'And ships' spars, and rope too,' said Lieutenant Middlewich.

'And even an anchor, yesterday,' said Thompson, 'They're busy all the time. And they're doing it in plain view. They must know that we can see what they are doing from up here.' Frobisher shook his head.

'I do not care what they are doing,' he said, 'I do not care why they are doing it. But I do care that we shall be ready if they try to break out. So we will tour the Fort once more, to make sure everything is as it should be.' This they did, and were on the gun-platform of the Fort's ground floor and inspecting the main battery guns, when a Havildar came running down the stairs from the battlements above. He rushed up to Major Thompson, and saluted.

'Sahib! Sahib! They're doing something. I respectfully beg that you come to see. I respectfully beg that you come quickly!' There was a clatter of boots on stone, and all five men ran upstairs to the open air and the battlements: Frobisher first and the Havildar last. 'Look, Sahib! Look!' said the Havildar, unconsciously whispering, 'There! There!' and he snapped fingers at a sentry, who ran forward and gave Frobisher his telescope. 'There, there, there!' said the Havildar and guided the telescope. Frobisher focussed and looked.

'Ah!' he said, 'It looks like a boat. But I can't see anybody aboard.'

'And behind it,' said the Havildar, 'There is another boat, Sahib! They are attempting some stratagem, Sahib, and I thought it best to summon you without sounding the alarm, so that we might catch them by surprise.'

'Well done!' said Frobisher, 'Now bring the men to action stations. Do it at utmost speed, but no drums or bugles. Quick! Fast as you can!'

252

'Sahib!' said the Havildar, and ran off.

'What are they doing?' said Thompson, taking a telescope from another sentry.

'There's a boat drifting out on the ebb tide,' said Frobisher, 'I can just see it. There's nobody in it, but something in the middle. Some cargo.'

As he spoke there was a great rushing of feet on the gun-platform below, as the gun-crews turned out and took up their stations with commendable discipline and order. Then, without a single word of command, they stood ready with handspikes to train their pieces, as the gun-captains cocked the flint-locks on the massive breeches and made ready to fire.

'There are two more behind,' said Thompson, 'I can just see them. And there are no men in them either, and they're slewed half sideways but still moving on the tide.' He turned to Frobisher. 'Shall we open fire, Sir? They're coming right into line with our guns. They're less than a hundred yards off, we could blow them to …'

Then the night split with light and a resounding, earth-shaking explosion. The leading boat thundered into nothingness with the stunning shock of a massive gunpowder charge, that threw splinters and water high in the air to fall back even on the battlements of the Fort. Every man who saw so great an explosion so close by, was temporarily blinded, and saw violet for minutes afterwards. Every man who heard it was temporarily deafened and heard bells ringing. Men staggered in the pain of it. But Frobisher was a good officer. He kept calm, even deafened and blinded. As soon as he could see what he was doing, he ran to the staircase leading down the gun-platform.

'Hold fire!' he yelled, 'Do not fire! There is no target worth firing at. DO NOT FIRE!' But the urge to retaliate was too strong, and two of the big guns went off with heavy detonations and banks of smoke as their gun-captains could not help but jerk their lanyards. 'Stop that! Stop that!' cried Frobisher, and personally ran down to the gun platform and pushed the gun captains away from their guns. 'Reload! Run out!' Then, when he was sure that the gunners were behaving, he ran upstairs and ran to look out over the bay just in time, to stagger back as a second and equally enormous charge went off, and a second boat went up like a volcano, and so close to the fort that the shock wave of the blast threw Frobisher back on his heels, whereupon he instantly struggled up again, only to be thrown over again when a third boat exploded, just seconds later.

Frobisher lay battered, deafened and blinded, with his officers and the battlement's sentries fallen all around him who groaned and rolled, holding hands to ears in pain. They were barely visible in the huge clouds of powder smoke that blew in from the explosions to cover the entire Fort. But Frobisher got up once more and yelled at the top of his voice.

'Stand to your duties! Man your guns! Beware of attack!' Hardly anyone heard him, and hardly anyone heard the relatively small thud and bang of an explosion far less than those that had annihilated the boats, and stunned the men of the Fort. The explosion came from below: from the courtyard leading to the main gate. It was followed by a great pounding of feet, and cheering and yelling and musket-fire, which Frobisher half heard, and half thought he was imagining, and then the thunder of boots on stone came up the stair from below, and a huge figure charged out of the smoke, bellowing loudly and holding a curve-blade sword in his hand. It was Fletcher: obviously Fletcher, undoubtedly Fletcher, and could be no other than Fletcher. So Frobisher drew his own sword and leapt forward in fury, and in considerable bravery too, considering the size of the man he was going to fight ... and then, by the perverse fortunes of war, Frobisher tripped over Captain Thompson who was flat on the ground, invisible in the smoke. Frobisher tripped completely and miserably and fell face-down on the stone flags, and cracked a tooth, and split his lip, and the sword flew out of his hand and skidded away.

The sword was picked up by Fletcher, now accompanied on all sides by the fixed bayonets of red-coat marines, who were drenched in the evil that drives men to kill in battle. They glared at Frobisher with mad faces, and looked to Fletcher for the word to go forward. But Fletcher stood straight. He saluted Frobisher with his curved sword, and raised Frobisher's sword in his left hand.

'Shall we take it that you've just surrendered this?' he said, 'You've had the benefit of a ton of powder in each of our boats. I've got two hundred and fifty men behind me which crept ashore and waited till our boats went up, before blowing in your gates. Your gunners are captured and the day's lost. So what shall it be, Major Frobisher?'

CHAPTER 40

In the early morning of July 17th, which was a Sunday, I called upon His Excellency Mr Rawson Charles Hornsby, Governor of the Presidency of Bombay. Brief and short though the journey was – from Port Kilbride, to the anchorage off Bombay's Custom House – I went in style aboard His Majesty's ship *Euphonides,* of forty guns. I went aboard *Euphonides* to impress, since I judged that an act of theatre was justified. Thus we saluted the batteries with blank charges, and the smoke drifted across the huge, blue bay, and we were answered with dipping flags and more blank charges from the castle, and due ceremony was performed between us, all neat and tight and proper. So weren't we all just bosom friends: the Navy and John Company? Weren't we though? Ourselves and the folk of Bombay who'd heard the massive explosions last night, and were wondering what had happened on Kilbride Island? But most of all, Governor Charley Hornsby must have been wondering, treacherous swab that he was, who'd ordered his bloody Fort to sink me, and yet here I was: come visiting! He must have been sat on his chamber pot, straining in fright.

So we lowered away my launch, with the tars aboard in their smart uniforms, and I made ready to be piped over the side, with a select company of my squadron's officers including Mr Pyne, Dr Goodsby, Mr O'Flaherty, and Captain Elmore of *Phoraos,* the senior in rank of the two frigate captains in my squadron. There were several other boats alongside, bearing all the other captains and first lieutenants of the squadron. It was a considerable company, sat waiting in the boats, and I was about to go down into the waist where a ladder was rigged for my own boat, when Pyne – being Pyne – made one last attempt to keep us from going ashore.

'Is this safe, Sir?' he asked with a troubled look on his face, the dismal swab, 'Are we not risking all our senior officers? Can we trust Governor Hornsby?' Perhaps I was a little unfair to Pyne, because I looked round and saw that he was not the only man who was wondering that same thing. So I made a little speech.

'Mr Pyne,' I said, 'In the first place, the Governor dare not lay hands on us, for fear of what the British Government would do to him. But it is none the less my duty – our duty and this ship's duty – to make entirely sure of the welfare of those of our comrades whom we must leave behind when we set sail.' I said that in a good loud voice for all to hear, and for Captain Elmore to take note of, and pass it on to others in due course. I was pleased to see that he nodded with vigour at my words.

'Aye-aye, Sir,' said Pyne, 'of course, Sir. Of course.'

So down the ladder we went: senior man first – myself – followed by the rest in due order, and Goodsby last. Then, as we pulled for the shore we saw that city had turned out to see us, which was hardly surprising considering the firework display we'd put on the previous night. It must have shook their temples and stunned their monkeys. There were thousands of people chattering, calling and pointing, and lining the wharves and fore-shore: everyone from English Company-men, to Hindu priests, to high-caste ladies in robes, to washer-women, porters, beggars and cripples – of whom there were great numbers in Bombay. The noise grew as we approached and O'Flaherty shook his head.

'And this is Sunday,' he said, 'the Lord's day! I wonder what market day might be like?' We all laughed at that. Perhaps we were nervous. But the Custom House officials saw us coming, and a guard of Sepoys formed up on the jetty and pushed back the common herd to make room for us. Then our boats were bumping up against the timbers of the wharf, and all of us got up the stairs, and then there was a great deal of arguing and insisting on my part, and refusing to accept what a set of very agitated officials were trying to tell me.

'His Excellency cannot meet you, Sir! Not without appointment!'

'It cannot be done, Sir!'

'No, Sir. No, Sir!'

'It is not possible, Sir!'

There was plenty of that, but I could see they were nervous, and didn't want to look me in the eye. My guess was that gossip had gone round, as it does in a seaport, and they all knew that my squadron was supposed to be bottled up by Fort Kilbride, so they were amazed that we'd got out. Also they'd all heard the explosions, they must have guessed there'd been fighting, and finally it was the British Flag that now flew over Fort Kilbride, not John Company's. So all these officials, whether English, Indian or half-and-half, were wondering what had happened but were afraid to ask. So the objections disappeared, and finally we marched to Government House with a company of Sepoys as escort under their English office: the same one who'd welcomed me last time I came ashore. But he didn't want to talk. He had the same shifty look as all the rest, and went ahead with his men, and left us alone with the scent of India all around and O'Flaherty pointing out the sights.

'Look there, gentlemen,' he said, as we went down a hot, narrow street crammed with little shops, each about six feet wide and full of fruits, spices and herbs and folk haggling and buying. 'See the vultures?' We looked up at a round tower, rising over the street, and saw a dozen black witch-birds sat round the rim: preening their feathers and occasionally flapping into flight. 'That's a Tower of Silence,' said O'Flaherty, 'That's where the Zoroastrians layout their dead to be eaten by vultures, since they believe it's pollution of nature to burn or bury a human body.' I didn't believe him at the time. I thought it was a sailor's tale and I smiled. But it was true. That's India for you.

At Government House, more officials vied with one another, in passing us on to someone else. But they all agreed that His Excellency was not in the building and would have to be sent for. We ended up in a shady, lavishly-furnished room, with carved furniture, beaten-brass ornaments, a punkha going in the ceiling, and a view out on to a most gorgeous garden of brilliant-coloured flowers, seen through windows with no glass but a fretwork of stone. There we were kept supplied with food and drink, though the drink was syrupy fruit juice and the food was little cakes that were more sugar than anything else.

Then at long last the great man arrived. He arrived with doors thrown open by servants, and came in with a small crowd of John Company Englishmen. They looked as if they'd come unwilling and unprepared, and they muttered to one another and glanced nervously at Hornsby. They were all dressed in the tropical version of European clothes: coat, britches and vest of off-white linen, and they looked like a flock of pale chickens. I stood as Hornsby entered. We all stood. We stood for the whole meeting, but the men who stood with me weren't fluttering birds like Hornsby's, but Navy blue, King's Commission officers, who growled approval at my every word. In short, I thoroughly enjoyed myself.

'Sir!' said Hornsby, and waddled towards me holding out his hand, 'There has been the most terrible mistake.' He looked at his fellows. 'Ain't that so, gentlemen?' I didn't take his hand, because I could see that he'd already surrendered. He'd struck his colours at the first shot so I could be stern, not accommodating, and that was a huge relief. Despite what I'd said to Pyne, there had always been the possibility that Hornsby might defy the British Parliament. Meanwhile I looked round and saw all the Company men nodding their heads off in agreement. They obviously had a cooked-up story to explain everything and they were sticking to it.

'Oh yes!' they said
'Indeed!' they said.
'A terrible mistake!'

Hornsby saw my frown and lowered his hand.

'It was all the fault of Major Frobisher,' he said, 'the commander of the Fort who threatened to fire on you.'

'Was it now?' I said, and looked at all of them: Hornsby, the greasy, cunning porker that he was, and all the rest of the fat-paid Company men with their secret Indian wives, and their accumulating riches. 'Governor!' I said in a loud voice to make him jump, 'Governor, I'll not let some lowly person take blame and certainly not Major Frobisher and his men. They fought honourably, so I took their surrender and I promised them decent treatment, and now they're held safe ashore. Also, and much more important, Governor, how do you know that Frobisher threatened to fire on me?'

That shut him up. He flapped and gaped like a landed fish, and I pressed my advantage. 'I never mentioned such a threat,' I said, 'not a word! So how could you know there was a threat to fire on me *unless you'd given the order yourself?*' Flap-flap, gape-gape, and I frowned like thunder. 'We are talking of treason, Sir! We are talking of firing on the British flag. There could be capital charges. There could be hangings.'

I let Hornsby think about that. I let him have a good think so he could fully appreciate that I'd got him by the marriage-tackles and was ready to twist. Then, when I was good and ready I continued. 'Governor,' I said, another pause, 'it is just possible – and I say only possible – that what happened last night could have been the result of a misunderstanding.'

'Ah,' said Hornsby, scenting a way out.

'Ah,' said the rest, cunning little grubs that they were.

258

'There were men killed and wounded last night,' I said, 'a dozen of yours and four of mine.' Hornsby blinked, and dabbed a handkerchief to his face for the sweat. 'So,' I said, 'everything now depends on what happens next.'

'Which is?' said Hornsby, recovering fast now that a bargain was offered, because he was a seasoned old trader and a lifelong politician besides.

'Which is,' I said, 'That we agree on three things.'

'Name them, Sir!'

'First that you give every respect and support to Captain Elmore of *Phoraos* whom I shall leave in command of my squadron when I leave.' I turned to Elmore. 'Sir!' I said, 'please come forward.' Elmore stood forward and Hornsby pumped his hand with vigour. 'Second,' I said, 'that we agree that Mr Stephen Kilbride, and Sir Robert Valentine are the persons most responsible for our present troubles, and are acting against British law in taking an army to Japan.' That was more difficult. Hornsby frowned and thought hard. He was like a chess player thinking several moves ahead. I could see it in his face, and I wondered what promises had been made? What agreements signed? What consequences must Hornsby consider if he abandoned Kilbride?

Hornsby thought of all this, and then he sighed and nodded.

'Yes,' he mumbled.

'Speak up, Sir!' I said, 'Be precise!'

'Yes,' he said, 'It was all Kilbride's doing. Him and Valentine. I was deceived.'

'Gentlemen,' I said, looking at my men, 'did you hear that? Did you hear what the Governor has said?'

'Yes,' they all said, and that was good, because that's why I had taken so many of them. I wanted witnesses and plenty of them.

'Thank you, gentlemen,' I said, 'And finally, Governor, my ship *Euphonides* is almost ready to pursue Kilbride and Valentine, but the rest of my squadron is not fit for sea. So my third requirement is that you should equip and provision them, so that they might follow me as fast as possible.'

'Ah! Ah!' said Hornsby and his big, fat face showed serious alarm, because the bargain that would save him from a charge of treason was slipping through his fingers like an eel. 'But I cannot, Sir!' he said, 'I cannot, because we agreed,' he stopped, gulped and changed tack swift as a racing yacht, 'which is to say that I was *deceived* into agreeing ...'

'Of course you were, Governor,' I said, helping him out because the bells of Heaven peal for a sinner that repenteth.

'I was *deceived* by Kilbride,' he said, 'into lavishing provisions into his squadron to the degree that my warehouses are emptied of stores, until the next shipments come out from England or are brought to Bombay from the interior.' He looked at me and spread hands helplessly. 'Kilbride's squadron was the biggest we have ever had to fit out,' he said, 'and it had to be done quickly. And so my stores were exhausted.' He was telling the truth. I could see it.

So we had to make do with that. We talked about it on the boat, pulling back to *Euphonides*, and later aboard ship in the great cabin, when I entertained all my captains and first officers for a final dinner. Once the meal was done, and the King's health drunk, I spoke to them all. I spoke to them but I did something else first. I got them all to sign copies of a transcript, drawn up by Goodsby, of my conversation with Governor Hornsby. In the time available, Goodsby had managed to draft three copies of this document. So I kept one, I gave one to Elmore and the other to the captain next in seniority. That way at least one copy should get home to England as evidence if need be.

'Now, gentlemen,' I said when the signing was done, 'You know how we're situated in this matter. You know that I'm commanded to pursue Kilbride and Valentine?'

'Yes,' they said.

'You know that I am commanded personally by the First Sea Lord, and since Kilbride and Valentine are aboard so powerful a ship – *Duke of Cornwallis* – I must pursue them in the strongest ship of our squadron, which is *Euphonides*.' They all nodded. 'So,' I said, 'between us we have barely enough stores for *Euphonides*, and no more are to be had from Bombay for an unknown number of months.' They all nodded again. 'Thus I must leave most of you here, under command of Captain Elmore, whom I raise to the rank of commodore, subject to the final approval of Their Lordships.' That brought a great smile from Elmore, and much drumming of fists on the table and heels on the deck, and another great toast in my best claret. 'So, Commodore Elmore,' I said, 'are you clear in your duties?'

'Aye-aye, Sir,' he said, 'I am to secure the health and security of all hands, and all ships, keeping them battle-ready until such time as provisions are made available, and then to make judgement as to whether some – or all – of the squadron should follow you, or return to England.'

And so, and so … aboard *Euphonides,* we upped anchor and made sail from Bombay, on Saturday June 23rd, over three weeks after Kilbride's squadron. It took that long to complete all matters of stores and provisions, before embarking on a sea voyage of six and a half thousand miles, and which voyage would be tedious to report in detail, since one day at sea sounds much like another to a landman. But over such a distance, under sail, you must expect storms, calms, accidents and sea damage and we met them all. We also lost three men: one falling from the main yard to be swallowed by the sea before we could get a boat to him; one crushed under a gun-carriage during live-firing practise; and one poor soul dropping dead of exhaustion, being old and weary and much worn out by the hardness of the sea life.

Thus we sailed south and east, around the tip of the Indian continent, then eastward through the Dutch East Indies, running south east down the coast of Sumatra, and avoiding the Malay Straits, as being so infested with pirates, and in such numbers, as to make the passage too hazardous to be worth the lesser sea distance. Of course, *Euphonides* might have thrown off any pirates that came, but you could never be sure. More important, I wanted to preserve my powder and shot for Kilbride if by chance we came up with him, and he'd never have risked the Malay Straits with a convoy of merchantmen. But most of all, I wanted to take on more provisions at the port city of Batavia – about half way between Bombay and Japan – and which lies on the north-east tip of East Java, where it reaches out towards Sumatra. You landman must consult a map to see what this means, since a few words can't convey the geography of it and if I gave you more words, you'd be bored.

What may not bore you is that even though we were supposed to be at war with the Dutch, I expected a friendly welcome at Batavia which was held by the Dutch East India Company. But the Dutch East India Company was near bankrupt in those days, and the war was all due to little Boney and his Frogs, who'd forced a revolutionary republic on the Dutch and an alliance with them against England. Worse still, the poor Dutch were in such a mess within themselves, that two of their governments were overthrown by rebellion in '98 alone. The result of all this was that the Port of Batavia, half-a-year away from Holland and Boney, was very much on its own, and would supply any ship that came in, and was ready to pay in gold. Just to prove my point, Kilbride and his squadron had likewise re-provisioned at Batavia, and were a month ahead of us, so we were on the right track.

After Batavia, we sailed a northerly course through the islands of the Dutch Indies, then north-west, into the South China Sea, with mighty China under the horizon on our port beam, then onward past Formosa, then past a whole string of Japanese islands, some small, some large until we sighted the great bulk of Hito Island on Monday, 24th September after a passage of ninety-three days.

And that, my jolly boys was the easy part. What came next wasn't easy at all, because at first it was deeply confusing and then it got deadly dangerous.

CHAPTER 41

'Beloved one. Keeper of my heart. Mistress of my soul. I am in doubt. Gather your wisdom, my lady, and gather your strength, because I will come to you soon for guidance.'

(From a letter of Thursday, September 20th 1798 by Kimiya Hitamoto, Daimyo of Hito Domain, to the Lady Meiko, The House of Flowers, Port Hito.)

The small group of Englishmen rode surrounded by Hitamoto cavalry. They looked at the bizarre equipment of these Japanese riders, with their tall, narrow banners fixed to their backs, their lacquered armour and their small, hairy horses. They looked at these oddities and worried because they were beyond their own power, and totally in the hands of these strangers. Besides that, it had been a long ride from Port Hito where the East India Company squadron was anchored.

'God save my arse!' said Captain Pryce, now in command of *Duke of Cornwallis*. He and his three mates, were riding beside Kilbride and Valentine. Kilbride glanced at Pryce, and said nothing. He agreed with the sentiment. He was saddle-sore himself. But he didn't like Pryce, who had once been a Sea Service lieutenant but resigned his commission over reasons undisclosed, and then – being a seasoned navigator and gunner – Pryce had turned to John Company and ended up in command of one of the current squadron's lesser ships. Pryce had eagerly seized the chance to command *Duke of Cornwallis* and had kissed her massive guns. But he was greedy and vulgar, and merely the best Kilbride could get when Stacey turned nasty.

Meanwhile Sir Robert Valentine managed a smile. He'd been a horseman since the age of four, and sat easy even in a Japanese saddle. So he stood in the stirrups and pointed.

'There!' he said, 'We're nearly there! That's where we're going. There: on top of that hill. That's the command post,' then he shook his head in amazement, 'and look all round! Look what they've done! They're amazing people.' So the Englishmen looked. They were on sloping ground, riding down towards a great plain, and they could see the vast complex of entrenchments across the plain a mile ahead, running from a mountain on one side, to a broad river on the other. There were three complete lines of ditches, sewn heavily with sharpened stakes, and provided with bastions, traps and pitfalls, and a causeway leading through the entrenchments, via heavily defended gateways, while a few hundred yards short of the entrenchments a hill had been fortified with further rings of trenches, to serve as a command post.

'Look at the size of it all,' said Pryce, 'The buggers must've been digging for years to build that.'

'They have been,' said Kilbride, 'They've been preparing for the Tokugawa invasion for years. They've built fortified lines like this all the way across Hito Island, so the Hitamoto can defend it. We know that because *he* told us.' Kilbride pointed. 'Him! Masahito and his brother.' The Englishmen looked ahead to where Lord Masahito rode beside his brother, Lord Kimiya, in the centre of a heavy bodyguard of horse and foot: the cavalry with their bright flags, and the infantry with their long spears, and arquebuses.

'Neat little buggers, ain't they?' said Pryce, 'all stepping out in time.' He looked at Kilbride. 'I say!' he said, 'I say! Mr Kilbride?'

'What? said Kilbride, clenching his teeth as his horse stumbled on the slope and rubbed more pain into his buttocks.

'D'you think our lads'll be any good against them Jappos?' said Pryce, 'Will our lads be any good?' Kilbride forced himself to swivel round, to look at Sepoys marching behind. They were the 1st Battalion, 79th Bengal Native Infantry, led by their mounted officers who politely raised hats at Kilbride's glance. Kilbride touched his own hat in return, and strained round further in the attempt to see the galloper battery that was coming on behind the 79th. But he gave up. He couldn't stand the pain. All he could see was still more of the Hitamoto cavalry and infantry that outnumbered the Company troops twenty to one. But the galloper battery was there, none the less: six nine-pounders, six teams of horses, six limbers full of ammunition, and six highly-trained teams. Kilbride just hoped that the horses were fit after the long sea journey.

Then Valentine rode close to Kilbride and spoke softly. It was the familiar subject.

'Can we trust them?' he said, nodding at Masahito and Kimiya.' Kilbride sighed. He was tired, fed up and in pain.

'I've told you,' he said, 'We've got to trust them.'

'We have *now*!' said Valentine, 'Now they've got our squadron trapped in port, with the harbour lined with troops so we can't land unless they say so, and you've agreed that every one of our navigating officers is locked up ashore, and ...'

'They're not locked up,' said Kilbride, 'they're guests. They can come and go as they wish.'

'Only ashore,' said Valentine, 'they can't go back to the ships, and the ships are trapped without their navigating officers.'

'That's the agreement!' said Kilbride, 'that's what we agreed!'

'You agreed!' said Valentine. Why didn't you make a landing, and show them who's in charge? We've got thousands of Company troops in the Squadron. Why didn't you make a landing in force?' Kilbride groaned in a pain that was not entirely due to saddle sores.

'And fight a war?' he said, 'Against the very people we need on our side? We're here to help Clan Hitamoto against Clan Tokugawa, not the other way round. We need the Hitamoto to get a base ashore, and then build a fort, and then once we've done that and brought out reinforcements ...'

'Look!' said Valentine, 'There they are. The Tokugawa army. They've arrived.'

A great chatter of conversation rose from the Hitamoto army and its John Company allies, as far ahead – out beyond the Hitamoto entrenchments – the dark mass of the Tokugawa expeditionary force slowly appeared like a column of organised black ants: the first sight of the enemy. They emerged from around the side of a mountain some five miles ahead, with prickling twinkles of light and colour among the marching men and the trotting horses. These flashes against the dark background were banners, insignia, clan badges, and the shine of bright metal: steel, brass and copper.

'There they are then, the sods,' said Pryce, 'Well we can't say we weren't warned.'

'No,' said Valentine, and nodded at Kimiya and Masahito, 'They told us the Tokugawa have landed.'

'Yes,' said Pryce, 'all over the soddin' beaches at the other end of this island.'

Meanwhile, just ahead of the Englishmen, Lord Masahito and Lord Kimiya, raised telescopes to study the oncoming Tokugawa army, with Masahito pausing to make sure that his brother was comfortable using the foreign device, with its odd sliding tubes.

'Huh!' said Pryce, 'Look at that pair of swabs! That's my own glass one of 'em's got there, the thieving sod, and it's is a twelve-guinea, three-draw!'

'I'll thank you to hold your tongue, Mr Pryce,' he said, 'The glass was a gift. A diplomatic gift!'

'if you say so,' said Pryce, as the two Japanese noblemen gazed on their enemies, and then they spoke in rapid speech, and in seeming accord.

'I seems there's peace between them now,' said Kilbride to Valentine.

'It wasn't at first!' said Valentine, 'it was all stamping and shouting.'

'But not now,' said Kilbride, 'Ah! What's this?'

Lord Kimiya was giving orders to one of the bodyguard. A horseman bowed in the saddle, wheeled, rode back down the column, wheeled again and came alongside Kilbride and Valentine. He gave a brief nod, then barked out Japanese words, beckoned, then rode forward a little, then turned and beckoned again.

'Come on,' said Kilbride, 'We've been summoned.' He kicked at his horse and went forward. The cavalryman nodded but then barked out more Japanese, and got in the way of Valentine and the rest and held up a hand, to prevent them following.

'Stand fast, Sir Robert,' cried Kilbride, 'It's only myself, that they want.'

'Take care,' said Valentine.

'You watch them buggers!' said Pryce, 'You watch out!'

Kilbride rode forward. The cavalry bodyguard let him through, but when he tried to ride level with Masahito and Kimiya, a senior cavalrymen shouted indignantly and gestured until Kilbride's horse was a yard behind Masahito's. But Kilbride saw that Masahito was himself a yard behind his brother. Kilbride was far too wise to take offence, and gave his best bow to Lord Kimiya. Then Kimiya nodded to Masahito, who spoke.

'My dear Mr Kilbride,' said Masahito, 'I do hope that you have not suffered unduly from this long ride, since I know that you are not a horseman by choice.' Kilbride thought it powerfully strange for perfect English to come from so alien a being, in his laced-together armour, and wide-brimmed helmet that was riveted with knobs and bumps and swirls, like nothing an Englishman ever dreamed of. Thus Masahito had grown more Japanese with every second that passed, but Kilbride was learning how an Englishman should behave in Japan, and especially how he should speak.

'I thank you for your gracious condescension, my Lord,' he said, 'and I extend my most respectful greetings to my Lord Kimiya, and to yourself, and I respectfully ask if we are now at our destination?'

'We are indeed at that place,' said Masahito, 'and I may tell you that it is the pleasure of my Lord and brother, the Daimyo Kimiya Hitamoto, that you and your followers should stand beside him on the viewing platform.' Kilbride bowed. This was no more than had been promised. But Kilbride was deep in Hitamoto territory with his troops outnumbered, and himself and his companions hostages for the good behaviour of the squadron left in Port Hito. So Kilbride was reassured that these promises were being honoured.

Later, Kilbride, Valentine and the other Englishmen were given a place to stand, on the ramparts of the hill-top command post. Pryce grumbled that there were no chairs, but the Japanese made no use of chairs, and the view over the entrenchments towards the Tokugawa army was awesome and spectacular. In fact, although honoured above the ordinary Japanese rank and file, the Englishmen were placed on a platform beside a slightly *higher* platform for Lord Kimiya, Lord Masahito, and their samurai. But that was the Japanese way.

Then there was a long period of waiting, while the Tokugawa Commander – the formidable General 'Chinese' Yoshida – sought to avoid another gunpowder disaster like Kagominato, by ordering detailed reconnaissance of the entrenchment approaches, seeking disturbed ground that might suggest powder mines below, and also by cutting exploration trenches to search for Hitamoto tunnels. These excellent precautions reflected credit on Yoshida but they were entirely un-necessary since his opponent, Lord Kimiya Hitamoto, had long since forbidden any further use of powder mines as being barbaric, dishonourable, and contrary to both samurai and Okobo Buddhist tradition.

Finally, at dawn on Thursday, September 20th, and to the booming of drums, and massed shouts of banzai, the Tokugawa army moved forward, with fascines and ladders to assault the Hitamoto entrenchments. They came on like rolling tide. They seemed invincible. None the less, they were instantly opposed by a Hitamoto force, that marched boldly down the causeway out of their entrenchments, to meet the Tokugawa face to face.

High up on the Command Post, Lord Kimiya stood with his brother Lord Masahito. They watched with samurai stone-faces as the Hitamoto force – smaller by far than the Tokugawa army – moved out. The Hitamoto soldiers marched under the banners of their families and clans. They went rank by rank, in tramping discipline, with drums and war-cries. They were splendid to see, but Kimiya, Masahito, and every other Hitamoto officer knew that their sallying forth was a nonsense and a sham, because military logic insisted that they should stay behind their fortifications to fight from maximum advantage. But they were not going out to fight. They were going out to conduct an experiment.

'Here come, the foreigners my Lord,' said Masahito, and the brothers looked down as the 1st Battalion, 79th Bengal Regiment, marched over the causeway.

'I grant that they seem like men,' said Kimiya,

'Do you see the spears on their guns?' said Masahito, 'The *bayonets*?'

'Yes,' said Kimiya, 'and what a sound they make! Is this their music?'

Nearby, on their slightly lower platform, the Englishmen cheered as the 79th marched out with colours flying, drums beating and fifers playing *Yankee Doodle*, since their colonel had served in the American wars and was fond of that tune. So Kilbride and the rest cheered as the Sepoys went forward, and they cheered later as the Hitamoto infantry fell back to allow the Sepoys to lead the Hitamoto advance, and they cheered as the Sepoys gave thundering volleys: front rank kneeling, second rank standing, third rank firing over the shoulders of the second, while the Tokugawa arquebuses fired in return.

Lord Kimiya studied this engagement closely. He saw Tokugawa arquebus men fall in numbers. He saw Tokugawa cavalry reel back, after attempting to charge the fixed bayonets of the 79th. He watched a good while to be entirely sure. Then he lowered his telescope.

'I have seen enough,' he said, 'Their flints shoot faster than our matches. Their spear-muskets are effective.' He bowed briefly to Masahito. 'It is true,' he said, 'It cannot be denied. They are superior to our arquebus men.' Masahito bowed in return. He bowed low. Then Kimiya turned to a samurai officer. 'Withdraw the flint muskets!' he said, 'Withdraw the muskets and send out the horse-cannon!'

'Hi!' said the officer and a cluster of rockets rose over the command post. They rose high and burst in the air, commanding the withdrawal of the Hitamoto force. But at the same time, the horse-drawn guns of the foreigners – kept in reserve until now – charged out across the causeway with Hitamoto cavalry around them, and went bouncing and pounding over the field, sweeping around the retreating Hitamoto and Sepoys. Then they wheeled, unlimbered, and opened up a rapid fire straight into the Tokugawa advance. They did so under ideal conditions: out of range of bow or arquebus, with Hitamoto cavalry on their flanks, and without a single artillery piece to return fire against them, because there was no field artillery in the entire Tokugawa arsenal.

When that happened, the Englishmen fell silent at what they saw, and in that same instant, on his slightly higher platform, Lord Kimiya Hitamoto, Daimyo of Hito Domain, also fell silent. He fell very silent indeed. Then he spoke to his brother.

CHAPTER 42

Hito is the most south westerly of the main islands of Japan, and Port Hito is on the south-west tip of Hito, facing out in to the East China Sea. The port lies at the north side of a fine bay, about a mile across, and shaped like the pincer of a giant lobster, with the south claw longer than the north claw, and a deep water harbour enclosed by mountains covered with pine forest, and flowering shrubs. Much of the southern lobster-claw was taken up by the town of Okanomo, but as we came in to anchor, the only thing that any seaman aboard *Euphonides* had eyes for, including able sea cat Jimbo, was an enormous construction at the very tip of the southern claw.

'What is it?' we said as we got first sight of it, coming in from the sea. The yards and shrouds were full of every man who wasn't on duty, because none of us had ever seen anything like it. It was exotic and foreign in the extreme. It was such a wonder as makes men go to sea, and even the officers on the quarterdeck, were chattering like children in their amazement at the monster.

'There's layers and layers of it.'

'All bright and painted and with tiled roofs'

'It must be a palace.'

'No! Look at the stones. It's a fort.'

'But where's the guns? There's no gun-ports.'

'It's massive, it must be two hundred foot high!'

'Is it a temple? Something for their gods?'

'No,' said O'Flaherty, 'These people don't have gods,' and he pointed at the great mass of stone and timber, 'That there is a castle.'

'Speak up, Mr O'Flaherty,' I said, 'Did you say it's a castle?'

'Aye-aye, Sir!' said O'Flaherty, touching his hat, and everyone lowered their telescopes, and looked away from the enormous structure that we were approaching, a few cable's lengths to larboard. Everyone looked at

O'Flaherty, and the ship's people edged closer to hear what he had to say. 'It's their style of castle,' he said, 'They use stone blocks to build an enormous foundation that's pyramid-shaped to be proof against earthquakes, which are frequent here, and they build pagodas on top of the stone. So it's a castle, and a big one like that will be the centre of government, and where all their great folk live, and an arsenal and storehouse besides. It'll be the most important place on this island probably.'

'What about guns?' I said, 'there are no gun-ports or embrasures.'

'They don't have guns, Cap'n.' said O'Flaherty, 'they have bows, and matchlocks, but they don't cast guns: not proper guns, just piddling little 'uns. So their castles aren't built to withstand artillery, but only men trying to climb aboard with ladders and such. So their castles have firing-galleries all round the sides, to use small arms on the boarders.'

'How do you know all this, Mr O'Flaherty?' I said, 'Have you been to Japan?'

'No, Cap'n,' he said, 'But I had a friend once that was Dutch, and he talked a lot.'

'Ahh!' we all said.

'So,' I said, pointing at the castle, 'Do we salute as we go in? Or wouldn't they understand gunfire?'

'Oh, fire away, Cap'n,' said O'Flaherty, with emphasis, 'Fire away and show the little darlings, 'cos if there's one thing these people do understand, it's strength! Let's give 'em a show.'

'Mr Gunner!' I cried, seeking out Unwin.

'Aye-aye, Cap'n!' said Unwin, standing with his mates by the larboard quarterdeck stairs.

'Blank charges, larboard battery, every gun!' I said, 'Let 'em know the Navy's here!'

'Aye-aye!' said Unwin. But:

'Sir! Sir!' cried several voices at once, and the masthead lookouts yelled.

'Ships on the port beam! East India Squadron!'

Indeed it was, as we got our first view into the bay, past the upper claw of the pincer, and there was Kilbride's squadron, dominated by *Duke of Cornwallis* all tucked up at anchor, each to a pair of cables, all snug and cosy with their yards sent down, and sails rigged over spars to shade their decks, and boats nudging between them. Well, well, well. There they were, my lads. We'd got 'em!

'Mr Unwin?' I cried, 'Give the port battery besides. One for the castle and one for John Company!' That got a cheer. It's amazing what men will cheer for. It was a big cheer too. Then it was thud-bang-boom! It was echoes bouncing, and lurid flashes of light, and a vast blanket of smoke, that hid *Euphonides* from view, for a good half hour until the wind revealed us again, and I backed tops'ls and brought her to. Then the anchor was let go, the cable rumbled out and *Euphonides* eased herself round, till the cable checked her, and then we had to be patient, though – as ever – Mr Pyne was worried.

'With your permission, Sir?' he said to me, 'Might we not send a boat ashore to speak to the authorities? Might we not, Sir? To show good intent?' He was pleading.

'Mr Pyne,' I said, 'We've discussed that for weeks. No man aboard has ever anchored in a Japanese port, so we don't know the protocol except that this country is closed, and we've not been invited, and we're a ship of war not a merchantman. So the shore people have cause to be wary, and our friends there,' I pointed at the East Indiamen, 'have got here first and may have told such tales about us as we cannot know. So while I respect your concern, Mr Pyne, we shall stay where we are, safe behind our guns, unless our East India friends try to get out and past us.'

Which is what we did. We stayed at anchor, the ship's routine continued. Watches changed, the noon observation was taken, the men were sent to their dinners, grog was served, and all the while we were subjects of the most intense scrutiny. We could see men lining the rails of the East India Squadron. We could see men in their hundreds peering down at us from the buildings and firing galleries of the castle, we could see disciplined bodies of troops, in great numbers formed up on the shores around us.

These were men in actual armour like the knights of the middle ages, only strange armour, painted in colours, and we could see wisps of smoke rising from the matchlocks of their infantrymen, to hang in a hazy cloud above them. We could see small bodies of cavalry riding up and down the shore, and stopping to look out at us. Some of the riders wore lurid costumes and I assumed that these were commanders: senior men, making their judgements of us. There were hordes of ordinary people too: sun-browned farmers, and their wives and children peering and wondering. I suppose – indeed I do not doubt – that we were as strange to them as their castle was to us.

Then late in the afternoon, a boat came out from Port Hito and pulled towards us, or rather it pushed, because the oarsmen did not sit at benches but stood and threw their weight forward to work their oars. The boat was a big one, with a dozen oars going on each side, a gilded dragon-head rising high over the bow and a brightly painted pavilion at the stern, with a guard of soldiers around it, and a man in elaborate costume sat on a big cushion on a platform within. A drum was going to give time to the oarsmen – a slow and booming drum and not a rattling side-drum such as the Navy used – and a banner flew over the boat bearing the image of what looked like a bird of prey reaching out with its talons. I was below decks when the boat appeared, and a middy was sent to fetch me. The quarterdeck officers politely stood aside, and O'Flaherty pointed out the boat and its banner.

'That'll be their *mon*,' said O'Flaherty, 'That's their clan badge.' He pointed to the castle. 'Same flag flying there,' he said, 'It's like a coat of arms.' I nodded, and studied the boat through my glass.

'Stand by to give honours,' I said, 'rig a full set of steps, marines in parade order, and all hands turned out.'

'Aye-aye!'

Soon the boat was alongside, and crewmen catching hold of the lines we threw down, and rigging a neat gangplank so their elite passenger could get up off his cushion and step up our ladder without falling into the harbour. Then the boatswain's mates blew a loud call on their pipes, the marines stamped to attention and presented arms, and all hands aboard of us saluted, and Jimbo wore his hat and jacket.

Then wonder of wonders: a set of creatures from another world came over the side, and I stepped forward to greet them. There were four men, all quite small, dressed in the most outlandish armour and helmets, little bits of plate all painted and fixed together with coloured silk lashings, and each man with two swords stuck in his belt. They came behind a man in silk robes that stuck out at his shoulders, and were belted at the waist, and embroidered with the bird-like *mon*. He had the oddest hair style: a little pigtail curled at the back and his brow shaved half way up his head. He had swords in his belt, and held a fan as if it were a badge of authority.

Then two shocks hit me at once. The first was that I recognised him. He was Nakano, the Jiu Jitsu master that I had fought aboard *Duke of Cornwallis*. The second shock was that he spoke English.

'Commodore Fletcher,' he said, 'I am Nakano – Fumito Nakano – and I represent my master Lord Hayato Hitamoto, who is Daimyo of Hito Domain.' He gave a brief, sharp bow and continued, 'I also represent Lord Masahito Hitamoto who is the honoured brother of my master.' He bowed again. 'I represent them, and I am here to negotiate.' In fact he said *Fretche*r not Fletcher and *Rord* not Lord, and his English was nowhere near as good as Masahito's. But Masahito was a phenomenon with languages, while Nakano was an ordinary man making his best efforts at English, which to him was an ungodly strange way to speak. So: as I can't speak anything other than English, and profoundly don't want to, and don't approve of foreign languages at all – especially French – then I gave him three cheers, at least in my mind.

[Readers should note that any mention of foreign languages caused Fletcher to fall into a prolonged rant, declaring his unshakable protestation that if English was good enough for the British and Americans, who are God's Own Chosen, it was good enough for all humanity. These arguments I merely summarised above. S.P.]

So I was polite as could be to Mr Nakano, both for his English and more importantly because – which you youngsters should take note of – I was in a strange land where I didn't know the rules or who had the power, and under those circumstances it's only an idiot who doesn't step quiet, and polite. You can always be rude later if you can get *them* in front of a 24 pounder and *you're* holding the trigger-line: but until then, be polite.

'Welcome aboard ship, Sir,' I said, 'Most especially as I recognise you as the man who threw me over so many times that I lost count!' Nakano kept a serious face, where an Englishman might have smiled, but he too was polite.

'I recognise you,' he said, 'I recognise you as the man who has the spirit of a tiger and the strength of a bull.'

'Ahhh!' said everyone, except the four Japanese soldiers, and the mood lightened.

'May I invite you to come below for refreshment, Sir?' I said, 'And to discuss your mission of negotiation?'

'Hi!' he said, nodding, and he bowed again. So I took that for *yes,* and down we went to the great cabin, with O'Flaherty pushing against me to whisper.

'Put 'em facing the door, Cap'n,' he said, 'It's not polite to put 'em with their backs to the door, for fear some enemy might creep in behind. The little buggers are obsessed with good manners.' I nodded, and got Nakano seated on the stern-window side of my big table, and myself facing him with the door behind me. His four armoured knights stood behind him, and I had Pyne, O'Flaherty and Dr Goodsby beside me. Then port, brandy and claret were served, and little cakes with raisins, baked by my cook for special occasions. Nakano took a sip of drink and a crumb of cake, but that was all. So I tried some small talk.

'If we're to negotiate,' I said, 'I'll first ask how I should address you, Sir, because I'd not wish to give offence where none is intended: is it mister? Sir? My Lord?' He nodded.

'Forms of address are complex in Japan,' he said, 'But for you, and for now, and in this ship, you may call me Nakano.'

'Then, Nakano,' I said, 'You speak excellent English. How did you learn it and why did you never mention it before?'

'I learned through study over the years I lived in England,' he said, 'and in those days it was not polite for me to speak when my then master, Lord Masahito, was speaking.' I accepted that at face value, though my guess is that it must have been useful if the English didn't know that Nakano could understand them. He'd hear some secrets that way. And so to politics.

'You said you are here to negotiate,' I said, 'may I ask why?'

'May I first ask why you are here?' he said, 'Why have you come to Japan in this great warship, with so many guns and so many men?'

'I'm chasing Kilbride and Valentine,' I said, 'who have broken British Law in coming to Japan.' I looked carefully at him as I said this. 'Which you must know already, since you sailed with them for months, and Lord Masahito must certainly know what Kilbride's doing, and that it's against British law.' He kept a plain face with no expression, then slanted off sideways, not answering my question at all.

'I am here to inform you of the present situation,' he said, 'which dictates that no supplies or assistance may be given to you – not water, salt, flesh nor grain; not timber, rope, nails nor tar – unless certain conditions are fulfilled by you.'

'Oh-ho!' I thought, and looked at my companions. Pyne and Goodsby were mystified, but O'Flaherty winked, because he knew me better than they did, and knew that of all life's pleasures – second only to the ladies – I relish nose-to-nose bargaining most. 'Nakano,' I said, 'Tell me all you wish about this *present situation*, but my ship needs no supplies or provisions. So if your conditions are unacceptable, then I'll up-anchor and be gone.' I paused, and shook my head in sorrow. 'And your port will miss the opportunity to be paid for the few extras that we might otherwise buy … and we always pay in gold … pure gold.'

So off we went, and it soon emerged that Nakano wouldn't discuss the *situation* ashore, that he had thousands of soldiers to prevent our landing without permission, that he knew that western ships arriving in Japan needed supplies for the voyage home, and finally that he wanted to keep *Euphonides* in port and wouldn't say why. His starting proposal was that we'd be re-supplied if first we sent our crew ashore under guard, leaving Japanese soldiers in charge of our ship.

For my part, given good luck and fair weather, *Euphonides* might have just enough food and drink aboard to get us to Canton in China where there was an East India Company station. So we badly needed supplies. Also I was already determined to stay put, keeping *Euphonides* in fighting trim in case Kilbride's squadron tried to leave, and I was certainly not going to empty my ship of men! So *my* starting proposal, was that I didn't need anything from Nakano, I had no intention of landing, and was ready to be gone with the next ebb tide. Then the argument went to and fro, and finally Nakano himself came up with an offer that he said he'd already been accepted by the East India Squadron.

'We shall sell supplies to your ship,' he said, 'and allow small numbers of your men ashore for recreation, if you commodore, and your navigating officers come ashore with as a sign that your ship will make no hostile move against my Master or his brother.' But that wouldn't do, my jolly boys, that wouldn't do at all. What would happen to us ashore? Would we be locked up? So I thought a bit and replied.

'No, no,' I said, with a frown, 'that's impossible. I could never risk my officers in such a way, and I myself could never leave the ship.'

'Huh!' said Nakano, and the argument went on again, until the following was agreed.

'So,' I said, 'you will provide supplies for my ship.' He nodded. 'And some of my men in small groups will be received ashore.' He nodded. 'While I alone – just me and not my officers – will come ashore now. I will come ashore under your personal protection.' He nodded. 'Good!' I said, 'I shall do that to show our goodwill towards your master.' I paused and gave my best smile. 'Of course,' I said, 'If I should *fail* to return to the ship, or if I should come to harm, then it is possible that my officers might be so offended, as to turn the guns of this ship on your castle.' I looked at Pyne, O'Flaherty and Goodsby, who all nodded their heads nearly off. 'But of course,' I added, 'I shall come to no harm because I shall be under your protection, Nakano.'

'*Hi!*' he said, which again I took for yes, though in fact it meant much more, because the Japanese are not only obsessed by good manners, but by keeping their given word. So that one, single sound from Nakano was as good as a contract signed in blood before a thousand witnesses. Of course we didn't know that at the time, so when I was gathering my traps to go ashore, with my servants bustling round and shoving things into bags, and with Nakano and his men up on deck, I had another argument, this time with my officers.

'You can't go, Sir!' said Pyne.

'Can we trust them?' said Goodsby.

'Could our guns even reach the castle?' said O'Flaherty, 'The parts we could damage, that is? Because round-shot would bounce off the stone foundations, and the pagodas are a hundred feet up.'

'Build special carriages,' I said, 'so the guns can be elevated good and high. Use 'em like mortars, firing upward with reduced charges, to drop shot among the upper-works. And use shells not round-shot. That'll do more damage.' Pyne shook his head.

'We've never fired at a target that high. I don't know if it's even possible.'

'And neither do they!' I said, 'these people have got no guns of their own, so they don't know what ours can do. It's the threat that counts, and I've got to go ashore, because I'm ordered to chase Kilbride, and I'm damn sure he's already ashore, so that's where I'm going.'

And that's what I did.

CHAPTER 43

'Our profession is hard, honoured Lady-my-mother. By the discipline you taught me, I control my dislike of the grovelling endearments that flow from him that I shall not name, and I give thanks that he may never physically touch me. But now he brings another to me, so that I might end the dispute between them. I therefore send you the details, well knowing that your wisdom exceeds mine.'

(From a letter of Wednesday, September 26th 1798 by the Lady Meiko, The House of Flowers, Port Hito, to her mother the Lady Kusami, The Street of the Print-Makers, Okonoma.)

Lord Kimiya sat beside his brother Lord Masahito. They sat in seiza position in the Tea House of the House of Flowers. Their bodyguards were outside. There was tranquil silence. The Fodai poem and the flower arrangement in the alcove were chosen to represent the resolution of dispute and the peace of contentment.

The Lady Meiko's kimonos were likewise chosen to represent resolution and contentment, and she sat facing the two brothers with the implements of the tea ceremony set aside, and her musical instruments untouched. She bowed to the two great men. Lord Kimiya was the Daimyo and Lord Masahito was his heir, since Kimiya had no legal sons, and of the three brothers between him and Masahito, two were dead of smallpox and one from a horse-fall. Thus Kimiya and Masahito were the leaders of Clan Hitamoto, and just possibly the next rulers of all Japan.

The two noblemen bowed in return, an act of deference that neither would have extended to any other person than the Emperor Himself in far-away Kyoto.

The Lady Meiko spoke with care.

'It is not for a woman to advise men, in the affairs of men,' she said. She paused and gave a gracious and elegant gesture of apology.

'And yet, Lady,' said Lord Kimiya, 'my honoured brother and I would seek your word in this matter.'

'It would be improper for a mere woman to utter such words,' said Lady Meiko, and raised a hand to protect herself from so distasteful a duty.

'Yet we ask you, Lady,' said Lord Kimiya, 'I ask you and my brother asks you.' But Lady Meiko – being trained in a lifetime of observation – spotted the irritation behind the passive face of Lord Masahito.

'You aren't going to take a woman's word,' she thought, 'not you, my pretty boy.' But she merely smiled.

'We ask you again,' said Lord Kimiya, 'My brother asks in respect, and I ask in the knowledge that you understand my feelings for you, my Lady.'

'Grovelling little mouse,' thought Lady Meiko, 'why can't you be a man, like your brother? At least he's a soldier, not a poet like you.' But those were merely her thoughts.

'I might perhaps speak if it is at your command, my Lord,' she said, 'and at *your* command, honoured brother of my Lord.'

'Speak, my Lady,' said Lord Kimiya, and looked hard at his brother, who sat silent, then nodded.

'Hi!' he said.

'Properly!' said Lord Kimiya in irritation. 'Speak properly!' Lord Masahito sighed.

'I too ask, honoured lady,' he said, 'I ask for your wisdom.' Lord Kimiya nodded.

'Good,' he said.

'So,' said Lady Meiko, 'You, my Lord Masahito have brought the foreigners here, and you, my Lord Kimiya, have tested them in battle and found that their mode of warfare is superior to that of Japan.' She paused and looked at them. She saw the unease where others would have seen only calm faces. 'You two have therefore brought a thing to Japan,' she said, 'that is new, and dangerous beyond imagination.'

'It was not me that brought the foreigners,' said Lord Kimiya.

'It was you that used them,' said Lady Meiko, and Lord Kimiya squirmed in guilt.

'And it was also you, Lord Kimiya,' she said, 'who told me of the appalling mutilations that the galloper guns inflicted on the men of Clan Tokugawa.'

'Who are our enemies,' said Lord Masahito.

'And yet they are Japanese,' said Lady Meiko, 'and this is the cause of the division between brothers, because one brother seeks defeat of Clan Tokugawa and the overthrow of the Shogun, while the other seeks only to defend Hito Island.' She paused and saw the brief nod that neither of them even knew they'd given. 'But in either case you must use foreign soldiers and foreign means of war that bring disgrace upon you.'

'It is not disgrace,' said Lord Masahito, 'it is expedient.'

'That *is* the disgrace,' said Lord Kimiya, 'doing a foul thing, just because it works!'

'My Lords,' said Lady Meiko, you have sworn not to argue in this house. She said that quickly before the anger caught fire again. She raised hands for calm, and the brothers breathed deeply and were silent. Then Lord Masahito spoke.

'We can control the foreigners,' he said, 'we can control them and use them.'

'What if they control and use Japan?' said Lord Kimiya, and again the Lady Meiko raised hands for silence and for calm.

'Look at the pair of you,' she thought, 'a limp flower that won't fight and a clever monkey that loves everything foreign. You were stamping and screaming at each other when the monkey came home and found the flower in his father's armour.'

'My Lords,' she said, 'you are men of the highest birth. You are imbued with the Samurai Spirit, you are honoured by your followers, and it is most tragic and serious when a division comes between men such as yourselves. I therefore, and humbly, beg time to consider this matter deeply, before I attempt any words of advice. Will you permit that?'

'Hi,' they said.

CHAPTER 44

Nakano was three sheets to the wind, he was smitten with barrel-fever. I'd been in his company only a few days, and previously I'd never seen him behave any other way than with a stone-face, straight back and rigid discipline. But now he was drunk as a lord, which is fitting since he was a lord among his own people. I knew that from the way the people bowed and scraped to him, and from the way his bodyguard of samurai, stood round him.

Also I'd seen his house, since I was staying in it and sleeping on the floor, with a mat under me and some sort of quilt on top: God help my aching limbs! It was his summer lodge, and it was huge. It was made out of timber beams, with sliding screens of lath and paper that let the light through, and was full of nothing but mats on the floor, because the Japanese tidy everything away to leave empty space. It was odd but it was impressive, and the gardens were even more impressive, with servants combing the grass, polishing the stones, and arranging bushes like blooms in a vase.

I never saw his family though. I think his wife had died during the long years Nakano was out of England, and his children were away with relatives, having grown up among them. But I merely guessed that out of hints, because he wouldn't talk about it and changed to subject if I asked.

So that was Lord Nakano, who I'd thought was merely a bodyguard. But now this formidable man, who'd repeatedly thrown me arse-over-tit, was rolling about singing a silly song, among a chosen elite of his friends, and myself looking on, and all of us sat on the tatami mats of an upper-class Oiran house in Okonoma, on the southern pincer of Hito Bay.

An Oiran house, incidentally is something you youngsters – boys at least – should see for your education, since the equivalents even in Paris, could never match one for sheer cleanliness, neatness, exquisite good taste, and the gorgeous little creatures in silk gowns, that serve there for the entertainment of gentlemen. I thought Perse and her chums were fairies, but not compared with the Oiran girls of Okonoma.

So what was going on? What was going on was that Lord Nakano was trying to recruit me, and my ship, into his service. It was that, and a mixture of the fact that he personally liked me and that he was showing me off, around the town as the finest example of a foreign barbarian that any Japanese had ever seen. Thus I was monstrously bigger than any of them, and the Oiran girls gasped at the calibre of my lower deck battery. Also I didn't know how to do anything Japanese, which the Japanese loved, and they laughed and laughed. I didn't know how to sit on the floor, I didn't know how to use chopsticks, I didn't have any Japanese manners, and I certainly didn't speak Japanese.

To get a grasp of this, just imagine that you had charge of a giant ape, shaved of his fur, crammed into gentleman's clothes and which you were leading through the clubs and coffee houses of west London. So that was your Uncle Jacob in Japan, my jolly boys, except that it was good-natured, because the Japanese were like the British, in being so profoundly sure of themselves that they pitied the poor barbarian in his innocent ignorance and just laughed when he couldn't pick up rice with two sticks, or couldn't stomach their national dish of octopus bollocks on toast.

And then there was drink: strong drink. The Japanese had something called sar-kay which was brewed out of rice.

[The word is generally rendered as 'sake' in English, but Fletcher typically insisted in setting down foreign words phonetically. See above for his views of foreign languages. S.P.]

In strength, sar-kay stands somewhere between wine and proof spirit, and there's a rainbow of different types, and ceremonies for the drinking of it, and neat little pots to pour it from, and neat little vessels to drink it out of: everything neat, mark you: neat and beautiful. But the funny thing is that the Japanese get drunk really fast on sar-kay, and don't mind getting drunk.

So, being a seaman and used to strong drink, I could sit on the floor among Lord Nakano and his friends, with my aching bum and my legs gone numb, but I was still sober while they were rolling around grinning and laughing. On that first occasion it was only myself and the Oiran girls who were fully conscious by the end of the evening. But – and here's the difference between them and us – nobody minded if a gentleman got drunk and made a fool of himself, because next day it was all forgotten and never mentioned, and it was back to stone-faces and discipline.

So perhaps Nakano let slip some truths when he was drunk, or perhaps he was trying me out. Because when he'd done singing, and all his friends laughed, and the Oiran girls poured some more drink into little porcelain cups, he had a little word with me. There we were, all chums together, round a low table with neat-little, tidy-little, delicacies lined up in rows, and the girls smiling and the lanterns glowing, and Nakano leaned towards me and grinned.

'The song was about a man who cannot kill a chicken because he is afraid of blood,' he said, then chattered to his friends in Japanese, saying the same thing, and they all laughed and Nakano looked at me again, 'Just as *Our Lord* is afraid of blood!' He rocked with laughter and said it in Japanese.

'Oooooo !' said his Japanese friends, at this statement which they found outrageous, and they nodded and laughed.

That was the first instalment of the story. I got more day by day, as Lord Nakano took me round the town to see the sights. He got me rigged out in Japanese clothes pretty quick because the climate was humid, and he said my own clothes wouldn't do. So off we went on our walks, always with a retinue of samurai behind us, and always with the local folk bowing low, and the soldiers saluting, Japanese style, because the town was full of soldiers.

Thus, the day after the visit to the Oiran house, we went up a long, narrow street to a hill for a view of the harbour and the town. The street was teeming with people, and was all neat and clean, with rows of buildings all the same height, all made out of wood and paper, all tidy and square, and with tiled roofs, and big painted signs in their incomprehensible writing. And there were little peasant-folk trotting along, carrying bamboo poles over their shoulders, with a heavy basket at each end, and ladies stepping past in bright gowns, and wooden clogs on their feet, and long pins in their hair.

'There, Fletcher-san,' said Nakono when we got to the top. He always called me that because adding 'san' to a name was polite. There was a viewing platform at the top of the hill, with a fresh sea-breeze, and flowers in pots, and little shops offering refreshment. 'There is the East India Squadron,' said Nakano, 'and there is your own ship.'

'Yes,' I said, because the view was magnificent: blue sky, blue sea, the ships at anchor, the huge castle, the port and the town, and the tented camps of the thousands of Japanese soldiers that lined the beaches. Finally, I pointed at the East India ships. 'Where are their people?' I said, 'their crews? And the Sepoy soldiers that came from India? What are they doing?' I asked because he'd ducked these same questions repeatedly since I came ashore, and now I wanted some answers. He thought about that and nodded.

'Look there,' he said, and pointed, 'there is Port Hito to the north.' He pointed again. 'And there is Okonoma, to the south. The East India people are confined to Port Hito ...'

'And I and my people are confined to Okonoma,' I said.

'You are not confined, Fletcher-san,' he said, 'you are in my care.'

'And what about them?' I said, pointing to the Japanese encampments, 'what are all the soldiers for?'

'What would you do in England,' he said, 'if foreigners came in great force and in great ships? Would you not send soldiers to keep order?'

'What about Kilbride and Valentine?' I said, 'Are they ashore?'

'Yes,' he said.

'And what about the Sepoys? Have they landed?'

'Yes.'

'And what have they done?'

'They have been tested,' he said, 'and much blood was shed.'

'Whose blood?'

'Tokugawa blood. The enemy's blood.' The mention of blood reminded me of what Nakano had said when he was drunk.

'Last night,' I said, 'you said that *Our Lord* is afraid of blood. What did you mean?'

'I do not remember,' he said, 'that was last night.'

'And what about this *situation*, that you mentioned,' I said, 'what is it?'

'Now is not the time,' he said, 'We may talk of this later. Now I have duties. My men will take you back to my house.' And that was that. Not another word. Off he went with half of his men and the rest took me back to the summer lodge. I could hardly argue. There were a dozen of them, and they all had swords, and there were soldiers everywhere. So I made the best of it and walked back like a good boy, with the people gazing at me and pointing me out. I noticed that the ladies especially

284

pointed me out, and looked me up and down, and whispered to one another and giggled.

'*Oh!*' they said, and '*Ah!*' they said, and with such cheeky expressions that I think the Oiran girls must have spread word that I mounted a thirty-two pounder where the local gentlemen had nines.

The next evening, Nakano took me to the theatre, which I enjoyed very much. It was called a Kabuki theatre, and was very much like the London equivalent and yet very different. It had a big auditorium with a stage sticking out into the audience, and rows of oiled-paper windows up near the ceiling to let in the daylight. But it was all made out of wood, and the seats weren't seats at all, because the Japanese sat on cushions on the floor. So in front of the stage there was a timber grid dividing up the auditorium into low boxes about six feet square and two feet high, and you had to clamber over everyone else's to get to your box, except that Lord Nakano had his own box and everyone stood and bowed, and made way for him, and me, and his friends.

So the people lounged in their boxes, and watched the performance, and tucked into the food and drink that they'd brought with them, and it was all immensely jolly and bright, and most of the time, the stage was crowded with actors and actresses in the most fantastical and lurid costumes and makeup, though there was very little scenery or stage effects such as we have. But the actors stamped and shouted, and postured and danced, and I didn't understand a word of it but I loved it and cheered along with the rest.

Meanwhile Nakano and his chums got at the sar-kay, and the silly grins came out and Nakano let slip some more information, either accidentally or deliberately.

'See Fletcher-san,' he said, rocking towards me and whispering loudly, 'The play concerns two brothers who fight over their father's property.' He laughed. 'Just like Lord Masahito and Lord Kimiya.' He laughed again, and nudged one of his chums and chattered away and the chum laughed and pointed at the stage, and chattered at me, nodding furiously. 'And one brother is a eunuch, and the other a soldier!' They all laughed at that, and everyone around us laughed too, so it seemed to be a joke that everyone understood, except me.

Over the next few days, I was taken to see a display of mounted archery, and then a display of Japanese sword-play using wooden sticks so nobody got killed, and finally a contest of Sumo, which is the Japanese form of wrestling. A special display of Sumo was put on for the benefit of Lord Nakano and when he told me where we were going, I asked if – once again – I would have to take part.

'No, Fletcher-san,' he said, and gave a rare smile: rare when he was sober, that is. 'You will not take part because you *may* not take part. On Hito Island, Okobo Buddhism teaches that Sumo is a sacred discipline practised by initiates. It is not like Jiu Jitsu. It is not a fighting skill but a spiritual art and a reverence of tradition.'

'Is it?' I said, 'Ain't that nice.'

Then we were off to a Sumo stable, or barracks, whatever is the word for the place where the Sumos lived, trained, and ate the enormous meals that made them so big. The stable was on the edge of Okonoma, and we marched there with the usual guard of samurai. We came to a big, free-standing building, with banners and coloured signs all round the entrance, and two lines of very big men standing outside, waiting for us. They wore the usual Japanese civilian robes, they had the pigtail and shaved-brow hairstyle, and they were so thick about the middle that they had trouble in bowing. These were obviously the Sumos. They looked strong and determined men, bigger by far than most Japanese: some as tall as me and most of them heavier, because the Japanese ideal of strength demands a big fat body, and huge limbs.

There was a lot of bowing and greeting, and a series of smaller men in fancy robes and funny hats came forward and bowed to Nakano, and greeting scrolls were passed to and fro, and I got one which I still have, after all these years, and I still don't know what it says. Then I was introduced, and I bowed to everyone, and everyone smiled. Then the most senior of the small men in fancy robes – a little fellow, all brown and wrinkled and old – bowed to me, looked me over, and said something to Nakano.

'This honourable gentleman,' said Nakano, 'is Master Hamada, supreme trainer of Sumos.' The small man bowed again at the mention of his name. 'Master Hamada says that you have the bones of a Sumo, and with diet and exercise you might do well.'

'Aaah!' said everyone, much impressed and they bowed at me. I was being paid a compliment.

Later we were treated to several bouts inside the building, on a place called a dojo, which was a clay circle about fifteen feet across. There was a great deal of action, even before the bouts, with the Sumos taking turns to bend forward and stretch their legs in the air, and stamp down hard, trying to frighten each other with a display of ferocity. Then they were at it: pairs of huge men, barefoot and near naked, with the cheeks of their arses bulging out of fancy loincloths, and a tiny referee in charge whom the wrestlers obeyed like dogs. The bouts were over fast, and victory was won by throwing over your opponent, or pushing him out of the ring. I thought it was interesting, though not so good as boxing. But Nakano was fascinated. He was so carried away that he let loose a bit more of the truth. Or was it policy? Who knows?

'See the fighting spirit, Fletcher-san!' he said, when one of the Sumos heaved his opponent off his feet, 'That is what wins the bout. That is what *he* lacks ...' then he interrupted himself as the wrong-footed Sumo skilfully recovered himself, gripping hard to his opponent. 'Ah!' said Nakano, and cried out something in Japanese in congratulation.

'Who are you talking about?' I said, 'Who lacks fighting spirit?'

'Kimiya,' said Nakano, 'Lord Kimiya.'

'But he's your ... your ... what is he? I said, 'Prince? King?'

'Daimyo!' said Nakano, 'But he has no fighting spirit, and he says Lord Masahito has no honour. So we are stuck like a man at the crossroads who doesn't know which way to go and ...' but this time a Sumo went right over, and Nakano and the rest cried out in appreciation. Then Nakano looked at me. 'So we need you here, Fletcher-san. We need you.'

'What do you want from me, Nakano-san?' I said, 'Won't you tell me what you want?'

'I cannot,' he said, 'not yet. I must wait until Lord Kimiya and Lord Masahito make their decision. But I want you here.' And that was as much as I got out of Nakano, because he was careful after that and wouldn't say any more. He wouldn't but someone else would.

Sometime later, Nakano took me for another evening at an Oiran house. He brought his same best friends, and it was the same with the sar-kay, until he and the rest were dozing. Then I had to get up and go to the privy, and would you believe it, just as aboard *Duke of Cornwallis* months ago, when I was done and stepped out into the neat corridor, there – would you just believe it – was Kilbride, the swab, leering at me and with a Japanese man beside him: he was young, sharp faced and civilian and he had one sword in his belt, a short sword.

The only thought in my mind in that instant was to wring Kilbride's neck, but he saw the look, stepped back, and pulled out a small pistol and cocked it. Though small, the pistol had a wide bore. It looked to be musket-calibre at least. Meanwhile the Japanese friend drew his sword.

'Now, now, commodore,' said Kilbride, and did his best to smile, 'no cause for anything nasty. I just want to talk.'

'There's a bodyguard of samurai outside,' I said, 'If they hear a shot they'll be in here on the instant.'

'And you'll be dead, and we'll be out the back way,' he said, 'So what'll it be? Don't you want to see your ship again?' He paused and smiled. 'And your sister, and her kiddies in Canterbury? There's a whole life waiting for you, and it'd be a shame to lose it.'

'So what do you want?' I said.

'To talk,' he said, 'To make you an offer.'

The bastard. The swine. The swab. He stirred up all the old arguments again, about whose side was I on? He'd caught my attention, damn him, and he saw it. 'Good!' he said, 'This way,' and he led along the corridor to another room, past another sliding panel. We went in and sat down on cushions, with a small table between us, and the Japanese gent sat beside Kilbride. There was a small, gilded box on the table. It was about a foot long and six inches high. It was like everything Japanese: neat, perfect and beautiful.

'How did you get here?' I said.

'Money,' he said, 'The magic key. Money and him.' He looked at his Japanese friend. 'This is Yamada. Say hallo, Yamada.'

'*Harrow*,' said Yamada, just about managing the word.

'He understands a lot more than he speaks,' said Kilbride, 'there's a little colony of Dutch seamen in Port Hito, wrecked off a ship years ago, and some of them speak English and Yamada learned it from them, as a lad. He had to learn Dutch and English. His father made him do it.'

'Why?' I said.

'Because his father's a merchant looking for opportunity,' said Kilbride, and he pushed the gilded box towards me, 'His father gave me this thing. Go on Fletcher: open it, and have a good look.' So I opened the box, which was remarkable in its beauty and I found all sort of things inside: other boxes, neat-packed to perfection and each exquisitely decorated, and a neat stack of tiny, much-decorated tools and tongs. It was a lovely thing to see and to handle, and was wonderfully exotic and different from anything made in Europe. 'It's an incense set,' said Kilbride, 'they play some sort of game with it. The boxes hold different kinds of incense, and one player sets a bit burning, and another has to guess what it is. But that doesn't matter. What matters is: how long have you been here, Fletcher?'

'A few weeks,' I said.

'And in that time,' he said, 'have you seen *anything* these people make that is not beautiful? Carving, pottery, lacquer-work, prints, jewellery? Anything at all that isn't beautiful – and better than the Chinese can make?'

'Oh,' I said, already guessing where he was going.

'And on top of that, they can deliver tea, spices, silk and the rest!' His voice was rising and speeding up as the passion gripped him. 'Japan is better than China, and it's wide open, and you'd know that if you'd not been knocking on the wrong door!'

'What door?' I said.

'You made one mistake when you spoke to Nakano,' he said.

'What do you know about Nakano?' I said.

'I know that you told him you'd trade for supplies, in gold.'

'How do you know that?' I said, and he grinned.

'Never mind how I know. Did you say it or not?'

'Yes, I did say that.'

'Well, you shouldn't have said it! Because the samurai despise trade! To them, the merchants are like whores and beggars. If Nakano is on your side, it's for politics not trade. But the merchants hate the samurai, and they *are* ready to trade, and I've spoken to Yamada's father.' He turned to Yamada. 'I spoke to your father, didn't I?'

'Hi!' said Yamada.

'That means yes,' said Kilbride.

'I know,' I said.

'I spoke to him, and he's a very big man here, and he spoke to some others who know people in Okonoma, and we've been tracking you, Jacob Fletcher, waiting the chance to talk to you when your friend Nakano has drunk himself stupid.' He smiled. 'It's amazing what people will tell you for money … if they're not samurai.'

'I see,' I said

'But do you really see?' he said, 'Do you see how everything's stuck fast here while Kimiya and Masahito make their bloody minds up?'

289

'No,' I said.

'Right,' he said, and un-cocked his pistol and put it aside. 'See that?' he said, 'I'm going to trust you,' and he leaned forward, 'It's like this, Fletcher: this island's been invaded by Clan Tokugawa for the Shogun. Did you know that?'

'Yes.'

'But my Sepoys and guns – together with the Hitamoto – can smash the Tokugawa invasion army, and Masahito wants me to bring more men and guns, so he can take the war to the Tokugawa, and invade the main Japanese Islands and take over, while Kimiya, doesn't like warfare at all, and doesn't like using foreigners to win battles. So they hate one another, and end up shouting when they meet, and they don't know what to do, and the samurai are terrified of an open split, for fear of civil war at the same time as facing an invasion!'

He sat back on his cushion to let me think about that.

'What's this to you, Kilbride?' I said, 'Why are you telling me this?' He nodded to himself. He leaned forward, and all the force of passion swelled up within him again.

'Because I'm giving you one more chance, Fletcher,' he said, 'I'm giving you the chance to make everything right. So you just listen!' I nodded, I admit that I was hooked. 'Listen!' he said, 'I was both right and wrong about Japan. I was *right* that it's wide open to being taken over. I've seen it! I've seen our guns and muskets in action. But I was *wrong* about the trade that can be done here.' He tapped a finger on the incense box. 'Look at this!' he said, 'Have you ever seen anything like it? And it's just an example!' He leaned closer he stared me in the face. 'I've got a shipload of things like this, aboard *Duke of Cornwallis*. I've been busy trading while you were going round the theatres and tart-shops. Fletcher, these Islands are vastly richer than I thought! So this is what we're going to do. We break out, aboard *Euphonides* and *Duke of Cornwallis*. We sail home, and the pair of us together tell Parliament and the Company what's out here, and how it's ripe for conquest, and we come back with men, ships and guns – John Company and the Navy together – and dominate these Japanese islands!' His eyes were fairly popping with emotion now, as he painted the full picture. 'We can do it *because* they're islands! Japan isn't a continent like China or India, it's a stretched-out chain of islands! It's all coast and bays! None of it's far from the sea and it's wide open to being dominated by a powerful fleet. So first we take Japan, and then we carve out a bigger empire than we had even in America, because once we've got Japan we go after China as well, and we'll still have India in our pocket!'

'What about the war?' I said, 'What about the French?'

'Bah!' he said, 'What do they matter? The French can have Europe and we'll have the world!'

'What about the East India ships we'd leave behind? And the Shadow Men?' I said. He positively beamed at that.

'Well done, Fletcher!' he said, 'You've hit the mark twice! The ships and men left behind will be our excuse for war. We'll say they were trapped by the Japanese, as an act of treachery. And as for the Shadow Men, d'you think they're immune to advantage? D'you think I can't bring them to our side? You'd be free, Fletcher! Free, and out of the Navy and into trade!'

I breathed deep.

I closed my eyes.

I thought, and thought, and thought.

CHAPTER 45

'Again and again, I thank you for your wisdom which was all that I had hoped for, and more. The cringing flower-man and the bouncing monkey-man are now satisfied. They will attempt to make real the compromise you suggested. Thus the future is in their hands, and I pray to The Ancestors that these obtuse and block-headed men might learn one thousandth of the political skill of The-Lady-my-mother.'

(From a letter of Thursday, October 25th 1798 from the Lady Meiko, The House of Flowers, Port Hito, to her mother the Lady Kusami, The Street of the Print-Makers, Okonoma.)

Lord Kimiya and Lord Masahito sat side by side, facing the Lady Meiko. They were as nearly reconciled as ever they could be. The Lady Meiko could see that in their faces, but she had to make sure.

'We are taught,' she said, 'that a man easily sees fault in his brother, but cannot see fault in himself. Thus speaks the Buddha!'

'Thus speaks the Buddha,' they repeated, and bowed.

'We are also taught,' she said, 'that to cherish anger is to wound the self. Thus speaks the Buddha!'

'Thus speaks the Buddha.' they repeated, and bowed.

'And so,' she said, 'as a mere woman and a servant of men, I am awestruck at the noble grace with which My Lord Kimiya and My Lord Masahito have acted, according to the teachings of the Buddha.' She gave a graceful gesture of admiration, and bowed. *You howling infants. You club-foot donkeys. You stupid apes.* Lord Kimiya and Lord Masahito bowed. 'And finally,' she said, 'we are taught that no good comes of a bad thing, and only the light can drive out the dark.' They nodded. 'And therefore, My Lords, the path you have agreed, in your wisdom,' – '*my mother's wisdom,*' she thought, – 'is as follows. First: the Tokugawa must

292

be convinced that they cannot win against the foreigners. To this end, more foreign troops and guns will be landed for one final battle. Second: the Tokugawa must be convinced that we are preparing the foreign ships to sail to Edo, Capital City of the Shogun, to bombard the city with the invincible foreign cannon.' She paused and smiled. 'This is a most powerful threat, because the Shogun would lose face before all Japan if he could not protect his own city, and we thank Commodore Fletcher who gave us this idea by threatening to bombard Okonoma Castle.'

'Hi!' said Lord Kimiya and Lord Masahito.

'So,' said the Lady Meiko, 'To this end we shall invite Tokugawa officers, under promise of safe-conduct, to view the foreign ships and their guns, so that they understand that we have the power to break the Shogun's honour.'

'Hi!' said Lord Kimiya and Lord Masahito.

'Then third,' said the Lady Meiko, 'We shall negotiate with the Tokugawa, proposing that Hitamoto will not attack Edo city, nor invade the home islands of Tokugawa, if Tokugawa withdraws from Hito Island, and declares it to be sovereign Hitamoto land.' She bowed. 'My Lords, I humbly offer these words for your agreement.' There was brief silence. And then:

'There will be more bloodshed,' said Lord Kimiya, 'caused by the foreigners.'

'But there will be more if we follow any other path,' said the Lady Meiko.

'We would abandon any hope of defeating the Shogun,' said Lord Masahito.

'But we would secure the freedom of Hito Island,' said the Lady Meiko. There was no further argument.

CHAPTER 46

'The Jappos was in a fury of busy-ness. Half the Sepoys was summoned ashore, and all the field artillery, and all us officers was put under special guard.'

(From a letter of Friday, October 26th 1798 from Captain Edward Pryce of the EIC ship *Duke of Cornwallis* who wrote letters – normally on Sundays – to his wife Mrs Emily Pryce to be given to her as a record of his voyages, on his return to England.)

'Have you heard from Fletcher?' said Sir Robert Valentine, shouting upward as he climbed the ladder.

'No,' said Kilbride, 'but he'll come round. He's greedy for trade, and he hates Spencer and the Shadow Men.' Kilbride looked down at Valentine, as he puffed and blew and heaved himself up into the loft space where he and Kilbride had their beds: the loft of the empty warehouse where the East India officers lived while ashore. Kilbride saw that Valentine was unsteady on the ladder.

'Where have you been?' he said.

'I've been engaged in financial discussions,' said Valentine.

'You've been to that damn grog-shop again,' said Kilbride, 'I can see it in your face. You go cross-eyed when you've had too many.' Valentine ignored that.

'There's something going on,' he said.

'I can bloody-well see that for myself,' said Kilbride, 'Look!'

The two men crouched to look through the window. It wasn't a proper, glazed window, just a woven grid of sticks, in a square hole looking out under the thatch of the roof. They could see the harbour, with boats going to and fro, and the nine, big Indiamen anchored offshore. But what took

294

their attention was bodies of marching Japanese soldiers with drums booming, banners waving and officers on horseback.

'Damn!' said Kilbride, 'There's one lot coming this way. We'd better get downstairs to see what's going forward.'

Five minutes later, Kilbride was arguing with a Japanese officer while the East India Squadron's captains and mates – three dozen of them in their long blue coats and shiny buttons – stood behind Kilbride and listened with anxious faces.

'We're under guard?' said Kilbride.

'Yes,' said the elderly Dutchman who was the officer's translator, 'Officer say so. Officer is samurai.' The Dutchman bowed to the officer. The bow was instinctive. The Dutchman had been thirty years in Japan. The samurai officer nodded, he wore battle armour, with swords in his belt, and he had six men behind him, and an infantry company outside.

The officer looked at the foreigners in disdain. He looked at the untidy jumble of sea-chests, bedding, and pots that filled the warehouse. No Japanese would live in such disorder. He sniffed. Foreigners smelt bad because they did not bathe. They smelt especially bad indoors because the cooking smells of their food tainted any place where they lived. The officer put this nastiness aside, and spoke in rapid Japanese to the Dutch interpreter and gave him a scroll of paper.

'Hi!' said the Dutchman, and looked at the paper, nodded, then translated for Kilbride and the other Englishmen.

'You are under guard,' he said, 'You stay in this house. You don't go out,' he gave the paper to Kilbride, 'But these forces must come ashore at once,' he said, 'You give orders! They come ashore! They come with all equipment, ready to march,' he looked at the paper, and passed it to Kilbride, 'This is Order of Daimyo and Lord Masahito,' he said, 'Signatures are here,' he pointed to the Japanese characters, 'and below is men and guns to come ashore. Men and guns is in English.'

'What?' said the East India officers.

'Why?' they said.

'What's going on?' said Kilbride to the Dutchman, making sure to nod politely to the officer, 'all this time we've been here, and able to go round the port, and nobody minded, and I want to know what …' But the officer stamped his foot, stabbed a finger at the ground and shouted in Kilbride's face.

'He say, you stay here,' said the Dutchman, 'No argue. No more words.

You bring men ashore. You bring guns ashore. You write orders to your ships. You do it now!'

'Hi!' said the samurai, and uttered a few more words.

'Now!' said the Dutchman, 'You do it now!'

'Hi!' said the samurai, and put a hand on a sword hilt.

'Oh,' said Kilbride, and knew that he must do as he was bid ... or at least seem to, because Kilbride's mind was swift and clever and he had already made a major decision. So he spoke very carefully, always remembering that it was not only the samurai that must be kept sweet, but the East India officers too.

'Please tell this honourable gentleman,' he said, bowing to the samurai, 'that I will do as he asks.' The Dutchman translated, the samurai nodded. 'And I will do it instantly!' The Dutchman translated, the samurai nodded. 'But so great a movement of men and guns,' said Kilbride with a most earnest expression, 'cannot be achieved by orders on paper, but only by my personal presence aboard the ships, together with some of my officers to organise the movements.' Kilbride paused to make sure that the samurai understood and approved. 'So,' said Kilbride, 'I shall go at once, with Captain Pryce and the officers of my flagship. We shall go aboard to set matters in hand.' The Dutchman translated, the samurai nodded, and meanwhile Kilbride saw the anxious look on Valentine's face and realised that Valentine was sharp enough guess what was happening and make trouble. So Kilbride added, 'And I shall need Sir Robert Valentine, too, since he and I are joint commanders of the squadron.'

Valentine sighed, the East India officers muttered and grumbled, and the samurai listened to his interpreter and replied. Then finally:

'Yes,' said the Dutchman, 'Do that thing! Do it quick!'

In the boat going out to *Duke of Cornwallis* the Japanese coxswain and oarsmen were deaf to English. But Kilbride spoke softly, not wanting to rouse emotions and cause alarm. So Valentine, Pryce and the three mates, leaned close to hear him.

'Kimiya and Masahito have settled it between them,' said, Kilbride, 'They must have, because they both signed that paper. So they're going forward together, and not a word to me!' Valentine frowned. 'To *us!*' said Kilbride, 'So we're not part of what they're doing, and we're being put aside. But they're taking our men and guns.'

'So what do we do?' said Valentine.

'We leave them to it,' said Kilbride, 'fighting their war against the Tokugawa.' He pointed at *Duke of Cornwallis*. 'Once we're aboard that ship, they can't touch us. We'll make ready for sea and be gone, and then home to England.' He smiled. 'We don't need Masahito and Kimiya any more. I'd have gone soon in any case. We've got enough Japanese goods aboard to show what's out here, so what we must do is get home, and bring back the Company and the Navy together and take hold of these islands and shake the money out of them!'

'What about Fletcher?' said Kilbride, 'Don't we need him?'

'Not really,' said Kilbride, 'I spoke to him to ease our path and avoid trouble. We don't so much need him *with* us, as not *against* us.' He looked across the bay to *Euphonides*. 'Captain Pryce?' he said.

'Sir?' said Pryce.

'If it came to a fight,' said Kilbride, 'Could Fletcher's ship beat *Duke of Cornwallis*?'

Pryce smiled.

'A frigate against a line-of-battle-ship?' he said, 'I think not, Sir. I really do!'

CHAPTER 47

I have not the slightest doubt that the reason I detested Kilbride so much was that he used my own dreams to push me into doing what he wanted. Yes, I wanted to be a trader. Yes, I wanted to be a manufacturer. Yes, I loved busy mills grinding out goods for the masses and wealth for me. And, yes, I never wanted to be a sailor in King George's Navy. So Kilbride caused me to think long and very hard, about his plans for an empire of the East, and the colossal opportunities for trade which that meant.

After all, what he was proposing was no more than what John Company had done in India: taking over nation after nation by force of arms, step by step, year by year and all in the name of trade. So why not do the same with Japan?

I thought all that as I went home with Nakano and his chums that night after meeting Kilbride: Nakano and his dozing friends carried in litters by their retainers, and myself walking. I was far too big for the boxes on sticks that they rode in, and I wasn't drunk. That night I slept on my mat on the floor in my room in Nakano's summer lodge, except that I didn't sleep much for worrying. So finally, my jolly boys, who knows what I would have done if the choice hadn't been taken from me?

But I was pulled up off the floor by Nakano himself, early next morning. Either he was immune to feeling ill the morning after, or he covered it up with self-control. He was in my room with followers waiting outside, and a servant holding my uniform coat, cocked hat, sword shoes and all the rest. I heard them even before he came into the room, and I was already awake.

'Fletcher-san!' he cried, and bowed several times in apology, 'I had to wake you. Much is happening. We are summoned to the castle. You must be yourself again. You must wear your own clothes!'

'Why?' I said, 'What's happening.'

'I do not know,' he said, 'We will learn at the castle. Be quick! I must

298

prepare.' Then he was gone and I was up, and doubling to the wash-house, and into my ablutions with Nakano's servants looking on, since they see no shame in nakedness, nor even the thunder-box. Then I dressed with servants hauling on my coat, and buckling my belt, and I was thrust a pot of green tea, and some rice-cakes, which I ate standing up, and then it was outside, where cavalry were formed up, and Nakano in full armour, and up we got into the saddle – something I forever loathe to do but sometimes I must – and off we went at a fast trot. Out of the town we went, and on to the coast road, with a fine view of the bay, and the anchored ships, and I was surprised to see that *Duke of Cornwallis* was striking the canvas shades over the quarterdeck and midships, and heaving the yards aloft. Something was going on.

'What's happening?' I shouted at Nakano, over the sound of the horses. But he just shook his head. So on we went, towards the castle, which was out on the end of a peninsula and defenced by the most amazing lines of entrenchments and banks, all bristling with sharp stakes, and little forts everywhere, and the road through blocked with heavy gates, and soldiers, and challenges and passwords, and Nakano waving a paper with official seals, to get us through.

Then we were riding round the enormous, pyramid of masonry that was the base of the castle to an entry port heavily guarded by pike-men, and dismounting, and the horses taken away, and much bowing and shouting, until Nakano, his personal bodyguard and myself were let through. Then we doubled up a sloping ramp, with all of us hanging on to our swords for fear of tripping, and myself soon winded because I'm too big to be a runner, and all the while men were looking down on us from the firing galleries, with matchlocks smouldering, and myself thinking we'd all be dead if we were attacking.

Finally we got to the top of the stonework, and into the timber innards of the castle, which were massive, and highly ornamented, and were full of rooms, and stairs, and men, and some women too in their fancy silks. So up we went again, floor after floor, until we reached an audience chamber right at the top. Or rather we reached the outside of it and stood gasping and panting, in front of a great, sliding screen with beautiful coloured images of birds and tigers and trees, and which was the entrance. There we faced a company of some twenty men in extremely elaborate dazzling-coloured armour, and huge helmets. These were obviously the local guardsmen, and who stood in our way and looked grim, and their commander studied Nakano's document with excruciating care. But finally he bowed, handed back the document and shouted a command, that caused the guardsmen to fall back, and the screen-door to slide open.

At this, Nakano stepped forward with me behind, while his bodyguard stood fast, and we entered the most beautiful, and elegant space, all bright with sunlight, and decorated Japanese style, with just the minimum needed for tasteful beauty of flowers, and with silk embroidery on the walls. At the far end there was a superb and complete view over the harbour, seen through slid-back screens, with a balcony beyond, and rails to stop you plunging three hundred feet to your death on the rocks below. But for the moment, Nakano and I didn't look at that. We looked at two men, in plain black robes bearing the Hitamoto clan badge. They sat on cushions to one side of the room, the cushions being raised up on a platform, and two lines of guardsmen around them, one on each side of the platform, and wearing armour even more gorgeous than that of their comrades outside. The scene could not possibly have been more exotic and more perfectly Japanese. Then one of the men spoke.

'My dear Commodore Fletcher,' he said, 'My dear Lord Nakano, how charming to see you both. Did you come far?' It was the authentic speech of Bond street, as delivered in Okonoma castle by Lord Masahito. Nakano bowed almost to the ground and said something in Japanese.

'My Lord,' I said, and I bowed, 'I am at your service.' What else should I have bloody-well said? What would anyone say? After all, he'd said, 'did you come far?' and he must have known where we'd come from.

'How kind,' said Masahito, 'though, in fact, I hope that you are in the service of Lord Kimiya Masahito, Daimyo of Hito Province,' and he bowed to the man sitting next to him.

'Hi!' said Nakano, emphatically, and down he went again.

I looked at Lord Kimiya. You could tell by their features that he was Masahito's brother: his elder brother. I thought he looked much older, and very worried. He frowned at the English words, said something to Masahito, and the two spoke to each other very fast, and without much goodwill. But finally they reached agreement, and Masahito looked at me again.

'Commodore,' he said,

'My Lord?' I said, and said it politely.

300

'We are in dangerous times,' said Masahito, 'So Lord Kimiya has commanded me to speak directly to you, without the formalities of normal etiquette.'

'And we'll all be jolly shipmates together,' I thought.

'So we must move fast,' said Masahito, and bowed to Kimiya. Then Kimiya got up off his cushion and walked the balcony, Masahito followed him, and beckoned me and Nakano to follow. The view was awesome. It was magnificent. Everything in Hito Bay was laid out below. Masahito bowed to Kimiya, asked something, most likely 'with your permission?' and Kimiya said, 'Hi.'

'Commodore,' said Masahito, 'I will speak to you, and Lord Nakano will translate for Lord Kimiya.'

'How nice,' I thought, and just nodded.

'Look,' said Masahito, and pointed to *Duke of Cornwallis*. I looked down, and there she was, still swinging to anchor, but with yards crossed and the hands making sail, though the canvas hung limp, since the bay was becalmed. 'She is putting to sea,' said Masahito, 'and we want you to stop her.'

'My Lord,' I said, 'why should I do that?'

'For several reasons, commodore. First because *Duke of Cornwallis* alone could defeat every ship in these waters, whether Hitamoto or Tokugawa. She could defeat every ship except yours. Even now, even in harbour, that ship is invincible, and only you could stop her.'

'Very likely, my Lord,' I said, 'But I why I should even try?'

'Because I ask, commodore. I ask. I do not threaten or demand.'

'Much appreciated, my Lord, and very kind of you, but I ask again, why should I take my ship to face a battery of thirty-two pounders?'

'Commodore,' he said, 'You were brought ashore, as part of an arrangement whereby your ship was provisioned for sea, yes?'

'Yes,' I said.

'And once ashore it was the duty of Lord Nakano, to keep you entertained and happy, so that you, and your ship, would stay in Hito Bay.' I looked at Nakano, standing by and translating for Kimiya. He heard what Masahito said, and bowed to me. 'And why do you think we wanted you to stay?' said Masahito.

'I don't know,' I said, 'Lord Nakano would never say.'

'We wanted you here as opposition to Kilbride,' said Masahito, 'In case he turned against us in his great ship.'

'But why did you think I'd take your side against him?' I said, 'And if I did fight him and won, then why would you trust me? How d'you know I won't turn against you and be as bad as Kilbride?'

'My dear Fletcher,' said Masahito, 'I spent many months at sea with Kilbride, and Valentine, and in such a time men say more than they intend, especially men like Valentine who drinks heavily.'

'So?' I said.

'So I know that your Government is so busy with the French, as to seek no adventures beyond Europe, and that Lord Spencer the First Lord of your Admiralty, has given you a direct order to disrupt Kilbride's adventures here.' I said nothing, but my thoughts must have showed. 'Ah,' he said, 'I see! But there is more. You dislike Kilbride, don't you?' I couldn't help but nod. 'So why should he get away from Port Hito and come back with more men and ships?' said Masahito, 'Why should he fulfil his dreams when he is a deceiver and a traitor? He betrayed you in Bombay and now he has abandoned the ships of his squadron, and his officers too.' Masahito looked at me. 'Think of these things, commodore, because this matter deeply concerns you. It concerns your inner *self*. Will you accept treachery and deceit, or will you walk with honour? You must decide this! You must decide what sort of man you wish to be, and then you must become that man, because only you can do it.'

So I did decide, and within the hour I was aboard a boat, with my sea chest, on the way out to *Euphonides*, where I was piped aboard with much joy, and my officers beaming, and the men cheering in the most flattering manner. So, well done, Pyne, for keeping the ship in tip-top order, and well done, Masahito, because he persuaded me to do my duty opposite Kilbride. Masahito had done it when he didn't even know the whole story. In particular he didn't know that despite the French wars, Kilbride thought he could dazzle the British Government with tales of empire, and come back to Japan with a combined armada of Navy and Company ships, and if Kilbride thought he could do it – devious bastard that he was – then maybe he really could.

Meanwhile Pyne and O'Flaherty and everyone else with a telescope wanted to point out what was going on aboard *Duke of Cornwallis*, a mile off across Hito Bay. The huge ship was bringing her anchors aboard. It was a still evening with barely a breeze, when sound carries far over the water. So we could faintly hear a fiddler playing and the men singing, as they heaved the capstan bars around.

'Mr Pyne?' I said, in a big loud voice, for all to hear, 'We are ordered to prevent that ship sailing.' I pointed towards *Duke of Cornwallis*. 'We are ordered by the First Lord Himself. We are ordered to take, sink, or burn that ship, and that's what we are going to do. I'll therefore trouble you to beat to quarters.'

Well, my jolly boys, it was almost true about 'take, sink, or burn' and it was certainly true about the First Lord, and anyway you have to say such things because it's traditional in the Service. Also, it puts beef in your belly, when you're about to engage an enemy that could blow you to splinters with one broadside. So I'm pleased to say that the hands approved, and they cheered again and again.

CHAPTER 48

'So soon as anchors was weighed I went round the gun decks to kick their black behinds so's there'd be no shirking of their duty.'

(From a letter of Monday, October 29th 1798 from Captain Edward Pryce in a letter to his wife as above.)

'Give a cheer, you swabs! Give a cheer for the old Duke!' This was what Pryce loved. This was what gunners dreamed of. Because on board of this ship, there were guns as fine as any in King George's Navy. Pryce gazed at the long rows, with their tackles and buckets and rammers and swabs, and their red boxes for cartridges, and the round-shot ready in the racks. The crews looked back at him, fifteen men per gun, twenty guns, three hundred men in total, all packed round the iron monsters of the larboard battery lower deck. Three hundred men stood ready, most of them Indian Lascars. The English among them gave a cheer. Then Pryce's first mate, yelled in Bengali and the Lascars cheered too. They cheered good and loud, because they were the elite of the Company's service and they were proud of their giant ship.

'That's better, you rogues!' cried Pryce, 'That's better you sods!' and he elbowed men aside, got in close to the massive breech of the nearest gun, leaned over and looked out through the gun-port across Hito Bay. 'Look there!' he cried, 'It's only a sodding frigate, and it thinks it can stop us!' He straightened his back and went up and down the deck, going from crew to crew. He pulled their noses, he poked their ribs, he slapped their backs and he grinned and shouted. Pryce had his flaws as an officer – especially where money was concerned – but who wouldn't love a fine, old hammer-and-tongs battering match against a smaller ship? Pryce certainly did. He was pumped full of delight, and he well and truly passed it on to his gun-crews. 'We're bearing down on the sods!' he cried, 'So what are we going to do? Are we going to smash 'em and wreck 'em? Are we going to beat 'em and bugger 'em?' Are we going to blow their arses off?'

There was no need for the first mate to translate. All hands cheered in delight.

Up above, on the quarterdeck, the second mate and the seamen grinned at the cheering from below. But Mr Stephen Kilbride, Director of the East India Company, and fellow Director Sir Robert Valentine neither grinned nor smiled. Instead they stood apart and spoke softly so as not to be heard.

'At least we're under way,' said Valentine.

'Yes,' said Kilbride, and looked at the sails. The breeze was soft and uncertain but enough to give steerage way to the huge ship. The two men looked round the harbour. They looked at the other East Indiamen. Their rails and rigging were full of men staring at *Duke of Cornwallis.* They were shouting and calling. The sound came clear over the water.

'What about them?' said, and Valentine.

'They're our excuse for bringing the Navy,' said Kilbride, 'remember?'

'But what *about* them?' said Valentine.

'They'll have to take their chances,' said Kilbride, 'the Japanese won't eat them!' He looked at the shore, still bristling with armoured soldiers, who were also staring at *Duke of Cornwallis.* There were thousands upon thousands of them. 'Never mind the Indiamen,' he said, pointing to the forlorn ships, 'You just be thankful there's been no action from the Japanese.'

More cheering came from below, and Valentine shook his head.

'That's Pryce!' he said, 'He's mad for action. He'd fire into a boat-load of nuns.' Valentine looked across the harbour again. He looked at His Majesty's Frigate *Euphonides* anchored so as to lie between *Duke of Cornwallis* and the open sea. 'We'll have to pass that ship to get out,' he said, 'D'you think Fletcher's aboard? And will he try to stop us?' Kilbride said nothing. 'Will he though?' said Valentine, and if he does, can we fire on a King's ship? Do we dare? What would Parliament say?' Kilbride still said nothing. 'What about Parliament?' said Valentine, shaking Kilbride's arm.

'Sir Robert,' said Kilbride. 'the honourable members of the British Parliament mostly got their seats by bribery, and they are in public life for what they can suck out of it. We are offering these gentlemen two new empires: Japan and China, with the chance to take a fat share of the riches that will flow from these empires.' Kilbride smiled. 'D'you think one ship will count against that?'

CHAPTER 49

On the quarterdeck of *Euphonides*, we looked across the bay.

'They've got the wind of us,' said O'Flaherty.

'Aye!' said the rest, because although *Duke of Cornwallis* was under way, there was dead calm on our side, since the wind blows odd in a bay.

'She's set to cross our stern for a raking shot,' said O'Flaherty, and he was right. We were idle at anchor: just waiting for the huge two-decker to cross our stern. We were perfectly placed for shot to fly straight in through our stern windows, ripping from one end of the ship to the other, in the worst blow that any ship could receive.

'Mr Pyne!' I said.

'Sir?'

'I'll have a spring on the anchor cable, to bring the ships gun's to bear on the enemy.'

'Aye-aye!'

Then it was busy work aboard *Euphonides* as the hands doubled to pass a hawser – the spring – out through the stern-most gun-port, and bring it forward to be made fast to the anchor cable in the bow. The other end of the hawser, inboard of the stern gun-port, was then bent to the capstan such that, by turning the capstan, tension could be put on the spring to turn the ship any way we chose. Thus we brought *Euphonides* round to direct her broadside in the direction from which *Duke of Cornwallis* must pass by, and the worst fear was prevented. We could not be raked by the stern and would receive shot in the thickest of our timbers, with all our guns able to return fire. But there was still something else to do.

'Hoist battle ensigns, Mr Pyne!' I said, 'Let's show the Indiamen who they're facing.' That was mostly a matter of principle, since there was no wind to spread the flags, and our colours went up to hang like washing. But it had to be done because the hands wouldn't be happy without it.

* * *

Then we had to be patient, staring at *Duke of Cornwallis* as she crept forward, and sometimes seemed not to be moving. But she was. She was coming on, with two gun decks – twenty-four pounders over thirty-two pounders, and some of my people were muttering. Two of the signals midshipmen were close by and I heard them.

'Who's going to fire first?' said one.

'We shall, of course!' said the other.

'Belay that!' I said, 'Silence on deck!'

'Aye-aye!' they said, and shrivelled. But they'd touched on something serious.

'Gentlemen!' I said. 'I shall put a shot across the bows of that ship.' I pointed to Duke of Cornwallis, now close enough that we could see every detail of her: officers on the quarterdeck, Company Ensigns aloft. 'I shall do that to give fair warning. But we shall not give our broadside because whoever fires first will be judged a murderer, since both ships are British!'

'But think of the harm they'll do us,' said Pyne, 'begging your pardon, Sir, but *must* they fire first?'

'Yes, Mr Pyne, they must,' I said, 'because Kilbride's aboard her, and he has such influence in England, that if we fire first, then every one of us officers will be charged with murder, and there's a host of people here to see who fires first. So it can't be kept quiet.'

'What about Lord Spencer, Sir?' said O'Flaherty, 'Won't he support us?' That was difficult because I knew that Spencer would *not* support us: not me anyhow. Not if I was openly acting against the law. But I couldn't tell O'Flaherty that.

'He'd do his best, Mr O'Flaherty,' I said, 'but there are matters of Parliamentary power here, which are greater than his.'

'Ah!' he said, and believed me, and perhaps it was true? Who knew what influence Kilbride had? But the ship's people were miserable, and that wouldn't do.

'Mr Pyne?' I said, 'Muster the musicians, and we'll have a song.'

And that, my jolly boys and girls, is the sort of nonsense that makes a seafaring hero out of a man who never wanted to go to sea at all. So the musicians fetched their instruments, everyone smiled, and the band master looked to me and saluted.

'What shall it be, Cap'n?'

'Heart of Oak!' I cried, 'Then anything else that's merry!' So off they went and the crew roared out the words.

'Come cheer up my lads.

'Tis to Glory we steer,

To add something new,

To this wonderful year!'

[As ever when his memoirs turned to music, Fletcher insisted in giving the song, and calling 'all hands' of the house-folk to join in, which they did with a will since it was a famous part of his reputation, that he'd once gone into action against impossible odds, with the band playing, and the crew singing. S.P.]

That kept us cheerful, until finally it was time to burn powder.

'Dismiss the musicians, Mr Pyne,' I said, 'and ask Mr Tildesley, our Gunnery Lieutenant, to choose his best gun-crew to put a shot across *Duke of Cornwallis's* bow.'

'Aye-aye, Sir!'

That's how it began. Number five gun, larboard battery – Jimbo's favourite – was chosen, the gun-captain took aim, jerked the lanyard, the gun boomed, the shot flew, and ... CHOP! It plunged into the water no more than ten feet from *Duke of Cornwallis's* figurehead throwing up a water spout a hundred feet high. But *Duke of Cornwallis* sailed on. A shot across the bowwas the signal to heave to, and *Duke of Cornwallis* ignored it. She sailed on with her two rows of gun-ports coming into line with *Euphonides*.

'Give 'em another!' I cried, and number five gun fired again, but *Duke of Cornwallis* ignored it.

'Give 'em ...' I would have said 'another' but a succession of yellow-orange flames burst out of the side of *Duke of Cornwallis*. They burst out in silence, with huge gouts of white smoke around them. Then the sound hit us: forty heavy guns firing, then the ferocious shriek of shot flying overhead: an appalling sound which makes men squirt their bowels in fright, and timbers smashed as shot struck home, and lines parted aloft, and great splinters, whoosh-whooshed through the air, men were struck down, and guns thrown over.

Duke of Cornwallis had fired first.

xxxxxxxxxxxxxxxxxxxxxxxxxxxxxxxxxxxxxxxx
'We gave it 'em hot. We gave every gun.'

(From a letter of Monday October 29th 1798 from Captain Pryce to his wife.)

Pryce snapped his fingers.

'Go on, lads! Go on!' he said, and everyone aboard *Duke of Cornwallis* choked in the dense powder-smoke that hid the ship. Pryce laughed and took Kilbride by the arms and danced him round the deck as Valentine held his hands over his ears against the enormous sound of the broadside.

Kilbride pushed Pryce away.

'Madman!' he said, wishing that he still had Captain Stacey.

'Reload! Run out! Give 'em another!' cried Pryce, and ran – or rather felt his way through the smoke – down a quarter ladder to the main-deck to encourage the gunners. 'Cap'n!' said the first mate, yelling over the organised chaos of a gun-deck, with hundreds of men heaving, sweating and chanting, and trucks squealing and guns rolling, and officers prancing about giving orders.

'What?' said Pryce, trying to wave away the smoke.

'Look!' said the first mate, and pointed aloft, 'Look at the sails. We're becalmed.' Pryce stared. It was hard to see through the smoke, but the great mass of the sails hung limp, because the wind was gone.

'Sod and bugger!' said Pryce, 'We'd have been clear and away in minutes.'

'Not now,' said the first mate.

'Then give 'em another broadside!' said Pryce, ' Give it 'em hot!'

'We can't see 'em, Cap'n,' said the first mate.

'Never mind, we're too close to miss!' said Pryce, and he was right, but that went both ways, and the huge sound of someone else's gunfire came heavy and steady. It was followed by the scream of shots, and the thunderous rending of oak, and the crack of a spar parting above, and wreckage falling. Pryce stumbled as something shot past and the first mate gasped and sighed, with an arm gone, and his coat and shirt ripped off one side, and white ribs and red lungs visible. Pryce shuddered, the first mate died standing up, and fell to the deck, and Pryce ran off. He got himself back up on the quarterdeck. He tried to see through the smoke. Flash-BOOM: another gun firing at *Duke of Cornwallis*! Flash-BOOM: another! One shot howled overhead, the other struck mightily into *Duke of Cornwallis's* ship-of-the-line sides.

Euphonides was firing in return.

xxxxxxxxxxxxxxxxxxxxxxxxxxxxxxxxxxxxxxxxxxx

'She's killed the wind!' said O'Flaherty, 'A heavy broadside kills the wind if it's light. D'you see Cap'n? Her smoke's not moving at all. She's as becalmed as we are!'

'Good,' I said 'and we've lost only four guns, and we're still afloat, and still in action.' I spotted Mr Tildesley organising the clearing up of remains – human and non-human – from the main-deck, and the hands heaving wreckage over the side, and our boatswain bellowing at his crew, to deal with the damage to our rigging, and the top-men splicing and mending above, and the carpenter waiting to report our leakage after hits into the hull.

As I've said before, my lads, you can't do it all yourself, especially when the ship is in action. As captain you've either done your part months ago in practise and drill, or you've failed before the first shot is fired.

'Let's hope she stays becalmed,' I said to Mr O'Flaherty, 'because if the wind gets up and she comes close, we can't win a battering match.' Which unfortunate words, my jolly boys, show why a seaman should never challenge fate, because in that instant the wind stirred, and filled *Duke of Cornwallis's* sails.

xxxxxxxxxxxxxxxxxxxxxxxxxxxxxxxxxxxxxxxxxxx

'At first we was blinded and fired by hope, but then all was clear. '

(From a letter of Monday October 29th 1798 from Captain Pryce to his wife.)

'They're firing broadsides, the buggers!' said Pryce, 'They're still firing. So damn you, Kilbride, I'm giving the sods another broadside.'

'Aye!' cried every man of the crew who heard that.

'But you'll blind us with smoke again!' said Kilbride, 'And we can't see where they are even now.'

''Course we can, you bloody lubber!' said Pryce, 'We can see the bloody flash of their bloody guns!'

'You mind your tongue, Pryce!' said Kilbride, you may be ship's Captain, but I'm your master in Company Law and you damn-well know it!'

'Bollocks!' said Pryce, and ignored Kilbride thereafter. 'Aim at the gun-flashes,' he said, to the first mate, 'Full broadside, and plenty more after that!'

'Aye-aye, Cap'n!' said the first mate, and *Duke of Cornwallis* fired again, shook the hills with echoes, and blinded herself in smoke. But Pryce wouldn't give up. He gave one broadside after another, especially when a shot from *Euphonides* ripped across the planking of the quarterdeck, throwing up splinters that wounded half the men there. The wounds were slight, except for one, when a jagged wooden spike, fully three feet long, struck Sir Robert Valentine in the neck. Valentine made gurgling noises in his throat, and jerked out the splinter with both hands, then he sat down heavily on the deck, trying to staunch the blood with his hands. Kilbride stepped clear. Valentine's wound looked mortal and Kilbride felt sick.

'Get that man below!' cried Pryce, 'get him down to the surgeon!' Two seamen carried Valentine below. Then the fickle elements pleased them-selves, and Pryce grinned as the sails rumbled overhead. They rumbled and flapped and filled, and the smoke began to move.

'There!' said Pryce, 'A wind, bless us all!' he cried, and he pointed at *Euphonides* and yelled to the men at the wheel. 'Lay me alongside of that bloody ship, and we'll blow her to buggery!'

xxxxxxxxxxxxxxxxxxxxxxxxxxxxxxxxxxxxxxxxx

Duke of Cornwallis was under way. She was close enough that we could hear the sound of cheering from her people. It was a bad moment. But Mr Midshipman Phaeton Ordroyd – in the deep of his wisdom – attempted to lift spirits with a thoughtful observation.

'Never fear,' he said, 'they're only darkies. They can't stand fire from a British ship.'

'Aye!' said some other idiots, and many of them grinned and turned to me, for endorsement of this patriotic sentiment. But Mr Pyne spoke first.

'Shut your trap, you blockhead!' he said, '*Darkies*? Darkies indeed? You didn't see how they manned their guns in Fort Kilbride! They cleared and ran out like lightning.' He looked at me. 'It'll be broadside-to-broadside presently. What shall we do, Sir?'

It was an excellent question and I wondered very much indeed what we should do? By Jove I did, because the captain of a King's ship was the Almighty One and the lonely one. I was in command of the finest ship in the navy. She was intact, ready to fight, and tradition proclaimed that one British ship was worth two French ships, three Spanish, or four of any other nation. While as for East Indiamen, they didn't even count! So what would England think of a captain who didn't go into action against *any* Indiaman that *ever* floated?

But in all truth the choice of what to do wasn't so much hard, as extremely painful.

'We cut and run, Mr Pyne,' I said, 'Quick as you can now, and make sail for the open sea.' That order caused such a cry of dismay from the entire ship, as to be a measure either of the valour or stupidity of British seamen, depending on your point of view and I never did make up my mind in that respect.

[Untrue. Fletcher was deeply proud of the fighting spirit of his ship's crew. S.P.]

But I did have to go round and bellow and roar, to stamp on the sulkiness, while Pyne sent men with axes, to hack through our cable and spring, abandoning tons of anchor and fathoms of hemp, as we made sail to catch a stiffening breeze. Thus *Euphonides* heeled over, and gathered way, and the powder smoke blew free, and all of Hito Bay looked as we ran from the enemy. The East India Squadron saw it. The shore-folk saw it. The Lords and samurai in the castle saw it. And above all *Duke of Cornwallis* saw it and her people danced the hornpipe in derision and we heard their jeering, loud across the water.

But *Euphonides* escaped. We were nearer the mouth of the bay than *Duke of Cornwallis* and the nimbler vessel. Thus the hornpipes ceased aboard *Duke of Cornwallis* and through my glass, I could see her officers darting about and urging their men back to their duties, and soon the big ship hoist more sail and came along in our wake, some cables' lengths astern of us as finally we went out through the pincer-jaws of Hito Bay, with the castle looking down on us and *Duke of Cornwallis* in persuit. Then call me a Frenchman if her captain didn't show how efficient his ship was, and how right I had been to run! Because the rascal got his bow chasers into action, quick as could be. All of us on the quarterdeck were up at the taffrail with our glasses on the big ship, and we saw the gun-ports open, and a pair of long nines run out, on either side of *Duke of Cornwallis's* bowsprit. Then two orange flashes, two clouds of smoke and two heavy detonations: boom-boom! Then the hideous screech of one shot howling over our heads, and every man ducking, and hearing shattering, scouring of the other shot, which went straight into our stern windows and down the entire length of our ship.

xxxxxxxxxxxxxxxxxxxxxxxxxxxxxxxxxxxxxxxxxx
'I pointed the first piece with my own hand.'

(From a letter of Monday October 29th 1798 from Captain Pryce to his wife.)

'Left-left!' Pryce cried, leaning over the larboard nine, laying the gun on the stern of *Euphonides* that seemed so close and bright through the gun-port.

'Left-left!' repeated the Lascar gun-captain, with his duty taken from him and heaving with the rest of the crew, as they sweated in the cramped space behind the gun-port, crammed between the in-curving timbers of the hull, and the great mass of the bowsprit.

'Right-right-left!' came the shouting of the starboard gun-captain on the other side of the bowsprit.

'*Well!*' cried Pryce.

'*Well!*' cried the starboard gun-captain, and all hands stood clear of the carriages.

'Fire!' cried Pryce. He jerked the lanyard, the gun's flintlock flashed, and the black mass of iron and oak, heaved back like a mad animal as three pounds of black powder drove nine pounds of iron round-shot out of the gun barrel in a fury of violence. The starboard gun fired an eye-blink later.

'Come on you buggers!' yelled Pryce, in an ecstasy of delight, 'Come on you bloody buggers!' But he needn't have bothered. The men knew their duties. They swabbed and rammed and loaded and ran out, even blinded in smoke and deafened by the sound of their guns. Then, 'Left-left! Right-right!' cried Pryce, aiming again, and the men heaving the gun to his directions.

Pryce fired three times like that. He did well. He did well even when gouts of smoke, and thundering detonations told him that *Euphonides* was firing back with her stern chasers. But then the universe howled at the appalling, stunning, clanging of a *Euphonides* round-shot, impacting directly on the next-door gun, throwing it into scrap, and mangling the crew into bloodied meat, some of it still alive, and attempting to scream. Pryce was untouched. His gun was untouched. The gun-crew were untouched. But Pryce took one look around the other side of the bowsprit, and his nerve went. He was a roaring boy when hitting others, but he didn't like being hit back.

xxxxxxxxxxxxxxxxxxxxxxxxxxxxxxxxxxxxxxxxxxx

I was glad I'd insisted on stern ports. Without those, we should have been under prolonged, steady fire from *Duke of Cornwallis's* nine-pounders. I'd insisted on stern ports because years ago, I'd been obliged to cut one in a merchantman to fire on a pursuing Yankee privateer. It's in my earlier memoirs if you look. On that occasion I laid the gun myself but this time it was Lieutenant Tildesley and he soon scored a hit which brought cheers from all who saw it aboard *Euphonides* since we heard no more from the gun he hit, and its fellow never fired so well afterwards, punching holes in our sails, and parting a few lines, but making no more impact on our hull.

Later we got out into deep water, with the wind on our quarter and Hito Island shrinking astern, and ourselves pulling away from *Duke of Cornwallis* since we were the faster ship. But I didn't want to get too far ahead. Not when there was the chance of raking our enemy by the bow.

'Bring her about, Mr Pyne,' I said, 'and order up Mr Tildesley to give a broadside, slow and steady, in his own time and aiming at the enemy's masts, to disable.'

'Aye-aye!' said Pyne, and the crew cheered up something wonderful. Then Tildesley was making ready our larboard battery. He went from crew to crew, telling them to take their time.

'Fire only as your gun shall bear,' he said, 'let the ship do the aiming, and fire on the upward roll.' They were my own words: words I'd learned from Sammy Bone.. So I was glad I'd spent so long hammering in the virtues of long range fire. Then we put up the helm, came about, turned our broadside on our big enemy, and fired nice and steady as each captain took his time. Thud! Thud! Boom! And every man with a glass who wasn't at the guns or in the rigging, was peering at *Duke of Cornwallis* for signs of a hit. There were some cheers as splinters flew from her bow, but she plunged on, and then did just as we had done.

'She's coming about!' cried O'Flaherty, 'She's giving her broadside in return.'

'Wear ship!' I cried, 'put her on the opposite tack to the enemy.' But we didn't need to, because our ship positively exploded with cheering, as the final two guns of our battery fired, and *Duke of Cornwallis's* main topmast went over, with stays parting, shrouds ruined, spars tumbling down, and the vast canvas topsail enveloping all below it in confusion and despair.

xxxxxxxxxxxxxxxxxxxxxxxxxxxxxxxxxxxxxxxxxx
There was nothing we could do.'

(From a letter of Monday October 29th 1798 from Captain Pryce to his wife.)

Pryce woke up. He could see nothing. He was numb and smothered by the great mass of canvas that bore down on him, and he was aching from a blow to the head. But his crew hadn't given up – not yet – and were working with axes and hand spikes to clear away the wreckage, and make ready their ship to fight again. This they without orders, taking the initiative as seaman do.

Pryce struggled up, someone helped him. He'd been buried deep. He'd been unconscious. Time had passed. He didn't know how long. He looked around. *Duke of Cornwallis* was sorely hit aloft. It wasn't just the main topmast that had gone, but the foremast yards were wrenched from their mountings, and the ship had no steerage way. So a dreadful fear fell upon Pryce.

'Where are the buggers?' he cried, 'Where have they bloody gone!'

'There Cap'n,' said a ship's boy. He pointed, and all Pryce's worst fears came true, because *Euphonides* was tearing along under all plain sail, and about to cross *Duke of Cornwallis* by the stern for a raking broadside.

'Oh no,' said Pryce, 'Oh bloody Jesus, no!'

xxxxxxxxxxxxxxxxxxxxxxxxxxxxxxxxxxxxxxxxxx

And now, my jolly boys, just in case you think that a sea battle is something splendid, then listen to your Uncle Jacob. Yes, we'd knocked *Duke of Cornwallis's* masts into wreckage by careful long-range fire, and we deserve credit for that. But then we fell upon our enemy when he was helpless and we pounded him without mercy. We did so because we could manoeuver and he could not and we passed his stern, time after time, and raked him from end to end, and that isn't glorious, or fair, or nice. But that's how it's done, my lovely lads and lasses, and is one more reason why you should seek a career in trade rather than go to sea.

When we'd finally done with *Duke of Cornwallis* and she was wallowing, with blood running out of her scuppers, there remained the formality of boarding. We came alongside and grappled, and I led with sword and pistols in my belt. I took enough men to control the ship, but there was hardly a fight. *Duke of Cornwallis* was well beaten, and her crew either wounded or disheartened – all those who weren't already dead – and the ship was appalling mess of overthrown guns and bits and pieces of men.

The English among them begged for quarter and God knows what the Lascars were saying. I left them to the lieutenants of our boarding party. My duty was on the quarterdeck. I wanted hold of whoever was in command.

'Who's master here?' I yelled as I ran up a quarter ladder, and there they were: a little clump of men in John Company service coats, all white in the face, and trembling in shock. 'Who's master?' I cried again.

'Me,' said one of cocked hats, 'I'm Pryce, and it was all Kilbride's fault and it weren't none of mine.' Snivelling little toad. He was already shoving the blame away.

'So where is he?' I said, 'Kilbride?

'Below. He ran below.'

'You!' I said to a mid who'd followed behind me, 'take command! Secure these men!' 'Aye-aye!' said the mid who was Phaeton Ordroyd. Then I went below to look for Kilbride. I ran to the cabins and yelled out his name.

'Kilbride!' I cried, 'Where are you? Show your damn self!' I kicked in doors and found him in a cabin on the larboard side. He was sat a desk, scribbling on a sheet of paper. He looked up at me, and I could see his mind working.

'Fletcher,' he said, 'I knew it would be you.'

'You'll bloody-well hang for this!' I said.

'No I won't,' he said, 'It's all been a tragic mistake. I'm setting down the details now. I'm writing to my friend the Prime Minister.' But I grabbed his paper, tore it to shreds, and caught him a full-handed smack round the face that knocked him off his chair. So if you think your Uncle Jacob was in a foul temper, my jolly boys, then you're entirely correct because just before we'd entirely smashed *Duke of Cornwallis* she managed to fire a gun, and a round-shot came aboard and knocked Mr O'Flaherty into meat and rags. I saw it happen. I saw it and I will never forget it. But Kilbride got up, spattered with ink from his ink-well.

'Fletcher,' he said, 'You don't know who you're up against.'

'And I don't care,' I said, and grabbed him by the shirt front, 'because I'll see you swing at the yard-arm.'

'But you don't know ...' he said.

'And don't care,' I repeated, and he looked at me, and his expression changed, and his cunning mind found another way forward.

'Let me show you something,' he said, 'I want to show you a letter that proves that I was *forced* to act. It's only a letter. What harm can it do?'

So – God forgive me – I let him go, and he smiled and slid open a cupboard drawer, and reached inside. Then he spun round and raised a gleaming blade over his head, and swung at me. I cringed and raised an arm, but *thump!* He hit the deck-head a mighty blow. He had a samurai sword in his hands. It was stuck in a beam. He tried to heave it free. He pulled. It came out! He drew back to slice sideways ... and I shot him.

I just barely managed to draw, cock and fire before he cut me in half. The sword was sharp as a razor: the finest Japanese steel. But plain lead did nicely for Kilbride. He dropped the sword. He fell down backwards. He tore open his shirt to find the wound. Then he blinked and gabbled and died, and a good job too and a damned good riddance, because that was the end of him!

[Note that in August of 1799 Mr Midshipman Phaeton Ordroyd famously declared, in Saint's Club and before witnesses, that he was outside Kilbride's cabin when Fletcher shot Kilbride, but heard no thump of blade onto wood, nor later did he see any mark upon the deck-head beams. When it was pointed out to him that this meant Fletcher had shot Kilbride in cold blood he claimed that he did, after all, recall hearing a thump. These contradictory statements have been much discussed ever since. S.P.]

CHAPTER 50

'Nearly a month has passed since the barbarian ships fought in Hito Bay. Lord Masahito has reached agreement with Fletcher-san and speaks firmly to the Tokugawa. I have come to respect Lord Masahito. He is a full and proper man.'

(From a letter of Saturday, November 24th 1798 from the Lady Meiko, The House of Flowers, Port Hito, to her mother the Lady Kusami, The Street of the Print-Makers, Okonoma.)

For once, the Lady Meiko met a potential client elsewhere than in the Tea House of The House of Flowers, because the Lady Meiko was received by Lord Masahito Hitamoto in the audience room of Okonoma Castle. She was received with a retinue of subordinate Geisha and their personal maids. This incredible break with tradition was only one of many changes taking place in and around the great Castle.

For this notable occasion, the audience room was filled with ladies and samurai of the highest rank. They were persons of the most splendid bearing, dressed in the most gorgeous of robes, though for once – and yet another break with tradition – no armoured men were present, nor any other weapon than the swords worn by the samurai as part of their civilian regalia.

After formal greetings, a blessing was invoked by Okobo priests, the chamber was purified with incense, and a finally specially written poem was declaimed by the court poet. Then, Lord Masahito declared that all persons might now withdraw, except for himself and the Lady Meiko, each supported by a witness as required by Hito law when contracts were to be made. The Lady Meiko was attended by her elder sister, and Lord Masahito by Lord Nakano.

When all the rest were gone, and the screens closed, all present bowed to Lord Masahito, and he bowed in return. Then he spoke.

'The Clan Hitamoto expresses gratitude to the House of Flowers,' he said, 'It expresses gratitude for the advice given by the Lady Meiko.' The Lady Meiko bowed. Her sister bowed. Lord Masahito continued. 'It is the judgement of the Clan Hitamoto, that the Daimyo should continue to consult the Lady Meiko, as the previous Daimyo has done before.' Lord Masahito smiled. He smiled perhaps as gracious act of condescension, or perhaps as an expression of the foreign mannerisms he had absorbed from the barbarians. Who knows? But he smiled. 'And I shall be most happy, personally,' he said, 'to consult the honoured lady as my brother used to do.'

The Lady Meiko bowed. Her sister bowed. All Hito Island knew that Lord Kimiya had shaved his head and become a monk immediately after declaring Lord Masahito to be his heir. All Hito also knew that this was a huge relief to the entire samurai caste, now that negotiations with the Tokugawa were under way.

Then the Lady Meiko spoke.

'It is with honour and respect that I hear your words, my Lord and Daimyo,' she said.

'Just as I give honour and respect to you, Lady,' said Lord Masahito, and the Lady Meiko replied not with mere words, but with a graceful gesture of gratitude.

'Ha!' said Lord Masahito, 'Look how you did that! You do it so well. How many years did it take to learn that? My brother always said there is nobody like you.' He laughed. Everyone gasped at the shattering of etiquette. Then Lord Nakano remembered Masahito's father: the unpredictable and beloved Lord Hayato, and Lord Nakano smiled. The son was the father.

'Lady,' said Masahito, 'On your advice, we brought the Sepoys ashore with their galloper guns, and used them to inflict defeats on the Tokugawa. Now we are bringing heralds from the Tokugawa to view the foreign ships, to show them we could bombard Edo city.' He smiled again. 'We shall have peace, Lady Meiko, and freedom for Hito Island.'

The Lady Meiko was quick to read the minds of men. That is why she was so successful a Geisha. So she responded instantly to Masahito's humour and informality. She responded in kind, delivering a series of comic mimes, expressing surprise and delight. Lord Masahito and Lord

Nakano laughed. She was very talented. Very funny. Then she signalled that she had a question, doing it entirely with expression and poses.

'What's she saying?' said Masahito.

'I don't know, my Lord,' said Nakano. So Lady Meiko mimed a ship, and then a giant, and gave the question-face again. 'Fletcher-san!' said Nakano, and laughed.

'Fletcher?' said Masahito, 'He is free to go with his ship. We will provision it for a voyage.' He looked at the Lady Meiko. 'Did you know he personally killed Kilbride?' She nodded. 'And Valentine died of wounds?' She nodded. 'Without those two,' said Masahito, 'their plans fail because no other men have such influence in England, nor even their interest.'

The Lady Meiko made the two men laugh again: she mimed foreign soldiers with their grotesque faces, and foreign cannon drawn by horses. Then the question-face.

'How does she do it?' said Masahito.

'She's magic,' said Nakano, 'she's a goblin, only beautiful!'

'You're asking about the Sepoys and the East India ships?' said Masahito. She nodded. 'We don't want them here,' he said, 'We've taken their galloper guns and will keep their big ship as a threat to Edo. The rest can go.' The Lady Meiko mimed congratulation and respect. Lord Masahito looked at her exquisite face, and decided that another of the Hito traditions which must change, was the one which prevented a Geisha from the physical expression of love with a man who was entranced by her.

CHAPTER 51

The butcher's bill was fifteen dead and twenty-five wounded aboard *Euphonides* and vastly more aboard *Duke of Cornwallis*. I never got the full list, but it was a long list, and we'd done something remarkable in beating such a vessel, which was so much bigger than ourselves.

[Note that Fletcher's claimed victory over *Duke of Cornwallis* was at first treated as exaggeration by the Admiralty and was outright disbelieved by the newspapers, since *Duke of Cornwallis* was the contemporary equivalent of a modern armoured battle-ship of the heaviest class. It was only on the return of the East India Company ships, that witnesses attested to the truth of Fletcher's account.]

So we mended our wounds, repaired the damage and buried our dead. Like Francis Drake they were slid over the side in the deep of a foreign bay. They went over in their hammocks with round-shot at their feet to take them down, and Chaplain Goodsby giving his prayers. Poor O'Flaherty wasn't among them since, in the heat of battle, the tripes and offal of the mangled dead were always, and instantly, heaved over the side for fear of dismaying the living.

But even the loss of these good shipmates didn't bring so many tears as were shed when a tiny hammock, lovingly made by the men of number five gun, was brought forward, draped in a union jack, and bourn on a cushion by myself and Mr Pyne in our full dress uniforms. Able sea-cat Jimbo was one of the fallen, and the men groaned aloud, and they wept from the bottom of their hearts, and wrung their hands and clung to each other in their grief, because such is the love that sailor-men have for their ship's cat.

As for the huge ship we'd taken: I gave command of her to Mr Pyne, as the rightful privilege of a first lieutenant. He was a fine seaman, and fully fit to see the ship repaired and got under sail, which you landmen must understand is routine for seaman, such that even a ship totally dis-masted, can be rigged with spars lashed to the mast-stumps, with cross-yards to carry sail. So I sent Pyne across with a good number of our marines, to make sure that Duke of Cornwallis' people behaved. But that wasn't really needed. The crew were good as gold, being keen as we were to see their ship fit for sea. So they worked with our hands, and got the ship under way for Port Hito.

But *Duke of Cornwallis* did cause problems opposite the Japanese. Since her hull was sound, and her masts could be replaced, my first thought was to take her home as a prize, with the vast wealth of her passing into my hands and those of my crew. But when I mentioned this over dinner to my officers, Dr Goodsby proved expert in the ways of the Admiralty.

'With respect, Captain,' he said, 'I doubt that the law would recognise her as a prize.'

'Oh?' said everyone, and forks hung in the air.

'Indeed not, Sir,' said Goodsby, 'In the first place: we are not at war with the East India Company, so she is not a ship of the enemy. And in the second place: is she a merchantman or a ship of war? Because very different considerations apply in each case.'

'Ah,' I said, 'So the lawyers will squabble?'

'I fear so, Captain,' he said, 'even leaving aside what actions may be taken by the East India Company to recover so valuable a ship.' That was the end of any hopes of prize money, but it did stir me into taking a good look around *Duke of Cornwallis* just to see what was on board of her apart from men and guns above, and ship's rats down below. And by Jove, my jolly boys, I found something that I wanted more than the ship herself.

Meanwhile, once we'd anchored in Port Hito with our giant captive, Masahito had me up in his castle again. This time it wasn't a formal meeting on the topmost floor, with his knights in armour standing by. I was taken to a set of rooms on a lower level, just like those in Nakano's summer lodge. We sat in a neat, tidy room with a view of one of their neat, tidy gardens and Masahito was even kind enough to have a table and chairs put out, knowing that we foreigners didn't sit on the floor. There was a bottle of decent wine too. Masahito had Nakano with him, and had insisted that I should bring a friend, since that's how they did business. Mind you, he did have quite a few knights in armour outside the sliding door, because the castle was full of them, and there were tens of thousands more in Port Hito.

So there was no doubt who was in charge, and to prove it, he'd already put the John Company Sepoys back aboard their ships, having taken the field artillery off them! And now he wanted to take *Duke of Cornwallis* off me.

'The ship is, in herself, my settlement with the Tokugawa,' he said.

'Is she?' I said.

'She is,' he said, 'she will be fully repaired with masts and gear taken from the East India ships. She will receive a delegation of senior officers of the Tokugawa army. They will understand her invincible power and this will lead to peace with the Shogun.'

'Will it?' I said.

'Indeed,' he said, 'Thus I will take the ship, together with volunteers of her crew to teach my sailors how to sail her and work her guns.' His smile disappeared. 'I will have the ship. Do you understand, Commodore Fletcher?' I sighed deeply and shook my head.

'Dear me, my Lord,' I said, with my best worried frown, 'that would present me with huge problems. The fact is, my Lord, that under the laws of my own people ...' I was beginning a good-old bargaining session in my good-old, usual style, and I was enjoying myself. But he stopped me.

'Commodore Fletcher,' he said, 'I know you have looked into the holds of *Duke of Cornwallis*. I know your reputation and I know that you want the Japanese goods that Kilbride packed into the ship.' He shrugged. 'Take them!' he said, 'I don't want them. I am a samurai not a merchant. I want only the ship.'

God stap my vitals! I was never so astounded in all my life. All I wanted now was *Duke of Cornwallis's* cargo! And he'd given me the lot without a word spoken of all the arguments I had waiting in my head! I was almost disappointed. But I didn't complain, my jolly boys, not one single word.

After that there's little to tell. We provisioned our ship, the East Indiamen provisioned theirs. We were the first to sail, since they were resolved to sail in company and one or two were in need of serious repair. Thus *Euphonides* upped anchor and made sail in mid-December of 1798, for the long voyage home, back the way we'd come, and which took eleven months.

I ask you now to think on that, because it took seconds to write, but took eleven months of men's lives. It took eleven months, and gave back the violence of the elements, the exhaustion of sleepless nights, boredom and terror in equal degree, and the vast loneliness of empty ocean, and the hunger for land and the *smell* of land when it comes to you over the horizon. Then finally, after all these pains, and hardships there's coming into soundings with the ship hove to and the deep-sea lead striking bottom. That's when the whole ship gives a cheer because it tells you – even out of sight of England – that the great deep of the ocean is behind you and you are close to home. It's also the time when double grog is served on any ship under my command.

Euphonides dropped anchor in Polmouth in November 15th of 1799 in foul weather, freezing cold, and icicles hanging from the yards. Afterwards I had the usual formalities to attend with the shore authorities and eventually with the Admiralty in London, where I presented a written report of my doings. On that occasion, in the grand building off Horse Guards Parade, there was frowning of officials and whispering behind hands, and I was sent to a hotel, and ordered back the next day. Then they put me in a quiet room, and after a while, in came His Grace The Earl Spencer, First Lord of the Admiralty, who entered without knocking. Just him. Just him alone. He closed the door and sat down, even as I shot to my feet.

'Sit down,' he said, and studied me. 'Hmm,' he said, 'you look older, Fletcher. It suits you.'

'My Lord,' I said, 'Have you read my report?'

'I have,' he said, 'and we must now be brief. I have much else to do, and cannot be seen with you. So please listen and do not interrupt.'

'Aye-aye, m'Lord,' I said.

'You've done very well, Fletcher,' he said, 'but be warned that His Majesty's Government cannot fight both the French and John Company at the same time, and agreement has already been reached with John Company such that he must behave in future, but his excuses shall be accepted regarding India and Japan. Please note that the ships of the British squadron you left in Bombay, are safe-returned, and are similarly under orders to say nothing of what happened there.'

'Aye-aye, m'Lord.'

'Meanwhile *Euphonides* is worn out with so long a time at sea, and will go into dock. Her people will go to other ships, her officers will be promoted, and you – Fletcher – will be constantly employed as …'

'M'Lord,' I said.

'I have told you not to interrupt.'

'M'Lord!' I said again. I said it loud. I was deadly serious.

'Well?' he said.

'I'll have no more to do with the Shadow Men!'

'Will you not?' he said, and looked at me, and thought a bit. 'I see' he said, 'a pity.' And that was that. I was surprised. I was amazed. I could hardly believe it. I'd expected an argument. I'd expected dire threats and thundering anger. But I suppose he needed a true volunteer for such work, and I wasn't one. So he accepted what I'd said, and – would you just believe it – he even asked me who he should put in my place! Then he told me to get out of London for some months and await further orders. So I went down into Kent to my family and the reunion was joyful. My sister Mary wept and embraced me,

'Oh, Jacky,' she cried, 'Look your hair! Look at the white streak! It's like something from a story-book, it's so dashing!' The children climbed all over me, and had grown up something amazing but they still wanted to be rolled up and down the garden in the wheelbarrow, and my brother-in-law Josiah Hyde shook my hand, and asked if I'd seen the day's newspapers.

'No,' I said.

'I'll show you later,' he said, 'Since Mrs Hyde has a fine dinner ready for you.'

So it was in the evening that I sat down to look at what was being said about me, and to give you the flavour of it, I attach the Editorial of the *Times of London*, for Friday, December 20th 1799.

Dreadful Deeds in Britannia's Name

The celebrated Commodore Jacob Fletcher of His Majesty's Sea Service is recently returned from a cruise to India and beyond during which we are assured by unquestionable sources that he has rendered his nation inestimable services. He not only convoyed this year's premier East India fleet safe to Bombay, defending it from piracy, but he supressed a mutiny of native seamen within a fort of the Honourable East India Company. He then further safeguarded a squadron of Indiamen from the hands of local warlords, when the Gales of Monsoon caused the

squadron to take refuge in Japan. There Fletcher re-took the East India
Company's armed ship 'Duke of Cornwallis' – the world's biggest ship
and mounting a prodigious strength of guns – when it too, fell into
mutinous and treacherous hands of native crewmen. We none the
less regret to report, that these bold strokes were not achieved without
dreadful deeds on Fletcher's part, yet we are assured that all was done
in Britannia's name. We may only hope that this latter statement
reflects truth.

I offer this to all you youngsters as proof that you should never believe
what you read in the papers, and I stress that it wasn't just *The Times* that
was spouting this rot. They were all doing it, presumably following rot
fed to them by John Company. They were turning me into a mixture of
monster and hero. In many ways I was the man of the hour and they
couldn't get enough of me. But still, the sun shone upon me as far as the
Admiralty was concerned. Thus Their Lordships steadfastly chose not to
ask why *Euphonides* had called in at Polmouth, before any other port.
Equally, they managed not to notice what I did in Polmouth.

Because Polmouth, my jolly boys, was one of the biggest merchant
seaports in the southwest, and was the town where I'd grown up before
I was pressed. Thus I hoped that people there would remember me, and
by God's grace, one of them did. He was Mr Nathan Pendennis, who'd
once been my employer, and was the most powerful man of business in
the town.

So he and I sat over a bottle of port, and arranged for the entire cargo
of Japanese valuables, brought home aboard *Euphonides,* to be unloaded
and locked in Pendennis's warehouse, awaiting shipment to London.
The result was the famous explosion of Japanese fashion in London's elite
auction houses in the summer of '99, and the fierce scramble to buy and
the insane prices paid. Thus a vast profit passed to me via Pendennis, who
took his percentage according to a contract signed between us, which
precaution you youngsters should never neglect. After that, fair shares
went from me my people out of *Euphonides,* so we got our prize money
from the *Duke of Cornwallis* after all.

That was the end of my adventures in India and Japan and I heard
no more of the Shadow Men. In my time I've done many things that are
not covered by the Articles of War, not listed at Lloyd's, nor given in the

Book of Common Prayer. But none of these things was as bad as being a secret agent, and in any case the risks are too great.

I have to admit, though, that other risks came later: such as the navigation of aerial carriages and being stung by Signor Galvani's electricity.

EPILOGUE

(Transcript of a letter written in late 1799, from the Earl Spencer, First Lord of the Admiralty, to Mr William Pitt, the Prime Minister. As with a letter represented in Chapter 3, neither date nor addresses appear and capital letters replace some names. 'F' is Fletcher, 'R' is Rowland, 'S' is Earl Spencer, and 'SS' probably refers to Mr Samuel Slym, the celebrated thief taker whose adventures are reported in 'Fletcher's Glorious 1st June'.)

Sir,

I regret that we must dispense with F as a replacement for R. This is most exceeding unfortunate, since F is the very exemplar of the man for such work.

But he is become so well known to the public as to be disqualified from the vital requirement that we must be able to disown him should arise, since the newsprints would rejoice to give utterance to his voice. I asked F if he could name a man to replace him, and he mentioned SS who sounds a promising candidate. More of SS when we meet.

Finally, since F has acted greatly in the British interest, both in Japan and previously in the French steam-boat affair, and because there is a need to keep F sweet, I recommend that he be given an honour. It need not be one of the highest since F insists that he wishes only to be done with us. A knighthood of The Bath should be sufficient.

Yours, etc, etc,

S.